BEST OF THE WEST 2011

D1462079

BEST OF THE WEST

2011

NEW STORIES FROM THE WIDE SIDE OF THE MISSOURI

EDITED BY

**JAMES THOMAS AND
D. SETH HORTON**

FOREWORD BY

ANA CASTILLO

UNIVERSITY OF TEXAS PRESS 〜 AUSTIN

Requests for permission to reproduce material
from this work should be sent to:
    Permissions
    University of Texas Press
    P.O. Box 7819
    Austin, TX 78713-7819
    www.utexas.edu/utpress/about/bpermission.html

∞ The paper used in this book meets the minimum requirements
of ANSI/NISO Z39.48-1992 (R1997) (Permanence of Paper).

Library of Congress Cataloging-in-Publication Data

Best of the West 2011 : new stories from the wide side of the Missouri / edited by James Thomas and D. Seth Horton ; foreword
by Ana Castillo. — 1st ed.
        p.   cm.
    ISBN 978-0-292-72879-0 (pbk. : alk. paper)
    ISBN 978-0-292-73790-7 (e-book)
1. Short stories, American—West (U.S.) 2. West (U.S.)—Social
life and customs—Fiction. I. Thomas, James, 1946– II. Horton,
D. Seth, 1976–
    PS648.W4B4752 2011
    813'.087408—dc23   2011019072

CONTENTS

vii Editor's Note, D. Seth Horton

xii Foreword, Ana Castillo

1 Coach, from *The Idaho Review*
RICK BASS

17 The Silence, from *The Atlantic*
T. C. BOYLE

31 Escape from Prison, from *Tin House*
RON CARLSON

44 Bonnie and Clyde in the Backyard, from *Glimmer Train*
K. L. COOK

68 Melinda, from *The Kenyon Review*
JUDY DOENGES

79 Uncle Rock, from *The New Yorker*
DAGOBERTO GILB

85 Drive, from *The Gettysburg Review*
AARON GWYN

96   Looking for Boll Weevil, from *From the Hilltop*
      TONI JENSEN

104   Two Years, from *Narrative*
      TIM JOHNSTON

122   Same as It Was When You Left, from *The Bat City Review*
      ALYSSA KNICKERBOCKER

141   Nevada, from *The Southern Humanities Review*
      KATE KRAUTKRAMER

152   Lunch Across the Bridge, from *The Antioch Review*
      PETER LASALLE

159   Alone, from *The New Yorker*
      YIYUN LI

171   Horn Hunter, from *The Antioch Review*
      MICHAEL J. MACLEOD

180   What You Do Out Here, When You're Alone, from *The New Yorker*
      PHILIPP MEYER

195   iff, from *Tin House*
      ANTONYA NELSON

210   Creatures of the Kingdom, from *Epoch*
      STEPHANIE REENTS

223   Five Shorts, from *Day Out of Days: Stories*
      SAM SHEPARD

229   Opposition in All Things, from *Ecotone*
      SHAWN VESTAL

254   The Last Thing We Need, from *Granta*
      CLAIRE VAYE WATKINS

265   Other Notable Western Stories of the Year
268   Publications Reviewed
270   Notes on Contributors
276   Credits

EDITOR'S NOTE

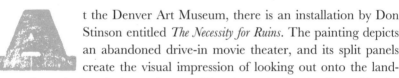

D. Seth Horton

A t the Denver Art Museum, there is an installation by Don Stinson entitled *The Necessity for Ruins*. The painting depicts an abandoned drive-in movie theater, and its split panels create the visual impression of looking out onto the landscape through the windows of a car. The viewer is thus implicated in the painting, which Stinson accentuates with a recording of environmental sounds, mostly wind, emanating from actual drive-in speakers. The overall effect of this work is unsettling, for while Stinson's landscape echoes works by generations of previous artists who envisioned the West in mythological terms, *The Necessity for Ruins* nevertheless complicates this tradition, for the land has been deserted; the only indication of human settlement comes in the form of crumbling artifacts serving as a visual reminder that Hollywood movies glorifying the settling of the West by adventurous, independent, and heroic Anglo men no longer bear cultural value.

In "Interstate Imprints," a 2010 editor's note in the *South Dakota Review*, Brian Bedard writes: "When it comes to traveling the Northern Plains or the American West, icons of place loom up in the light like subtle beacons from a landscape that will outlast us all. What materializes in one's line of vision are a combination of the New and Old West in a juxtaposition which counters the vainglorious sense of time contemporary technology promotes and reinforces." Stinson shares this interest in interpreting western landscapes through the juxtaposition of the Old and New West. To borrow two terms that can be traced back to Gilles Deleuze and Félix Guattari, Stinson's installation "deterritorializes" the West in that it weakens the concept of the region as a place to be permanently settled, which is one of the tropes in classic "Old Western" texts such as Frederick Jackson Turner's "The Significance of the Frontier in American History" (1893), Owen Wister's *The Virginian* (1902), and Harvey Fergusson's *Wolf Song* (1927). Stinson subsequently "reterritorializes" the region by visualizing it through the windows of a car, thereby emphasizing change, technology, and mobility. Stinson sees the West as a place of travel, migration, and immigration, which supports Patricia Limerick's famous argument in *The Legacy of Conquest* (1987) that the region is a place of convergence—"The West was not where we escaped each other, but where we all met" (291)—as well as the recent work of Neil Campbell, whose *Rhizomatic West* (2008) builds on the theories of Paul Gilroy and James Clifford, among others, in order to examine "a mobile genealogy of westness, a cultural discourse constructed through both national and transnational mediations, of roots and routes, with its territories defined and redefined (deterritorialized) from both inside and outside the United States" (8).

When read together as an assemblage, the stories in *Best of the West 2011: New Stories from the Wide Side of the Missouri* participate in this "route work" by representing a shifting West, a West in transit, a West where borders and meanings conflict and overlap. Interestingly, the trope of the road is ubiquitous throughout the collection. Consider, for example, Aaron Gwyn's "Drive," in which a couple rediscovers their passion for each other, at least temporarily, by driving faster than a hundred miles an hour in the wrong lane: "They were going forward, fully forward, faster and faster like the car in which they traveled, on toward the lights which seemed to have stopped moving." The central question of the story isn't about why the couple needs to do this, but rather what would happen if they were to stop moving. It is a problem similar to the one taken up by Kate Krautkramer in "Nevada," whose narrator drives all over the state for her job. The barrenness of the landscape and the long-distance driving mirror the emotional coldness of a relationship that she has trouble ending. Likewise, the protagonist in Rick Bass's "Coach" is a nomad moving throughout the state of Montana to coach girls' high school basketball. When he meets his new team for the first time, he thinks, "This is the best part . . . even better than the addiction of the game itself. This is the absolute best. The beginning." The implication here is that "the journeyman coach" will not put down any roots; rather, he will eventually move on to a new beginning, a new school, and a new town. In Yiyun Li's "Alone," Suchen drives along the Pacific Coast and heads inland toward the Rockies, and yet she is denied the possibility of a new beginning in the West. Her past will seemingly haunt her forever, allowing her little more than the vague comfort of passing acquaintances.

As Cormac McCarthy's latest novel chillingly reminds us, roads foreground issues of displacement and movement, diasporas and nomadology, but they also function as sites of violent encounters. In K. L. Cook's "Bonnie and Clyde in the Backyard," a young Texas boy meets Clyde Barrow, his father's cousin, and Bonnie Parker just weeks before they are ambushed by police in their death car. Their arrival at the narrator's family farm generates a moral dilemma, but it also represents the crossroad between local culture and international fame, which become blurred when the boy travels to Dallas to attend their funeral. In Peter LaSalle's "Lunch Across the Bridge," the cars in Nuevo Laredo are armored, a necessity for those involved in the drug trade. Antonya Nelson's "iff" is brilliantly framed around a small car accident that occurred shortly before the beginning of the story and the "impending certain crash" that ends it. And in Claire Vaye Watkins's epistolary story "The Last Thing We Need," the narrator stumbles across the detritus of what he believes to be a car accident, which triggers memories of the time he was once held up at a gas station.

But it is perhaps the short shorts of Sam Shepard that focus the most attention on the cultural value of roads and their possible meanings in the twenty-first-century West. The five stories included in this volume were selected from his most recent book, *Day Out of Days* (2010), a book so fragmented that there is hardly any continuity other than the names of highways in the story titles. The roads that Shepard's characters travel upon lead neither to youthful adventures à la Kerouac nor to liberatory new beginnings; instead, his unnamed narrator simply drives, stopping in towns that others mostly pass through (Butte, Montana; Rock Springs, Wyoming; Bonners Ferry, Idaho). These short shorts allow us an intimate glimpse into the vagabond life of loners in the contemporary West.

Whereas roads pass through many of the stories in this year's *Best of the West*, the collection as a whole consists of crossroads, narratives that both converge and diverge, that redraw the cultural map of the contemporary West. It is therefore fitting that a number of people have collaborated to help bring this book into print. I would first like to thank my coeditor, James Thomas, for our many fertile conversations about western fiction. For the 2011 volume, I searched for stories and stand-alone novel chapters originally published between fall 2009 and fall 2010. More than 270 literary journals, magazines, short-story collections, and newspapers were consulted. My research was augmented by this year's associate editors, all of them graduate students, who read a number of journals that I was unable to access. Their work has made this book better, and I would like to thank Dani Johannesen at the University of South Dakota, Brett Myhren at the University of Southern California, and Liz Stephens at Ohio University. Thanks also to Matt Bell, the editor of Dzanc Books' *Best of the Web*, for links to suitable stories that were originally published online. This year's *Best of the West* volume includes one piece published online, Tim Johnston's "Two Years," and I expect to include more online stories in the future as journals continue to move to electronic formats. Finally, I would be remiss not to acknowledge the thousands of editors of North American literary journals, many of whom have generously provided me with complimentary copies of their publications. Without their often-unacknowledged work, the richness of American and Canadian literature would certainly suffer.

This year's foreword was written by Ana Castillo, an essayist, poet, short-story writer, translator, and novelist. Like many of her characters, Castillo is a transplant to the region, and much of her work deals with the crossing of borders, whether regional, national, linguistic, or cultural. Her writing fuses the imaginative quality of magical realism with the fierce independence celebrated in western American literature, thereby carving out an important place for Chicana identity in the contemporary West. I would like to thank her for agreeing to write this year's foreword.

James and I are privileged to have the opportunity to work with the University of Texas Press. As Charles Bowden told me a couple of years ago in Spearfish, South Dakota, they are the best in the business. My sincerest thanks go to my editor, Casey Kittrell, for all of his advice, encouragement, and support over the years. I would also like to thank Lynne Chapman for making sure that each *Best of the West* volume is copyedited with care.

Several conferences have given *Best of the West* contributors a forum at which to showcase their work. I would like to express my gratitude to the organizers of the Association of Writers and Writing Programs for giving us a panel at their 2011 conference, and I would also like to thank Gioia Woods, the president of the 2010 Western Literature Association conference, who invited three recent *Best of the West* contributors—Aurelie Sheehan, Ron Carlson, and Dagoberto Gilb—to open the conference with readings from their work.

   And, of course, a special thanks to this year's twenty contributors. Their writing is exceptional, and I hope that this volume serves to introduce them to a larger audience. As always, my most important thanks are reserved for my parents, for their encouragement over the years; for my friends; and especially for my wife, Catherine Chen. She continues to offer unwavering support for me and also for my work, despite the sacrifices this often entails. Thank you, Cat.

FOREWORD

Ana Castillo

t was after participating in a sweat lodge in Sacramento, California, that I decided to move to Albuquerque in 1990. The lodge
was run by a Chicano activist and artist of the previous generation,
and I had participated numerous times in his lodge. I had dreamt
of New Mexico in early adulthood, before having ever traveled there: my
destiny in later years. While I don't recall the exact message that I received
during that ceremony, it felt right that I should move to New Mexico (where
I had only the most tenuous connections). It turned out to be a challenging
relocation but a defining one. I not only finished a book of essays but also
placed them at the University of New Mexico Press. I also produced a novel
soon after, thereby joining a long, honored tradition of work that falls within
the realm of that which I refer to as mystical.

A few years later, life caused me to relocate once again. However, a decade after that, I returned to New Mexico. As before, the decision came after
a "message." This time it was a recurring dream in which there was a home
waiting for me in the southern part of the state, which turned out to be true.
It became the place where I received the inspiration for my next novel, *The
Guardians*.

Mystical experience, which is centered on seeking union with God, falls mainly into two types: extroverted and introverted. In extroverted mystical experience, a mystic looks through the physical senses into the external world to find unity. In introverted experience, a mystic looks inward.

Merriam-Webster's Collegiate Dictionary defines "mysticism," in part, in the following manner:

> 1: the experience of the mystical union or direct communion with ultimate reality reported by mystics. 2: the belief that direct knowledge of God, spiritual truth, or ultimate reality can be attained through subjective experience (as intuition or insight). 3: vague speculation: a belief without sound basis.

"Vague speculation" and "belief without sound basis" lay the fertile ground in which fiction may take roots and flourish in the hands of imaginative writers.

The literature of the West has a number of familiar characteristics. We call in the sheriff, paint the adobes in the background, or find our characters on homesteads, ranchos, or reservations. The horses are noble, and folks work hard for a day's pay. We are often treated to the ever-roaming white missionaries, Holy Rollers, snake oil salesmen, drifters and grifters, and the sons and daughters of African slavery and early Chinese immigrants. Throughout the twentieth century and into the present, as open spaces were overtaken by asphalt and concrete, *la puta* with the heart of gold has remained; however, railroad bandits have transformed into gangbangers, and the not-so-new comers now constitute a flow of migrant workers. Despite these changes, luscious landscapes, prismatic mountain ranges, expansive deserts, red rocks, cacti, and endless skies are still present.

The conquest of the western territories of the United States by Europeans brought about a body of literature that was as much a spiritual response to place and time as a political one. Community-minded writers, especially from marginalized groups, more often than not, chose collective storytelling, whether delivered orally or with the pen. Or they offered their accounts by dictation.

Two examples come immediately to mind. They are important because I think they demonstrate how both internal and external mysticism affected entire communities whose spiritual perspectives were being dismissed for the sake of the supplanting religion of the conqueror.

A quintessential example of both a mystic and a prolific writer is a nun of the early seventeenth century who never set foot in the New World. Her name was María Jesús de Ágreda of the Poor Clares, and she wrote what became arguably the church's most controversial and famous book in the realm of mysticism: *The Mystical City of God*. During her career, Sister María played an unusual role in the exploration and colonization of New Spain and the Southwest. She claimed she had visited those lands via teleportation (the ability to be in two places at once, as recognized by the church). During her raptures, she claimed to visit "tribes" in North America. An investigation was eventually pursued, and it was verified that indeed, in northern New Mexico, an encampment awaited conversion at a mission after being visited via teleportation by the "lady in blue."

The other example is an American classic: *Black Elk Speaks*. It is the work of two collaborators: Black Elk, an Oglala Sioux holy man who tells his life story, and John G. Neihardt, a white man who interviewed Black Elk at the Pine Ridge Reservation in 1931 and fleshed out and gave artistic form to Black Elk's account. He claimed to have been spiritually moved to write down the medicine man's life. As for Black Elk, he felt his own story was important only because it was also the story of his people. Neihardt later produced an epic poem, *Cycle of the West*. It told the story of the Ghost Dance and culminated in the massacre at Wounded Knee. Such an endeavor leads one to wonder whether it was not spirit (or something akin to it) that inspired the author to continue exploring a topic for a period of more than thirty years.

Many narratives written by Native Americans have since come to fruition. No doubt the tragic history of the Natives of these lands makes collective consciousness a trademark of the literature. From Leslie Marmon Silko's classic *Ceremony* to the poems of John Trudell, an activist in the American Indian and environmental movements, from the novels of M. Scott Momaday to the varied works of Louise Erdrich and Sherman Alexie, politics are bound up with a driving force that must address the soul of a people, a land, and a time in history.

Other ethnic groups have also contributed to a literature that deals with a harsh history of settlement and displacement as well as with religious and spiritual conflict. Rudolfo Anaya's animist classic *Bless Me, Ultima* reminds us of the Hispanic and Native traditions of New Mexico during the mid–twentieth century, a time when Anglo culture began to pervade and dominate the culture. The land's indigenous and Mexican spiritual beliefs are entwined with its recent incorporation into the United States and its prevailing Anglo norms.

As opposed to Protestantism, which established the country's tenor in the East, Catholicism, brought by Spaniards in the settling of the Southwest, has played an influential part in the imaginative literature produced there. In some ways, although centuries have passed, writers are, at present, as haunted by this legacy as ever. María de Jesús Ágreda was the daughter of a Jewish tax collector for the monarchy. He became a converso (thereby keeping his job and his head), and his daughter became a spiritual advisor to the king. The Inquisition was underway during the conquest of the New World. It should not be a surprise, then, that not a few Hispanic families today have discovered that their ancestors were also conversos.

One such writer is Kathleen Alcalá, who resides in the Pacific Northwest but takes her family's history as the inspiration for her writing. In *The Desert Remembers My Name*, a collection of essays, she explores her family's crypto-Jewish heritage in Saltillo, Mexico.

Despite Anglo cultural dominance, as seen, for example, in English-only laws and a racialist movement that recommends Anglicizing Spanish place names in order to eliminate all references to the early Catholic friars, writers of various cultural backgrounds who migrate or immigrate to the area can scarcely ignore the religious permeation of Catholicism and an ongoing lived indigenous spiritual presence.

Chicanas, because of our own *mestizaje* and marginalization by Anglo culture, may take on the topic of mysticism in our lives as part of our personal and political journey. The most popular example of this is the essayist Gloria Anzaldúa. She embraced what she may have thought was a complexity of marginalization, which she both embodied and simultaneously addressed in her writings. Unlike John Rechy (born in El Paso), who dealt with sexuality in his books long before he turned to a Chicano theme (*The Miraculous Day of Amalia Gómez*), Anzaldúa, as a feminist of her generation, found it necessary to discuss her body (sexuality and gender) as part of the colonization of Mexicans and the indigenous by utilizing the U.S.-Mexican border as a symbol of that conflict.

At present, the trauma of the conquest and its consequent alienation of mestizos and the indigenous of North America are evident in symbolism and metaphors related to the human spirit produced by writers of the area. This is found no less so in popular genres. Tony Hillerman, a white man, found it impossible to write detective novels in New Mexico without integrating the spiritual beliefs of the Navajo characters in his stories. Aaron Albert Carr, a contemporary Navajo Laguna writer, finds mystical connections in the vampire genre, which can be read as either fantasy or an intrinsically mystical worldview related to Navajo beliefs. Vampirism may also be understood as a metaphor for racialist invasions of existing cultures.

Five hundred years after the initial evangelization of Native Americans, its impact continues to be rich fodder for new generations of western writers. My latest novel, *The Guardians*, which takes place near the U.S.-Mexican border, is as much about the fervor of the faith of Sor María de Jesús and her use of national loyalties to justify the conquest of the New World as about the equally heated claims of the U.S. government to the borderland territory.

In no way, however, should the political intent (whether conscious or unconscious) in these examples be seen as more significant than the conscious spiritual force that drove the storyteller to take on the arduous task of writing. For nothing brings a writer more pleasure (and more anguish) than the process of joining the tradition of a body of literature. However, long before the acknowledgment of this intent is the initial motivation: that of witness. In *Ceremony*, Silko reminds the reader of the power of recording legacies in the face of hostile takeovers: "Their evil is mighty but it can't stand up to our stories."

BEST OF THE WEST 2011

COACH

Rick Bass

It's late in his career, and Coach's mother is ill. He and she have left their home in the plains. There has been another unspecified controversy, nothing too outrageous, and Coach has been forced to seek a job in the mountains, where the players are, for whatever reasons, less talented and less committed to the holy sport of basketball. The job in Placerville for which he has interviewed is ostensibly teaching—he is a good teacher—but he's a coach first. Forty-three years old and with his own flesh beginning to mortify, ravaged by hypertension, the survivor of seventy overtimes, fifty-four double overtimes, twenty-five triple overtimes, and nine quadruple overtimes, as well as countless twenty- and even thirty-point comebacks, and countless run-of-the-mill heart-stopping one- and two-point victories at the buzzer, Coach has spent most of his adult life wondering whether he is a genius or just someone obsessed by, aflame with, passion, and someone who tries really hard. When the genius is in him, he knows it for what it is, and is scoured by it, burnished by it—but when it leaves him, he feels ridiculously ordinary, vulnerable, and exposed, an imposter: completely undeserving of the responsibility that he has dared to assume and dared to pursue.

This is the beauty of small-school high school girls' basketball: there is almost never any game that cannot be won, almost never any game that cannot be lost.

Basketball on the eastern side of the state—the windy prairie—is an entirely different sport—a steady-burning, year-round religion, Indian ball, dominated by the hot-shooting, trick-passing, full-court-press teams from the reservations, teams filled with players possessing intimidating names like Mankiller and Bearpaw, girls who play every second of every game as if basketball is the only thing in life, and yet also as if they have nothing to lose—while up in the mountains, the same sport can be a precise and careful game, one in which the focus is more on the sustained avoidance of mistakes rather than flights of brilliance.

And that's okay: Coach knows how to win anywhere, with any kind of team. He would have liked to stay out on the prairie, but had to take this job so that he could keep his mother on his insurance. He was born when she was forty, which was when she first got sick. The doctors told her not to have the child, but she did anyway, and then got better. Now she's sick again, has been sick for the last ten years, battling the illness year after year, one day at a time. It's too bad about his last job, not twenty miles from the family farm; that would have been a good one to finish out on.

But few coaches stay put forever. Their nights are haunted by the memories of the shots that do not drop—shots that bounce two, three, four times before falling back off the rim, or that swirl around on the rim before spinning back out as if repulsed by a negative polarity. Memories of the girl who travels in the backcourt with four seconds left, or the girl who goes glassy-eyed while inbounding and bounces it straight to the defender, who then takes one step forward for the easy layup, and the win, or loss, that extends one coach's career but finishes another, at that particular school—because no matter what the school board and principal and fans and parents say about building character, you have to win. In the poorer communities, winning is character—there is nothing else left, or so it seems to them—and so it's a pretty desperate fix, a pretty desperate lifestyle that Coach has gotten boxed into, here in his forty-third year. Win or go home. Win forever, or leave, banished from one's homeland.

The first and foremost talent, then, Coach knows, is nothing less than being able to look into the soul of these girls and know what each is capable of, and then labor to tease it out over the four years you have with them—which is to say, you have to be able to fall in love with them. You have to proceed with the secret knowledge that such love is temporal, not enduring. In this sense, it is a corrupted kind of love, able eventually to be compromised, diluted, or even dissolved by one too many losses or one too many failures. Over the course of the relationship with each team, and each girl, then, every gesture matters. One day that intensity and sweetness, that love and attachment between him and the girls will fade, and they will either graduate and go away, or he will be fired and sent off wandering into the desert, spurned and abandoned by those whom he once loved, sent to search for new love.

Coach has been to the state championships only once, but it was the single most transformative event in his adult life. Utterly intoxicating and transcendent, the season had been marked by scrap-and-claw, jockeying for an upper-tier berth in his division—in his girls' division—with setbacks and reversals, last-second blocked shots, long shots at the buzzer, and titanic battles in the paint.

His Lady Bearkats (he hates how the girls are always given short shrift that way—differentiated by that identifying pronoun of gender, Lady this and Lady that, rather than simply their team's name itself; why are the boys not called, for instance, the Gentlemen Bearkats?) had just squeaked into the district playoffs, but had then caught fire, clamping down on one team after another with a superior defense and winning one low-scoring game after another, with the girls playing their hearts out—the senior girls assuming leadership on their team, and weaving together a trust and mutual support more tightly than any family—and with Coach coaching his heart out, making genius substitutions, creating matchups that were based sometimes on long nights' scrutiny of game films for each opponent, though other times on intuition. More exhilarating than any drug was this sweetest chemical, adrenaline, chased second by heart-pounding second with boilermakers of desire, yearning, desperation, and pure and elemental hope. He has never known anything more wonderful, has never felt more fully the incredible power of being alive, and of being able, through dint of will and force, to shape one's world into the precise outcome one desires—though with everything at risk, the deep and lightless abyss of failure all around, attending every choice—the absolute compression of power and consequence into every melting second on the game clock.

To say that basketball for him is a matter of life and death is not to put too fine a point on it. For Coach, it's more than that; the game is a small, dusty window in a high attic in an abandoned house in the country through which his soul, long trapped and dying, might yet find escape, and be illuminated.

And at that long-ago state championship: having defeated teams thought to be superior in the district playoffs, and in the divisional playoffs, until finally—what sweet and temporary alchemy!—the Lady Bearkats were starting to be considered superior—the entire town chartered buses and took off work to attend the finals in Bozeman, where, in the big city's university arena, every individual from the small town of Tiber, population 5,167—all five thousand–plus of them, as well as the players' relatives from all over the state—were on their feet in that one building roaring at the top of their lungs, their love, their howling passion, for the courageous hearts and cunning of their team and coach.

Pride existed there like thermonuclear expansion, so much so that standing beneath the bright lights, while the national anthem was being played— for that shining and suspended moment, while that one song played on almost interminably, and wonderfully so, all coaches and players had the briefest and most blasphemous of thoughts, lasting no more than half a breath, as they took their eyes off the flag for a moment to look back up into the stands, that right then, right there, is as good as it gets, that this is the pinnacle—that it all could and perhaps should end right here, before there is a winner and loser—for who needs even more euphoria than this?

And certainly, upon whom would one wish such heartbreak, following such ecstasy? But then the thought was washed away, almost before it was even a full thought, for at this level of achievement they were all, or had all become, voracious basketball warriors, just like Coach himself, living, breathing, and consuming the sport.

Is it healthy? Absolutely not. Would you ever wish such fragile intensity, such narrow obsession—such addiction and dependency—upon anyone you loved? Never. But should you ever be faced with such an unlikely temptation—the opportunity, or even the nearness of opportunity—there are few who would say no. There are many who think they would be able to say no; but on those rare occasions when a team draws ever nearer, accumulating victories through the long season, things change. The bird finds itself again in the attic, and either forgets or does not have the intelligence to consider how it got into the old house in the first place.

The bright lights of the state championship, and the adoration of the entire town, for one long, focused, unified moment: Coach has known it once, and would give anything to know it again, and he wants it desperately for every girl he ever loves, and for every town he ever moves to, in his wandering drift, his peregrinations of adolescent drama, small-town booster-parent drama, and in the repetitions of passionate and sustained failure, year after year. The bird's tiny wings fluttering against that windowpane, barely audible but earnest, beginning each day at dawn and continuing until long after dark.

The interview in Placerville had gone well. The school board said all of the things they always said, no matter where he interviewed—that a quality education was the key goal of the school district, and that there were singular challenges these days, particularly in underserved rural areas, to be competitive in the ever-changing global marketplace. And that with regard to sports, they were more interested in building character than winning per se. Their team had won only three games in the last two years while losing thirty-four, and in the interview—that too brief part of it that covered basketball—the school board stressed how their main concern was that the girls have fun and continue to learn good sportsmanship. It was what they all said when they were losing, and it had gotten to where it rankled him to hear it. Just once he longed to sit down in an interview in which his teaching credentials—Montana history and Native American studies—were briefly examined, only to then really get down to business, with a unified school board telling him, Listen, we're tired of losing. It's bad for our school, bad for our girls' spirit and self-esteem, and we want you to come in and do something about it.

The ugly truth was that losing all the time eventually got to be where it was no fun at all, while winning was as much fun as anything these girls would have known up to this point. But he never told them this.

Instead—in that little window of time he got to talk to the board about basketball—he always laid out the threefold path to turning around a losing program. "Number One: family first. The parents have got to love their children. I need to know, and the kids need to know, someone besides me will always have their backs. Number Two: I'll stress academic excellence. Only until we reestablish those two things, will the third part, athletic excellence, return."

And always, in these small schools, athletic excellence had been there before; always, the residue of it hung in the hallway above the entrance to the ancient, dimly lit gymnasium, in the dusty, sun-faded photos of the hauntingly obscure teams from thirty, forty, even fifty years ago, with those past fleeting glories so isolated by forgetfulness as to threaten to make a mockery of the same passion the players and the fans in the here and now pursued.

In every interview, Coach talked briefly of his experience that one time he had gone to state. He mentioned it only casually, for he knew that in their initial earnestness, the school board members truly believed what they were saying about wanting only for the girls to have fun (as if they believed there was anything fun about losing).

It was only after he would begin to win games that they would change their tune, and dare to believe, and dare to be tempted. Would always yield to that temptation.

For now, he dialed it way down; but even so, he could not tamp or completely squelch the radiant love, radiant fury, he had for the game and all its virtues. And in the beginning, in Placerville, as in all the other places he had coached, the school board had been initially amused—not yet captivated— by his passions, and had given him the job immediately, after assuring him that his mother would be able to continue her health coverage under his state teacher's policy.

The first thing they took him to see, the very next day, was the volcano, or what they called a volcano. Up in the mountains south of town, the old mine had had so much ore gouged out of it that following the big snow year of 1963, the overburden of stony earth had collapsed like a fallen cake, and was still collapsing, the caldera widening every year, so the effect was that of some great beast gagging and choking on the earth, on the burning stone it sought to disgorge.

In subsequent years, wildfires had burned across the rubble of the ever-deepening caldera, igniting newly exposed seams and strata of high-sulfur coal, which burned slowly down deeper into the mountain's heart, issuing at almost all hours of day and night towering billows of acrid yellow-brown smoke, redolent with the odor of rotting eggs, and with the mist from those vapors so acidic that the downwind drift of it stung the eyes and lungs of the residents of Placerville, several miles from the mountain.

The acid turned the foliage of the maple trees in town, and the summer-green grass of the lawns, a speckled, mottled yellow, and dulled the luster and finish on the paint of the cars and trucks, so that after no time, all the vehicles had the same appearance—as if they were a fleet owned by one company and utilized by a vast though curiously unambitious workforce: for none of the cars ever appeared to be traveling anywhere specific, their drivers seeming to possess no mission other than a trip to the grocery or the post office or, for entertainment, the bowling alley or movie theater, or the bars and the churches.

Sometimes in the spring, one of the trucks might drive past with a sapling in the back, to be replanted in a yard, replacing one of the acid-speckled trees; in the fall, the backs of the same trucks would be filled with cut and split firewood gotten from the dead and dying trees up in the forest. But beyond that, all else was slumber.

It was only after Coach had said yes that the school board and town boosters took him up to look at the volcano. It was late in May when he had interviewed over the holiday, and a wet snowstorm had passed through the

mountains, bending over and sometimes snapping the green limbs of younger trees and bushes. The travelers rode toward the mountaintop in a caravan
of four-wheel-drive vehicles, tires spinning against the slurry of springtime
runoff, slipping and fishtailing in the deep snow that would be gone within
the day. Already the late-morning sun was beginning to rout the snow, slender double-bent branches arcing suddenly skyward as they shed their loads
with the suddenness of traps being sprung—all around them, the woods were
dancing, leaping in this fashion—and steam was rising from the forest as if all
the forest was afire, and the thunk and scatter of gravel churned against the
truck's undercarriage in a steady fountain of protest, the truck hopping and
bogging down, roaring, then lunging forward again: an army-like procession,
a mindless slog, an initiation.

As they labored up the mountain, encountering the first burned-out scab-
lands of lukewarm coal water and pustulous rivulets of toxic runoff from the
old days of cyanide and arsenic heap-leach mining—past the charred and
broken mineshaft timbers protruding through that rubbled ground as if seeking to reemerge, to escape their once-utilitarian existence, if only to burn,
freely now, to ash—Coach came to understand that his employers were
proud of rather than repulsed by the smoldering volcano.

"The kids come up here to drink on weekends," one of the boosters told
him. "We need to put a gate on it, but haven't gotten around to it." They
were still driving, close enough to the craters that no snow remained—even
in deepest winter, they told him, the area around the crater stayed snow-
free—and the inexorable creep, the burning itch, of the coal, would occasionally encounter the roots of one of the sulfur-strangled trees that it had
killed in previous years. In these places, the fire would find the one thing it
needed most, oxygen, within that tree's hollowed husk, and the entire tree
would burst into crackling flame. It could happen at any time, the boosters
said.

They stopped at the edge of the pit and got out. It was windy, and the
acid stung Coach's eyes and made him squint. He could hear little flames and
embers hissing underground, could see vapors rising from the dried-out soil,
and imagined—or was it real?—that even the ground on which they stood
was trembling, also about to collapse, and that he could somehow detect a
hollowness, just below him, just beneath the spot where they were all parked.

The rotten-egg smell was overwhelming, as was the burning in his eyes—
tears streamed down his face as if he were weeping, so that he had to wipe
them clean with the crook of his arm, and when he did so, the gesture left a
black smudge on his shirtsleeve—and yet there was another odor, too, above
that of the charred wood and sulfur; and peering through the blowing mist

and steam down into the gullet of the crater, where a few live coals blinked and flared like the winking teeth in a jack-o'-lantern, he saw that the crater was being used as a town dump, as well; that it was stippled with the carcasses of old televisions, recliners, charred and smoldering car batteries, couches, refrigerators, card tables, broken-down treadmills, as well as semi-melted plastic garbage bags of barely identifiable materials of organic provenance— deer bones, watermelon rinds, banana peels, cereal boxes, corncobs, and seemingly all the other detritus of the century.

The boosters admitted that although there was a no-dumping ordinance, people had been doing it for so long that there was really no way to stop them, that it had gotten to be a tradition; and Coach saw that long ago they had embraced its strange toxicity and had made no efforts to alter or correct it.

Coach could smell rubber burning, and whether from the tires of the trucks they had driven up here or the myriad tires tossed into the crater, he could not be sure.

"Have you tried to do anything with it?" he asked: by which he meant methane-gas capture, geothermal energy production, or even piping warm water down the mountain and beneath the streets and sidewalks in town, to provide faint passive warming. Any kind of tinkering, any kind of improvement.

No, they said, nothing like that: and they glanced at one another, smiling, almost mirthful, at the bargain they appeared to have gotten—all that useless extra energy in him, all that spitting passion, and the clamant need for self-improvement. He would wear himself out, they knew, here in the mountains, where nothing ever changed.

Coach felt the stench beginning to permeate not just his clothes and his short, cropped thinning hair, but also his skin. He could not wait to get back to his motel room, to take a hot shower. He turned away from the pit, saying that he was chilled, and went and got back in the truck while the boosters lingered awhile longer, admiring their abyss and listening to the faint subterranean cracklings.

When they finally turned away and joined him in the truck, the sulfur and garbage odors were deep set in the fabric of their woolen sweaters. Coach asked whether they could go see the gym now and said that he was eager also to meet the girls.

"They will never be loved by another as I will love them," he said. "They can despise me, and it will not change my love for them."

The boosters smiled at one another. What energy—what a bargain!

Coach has had an interesting life. Before the basketball, he was in the army, and before the army, he was in basketball again. And before that, there was only the prairie and the farmhouse where he lived alone with his mother after his father left them both when Coach was six, and his mother still sick, sick even then, leaving her to raise him alone. Coach has not seen his father since that time, thirty-seven years ago, though he knows he's still alive, knows where he's living, in California.

Coach and his mother ran the falling-down farm by themselves, hiring out when they could, but running parts of it themselves, in good years, when Coach's mother was strong enough. It was she who instilled a love of all sports in him. They would listen to the radio in the evenings, following the nightly fates of whatever acoustic drift would come their way—picking up occasional marquee events, heavyweight title bouts, World Series games, and so forth, even the Davis Cup, each September, when the cottonwoods were first beginning to turn yellow and the summer's terrible heat was finally leaving the land—but more regularly listening to the steady scroll, the nightly scratchy windstream, of Pioneer League baseball, local high school basketball and football, hockey from Missoula, girls' volleyball from as far away as Lewiston and Miles City—anything regular, anything scheduled and dependable, with only the most infrequent of weather-related cancellations.

A hero is a hero in any age, under any setting; the fact that the athletes they listened to would never play in college, much less professionally, meant nothing to Coach and his mother: the various athletes each had names and specific characteristics, valor and passion, strengths and weaknesses, and as long as the radio was working, they were always there, separating Coach and his mother from the darkness that surrounded them, separating them from it as ably as if the names of those players, and the broadcast descriptions of their gestures, were luminous threads, currents of light, the tracing of which lingered in the night air, extending from Great Falls or Choteau or Havre or wherever the gesture had originated, out past Coach's and his mother's farmhouse, extending all the way to the wall of blue mountains, the immense and snowy Front Range that separated west from east, and mountains from plains.

In the years when his mother was up to farming, Coach helped her clear the fields of the wind-varnished glacial moraine deposited there ten thousand years earlier. The stones and boulders—most of which were about the size of a basketball—were infinite in number, remnant and residue from the great ice shield that had overlain the prairie at some not-so-distant point—and no matter how many times they pried them up out of the loose, rich soil each spring, there were always more the next year, with the ice-polished boulders rising through the faint muscular rippling of each season's frost heaves and being expelled like ancient eggs waiting to incubate in the mild sun.

In addition to listening to the games at the kitchen table with his mother every evening, those are Coach's other deepest memories: trudging on stolid ankles through the new-furrowed soil, arms wrapped around one boulder at a time, reclearing the field each spring and summer while his mother, often lacking a tractor, plowed behind a single mule, in other seasons pulling the plow herself, then planting whatever section of field they had been able to clear.

Long spells of daydreaming by Coach, walking the fields in a trance, mesmerized by the shimmering opacity of warmer light radiating from the ground, and betranced, also, by his own physical exhaustion: though for as long as there were stones—or rather, for as long as there was daylight, for there were always stones—he would march back and forth across the fields, belly-gripping each boulder as if anchored to it; and in the absence of any tractor clatter, the only sound would be that of the ever-present wind and his own huffing as he labored onward, the muscles in his neck and back and upper legs burning. His calves sometimes so aflame that it would seem he could light a cigarette just by touching it to them. He was not a tall boy, but his arms stretched longer over the years.

Occasionally in his work he would spy something else glinting in the loosened dirt—arrowhead, tip of buffalo skull—and would stop to pry it out, the regularity of his days leavened by such small discoveries. Not boredom, for even then, he knew he was waiting: that something big would happen, and when it did, he would be in charge, for once, of the change.

A pocketful of arrowheads, and then a box, then several boxes, to sell to the museum in Great Falls for spending money. (Later, when he got older, he returned all his unsold arrowheads to the tribe that had last occupied that land, the Blackfeet.) It was rumored that farther down were the bones of dinosaurs from millions of years ago. But his and his mother's work never plowed that deep, never scratched deeper than the last few hundred years.

In junior high school, still a boy, he pined for his father, but then hardened up, welded shut that little lockbox, cut off the flow of oxygen. He played high school ball and, with his long arms, was a leading rebounder, pretty fair shooter, rogue defender, always fouling out in the fourth quarter, when his team needed him most. Mixed success, and with the welds on the lockbox not yet firmly or fully set: little seeps of oxygen still trickling in at inopportune times. Confusing the coach with his father, raging and rebelling and acting out, frustrated by his inability to be perfect for the man, or the team, he ended up quitting the team midway through his junior year, thinking the coach would come pleading for him to return.

No such drama ensued—he was replaced with a lesser player who, as if by mere mechanical tooling, soon developed to approximately the same caliber of player Coach had been, to the point where the team neither anguished nor prospered in his absence, but instead continued on as if he had never been there: a realization that sent him reeling into more rebellion, and more trouble, including numerous fights, his senior year. A little juvenile detention, some near-jail experiences, but then his old coach intervened, took him back under certain conditions, gave him some tough love, taught him the game, and teamwork, and straightened him out.

He had been mere hours away from the abyss. One of the attributes of a small town, for better or worse, was that you could never really get all the way lost.

So many paths and choices and dead-end trails available to him in a small-town high school: all that walking back and forth across the furrowed fields had not prepared him for the multiplicity of options that would be available to him—before his coach got hold of him, the only two plays he knew were Quit or Push On—but that coach—long gone now—essentially adopted him, mentored him in the seemingly useless art of pick-and-rolls, give-and-gos, diamond-plus-ones. Blew heavy, iron-forging bellows into the last cracks and fissures remaining in the secret lockbox, set him afire, a crackling pyre of unrestrained hunger, and showed him the new boundaries of the world, which were now the confines of the basketball court—as his and his mother's field had known the confines of the rushing, sagging barbed-wire fence and the wind-whittled, leaning fence posts. Taught him how to coach, how to squeeze the game—where the little cracks and secret crevices were—so that giants might be toppled.

School ended, there was no money for college, and no scholarships, so he went into the army—they allowed him to put his mother on his insurance policy—and stationed in Germany, he served long enough to qualify for college on the GI bill. He played some basketball at various overseas bases, came back to Montana, got a degree in psychology—there was little new he learned in those classes, other than the official names for the things he already understood—and then went to work teaching, and coaching, on the reservations. His brother had had a stroke when he was thirty-three, his father at thirty-five, and neither of them had ever even coached—he was a ticking time bomb—but how glorious each pulsing victory was, and how excruciating and torturous each loss, whether large or small, expected or unanticipated. They were easily the best years of his life.

He was back on the east side, his mother was in remission, his heart was not yet bothering him, and he had a couple of flashy sophomores whom he could envision standing beneath those bright lights again in a couple of years. There was no guarantee he could hold his team together for that long— whether on or off the reservation, the pressures of small-town, rural communities on adolescents was intense, and promising athletes were forever falling through the cracks—scholastic probation, bulimia and anorexia, teen pregnancy, drug and alcohol abuse, divorce and family dramas and relocations—and Coach ferociously involved himself in every hour of his girls' lives that was possible, rode herd on their friends, knew whom they hung out with and what they did, and scheduled as many team dinners and bowling nights and movie nights as was humanly possible. It was high energy, high maintenance, but things were coming together: he was weaving a fabric, a culture, of success.

Then he got called up by the army, and that was that. He was stationed in Lebanon, was shot at, and dodged bombs for two full years before there were any studies confirming what everyone already knew, that two years of bombings was not good for the psyche—that one single blast event could take a lifetime to recover—and when that war ended, he was still alive, and still loved basketball, still had the blind spots of a genius, and now, courtesy of his patriotism, a new Achilles' heel, a new impatience and irritability that he chose to confuse with his old impatience and passion.

Almost as if he had two brains, now, two ways of being: though he relaunched himself into his passion with such momentum and focus that for the most part he was able to mask that trauma, was able to stay out ahead of it: as if he had slapped the ball away from an opponent and was sprinting down the court now in a fast break, with no one between him and the orange rim of the basket. And even in his brief downtimes of rest and relaxation, he was able somehow to box out those memories of war—the shock of the first attacks in Lebanon, the shock of being hated indiscriminately, collectively— unfairly, it seemed, rather than specifically—when the first bombing victims were carried into his barracks.

How had he made it back to something as sissy and trivial as girls' high school basketball, and with his passion somehow intact? Good upbringing, he guessed. He put the horrors aside and kept them blocked out the way he told his two smaller low posts to hinge-and-flange lock down another team's dominant center or high post. Remembering a game on the res when his 5'2" guard and 5'5" low post manhandled a 6'3" girl, the district's leading scorer, held her to zero points, reduced her to a sobbing hulk on the bench midway through the third quarter, her confidence wrecked for the rest of the season and, to some extent, much of the rest of her career.

Even in those brief rests, in the off-season, he felt confident that he was able to keep it neutralized—that indeed, the paradoxical mix of high passion and deep irrelevance wrought by basketball was like therapy, and that he could use it to heal from or mask a lifetime of setbacks, as he urged his girls to do. He convinced himself that by making basketball his life, his life would not be able to bleed over into the game. It was a brave and foolish stratagem, simple and reckless. A genius does not always necessarily make a great coach. Obsession can carry the obsessed a long way, but has its costs.

What choice did he have, though? None. And because he loved his obsession because it had rescued him, time and again, thus far—he wanted that for his girls, too.

He had trouble making friends anywhere—so much in this regard conspired against him, from the peripatetic nature of a journeyman coach moving from one school to the next, to the social discomfort of a veteran in a politicized era.

But he did not miss or need adult companionship. It was different, here in the mountains; on the east side, whenever he had taken a new job, he was swarmed with dinner invitations, neighborliness, potlucks; here, he'd thus far had no such invitations. Placerville was a place of brooding, self-absorbed doubt and paranoia, as he had heard was the nature of most of the mountain folk, particularly in basketball season, the dreary lock of winter and then, further on, late-season slush and soggy gray—but no matter, the girls were all, he had staked his life on them, wanted to change their lives, wanted to save their lives, as his mother had saved his, by putting hers on the line—not even knowing who he was or would be, but loving him nonetheless.

A little dizziness and shortness of breath, in the middle of some games. A little bit of clustered star-shot strobes of eerie green light, in the swimming darkness. Pain, sure, high in his chest, but what coach didn't feel that, sometimes?

He was still a young man, but already—how did it go by so fast?—it was getting late in the game. As if he had had a fair-sized lead—not overwhelming, but enough only to then have squandered it through mere inattention and lack of focus. As if he had paused, had decided not to breathe fire for just a little while, but in doing so, had made a mistake, had let the opposition— swarming like demons—overwhelm him.

On his third day in town, the boosters invite him to a team dinner so that he can meet the girls. He has already received his $500 one-time signing bonus, courtesy of the governor of Montana, desperate to keep talented teachers in state, and has already taken his mother to meet her new doctors, and is pleased with them. He's transferred his insurance policy to the new school, has filled out the necessary paperwork for the twice monthly drib-trickle of contributions to his so-called teacher-retirement fund (he hopes for the best, that he might see that day—labors toward it—though he also derives a grim satisfaction from knowing he likely won't live long enough to have to suffer that diminishment, that borderline humiliation). Not that the teacher's life, or even teacher-coach's life, is paved with any economic security—as with the game itself, there is only now, each one step or gesture before the next.

He has met with the utility company and had the power turned on, has spent the weekend hammering and sawing, installing a wheelchair-access ramp for his mother, has gotten the phone turned on and the satellite dish installed so that they might watch all the world's various sporting events together and so that she can watch them by herself when he's away at practice or traveling to one of the away games, long bus trips to distant schools of similar enrollment. There are so few such schools in the state that the bus trips are always long, with the team not arriving back home until around midnight, exhausted, yet refreshed too—he will discover all this later—for having gotten out of Placerville, even if briefly.

Late on the afternoon of the dinner, he finishes photocopying and hole-punching the playbooks he has prepared for each girl, along with various short inspirational essays, proverbs, and mottoes as well as a list of training rules, philosophies, and regulations.

He showers and shaves, kisses his mother good night—she naps every evening from five to eight, then reawakens to watch the delayed telecasts from Europe or the late-start games from the West Coast, surfing back and forth. The new doctor, who is more honest than the old one, as well as closer to her own age, says, when asked his assessment of her future, that at this stage every day is a blessing, and that surely she must be aware of how extraordinarily fortunate she is to have traveled so far into the world and seen so much, and how proud she must be to have a son who loves her.

And then, although the doctor is not really a basketball fan, he begins to talk about the team and their hopes for the coming year.

Coach leaves a note for her, just as he used to do when he was a boy and would be going out somewhere, if she was not home, and then, feeling twenty or thirty years younger—every time that he has to leave one job and start anew, it is this way, terrifying and invigorating both— he lugs the cardboard box, bulging with folders and playbooks, out to his old 1982 Datsun truck—310,000 miles, two-wheel drive, rust-gutted from road salt and the howling winds of the prairie, speckled like Swiss cheese, so that driving down the road, a special harmonic is created that's almost musical or like eerie radio transmissions, perhaps, from another planet—and every bit as eager and nervous as a bridegroom preparing to first lay eyes on his bride, with the church bells beginning to ring, he hurries the short distance over to the school, wanting to get there before they do, not wanting to keep any of them waiting. He does not think he has seen any of them yet—in the grocery store, he's kept an eye out for which girls might possibly be basketball girls—but he's pretty sure he hasn't spotted one of his players. The girls he's glimpsed, here and there, traveling through town, or in the café, or at the bowling alley, did not look like any basketball girls he'd ever seen—though again, you never can tell. He's willing to be surprised.

He's the first one there. He spreads the playbooks out on the tops of each of the nine desks, up at the front of the classroom. He makes sure there is chalk for the chalkboard, and then the boosters arrive, smiling and nervous and eager themselves, carrying grocery sacks and armloads of unidentifiable casseroles, salads, brownies. A Crock-Pot of moose chili. Bread, cake, spaghetti, the meals of a thousand nightmares, but never has he been so glad to see them.

And then they enter, the girls themselves trickling in, laughing and loose, graceful yet also, at some level just beneath the surface, as wary as wild animals coming to a spring to drink: thirsting for the water but knowing also to be observant, maybe even cautious. But laughing, secure in one another's company.

Look at them, Coach thinks, my God, they are beautiful. Look at them, loving each moment, not thinking anything about winning, or even basketball.

He is dazzled by their beauty, their youth, their waiting innocence. He smiles at them, more nervous than he can ever remember being. He cannot help but read them with computer speed, is already diagramming plays on the chalkboard in his mind and then erasing those plays and starting over. He continues to smile, watching them slide into their seats. He had thought that because they were small town, they might not be beautiful, might not be happy, might not be perfect.

Now the athletic director is introducing him, though Coach barely hears the words. Coach looks out at the girls and still is not fully sure what he will tell them.

This is the best part, Coach thinks, even better than the addiction of the game itself. This is the absolute best. The beginning.

He can tell by the cadence as well as accruing stillness—as when concentric ripples in a pond finally begin to vanish—that the athletic director is finishing up his talk. As if through a muffled tube, Coach can hear that ancient phrasing, the one about how the principal goal is not to win but to build character.

No phrase infuriates him more, but he tries his best to remain calm and keeps smiling, almost stupidly: almost as if agreeing. He tries to will the throbbing veins at his temple to stay submerged. Can they see the steam leaking from his ears, he wonders, can they scent the fumes of his burning? He tries to consider the image of the stilled pond and to consider the joy of the girls gathered before him. The speed with which they are leaving childhood and entering young adulthood: faster, really, and more intricate, than any play he could ever devise or diagram.

It's absolutely intoxicating to behold, this arrested or suspended youth— this timelessness—and once more he stands at the edge of it; and hiding his secret heart, *I must win,* he smiles at them and steps up to the podium to introduce himself, in a place and a time where no one will ever grow older or in any way diminished, but instead will burn brightly, purely, cleanly every day, and where each of them, even Coach himself, will—if only they can win—always be loved.

T. C. Boyle

DRAGONFLY

hat a dragonfly was doing out here in the desert, he couldn't say. It was a creature of water, a sluggish slime-coated nymph that had metamorphosed into an electric needle of light, designed to hover and dart over pond and ditch in order to feed on the insects that rose from the surface in soft moist clouds. But here it was, as red as blood, if blood could shine like metal, hovering in front of his face as if it had come to impart some message. And what would that message be? *I am the karmic representative of the insect world, here to tell you that all is well amongst us. Hooray! Jabba-jabba-jabba!* For a long while, long after the creature had hurtled away in shearing splinters of radiance, he sat there, legs folded under him in the blaze of 118-degree heat, thinking alternately: *This is working* and *I am losing my mind.*

And this was only the first day.

YURT

What he wanted, more than he wanted the air to sink into the alveoli of his lungs or the blood to rush through the chambers of his heart, was to tell his wife about it, about this miracle of the dragonfly in the desert. But of course he couldn't, because the nature of this retreat, under the guidance of Geshe Stephen O'Dowd and Lama Katie Capolupo, was silence, silence rejuvenant, unbroken, utter. Three years, three months, and three days of it, the very term undertaken by the Dalai Lamas themselves in their quest for enlightenment. He had signed on, drawn down his bank account, paid his first wife a lump sum to cover her maintenance and child support for the twins, married the love of his soul on a sere, scorched afternoon three weeks ago, and put the finishing touches on his yurt. In the Arizona desert. Amidst cholla and saguaro and sun-blistered projections of rock so bleak they might have confounded the Buddha himself. The heat was an anvil, and he was the white-hot point of steel beaten under the hammer.

Though he felt light-headed from the morning and afternoon group-meditation sessions and the trancing suck of the desert sun, he pushed himself up and tottered back to the yurt on legs that might as well have been deboned for all the stability they offered him, this perfect gift of the dragonfly inside him and no way to get it out. He found her—Karuna, his wife, the former Sally Barlow Townes of Chappaqua, New York—seated in the lotus position on the hemp mat just inside the door. She was a slim, very nearly emaciated girl of twenty-nine, with a strong sweep of jaw, a pouting smallish mouth, and a rope of braided blond hair that drew in the light and held it. Despite the heat, she was wearing her pink prayer shawl over a blue pashmina meditation skirt. Her sweat was like body paint, every square millimeter of exposed flesh shining with it.

At first she didn't lift her eyes, so deeply immersed in the inner self she didn't seem to be aware of him standing there before her. He felt the smallest stab of jealousy over her ability to penetrate so deeply, to go so far—and on the first day, no less—but then he dismissed it as selfish and hurtful, as bad karma, as *papa*. They might have been enjoined from speaking, he was thinking, but he could find ways around that. Very slowly, he began to move his limbs as if he were dancing to an unheard melody, then he clicked his fingers, counting off the beat, and at last she raised her eyes.

CHICKPEAS

Dinner for their first evening of the retreat, after the meager portions of rice and lentils doled out for the communal morning and afternoon meals, had been decided on in a time when they could express themselves aloud—yesterday, that is. It was to consist of tahini, lemon juice, and chickpeas blended into hummus, basmati rice, and naan bread. He was at the stove, watching the chickpeas roiling in a pan of water over the gas jet, which was hooked up to the propane tank half-buried in a pit behind the yurt. The time must have been seven or so in the evening—he couldn't be sure, because Geshe Stephen had encouraged them all to remove their watches and ceremonially grind them between two stones. The heat had begun to lift, and he imagined the temperature dipping into the nineties, though numbers had no value here, and whether it was diabolically hot or, in winter, as he'd been forewarned, unsustainably cold, really didn't matter. What mattered were the chickpeas, golden in the pot. What mattered was the dragonfly.

He'd done his best to communicate the experience to Karuna, falling back on his admittedly rusty skills at charades. He led her to the entrance of the yurt and pointed to the place where he'd been sitting in the poor stippled shade of a paloverde tree, and then used the distance between his forefinger and thumb to give her an idea of the creature and its relative size, jerking that space back and forth vigorously to replicate its movements and finally flinging his hand out to demonstrate the path it had taken. She'd gazed at him blankly. *Three syllables*, he indicated digitally, making his face go fierce for the representation of dragon—he breathed fire, or tried to—and then softening it for the notion of fly, and he'd been helped here by the appearance, against the front window, of an actual fly, a fat bluebottle that had no doubt sprung from the desiccating carcass of some fallen toad or lizard. She'd blinked rapidly. She'd smiled. And, as far as he could see, didn't have the faintest idea of what he was attempting to convey, though she was trying her hardest to focus on the bliss in his face.

But now she was bending to the oven, where the flattened balls of dough were taking on the appearance of bread, her meditation skirt hitched up in back so that he was able to admire the shape of her ankles, a shape as miraculous as that of the dragonfly—or no, a thousand times more so. Because her ankles rose gracefully to her calves and her calves to her thighs and from there . . . he caught himself. This was not right-mindfulness, and he had to suppress it. There would be no touching, no kissing, no sex during the length of the retreat. And that length of time looped out suddenly before him like a rope descending into an infinite well: three years, three months, three days. Or no: two. One down, or nearly down. A quick calculation: 1,189 to go.

He reached for the handle of the pot and had actually taken hold of it, so entranced was he by the poured gold of the chickpeas, before he understood that the handle was hot. But not simply hot: superheated, all but molten. He managed to drop the pot back on the burner without upsetting it, the harsh clatter of metal on metal startling his wife, who shot him a glance out of enlarging eyes, and though he wanted to cry out, to curse and shout and dance through his pain, he just bit his finger at the knuckle and let the tears roll down both flanges of his nose.

TARANTULA

The first night came in a blizzard of stars. The temperature dropped till it was almost bearable, not that it mattered, and he stared hard at the concentric rings of the yurt's conical ceiling till they began to blur. Was he bored? No, not at all. He didn't need the noise of the world, the cell phones and TVs and laptops and all the rest, transient things, distractions, things of the flesh—he needed inner focus, serenity, the bodhisattva path. And he was on it, his two feet planted firmly, as he dropped his eyes to study the movements of Karuna while she prepared for bed. She was grace incarnate, swimming out of her clothes as if emerging from a cool, clean mountain stream, naked before him as she bent for the stiff cotton nightshirt that lay folded beneath her pillow on the raised wooden pallet beside his own. He studied the flex of her buttocks, the cleft there, the way her breasts swung free as she dipped to the bed, and it was so right, so pure and wholly beautiful that he felt like singing—or chanting. Chanting in his own head, *Om mani padme hum.*

And then suddenly she was recoiling from the bed as if it had burst into flame, pinning the nightshirt to her chest and—it was her turn now—jamming a fist into her mouth to keep from screaming. He jumped to his feet and saw the tarantula then, a miracle of creation as stunning in its effect as the dragonfly, if more expected because this was its environment, its home in the world of appearances. Big as a spread hand, it paused a moment on the pillow as if to revel in its glory, and then, on the unhurried extension of its legs that were like walking fingers, it slowly ascended the adobe wall. Karuna turned to him, her eyes fractured with fear. She mouthed, *Kill it,* and he had to admire her in her extremity, because there was no speech, not even the faintest aspiration, just the drawn-back lips and the grimace of the unvoiced verb.

He shook his head no. She knew as well as he that all creatures were sacred and that the very worst *papa* attached to taking a life.

She flew to the drain board, where the washed and dried pot lay overturned, snatched it up, and shoved it in his hand, making motions to indicate that he should capture the thing and take it out into the night. Far out. Over the next ridge if possible. And so he lifted the pot to the wall, but the tarantula, with its multiple eyes and the heat of its being, anticipated him, shooting down the adobe surface as if on a hurricane wind to disappear, finally, into the mysterious dark space beneath his wife's bed.

In the morning, at an hour he supposed might be something like three thirty or four o'clock, the first meditation session of the day began. Not that he'd slept much in any case, Karuna insisting, through gestures and the overtly physical act of pinching his upper arm between two fingers as fiercely tuned as any tarantula's pedipalps, on switching beds, at least for the night. He didn't mind. He welcomed all creatures, though lying there in the dark and listening to the rise and fall of his bride's soft rasping snores, he couldn't help wondering just what exactly the tarantula's message had been. (*I am the karmic representative of the arachnid world, here to tell you that all is well amongst us, which is why I've come to bite your wife. Hooray! Jabba-jabba-jabba!*)

Geshe Stephen, who'd awakened them both with a knuckle rap at the door that exploded through the yurt like a shotgun blast, was long nosed and tall, with a slight stoop, watery blue eyes, and two permanent spots of moisture housed in his outsized nostrils. He was sixty-two years old and had ascended to the rank of *geshe*—the rough equivalent of a doctor of divinity—through a lifetime of study and an unwavering devotion to the Noble Eightfold Path of the Gautama Buddha. He had twice before sought enlightenment in a regimen of silence, and he was as serene and untouched by worldly worry as a breeze stirring the very highest leaves of the tallest tree on the tallest mountain. Before the retreat began, when the thirteen aspirants were building their domiciles and words were their currency, he'd delivered up any number of parables, the most telling of which—at least for this particular aspirant—was the story of the hermit and the monk.

They were gathered in the adobe temple, seated on the floor in a precise circle. Their robes lay about them like ripples on water. Sunlight graced the circular walls. "There was once a monk in the time of the Buddha who devoted his life to meditation on a single mantra," the geshe intoned, his wonderfully long and mobile upper lip rising and falling, his voice so inwardly directed it was like a sigh. "In his travels, he heard of an ancient holy man, a hermit, living on an island in a vast lake. He asked a boatman to row him out to the island so that he could commune with the hermit, though he felt in his heart that he had reached a level at which no one could instruct him further, so deeply was he immersed in his mantra and its million million iterations. On meeting the hermit, he was astonished to find that this man too had devoted himself to the very same mantra and for a number of years equal to his own, and yet when the hermit chanted it aloud, the monk immediately saw that the hermit was deluded and that all his devotion had been in vain—he was mispronouncing the vowels. As a gesture of compassion, of *karuna*"—and here the geshe paused to look round the circle, settling on Karuna with her shining braid and her beautiful bare feet—"he gently corrected the hermit's pronunciation. After which they chanted together for some time before the monk took his leave. He was halfway across the lake when the oarsman dropped both oars and stared wildly behind him, for there was the hermit, saying, 'I beg your pardon, but would you be so kind as to repeat the mantra once more for me so that I can be sure I have it right?' How had the hermit got there? He had walked. On the water." Again the pause, again the geshe's eyes roaming round the circle to settle not on Karuna, but on him. "I ask you, Ashoka: What is the sound of truth?"

ASHOKA

His name, his former name, the name on his birth certificate and his New York State driver's license, was Jeremy Clutter. He was forty-three years old, with a BA in fine arts (he'd been a potter) and an MA in Far Eastern studies; a house in Yorktown that now belonged to his first wife, Margery; and a middle-age paunch, of which he was—or had been—self-conscious. He'd met Sally at a weeklong Buddhist seminar in Stone Mountain, Georgia, and she'd pointed out to him that the Buddha himself had sported a paunch, at the same time touching him intimately there. In his former life, he'd made a decent income from a dot-com start-up, thepotterswheel.com, which had not only survived the '01 crash but also had become robust in its wake. Money built his yurt. Money paid off Margery. Money embellished the geshe's grace. And the geshe gave him his true name, Ashoka, which, when translated from the Sanskrit, means "Without Sadness."

IRONWOOD

The second morning's meditation session, like all the ensuing ones, was held out of doors, on a slightly pitched knob of blasted dirt surrounded by cactus and scrub. There was a chill to the air that belied the season, but to an aspirant, they ignored it. He chanted his mantra inside his head till it rang like a bell, and he resolved to bring a jacket with him tomorrow. Geshe Stephen kept them there till the sun came hurtling over the mountains like a spear of fire, and then he rose and dismissed them. Bowing in his holy, long-nosed way, the geshe took Ashoka gently by the arm and held him there until the others had left. With a steady finger, the finger of conviction, the geshe pointed to a dun heap of dirt and rock in the intermediate distance and then pantomimed the act of bending to the ground and gathering something to him. Ashoka didn't have a clue as to what the man was trying to impart. Geshe Stephen repeated the performance, putting a little more grit and a little less holiness into it. Still, he didn't understand. Did he want him, as an exercise, a lesson, to measure the mountain between the space of his two arms extended so as to reduce it to its essence? To dirt, that is?

Finally, exasperated, the Geshe pulled a notepad and pencil from his pocket and scrawled his redemptive message: *Go up to the mountain and gather ironwood for the winter fires in the temple. Then report*—"report," that was the word he used—*to the temple kitchen to peel potato and daikon for the communal stew.*

FLYPAPER

The days stuck to him like flypaper. The moment was all there was. He went inward. Still, very gradually, the days became unglued, loosening and flapping in the wind that swept the desert in a turmoil of cast-off spines and seedpods. Nights came earlier, mornings later. One morning, after group meditation, the geshe pressed a note into his hand. The note asked—or no, instructed—him to meet the water truck that came bimonthly from the nearest town, Indio Muerto, which lay some thirty-five miles across the motionless plain.

The truck, painted an illusory forest green, appeared as a moving speck in the distance, working haltingly over the ruts and craters of what was once and occasionally a dirt road. He sat cross-legged in the infertile soil and watched it coming for what might have been hours or even days, all sense of time and the transient rush of things foreign to him now. A moment would come when the truck would be there before him, he knew that, and so he spun a prayer wheel and chanted inwardly until it was in fact there, planted before him and obscuring the horizon as if it had sprung up out of the ground.

He saw that a new driver had replaced the expressionless old man who'd come in the past, a lean monkey-faced boy of nineteen or twenty with tattooed arms and a cap reversed on his head, and that the kid had brought his similarly tattooed-and-capped squeeze along for the desolate ride across the waste. No problem there. Ashoka didn't begrudge him. In fact, as he watched them climb down from the cab of the truck, he couldn't help remembering a time when he and Margery had driven across the country together in a car that had no radio and how Margery had said afterward that he'd never shut up for one instant the whole way, singing and laughing and spinning out one story after another, because for him, at least in those days, conversation wasn't about truth or even communication—it was there for its entertainment value, pure and simple.

"So, uh," the kid began, startling him out of his reverie—or no, shocking him with the impact of those two syllables spoken aloud and reverberating like thunderclaps—"where you want me to pump it?"

He pressed his hands to his ears. His face reddened. In that moment, rising, he caught a glimpse of himself in the big blazing slab of the truck's side-view mirror, and it was as if he'd been punched in the chest. What he saw reflected there was the exact likeness of one of the *pretas*, the restive spirits doomed to parch and starve because of their attachments to past lives, his hair white as death and flung out to every point of the compass, his limbs like sticks, his face seared like a hot dog left too long on the grill.

"Whoa," the kid said, even as the girl, her features drawn up in a knot of fear and disgust, moved into the protection of his arm, "you all right there?"

What could he say? How could he begin to explain?

He produced a gesture to wave him off. Another for reassurance. And then, turning so gradually he could have been a tree growing toward the light, he lifted a hand and pointed, shakily, to the water tank, where it floated on wooden struts behind the two whitewashed yurts that housed Geshe and Lama respectively and rose like twin ice-cream cones from the dead, blasted earth.

AIR HORN

Everyone in the community, all thirteen of them plus Geshe Stephen and Lama Katie and including their nearest neighbors, the former Forest and Fawn Greenstreet (now Dairo and Bodhi respectively), had an air horn. For emergencies. In the event of an accident, an illness, a fire, the air horns were to be used to summon help. He spent a long while each day in contemplation of the one he and Karuna had been given, for what reason he couldn't say. Perhaps because it represented a link to the renounced world, a way out. Or because it had a pleasing shape. Or because it was the only object of color, real color, in the yurt.

Karuna was at the cutting board, dicing cucumbers. She'd lost weight. But she was firm and lean and beautiful, not that it mattered, and he was enjoying the sight of her there, her elbows flashing beneath her robes, which pulled back to reveal the pink thermal long johns beneath. Outside it was dark. There was a fire in the woodstove. Karuna's elbows flashed. Earlier, she'd been trying to tell him something of her day, of what she'd experienced on her walk out into the desert, but he couldn't really catch much of it, despite the fact that she was leagues ahead of him when it came to charades. Something about a hillside and a moment and something she'd seen there, tracks, he thought, and a discarded water bottle. He'd smiled and nodded, feigning comprehension, because he liked the way her eyes flared and jumped and sank back again, liked the purse of her mouth and the ghost of her breasts bound up and held tight in the thermal weave that fit her like a new skin.

These thoughts were unhealthy, he knew that. And as he watched her now, he couldn't help feeling even more unhealthy—aroused, even—and so he shifted his gaze to the air horn, where it stood on an adobe shelf like a work of art. And it *was* a work of art. The milk-white canister topped with a red rooster's comb of plastic that was to be depressed in an emergency, the matching red lettering (Sports/Marine, and below it, big horn), and the way the sound waves were depicted there as a flaring triangle of hard red slashes.

Big horn, he said to himself. *Sports/Marine. Big horn. Sports/Marine.* And for that moment, for that night, it became his mantra.

BUP-BUP-BAH

That was a problem, a growing problem, as the days wore on. The mantra, that is, because as the Buddha taught, life means suffering, and the origin of suffering is attachment, and the cessation of suffering is attainable only by taking the bodhisattva path, and yet his mantra became mangled in its eternal repetition until other mantras, meaningless phrases and snatches of tunes, blotted it out altogether. *Big horn* lasted a week or more. And then one chill afternoon, sitting buttock to buttock with Fawn Greenstreet—Bodhi— on one side of him and Karuna on the other, staring through the long-nosed ascetic face of Geshe Stephen and digging inward, shovelful by shovelful, *bup-bup-bah* came to him. It was a musical phrase, from a tune of the great and towering giant of inwardness, John Coltrane, a tune called "Bakai." The horns chanted it rhythmically, *bup-bup-bah, bup-bup-bah*, with a rising inflection on the first *bah* and a descending on the second. He tried to fight it off with *Om mani padme hum*, tried with all his concentration and practice, but it wouldn't budge. It was there, *bup-bup-bah, bup-bup-bah*, like a record stuck in the groove, repeating over and over, repeating endlessly. And worse: his proximity to Bodhi on one side and his wife on the other, given the day and the cold of the ground and the warm inviting odor arising from them both— *bup-bup-bah*—was giving him an erection.

TWINS

Another note, this one handed to him by Lama Katie after the morning
cleanup in the temple and the incantatory scraping of the baked-on oatmeal
from the depths of the communal cook pot. Lama Katie, squat, big breasted,
her hair the color of midnight in a coal mine and her eyes even darker, gave
him a smile of encouragement that radiated down the two deeply etched lines
defining her chin and into the billowing plumpness beneath. She knew the
contents of the note: she'd written it herself. According to the date marked
on the calendar secreted in a chest in the back corner of her yurt, the twins—
his twins, Kyle and Kaden—were due to appear this evening for the first of
their twice-yearly visits. He should wait for them half a mile out, Lama Katie
suggested, so that the noise and presence of the rental vehicle their mother
was driving wouldn't impede his fellow aspirants on their journey down the
bodhisattva path.

It was midafternoon, the winter sun bleached white and hanging motionless overhead, when he turned away from Karuna, who was shucking
a bushel of corn delivered to them on muleback by one of the geshe's more
worldly followers, plucked up a prayer wheel, and went on down the dirt
track to wait for them. The desert ran before him. Birds visited. Lizards. He
sat on a rock and stared off in the distance, chanting beneath his breath, his
mantra beating as steadily in the confines of his skull as the heart beating in
his chest, the Coltrane riff retired to another life in another universe and the
Buddha, the very Buddha, speaking through him.

The car was unremarkable, but strange for all that, its steel shell, the glint
of the sun on its windshield, the twin plumes of dust trailing away behind it
till it was there and motionless and he could see his ex-wife's face, a shadow clenched in distaste, as the two boys, nine years old now—or were they
ten?—spun out of the doors in a flurry of leaping limbs. He caught them
in his arms and rocked them round him in a mad whirl, their voices like
the cries of birds descending to a feast. He showed them the prayer wheel,
let them spin it. Sat with them and listened to their ten thousand questions
(When was he coming back? Where was Karuna? Could they see his yurt?
Did he have a pet lizard? Could they have a pet lizard?). He found that his
mimetic skills had blossomed, and he answered them with his hands, his eyes,
the cast of his mouth, and the movement of his shoulders. Finally, when the
novelty had begun to wear off and they started to look round them for a
means of escape—he could only imagine what their mother must have been
telling them about their father's mental state on the long flight and longer
drive out here—he produced a pad and pencil and wrote them a note.

What he was doing, he reiterated, was seeking the truth, *prajna*, wisdom. Liberation from the cycle of rebirth, in which all beings are trapped. If one soul achieves liberation, that soul can guide others toward achieving it too. They crouched beside him, staring at the pad in his lap, their faces numb, eyes fixed on the words as if the words had no meaning. *I'm doing it for you,* he wrote, underlining fiercely, *for you, for both of you.*

"Mom, too?" Kaden asked.

He nodded.

They gave each other a look, smiles flowering, and in the next instant they sprang up in a sudden delirium of joy and ran to her where she sat in the car, carrying the note like a gift of infinite worth, the paper fluttering in the breeze their moving limbs stirred in the air. She took it, her face a simulacrum of itself behind the reflective windshield, then ordered them into the car. There was the abrupt thunderclap of the engine turning over, the screech of the front end as the car wheeled round, pale miniature hands fluttering their goodbyes out the open window, and then, finally, silence.

RATTLESNAKE

The rattlesnake was itself a shadow, pooled there on the trodden dirt floor of the yurt as if shadows ruled and light was abject. He didn't see it until it was too late. Karuna, her hair released from the tight braid and exerting a life and movement of its own, was washing her face over a pan of water he'd heated for her on the wood stove, and he'd been watching her idly, remembering their first night together after they'd realized to their delight—karma, it was karma—that they lived no more than half an hour's drive from each other through the dense hilly woodlands of Westchester County. They were in Georgia then, the last night of the conference, and they'd lingered over beers, exchanging information, and she was so stunned by the coincidence that she'd slid away from the table in a slow sinuous dance, then taken him by the hand and led him back to her room.

When the snake bit her just above the ankle, where the swell of her calf rose from the grip of the heavy white sweatsock she wore as protection against the evening chill, it was just doing what it was designed to do. There was warmth in the yurt. It had come to the warmth. And she, inadvertently, had stepped on it. She didn't cry out, not even then, not even when the snake snapped back into the shadows as if it were attached to a spring, but just looked down in bewilderment at her bare calf and the two neat spots of blood that had appeared there in commemoration of the puncture wounds. He didn't think of what the snake's message had been, not yet, not before Karuna stretched herself out on the bed and he twisted the tourniquet round her calf and her eyes fluttered and the fire hissed in the stove and the leg began to swell and darken and he took the air horn to the door of the yurt and annihilated the silence in a single screaming stroke.

The snake's message—and he knew it even as Dairo and Bodhi flew up out of the darkness with faces like white darting bats, Geshe Stephen and the others not far behind—was this: *I am the karmic representative of the reptile world, and all is not well amongst us. There is nothing inside and no cessation of pain. Hooray! Jabba-jabba-jabba!*

WITHOUT SADNESS

A tangle of hands moved like thought, juggling mute phrases and tracing the edges of panic. Everyone was gesturing at once, the yurt shrunk round them, the snake vanished, the fire dying in the stove. Karuna's eyes had stopped blinking. She seemed to be in a deep trance, gone as deep as any soul can go, focused on the rising swirls of the ceiling and the circular hole that gave onto the night and the stars and the dead black face of the universe above.

His hands trembled as he gripped the pencil and scribbled a note for Geshe Stephen, who was standing stooped over the bed, looking lost. *We need to get the doctor.*

The Geshe shrugged. There was no doctor. There was no telephone. The nearest town was Indio Muerto. They all knew that—they'd all signed on with that knowledge, and its implications implanted like splinters in their brains.

What about the car?

Another shrug. The community's only automobile was a boxy white Prius belonging to Geshe Stephen, which was housed beneath a formfitting cloth out back of his yurt, where its shape wouldn't tempt anyone from the path or interfere with the business at hand. Its wheels were up on blocks, and the geshe, in a first-day ceremony, had drained the fuel tank and removed the distributor cap as a symbolic gesture while the gathered aspirants looked rapturously on.

We need to get her to the hospital! he screamed across the page in angry block letters.

The geshe nodded. He was in agreement. He dipped his shoulders, produced a tight grin that tapered to a grimace at both corners of his mouth. His expression said: *But how?*

Into that silence that was fraught with the shuffling of feet, bare and slip-pered both, the faint hiss of the stove and the subaural racket of neurons firing in brains that were no longer in touch with souls, no longer calm and meditative, neurons nudged from the path and straining to find their way back, there came a deep harsh ratcheting cry from the figure on the bed, from Karuna. They turned to her as one. Her face was twisted. Her leg was swollen to twice its size. The skin was black around the wound. They all looked shocked, Bodhi especially, shocked and offended, wondering why she hadn't stifled that human noise with a fist, with a knuckle stuffed between her teeth. The silence had been broken, and Karuna had broken it, consciously or not.

What he wanted to say—to roar so that they could have heard him all the way to Indio Muerto and back—was, "Christ, what is wrong with you people? Can't you see she's dying?" But he didn't. Habit, conditioning, the reflex of the inner path, kept him silent, though he was writhing inside. This was attachment, and that sigh was the sound of truth.

YOUR BOAT

Later, after they'd all filed uselessly out, he built up the fire and sat beside her while her breathing slowed and accelerated and finally caught in her throat for the last time. This might have taken an hour or mere minutes, he couldn't say. Into his head had come a new mantra, a jingle from a commercial on TV when he was growing up, a child of baseball fields and macadam bas-ketball courts with their bent and rusted hoops and the intense otherworldly green of a New York summer, a green so multivalent and assertive it was like a promise of life to come. The jingle was for toothpaste, and it made its own promises, and yes, you did wonder where the yellow went when you brushed your teeth with Pepsodent. The new mantra sang in his head and danced a tarantella, double speed, triple, and then it became a dirge. Just before dawn, he found himself running back even further, reaching down to take hold of the earliest mantra he could recall as it marched implacably across the field of his consciousness, beating out its own tempo with two pounding knees on the underside of a metal desk in the back corner of a just-arisen classroom, *Row, row, row your—Om mani padme hum—Gently down the stream. Row, row, row—Om.*

At dawn he got up from the bed and without looking behind him pushed open the door and walked out into the desert.

DRAGONFLY

In the desert, he walked without purpose or destination. He walked past the hill where his wife had found the discarded water bottle, past the place where the green truck had appeared on the horizon, beyond the mountain where he'd gathered ironwood, and down into the hot bleached plain it gave onto. He needed a mantra, but he had none. Into his head it came, the mantra the geshe had given him, but he couldn't sustain it, his mind swept clear of everything now. The sun was the eye of God, awake and staring. After a while, his feet seemed to desert him, and he sat heavily in the lee of a jagged boulder.

What he awakened to were voices, human voices, speaking aloud. He blinked open his eyes and looked up into three terrified faces, man, woman, and child, their wide straw hats framing their skulls like halos. They were speaking to him in a language he didn't understand. They said, "*¿Necesita usted socorro?*" They said, "*¿Tiene agua?*" And then one of them, the woman, went down on her knees and held a plastic jug of water to his lips and he drank, but sparingly, and only because he knew they wouldn't go away, wouldn't stop *talking*, unless he did. He didn't need water. He was beyond water, on a whole different path altogether. He reassured them with gestures, thanked them, blessed them, and then they were gone.

The sun moved till the projection of rock gave up its shade. His eyes closed, but the lids burned till he opened them again, and when he opened them, the dragonfly was there. He studied it for a long while, the delicate interplay of its wings, the thin, twisting calligraphy of its legs, and the perfectly jointed tube of its thorax. And what was its message? It had no message, he saw that now. It was merely a splinter of light, hovering for just a moment—just this moment—over the desert floor.

ESCAPE FROM PRISON

Ron Carlson

Now we hear the voices again, and a dark figure appears around the corner of the cabin. In the forest night, it appears to be a tall man in my old army overcoat. He's wearing the ruined Stetson I wear when I cut trees, and he's carrying a small flashlight, the beam bouncing here and there. I'm sitting with Pam in the old deck chairs by our weathered picnic table at the edge of the meadow. We've been watching the deer move through the far meadow. It is wonderful to have showered and not have sawdust in my socks and inside my waistband. Our glasses of red wine stand on the stump between our chairs. The man staggers out, his light scanning the tall bunchgrass.

"Hello," Pam calls. "Who is it?"

The flashlight shines our way. "Who are you?" the man says, his voice very high.

"We live here. I'm Pam and this is Michael, my husband."

The man approaches slowly. He's hunched and his arms are very short. The hat sits over his ears. "Do you have proper ID?"

"Yes, we do," Pam says. "Who are you?"

"I'm the warden," the high voice replies. "We've had some people escape from prison. Have you seen them?"

"We saw some people earlier," I say. "They were hiding in the grass."

"Are you escapees?" the man says.

Pam looks at me as his flashlight crosses our faces. "No," I say. "We just live here."

The man is circling the perimeter, edging toward the picnic table. The dark meadow beyond glows in the mountain night, and the stars are a full net above the forest. The man is shorter now, shuffling and starting.

"Have you been drinking?" Pam asks.

The man says, "I'll ask the questions. I need to see your ID." And then he stumbles and stands up again, now very tall, and he's scooting very fast for the picnic table. The hat falls off, and he squeals in two voices as the kids tumble forward, Big Bill landing on his hands and knees and racing in a crawl toward the table. Dora's down, lost in the coat. I shoot Big Bill with the Powerlight, a spotlight ray that illuminates his ardor as he reaches for the bench.

"Made it," he cries. "I escaped from prison." He sits up on the bench. "I did. I made it. Mom?"

"Valiant effort," she says.

"Apprehended," I say.

"No, I escaped. Mom?"

"Apprehended," she says.

His chin drops, but he stands up and puts his arms behind his back for the cuffs, walking that way back into the cabin.

"Just a minute, young man," Pam says.

Big Bill turns, our son, the smallest kid in the third grade. I wish he wouldn't put his arms behind him like that; he got it from *Cops*. We don't have a television here in the mountains, but it's always with you. We started this game one night last summer when I brought the light out to spot the deer. As soon as I turned it on, Big Bill ducked into the grass.

"Yes?"

"Did you have an accomplice in your escape attempt?"

I've trained the high beam on my overcoat now, and Dora lies hidden and still underneath.

"No," Big Bill says. "I acted alone."

Before he turns again, Pam says, "You forgot your coat."

He stands for a moment and says, "It's not mine. It's evidence now."

"Could you retrieve it, please?"

"I'm late," he says. "I gotta be in prison."

"Take a minute," I say.

Big Bill goes across the mowed yard to the overcoat and stands between it and my Powerlight. There is whispering. One of the kids laughs. Slowly he reaches and lifts the coat out like a cape, as wide as it will go. He stands like that for ten seconds, and when he lifts it over his shoulder, the girl beneath it is gone.

I run the prison spotlight back and forth from the cabin corner to the picnic table slowly. When the beam hits the edge of the cabin, we can see Dora in the dark sneak again toward the table and freedom.

When you take something that doesn't belong to you, there is nothing to say about it. You took it and you shouldn't have. I took it and I shouldn't have. I took two hundred thirty-seven thousand dollars over a period of sixteen months from the idle accounts of two of my clients, both elderly women whose trusts we managed. I acted alone and I told no one, not even Pam, especially not Pam. It became what I did every month, and there were months that I did not think about it. The thinking commenced when the auditors came in, and though I had covered my tracks in a four-step subterfuge, it didn't take calculus to find me. I had a twenty-one-year career with Kruger and Pederson, and it was Mr. Pederson who fired me and saved me from jail. He arranged the terms of my treatment and of my restitution, which was merciful, though it nearly cost our house and will cost much more every month for years. I took it and I shouldn't have and I lost everything, since my friends and all of my associates, when they heard, were sure I was an evil person. I have no defense. There is no *on the other hand*. I can say I did something wrong, but what is that? I changed everything.

I've traced it back to the start, when I shifted the first installment. I remember seeing the numbers on my computer, and I remember my hands on the keyboard. Why did I do it? I've been in therapy, and I've been as honest as I could be, and I don't know why I did it. It has made me a stranger in my skin, and the days no longer fit the way they did. It wasn't a thrill, and there wasn't special pleasure in doing it, and though it turned out to be a lot of money, the money made little difference in our lives. Until now.

It'd been five months, and when summer came around, we decided to leave Denver and come back up to the family place for the whole summer, not just a few weeks. Pam said we were going, and we came. I know she is tumbling it all in her heart, in her head. Will she stay? She had put her face in it for these past months at her firm, where she was headed for partner, and then she called in her leave time, and we are in the big woods. Every night in bed, she says one thing: Michael, why did you do it?

I have ruined my life.

Saturday, there's a cabin meeting for the nine cabin owners at McAllen's place to talk about the well. The Forest Service has mandated a well; the two catch boxes by the creek have to be removed. All the other families are local and live in the village of Rutledge; they're the upper crust of Rutledge, really, with these summer homes on the mountaintop. McAllen is editor of the paper, and four others own businesses in the town, the hardware, the car dealership, and the like. We are outsiders. I know a few of these guys, who came around other summers when I was clearing trees, when I taught myself the chainsaw, while in my other life I was taking money that was not mine.

After we talk about how many deer there are this summer, the discussion is about where to put the well for equal distribution to the nine cabins and whether we should just hire the whole job out: clearing, drilling, the well shed, and the road.

McAllen's got the numbers.

His cabin is one of the biggest, most like a real summer home, and has a deck overlooking the meadow. From here, I can see our place, the red barbeque grill and the picnic table, five hundred yards across the sage and grass field. The potluck is all kinds of chicken and macaroni salads; there's a tub of beer and soda, and the men have moved their paper plates to one side of the unrolled topo map McAllen's laid out on the picnic table with a river rock on each corner. A couple of the guys I've met have greeted us, Jenson and Guyman. *Glad to see you up for the summer*, like that, but it feels odd. I suspect some of them know, and if one, all. Ed Guyman, a tall man, stands apart, talking to no one.

The kids are all below us on the slope playing Frontier Croquet, a game Pam and Mrs. McAllen are monitoring. Evidently there are teams, and I can see Dora with another girl standing by their orange ball way down by the meadow grass, sensible sixth graders. Big Bill is following two other kids who are a little older, and I can see they're not letting him hold the mallet.

"If we give this whole job to Clear-Pipe," Guyman is saying, "they'll subcontract the clearing and the shed and the road, and they'll charge us double. They're drillers. They can put in the well; we should subcontract the rest."

"It's one-stop shopping, though," McAllen says. "We all write a check and it's done." We already know Clear-Pipe has bid the project at seventeen thousand dollars. "I don't have time this summer to cut trees and haul gravel. Besides, I'd hurt myself."

"Where will it be?" Jensen asks. He owns the sporting-goods store and sold me my chainsaw six years ago.

McAllen points to the two red circles; both are above the cabins but not far into the old growth, which is now given generally to standing dead and deadfall timber. The residual beetle kill punished great sections of the forest. I know both sites because we've hiked through them on the way up to Canyon Ridge, the little mountain that guards the valley.

"It's easier for some to write a check than others," Guyman says. "How much is the drilling itself and all the plumbing work?"

"Eleven," McAllen says. "We have until September, and then the water gets turned off."

"I can clear the trees," I say. "I don't know about the rest. Do they want the stumps out?"

"Only the ones that might be in the road."

"We could work around that," Guyman says. "A Toughshed isn't five hundred dollars, and we can have gravel hauled for a thousand."

"You can," McAllen says. "You want to head this up?"

"We could clear the trees and see," Guyman says. "How long would that take?" He's turned to me.

"I don't know," I say. "A week of mornings, I guess. If we can get the wood and slash hauled."

Don Treathway, who owns the little cellular store in town, brings over four longnecks and stands them on the map. "Beer?"

"Take one, Mike," McAllen says to me. "You've got some timber ahead of you."

The party breaks up late in the day, and Pam comes out of the McAllen's kitchen, where she's been cleaning up with the other women. I can see Big Bill in the trees playing some kind of tag with the kids; their cries have been continual through the day. The game has king's X if you are touching an aspen, and those who are it walk through the grove counting one–one thousand, two–one thousand. There's some kind of clock on it all.

"You got a new job," she says to me.

"I do," I tell her. "Some exercise."

"Be careful."

"Guyman's going to help," I tell her. "It will be go slow and heavy lifting." I look at her. "I need it. I'm glad for it."

Dora is now against Pam's side suddenly, a hug, her cheeks red and breathing hard. When did she get this tall? "Mom, can I stay at Karen's overnight?"

"What did her mom say?"

Before I can ask, "Who's Karen?" the deal's done.

A minute later Big Bill appears. Pam's got our Tupperware and table-cloth. "Dad, dad," he says. "This is Vernon Guyman."

A kid who appears a foot taller than Big Bill steps up, one pant leg all mud. "Glad to meet you," he says, shaking my hand. "I fell down. I'm in the same grade as Big Bill. I want to play Escape from Prison."

"Is your sister Karen?" Pam asks.

"She's my sister," the boy says. He stands straight as a cadet.

"Why don't you both come over tomorrow, and we'll have a cookout and you can stay over?"

Without hesitation, he nods and says, "That'll work." He shakes her hand now and runs off. Big Bill goes to follow, but Pam takes his shoulder.

"Let's go home. We've got to get your sister ready for her night out."

The well site is seventy big steps into the timber, and Guyman and I pace it off several times, trying for the shortest distance to our dirt road, and to circumvent the trees. These lodgepole pines are thick, but we find one path bending in an arc, which means we won't have to pull any stumps. Clear-Pipe has sprayed a big yellow X in the area and flagged the four corners; it'll be a clearing of a hundred by fifty when we're done. It's shady and cool in the thick trees, two-thirds of which are dead, and the quiet feels alien. It's this way for miles up toward the mountain.

"Let's just get a count," he tells me. I stand at one corner, and he walks in an arc counting aloud. There are almost sixty trees. "A week?"

There are a dozen leaning dead, which we'll have to drop first. This is going to be a pile of sticks. "We could drop them in a week, but we'll have to haul as we go. There's no place for them to fall."

He looks at me. "You volunteered for this. A banker."

"I was a banker. We'll go one tree at a time from the middle out."

"I'll get the week off and come back up tomorrow," he says. "I'll bring my gear." We meander back slowly through the trees. "You guys moving up here?"

"No, we'll go back in September." Guyman wants an explanation. I say, "We're taking the whole summer this year."

"Must be nice."

We emerge onto the circle road, where we will turn to part.

"We're glad to be up here," I say. "I had some legal trouble."

"Hey," he says. We shake hands and start to walk away, when Guyman comes back a step. "I grew up here," he says. "When I was twenty-four, I stole four cars."

"And now you're the pharmacist."

"I am. I'll see you this weekend."

It is a simple pleasure to peel off my woodcutting clothes. I take my pants off behind the cabin and shake them out; there is half a cup of sawdust in each pocket, and my socks are shot through. The shower is a weak-force one this time of summer, but my water heater works, and the warm water and soap burn around my wrists and my collar and my ankles where I'm chafed. My old flannel shirt feels good, as do the clean hair and a drink. We grill some chicken in the mountain twilight. Pam is quiet, tending to the kids. They've done some plaster of Paris today, making bears using the empty honey bottle. The little white statues are drying on the mantel.

"We're going to paint them tomorrow," Big Bill says.

"What color?" I ask him.

"We'll have to see about that," he says. I know what he'll do. He'll watch what his sister and her friend do, and then he'll do that, but painting the feet or the face another color.

Later, in the new dark, it's Escape from Prison. Karen is a giggler, and Dora cannot get her to stop giggling. It is too exciting for her friend, and I move the light extra slowly back and forth so they can run a few steps and duck into the meadow. We never see Big Bill; he must be crawling the whole way.

"Is Bill in the cabin?" Pam calls.

There is no answer.

"Bill?" she says again.

I search the area with the powerful light, trying to avoid Karen and Dora where they hide.

"Bill's okay," we hear Bill say. He's lowered his voice for the announcement. As Dora and Karen approach the table, the light goes by and they make their move, Dora dashing to the bench. Karen starts, and then stands giggling, unable to move. The light comes back, and there she is in hysterics.

"You're apprehended," Dora says. "You're going back to prison." She walks her friend into the cabin, where they will go out the back door and escape again. They try four more times while Bill is out there somewhere. Twenty minutes later, when the light catches Dora trying to get her friend up to run, we see a figure on the picnic table. Big Bill is grinning.

"How you doing?" he says.

I bring the light over.

"What did you do to yourself?" Pam says. He's soaking wet and all mud, a mud man.

"Don't go that far out into the meadow," I say. "It's too wet." I shine the light out across the expanse, and we see the two dots of the moose's eyes. "Look, kids," Pam says. "The moose." The big animal lifts her head and walks up the far slope.

So the prison is shut down, and there is one more shower before bed. Karen and Dora go up in the loft, and within a minute we can hear Karen sleeping. She's a real breather. Big Bill sleeps on the foldout down with us, and being clean, he crashes right out.

In bed, Pam keeps her place, the way we've slept for all these months. I tried to talk at first, but we just repeated ourselves. Now I hold it all and say my prayer silently and try for sleep. I've got a little rotary blade sharpener for the chainsaw that hooks onto the car battery, and what I do in bed is close my eyes and see it and grind and sharpen the chain tooth by tooth.

Pam says, "What's Guyman like?"

"He's a good guy," I say. "A good worker."

"He's the pharmacist, Mrs. McAllen said."

"He is. He grew up here. He said that he stole cars when he was a kid."

"Really. Why did he say that?"

"I think people here know about me."

"About us."

"No, it's about me, Pam." Big Bill is sleeping, but we hear him turn. "Did you ever steal anything?"

Pam turns to me for the first time in months. "What?"

"Did you?"

"I pissed off my sister by taking her sweaters. All the time."

"No, I mean steal something. It wasn't yours and you took it."

"I don't know," she says. After another moment, positioned for sleep, Pam says, "I'm sure I did."

I work with Guyman, clearing the well site for four days. On the first afternoon, he watches me enough that he runs the saw and drops a few trees: first cut, wedge cut, and then the back cut. When two guys work with one saw, they stay close together so the sawyer knows where his partner is. There's a timber accident in McAllen's paper every week. People run the wrong way. Last summer a woman was killed. You stand over the shoulder of the man with the saw and step back with him when the kerf opens, releasing the saw, and the tree starts to go. If there are downed trees, it gets dangerous because the falling trees teeter-totter and the trunk can go up ten feet and then come down again.

I actually love the days. I like knowing what I'm doing when I get up. Every day, the same Levis and flannel shirt. When I shake the shirt every morning, there is still sawdust in it. After gloves and boots, long sleeves are the most important part of the outfit. Guyman wears an old straw cowboy hat with a hole in the crown. It won't prevent him from getting killed, but he said at least he'll look good. I told him he should also consider that part of it.

I clean my saw every night on the old wooden cable spool I use as a work-table behind the cabin. I take the blade off, brush the gunk out with a bristle brush, and wipe it down. The third day, when McAllen walked over to see our progress, he said, "There's a pretty saw."

We move all day, dropping two or three trees at a time and then cutting them up. Guyman's got a little Igloo cooler on the tailgate of his Ford pickup, and we go back there every half hour and drink water. He drives back to his cabin for lunch, and I sit in the shade against a tree and eat the thick turkey and cheddar sandwich Pam made. I could walk down a quarter mile to our cabin, but I'd interrupt arts and crafts, and going back would make me want to stay, thinking something will be said. In bed when we talk, Pam has re-peated one thing a few times, and it's hard to hear. She says, "Did you want this to happen? Did you want this damage?" I don't know what to say to this. When Pederson called me in, he came to my office and said, "Do you want to talk about this in person?" I told him I did. He was straight up; he said, "We are going to call this an accounting error, which it is. Do you know what it means?" I said I did. It meant I should clean my desk and arrange restitution. "You can do this," he said. He never asked me why I had done such a thing.

Guyman and I dropped about half the trees and then started bucking them into eight-foot lengths. Cutting is the easy part, of course; clearing the brush and hauling the logs is the work. In the bed, Pam turned to me one night and said, "You're getting skinny." The bank fat is off, and I feel different, though I get up every night twice with cramps in my calves. McAllen came over on the fourth day and loaded the lengths into his pickup to stack at his place. He and Jensen volunteered to cut them stove length and divide them up.

"You've got firewood your grandkids will burn," he said. "Even if they're here every winter until the well runs dry."

The next day, as we're dragging the logs to the edge of our new clearing, Guyman says, "What are you hoping for, some sort of happy ending in the mountains?"

"What?"

"You think that you're earning points with these people?" I drag my timber up onto the big stack we're making and drop it. "We cut these trees and you're all set?"

"Not really," I say. "I don't see this ever ending. Happy or no."

"Right," he said. "Now we can do this. Let's cut five more. Nobody's happy. And Mike. Nobody likes me either. The pharmacist. They all think I'm rich. And they think that I think I'm a real doctor." He stops and appraises me. "Are you on meds?"

"No," I say. "I was."

"Well, see. Good." He put his gloves on. "Half of these guys think I'm still a hell-raiser. They lock their cars up here."

The well site is utterly changed. Cleared out like this, with the daylight pouring in, it's as if we've uncovered a secret. We don't have any trouble until the fifth day. We had one tree go back the first day, a standing dead that simply stood in its cut and then went exactly back. Dry, dead trees are more dangerous. We're in the last five trees, and I'm kneeling, making the back cut, angling it down to the wedge, when the kerf closes and the saw stalls and dies. "Oh oh," I say, but Guyman is back by his truck. "Ed," I call, and I stand bracing against the tree. You can't stop a tree, but when he joins me, we hold it. It wants to go back, and if it goes back, it's going to crush Guyman's Ford pickup. He's parked closer every day. We stand like that, at forty-five degrees, shoulders on the trunk, and we're both at full push, staring at the saw blade squeezed in the cut. There's no wind as far as I can tell.

"Goddamnit," he says.

I've never been up against anything like this, the tree a seventy-foot, one-ton column, and we're looking at the three-sixteenths of an inch where the blade of my saw is trapped, pushing with every muscle, breathing like weight-lifters. I think I hear children's voices, but I can't turn to look. No children, no children. I think about everything, really, my boss, Pederson, saying to me, "You know what this means." This is worse. A minute goes by, and the adrenaline rinses through, making this all feel like doom. My arms are trembling. The mountain air saws sharply in and out of my nose. There is a steel band around my forehead now, my teeth clenched. We did so well. I feel a little air at my neck, a breeze, and I can't tell, but something is happening.

There is no way to look up, to check for wind. The kerf opens a hair, and we can see the splinters along the cut rise like whiskers.

"Go," I say, and from somewhere inside me, there is one more push. The saw, suspended in the tree like a dagger, slides, and we see the cut open half an inch and stop. Now, I am rubber, but we hold it, and the space opens to an inch and then two. It wants to stay up so badly, and then the first crack and Guyman is pulling me back away. I leave the saw and stumble with him as the huge tree rips forward like an exploding door and swings heavily into the earth.

I sit on a stump, soaking wet. Guyman is over leaning against the truck, and then he sits on the tailgate, and then he lies back with his feet hanging down. I lie down in the sawdust, and my heart pulls at my legs, my head. After a while, the shade falls and I look up at Guyman.

"Okay, Michael," he says. "We got it done. McAllen can come and get these. I'll see you tonight."

"Good, good," I say.

"Are you okay?"

"Oh yeah," I say. The sky around his head is a primal blue. "We got it done."

Later, when I sit up, the light has changed. My gut hurts where I pushed, and my shoulders are cramped. I've never reached deeper in my life. The blood is working through my head. I'm awake. Walking down to the cabin, my legs feel like they were just made, and I test them out. The webbed shadows on the forest floor appear as a pattern from a tale, something unreal and familiar. I had forgotten that I loved my life.

We're having a cookout for the Guymans and McAllens, and there's a slug of sleepover kids coming later. When I come into the dooryard, Dora and Big Bill are out at the spool table, trying not to touch their painted bears. Dora's bear is silver, and Big Bill's is silver with red ears and red feet. "Looks good," I say.

"Is it dry?" Dora says.

"No," I say. "But it will be in half an hour. As soon as you forget them, they'll be dry. That's how it works."

I put the saw in the shed; I'll clean it tomorrow. Pam is in the kitchen, wrapping the potatoes. "Do you want to start the grill?"

"I do," I say. "I'll do it right now." Outside, the valley is a glowing shadow, and I'm a man starting a little fire in his dooryard. I walk back into the cabin and stand behind my wife. "Pam. Are we going to have grandkids?"

"Not right now," she turns, puts her hand on my hip. "Right now, we've got plaster bears. But Michael," her hand is now on my face. "Yeah, given time."

"Good," I say. I haven't talked like this all year. "I'm going to need some."

After the charcoal has started, I go out back and shake my shirt, and I sit on the ground and peel off my socks. I pull the pockets of my Levis inside out. I'm done with this outfit. This all goes in the laundry tonight, and when it does, that shirt is going to come apart.

McAllen brings a cooler of the beer made at the brewpub in town, called Mill Dew, and it's heavy and good, and after all the grilled chicken, everyone is feeling heavy and good. At any moment there is only one person up, Guyman's wife, Carol, taking in the dishes, or McAllen to get more beer. We're all out sitting in lawn chairs. "Jeez," McAllen says, pointing across to his place, "I need to paint under the deck."

"Your place looks good."

"And I'll get that wheelbarrow out from under there." His yellow wheelbarrow has always been there.

"It's fine."

"You don't come to the woods to look at my wheelbarrow."

"Yes, we did," Pam says. "That's why we came."

Henry McAllen brings out a sheet cake with a green design on top that is probably a pine tree. The kids line up at the old picnic table; now I can hear giggling, and Karen has arrived, and colored shirts are coming down the long driveway through the trees, kids carrying their sleeping bags and pillows. It looks as if we're having the whole mountaintop over.

"When will they drill the well?" Guyman asks.

"Next week," McAllen says. "You guys did us all a favor with those trees."

"I wasn't fishing for a compliment, Henry."

"I wasn't dishing any out."

Then in the twilight, the cabin lights go on. Pam makes a pot of coffee, and the adults arrange their chairs to watch the kids chase fireflies and carry on. Vernon has arrived, and he and Big Bill start a game of tree tag out back, and then Dora appears with her silver bear, which goes hand to hand for appreciation. I can feel my arms pinging, and there's a place in my lower back that goes hot from time to time. My heart tours freely: my elbows, my throat, every minute or so some thump-thump. By dark, I give all the kids little flashlights and have them play Spy, which lasts about five minutes. Vernon and Big Bill come up to me. "We want to play Escape from Prison," Big Bill says. "Everybody does."

"Try Spy for a while."

"It's no fun," Vernon says. "We need the Man." Big Bill's back in a minute with the Powerlight. When it goes on, the children yelp and run behind the cabin. Evidently, everyone knows the rules. The game has begun.

"You're the Man," Pam says.

"He's a lumberjack," Guyman says.

"There's no money in it," I tell her. "And no points."

Pam puts her hand on my knee, where my heart beats now, and says, "There's points."

The escapees come in waves, a dozen kids running and then suddenly mowed down by the light. When they see it coming, they dive into the weeds. Karen's little sister is five, and she doesn't dive, but stands amused in the strange traffic, wandering around as the light passes.

"This is more of a general jailbreak," McAllen says. Several kids make the table, crying, "I'm free!" Vernon sits there for a minute and then stands with his hands behind his back for the cuffs and starts to walk to the cabin.

"You made it, Vernon."

He comes over to my chair. "No, I was apprehended," he says. "I've got to go do my time." We all watch him walk slowly through the cabin front door. In the window, we can see him run out the back.

"It's a revolving door," Guyman says.

The kids run and dodge the light. They don't try any costumes, but there are all kinds of coded chirping and humming from the escapees. Karen's little sister eventually reaches the table, and she sits on the bench, swinging her legs. Beside the cabin, I see the three rolled pup tents that we'll set up in the front dooryard, kids sleeping in the forest. A moment later, I catch something across the meadow, and I focus on the dozen dots of the eyes of the grazing deer. When the light is still like that, we can see the kids, one by one, standing up in the dark.

"It's the deer," Dora comes to my side and stands against my chair. She runs her arm across my shoulder, measuring me from her new height.

"They're apprehended," Vernon says, coming up.

I turn the light off, and the dark stamps the silhouettes of children onto the world. They drift quietly toward the adults now. Big Bill drags one of the tents forward; it looks as if we're going to make camp.

BONNIE AND CLYDE IN THE BACKYARD

K. L. Cook

y mother, Whit, and Clara are at church, so I put the Chopin that Doc Melbourne lent us on the Victrola to soothe my father into sleep. Whit and I slaughtered a hog early in the morning, and the meat will rot in the May sun if I don't tend to it. I sheathe the hog, dispose of the trimmings, and am hypnotically rinsing the blood from the slaughter slab when I see a car barrel down the road to our farmhouse. A plume of dirt billows behind. Who in the world would drive the farm road that fast? I clean my hands and run to the house as a beautiful sand-colored sedan brakes in front. It looks new, despite the dried mud blasted against the fenders and sideboards. The dust rises up and over the hood like a shroud. I squint and cover my face with my sleeve. Though I've never seen them in person, I know before they speak a word who they are. I scan the backseat for more passengers, but it's just the two of them.

"Your father named Zachary?" Clyde asks. He's boyish, with a dark brown curl of greasy hair flopping on his forehead below his fedora, and his voice is higher pitched than I imagined it would be. I wonder for a moment if maybe I'm mistaken. Maybe they're just joyriding kids.

"Yep," I say.

"What's your name?"

"Riley."

"Glad to meet you. I'm your cousin, thrice removed. Clyde." I shake his small, calloused hand. "This here's my wife, Bonnie."

"I see handsome runs in the family," she says, and Clyde smiles.

I know they aren't married. I know everything about them. I know she was married once when she was sixteen to a thief named Roy Thornton. I know she was a waitress at Marco's Café in Dallas. I know Clyde has killed at least ten men by now, including four police officers. I know that Buck is dead, his face and skull practically shot clean off in an ambush in Platte City. I know about the banks in Oklahoma and Missouri and Louisiana and New Mexico. I know about Bonnie's aunt in Carlsbad and the policeman they kidnapped there and dropped off in San Antonio, the one that made them famous. And I know, as everyone else in the country knows at this point in 1934, that it's just a matter of time before they will be caught or killed.

"My father's been sick," I say.

"I'm sorry to hear that," Clyde says. "What's wrong?"

"Something's the matter with his head."

He laughs. "You can say that about most folks in Texas."

Bonnie slaps his arm. "Be respectful," she says. And then to me, "Don't mind him none. He's just like that. How's your daddy doing?"

"Not too well."

"Can we see him?" Clyde asks, suddenly serious. "He was nice to me when I was a boy. My mom's favorite cousin. She made me promise to stop by and pass on her good wishes."

I nod.

"Good deal," he says.

They step out of the car. The sight of them surprises me. So little. From the stories about them in the papers, I expect size, a certain grandeur. Yet she isn't even five feet tall, a girlish wisp, though prettier in person than in the newspaper photos, her skin pale, almost translucent, with freckles and a big, pretty smile and almost straight teeth. Her reddish-blonde hair twirls in ringlets to the bottom of her neck. A bright red skirt and a matching sweater cling to her body. I glimpse, at the hem of her skirt, white gauze wrapped around her leg.

Clyde isn't much bigger, certainly no bigger than I am at thirteen. The coroner's report will later say that he was five seven and weighed a hundred and thirty pounds. When he takes off his hat, his thick brown hair makes his head look too large for his body, as if he is a little girl's doll. He has an oval-shaped face with baby fat and freckles, a kid's face, complete with a couple of nicks on his cheeks and a scab on his forehead. He sports a green-and-red-striped tie, like a Christmas dandy, but his shirt is spattered with either dirt or blood. He walks with a slight limp, a pistol tucked into the front of his pants. My mother won't appreciate that pistol. She won't appreciate this visit at all. But I am not about to tell Clyde Barrow, third cousin or not, that he can't carry a gun onto our property.

"The rest of your family here?" Clyde asks.

"They went to church."

He nods.

"Clyde, the car," Bonnie says.

"You got a barn, son?" Clyde asks. I point to the north side of the house, beyond the stand of peach trees. "You think your father'd mind if I parked my car in there?"

"I guess not."

"Why don't you give the boy a ride?" Bonnie says.

"I'll do one better." Clyde tosses me the keys. "You know how to drive, don't you?"

"Yes, sir."

"Well then."

I get in the car, and Bonnie climbs in with me. Her skirt rises up. The bandage extends beyond her knee to her thigh.

She catches me looking. "An accident," she says. "But I'm better now. Clyde nursed me back to health, the sugar."

I turn the key, and the engine starts right up, without any trouble, just hums.

"This is nice, ain't it?"

"Yes, ma'am."

"Feel these custom seats." She places her little hand on mine and runs my fingers over the upholstery. "It's also got a built-in water-style heater." She turns it on, and hot air pours like the breath of a horse from the vents. "Not that we need it in this weather, huh?"

Clyde pokes his head inside my window. He smells, strangely, like sweat and oranges. "She sure is sweet on this damn car," he says. "Let's put her away."

I inch the sedan along. At the barn, Clyde says he'll get the doors. He limps over and swings them open. The chickens squawk and flutter, sounding an alarm, but he walks in like it's his place, not ours, and I roll the car over the hay-strewn ground until he holds up his hand for me to stop. Bonnie and I get out, and I drop the keys in Clyde's small hand.

"Thanks," I say.

"The pleasure's mine, son." It sounds odd, him calling me "son," since he doesn't seem much older than me, though of course I know that what he's done over the past few years—including the stint down in Eastham prison—is enough for any lifetime.

Bonnie and I stand on either side of him while he opens the trunk. About a dozen guns clutter the padded floor, including revolvers, rifles, and two of the automatics called BARs that I've seen in the newspapers and magazines. There's a crate of oranges there and a box of license plates. Clyde smiles at me, proud of his stash. I try not to reveal any surprise, but my face must please him because he and Bonnie both laugh.

"What'll it be?" Clyde asks Bonnie. "Texas, Arkansas, New Mexico, or Missouri?"

"Let the boy decide," Bonnie says.

The plates on the car are from Kansas. I know Clyde likes to change plates frequently, usually after every job.

"What'll it be, sugar?" Bonnie says to me. "You choose."

"Texas," I say with no hesitation.

"Why?"

"Because you're less likely to attract notice with in-state tags."

Bonnie steps around Clyde and kisses me on the cheek. "I think we're gonna have to recruit you. You're good-looking *and* intelligent."

She hooks her arm in mine as Clyde changes the plates.

"Why don't you go tell your father we're here," she says, almost a whisper.

"Yes, ma'am."

I quit school the previous fall to help my mother. My father had been bedridden for several months. The three of us kids—my youngest sister, Jenny, had died of diphtheria by then—would sit with him in the parlor or in his room or sometimes, when it was warm, in the backyard beneath the cherry tree when we thought he was closer to death and his fingers and toes started to lose their feeling. We just stared at the wood plank floors or the ground, those knotholes and seams and blades of grass riveting our attention. In those early months, we feared to look at him, afraid of what bad luck had done. It felt like an apology in our home. None of us knew what to say or how to express the sadness that lay like sharp stones in our stomachs, none of us looking up because what we'd see was not him but rather that huge unworldly lump, swelling so that it seemed like a cantaloupe had taken root under his scalp, small patches of black fuzz trying to find purchase on his skull.

He was still our father, of course, but he wasn't long for this world, and after a while we got used to the idea. He was no longer the man we'd known. During the day, he remained fairly lucid, but at night he lost hold of whatever tethered him to us. I understood sooner, since I was the oldest, and I sat with him some nights to spell my mother. It was spooky there with him, especially when he'd mutter and shout in some strange gibberish, waking me from a fitful dream of my own. He'd startle up, the kerosene lamp by his bedside just barely going, and then carry on a conversation with me, as if nothing had happened, but it wouldn't be me he'd be talking to but rather his own father, who'd died in the Spanish-American War, or to his grandmother who raised him.

His head made shadows on the wall, lopsided shadows, and I'd listen and watch and not know what to say, afraid if I spoke, if I angered or contradicted him, then he'd be lost to us forever. It was a frightful time in my life, and I didn't think a day would ever go by that I wouldn't think about those nights with my father as he lay dying, his head expanding.

No one knew why it happened. A couple of the other farmers in town speculated he got kicked too many times by irritable mules, which was true. Others said it was because he'd gotten in a fight with Peter Cooley, from the next county over, and Cooley had hit him over the head with an iron rod. That, too, was true. Sam Fogarty, the sheriff, said it was drink because my father had bootlegged vinegary whiskey in 1931, when a series of floods and hailstorms ruined our cotton and corn, but my father was never much of a drinker himself. Ladies at my mother's church whispered that he'd gotten his just deserts for tomcatting all over the county, crawling between the sheets with any lonely sinner who'd spread her legs for a good time at the price of damnation. My father was no saint. I knew that. But I couldn't then, and didn't imagine I would ever, believe in a god that doles out punishment in that way.

Doc Melbourne thought it was water on his brain, brought on by a bad bout with a virus that fevered him on New Year's Day 1933. He predicted that the swelling would eventually recede. It didn't. A surgeon from Houston made a trip to our house because of research he was doing on brains and said what caused the swelling was something reproducing inside his head and that it couldn't be cut out. He told us it was probably cancer, but it could also be something else that had a long name that contained about fifteen consonants. The surgeon wrote it down, but my mother threw it away. He said he'd never seen a case like my father's, a head *erupting* (his word) so large and irregularly that the scalp had stretched thin enough to see the deformed skull. He said it would get worse. My father'd be in miserable pain, and then he would die, and what we should do was to make his last months as comfortable as possible.

"And make your peace with him."

"You a preacher as well as a surgeon?" my mother asked, her left eyebrow arching.

"No, ma'am," he said. "Just encouraging you to do right by him and yourselves, so you don't regret it later."

"You just take care of the diagnosing," she said. "Since you're so good at it. And we'll take care of the peacemaking."

"No offense, ma'am."

"None taken," she said, but it was clear to even those of us who weren't brain surgeons that she didn't mean it.

The only thing that was keeping my father halfway interested in life during this time was the newspaper stories of the Barrow Gang. He hadn't seen Clyde in more than a decade, not since Clyde was a kid. Even before my father fell ill, we were keeping track of what was happening to Clyde, his brother Buck, Bonnie, and the various members of the Barrow Gang. My father enjoyed his connection to these celebrities, and celebrities they were, even if notorious. My mother didn't approve, though she didn't want to bad-mouth them either. She told Whit, Clara, and me that we shouldn't brag to our friends about being related to them. That would only result in Sheriff Fogarty getting suspicious about us. Nobody wanted that, she said. Life was difficult enough.

By summer of 1933, my father had already gotten so bad off we could sense that it wouldn't be long, excepting a miracle, before he'd be dead. So my mother let me and Whit read the newspaper stories to him while she and Clara made dinner. She thought Clara was too young for the stories and couldn't be trusted not to tell her schoolmates.

Of course, I'd learned to read before I quit school, was a damn fine reader in fact, poring over the few books we owned, including the collected works of John Milton, though my mother didn't appreciate his depiction of Satan as a seductive orator. She said it wasn't right that Satan turned out to be the most entertaining character in the book.

My father laughed. "God loves the virtuous," he said, "but everyone else loves a sinner. Even old blind Milton." My mother smiled at that, which surprised me, given the history of their relationship and the rumors about his affairs, most of them apparently true. Perhaps she was pleased to hear that he was still capable of humor, that some semblance of his former self had not been totally eclipsed by his illness.

I'd walk the couple of miles into town, or if my mother needed groceries, I'd drive the Ford and get the papers and read aloud to him about Bonnie and Clyde's latest escapades. In late July, we heard the news about Buck Barrow's grisly killing, and my father listened carefully and then reminisced about Buck, who he called Ivy, and how awful sad it was to hear about his death. He made my mother send Clyde's parents a condolence card. He wrote on it himself, in a barely legible scrawl:

Dear Cousins,

I know you ain't heard from me in a long time. I've been bad off and nobody except me thinks I'll make it much longer. I read about poor Ivy's death and I am sorry for him and for you. We follow Clyde and Miss Parker in the papers. And, good or bad, we root for our kin. Me and mine are thinking about you in your grief.

Yours,

Zachary

Miraculously, my father didn't die as soon as everybody expected. Whatever was growing inside his brain stopped for a time. His head didn't get any smaller, but it didn't get any bigger either, and there were whole weeks when he seemed almost normal again, though he still couldn't work and spent most of the day sleeping.

When there wasn't any news in the papers about the Barrow Gang, my father would ask us to read from the clippings that Whit and I saved in an album. We memorized the more colorful ones and would recite them with a melodramatic flourish that delighted him. He'd close his eyes, and his enormous head would swivel on his neck. His lips would part, revealing the gap between his front two teeth. Whit and I would grab brooms and pretend they were BARs, acting out the Barrow Gang's exploits, even as our mother, clanging her pots in the kitchen, reluctantly indulged our shows before calling us in to dinner, where she said the blessing, never once offering a word of prayer for our father's doomed cousin.

That was how we passed the fall and then winter and then most of the next spring, watching my father and his cousin continue to elude the forces determined to kill them off.

He's awake when I enter his room and asks, before I can say a word, "Who's here?"

"You ain't gonna believe it," I tell him and turn off the Victrola.

"Ralph?"

Ralph lives in Honey Grove and comes out every couple of weeks to check on us, usually toting a basket of vegetables or beef tips for stew. He knows money is tight with only me, my mother, and Whit doing the farming, and my mother picking up a little extra as a seamstress.

"Nope," I say. "Clyde."

He seems momentarily befuddled. "I don't know no Clyde."

"Clyde Barrow."

And then it dawns on him, but I can see, in the tightness of his lips, his confusion turns to suspicion. "Don't be funning me, Riley."

"I'm not. Clyde and Bonnie Parker are in the backyard right now. I just helped them put their car away."

"You best not be lying," he says, but I can see he's excited by the possibility. Despite the bad night of sleep, this might be a clear-headed day. His eyes aren't as rheumy as usual. I help him up and into his overalls and slippers, and then I place him in the makeshift wheelchair that Whit and I jerry-rigged by hammering wheels to one of the kitchen chairs. I roll him across the hardwood floor through the kitchen, squeeze the chair through the back door, and down the ramp we also made because he likes to be in the yard whenever it's warm enough.

"If it ain't Uncle Zach in the flesh," Clyde says.

"I thought you were cousins?"

"Well, your father's the same age as my mother, and they was as close as brother and sister, so we always called him uncle."

"Truth is," my father says, "your mother and me was kissing cousins."

"You shitting me?"

"When me and her was kids no older than my boy here, we used to sneak down by the lake in Honey Grove and . . . well, I better not say what exactly we done."

"My dad know that?"

"Your father was my best friend. Used to play baseball. I'm the one that introduced him to your mother. Before long, they was married and popping out you kids faster than we could keep count. How many of you are there now?"

"Eight," Clyde says.

"Which one are you again?"

"Five."

"I remember coming to see y'all when you was living under the viaduct. A damn pitiful sight. I talked to that man who owned the Star gas station, out there on Eagle Ford Road, and got Henry a job. It was still pathetic to see y'all cramped in that storage room with them Dr Pepper and Nehi signs."

"It beat the hell out of the viaduct," Clyde says and scratches at his nose. "You're right, though. Those were some glum-ass days. I remember you used to bring us groceries and milk and play rummy with me and Buck. We ain't never forgot it either, Uncle Zach."

"How's Ivy?" my father asks. He's forgotten the articles I read to him last July, not to mention the card we sent after Buck died, the card that has no doubt prompted this visit. I thought my father would never forget the details about Buck's killing, since he knew a thing or two about disfigured heads. But this slip reminds me that even though this is a good day for him, you can never speculate accurately about what he will or won't remember, or even if he'll know you from one minute to the next.

Clyde starts to speak but then buttons up. His lips twitch. "Excuse me," he says and limps over to the side of the barn.

Bonnie watches Clyde, trying to gauge his mood, and then she reaches over and places her little hand on my father's forearm. "I'm afraid Ivy's passed away," she says.

"How'd that happen?" my father asks. "He was always a strapping boy, the laughingest sumbitch."

"I'm afraid it wasn't too pretty, sir. It was about the worst thing I ever saw in my life. And Clyde feels he's to blame."

"Well," my father says, "there's always somebody to blame for something." Bonnie flinches slightly at what seems the casual indictment of my father's statement.

Clyde limps back over, frowning.

My father says, "Don't let it eat you up, son."

"Can I ask you a question?" Clyde says, and I sense something ugly's about to happen.

"Shoot."

"What the hell happened to your fucking head?"

I step back. Bonnie's surprised, too, but she's undoubtedly seen this shift in Clyde before. She shakes her head slightly, as if to warn him off, and then puts her hand on his shoulder, a secret communication between them. I figure Clyde blames my father for not knowing what everyone else in the country knows, and now he wants to return the favor of an inappropriate question. I worry at this moment that his famous temper will erupt. I watch his twitchy lips. I watch his hand to see if it moves to the gun.

"Ate too many goddamn watermelon seeds," my father says.

We all stare, dumbstruck, at him. Is this my old joking father, before the swelling, or the new, frequently addled one who will say something like this, believing it himself?

There is a shocked silence, and then Clyde and Bonnie explode into laughter. My father laughs, too, a big belly laugh. I still don't know if he meant it as a joke, but it's clear he loves the good humor of the moment and the fact that he's apparently caused it. His wide-gapped teeth and the tops of his pink gums reveal themselves like a happy banner. I can't tell you how relieved and delighted I am to see that face.

For the next few minutes, the four of us give ourselves over to an all-out giggle fit. Bonnie laughs so hard that she drops down on the grass and rolls around onto her side. Clyde is just as bad, his big ears turning red, his boy's face streaming with tears. He can't catch his breath and hops around on the grass like he's eaten a bunch of Mexican jumping beans. It's the funniest thing I've ever seen in my life.

"Clyde, you look like a goddamn grasshopper," my father says.

After we regain control of ourselves, my father sends me inside for lemonade. As I make a pitcher and stare out the window at the three of them, I think it would be a good idea to show them our album of clippings, let them know the significant role they've played in the life of our family. I flip it open randomly to the page with the newspaper photo of Buck, blindfolded, on his knees, and a caption that proclaims: "One Barrow Brother Down, One to Go." It spooks me that I open it to this page, and I'm reminded that what has most fascinated me this past year has not been the details of their escapes but the possibility of their deaths. I've expected each day to see their mangled bodies on the cover of the paper when I go to town. Staring at the clipping of Buck in the album, I realize I've been hoping that they would be murdered, that their ending would not be anticlimactic, with a capture and a prolonged trial, but bloody and grand instead. I realize, too, that my feelings about Clyde and Bonnie are mixed up with my unacknowledged wish that my father will die soon to relieve us of the burden of caring for him. I feel ashamed at this moment and close the album and put it back in the drawer, returning to the kitchen to finish the lemonade.

When I come back out with the tray of glasses and the pitcher, Clyde has his shirt off, showing my father the bullet wounds on his arms and chest.

"Go ahead and touch 'em if you want," he says, and my father does, running his fingers over the raised welts.

"Ouch!" Clyde screams. My father jerks his hand away, and Clyde giggles. "I'm just kidding. It don't hurt none now."

He sits down on the chair by my father and pulls off one of his wingtip shoes and a black, threadbare sock, revealing only three toes and two little stubs where his big toe and second toe should be.

"See that?" he says. "I sliced those bastards off with an ax when I was down in Eastham. Got Governor Sterling, that gullible jackass, to sign my parole."

Clyde plops his foot in my father's lap, and my father runs his fingers over the striated ridges of Clyde's missing toes. My father doesn't have much feeling left in that hand, but I wonder if there might be magic in Clyde's stubs because my father seems to respond pleasurably to what he touches.

"Hey, Bonnie, hike up your skirt."

"No, Clyde."

"Come on now, honey." He turns to my father and me. "She nearly burned to death up in Wellington. A bridge wasn't where we thought it was, and we went right into the ravine. We barely got Bonnie away before the whole goddamn engine exploded. Cut her knee clear to the bone and burned up the prettiest thigh this side of the Ziegfeld Follies."

Reluctantly at first, Bonnie places her foot on my father's wheelchair and unwraps the gauze, shows us the gash she suffered almost a year ago. My father and Clyde oohh and aahh, and she gets into the act and hikes up her dress even more, enough to reveal her lacy peach undergarments. She shows us her thigh.

"Ain't that a beaut?" Clyde says, touching around the edges. The skin is shriveled, oily from some kind of ointment. "Hell, I think it's gonna be prettier than before," Clyde adds.

"I like a woman with battle scars," my father says, which makes Bonnie smile and Clyde giggle again. I can't get over the comedian my father's suddenly become.

"You know what we need?" Clyde asks. "A photograph. To commemorate this family reunion and show off everybody's war wounds. I know my mother would love a picture of us with her old kissing cousin."

"That sounds grand," Bonnie says.

"Son, would you go to the car and fetch the camera from the back seat? Be careful with it."

"Yes, sir," I say and race to the barn to find the Kodak box camera that they've used to take all the famous pictures of themselves—my favorite being the one where Bonnie, a cigar bobbing from her lips, holds a pistol and props her leg against one of their stolen cars. I carry the camera delicately to the front porch. I feel uneasy about having the picture taken since we haven't had any made since my father got sick. If my mother were here, she'd not allow it. She'll be showing up pretty soon, and that worries me. But she isn't here yet, and I like the idea of not only the photograph but of me as the photographer. I entertain the fantasy that the picture might make it into the newspaper, and that I will be the one to bring it home for my father.

Bonnie shows me how to take the picture, and then she and Clyde pose on either side of my father—Bonnie with her dress hiked up, revealing her wounded leg, her elbow propped on my father's shoulder, the deformed part of his head glistening in the sun. Through the lens of the camera, she seems so tiny next to my father, and I have the odd feeling he might pick her up with one hand and make her talk like a ventriloquist's dummy. Clyde sits on a stool next to my father with just his undershirt on. He thrusts his bullet-scarred arm toward the camera. His three-toed foot is propped on my father's lap.

"Smile," I say. Clyde and Bonnie remain solemn faced, as their custom has been in photographs. My father, however, offers me that fat, gap-toothed grin of his.

Afterward, Bonnie leans over and lightly kisses my father's cheek. It's such a sweet gesture that I wish I'd had the wherewithal to take a photograph of that as well.

Clyde tells me to put the camera away, which disappoints me since I'd hoped to have my photograph taken with them, too, though I realize my father wouldn't be able to operate the camera. When I get back, Clyde has lit up a couple of cigars for himself and my father. I expect Bonnie to smoke one, too, like she did in the famous picture.

"They sour my stomach," she says, as if reading my mind. "I wish Clyde would quit the nasty habit. They stink to high heaven."

"We read the poem you wrote," I say as I pour the nearly forgotten lemonade into the glasses. I've hardly spoken a word and want to offer something to the conversation. Bonnie's poem was reprinted in newspapers across the country.

"He can recite it from memory," my father says, and both Clyde and Bonnie seem genuinely impressed.

"A command performance," she shouts, raising her arm high. I'm eager to do it, though nervous that I might forget a line or skip a whole verse. I do well, though, and am especially dramatic, gunning an imaginary BAR as I recite my favorite lines:

> If they try to act like citizens
> And rent a nice little flat
> About the third night they're invited to fight
> By a sub-gun's rat-a-tat-tat.

They applaud enthusiastically, my father included, and I take a ceremonial bow. Then Bonnie jumps up, cups my cheeks between her hands, and kisses me on the lips. She holds the kiss until I can feel the heat rise in my face.

"Hey there, hoss, slow down a little!" Clyde jokes. "She ain't *your* kissing cousin."

Just after noon, my mother drives up and parks the Ford beneath the shade of the willow tree that whispers against my shutters late at night. My brother and sister bolt from the car and then stop short when they see we have guests.

"Who are you?" Clara asks.

"I'm your dad's kin," Clyde says. "Me and him go way back. You're my cousin, thrice removed," he adds, the same thing he said to me when I first met him, and I wonder if this is a phrase he's rehearsed. He seems to delight in the formality of it. "Pleased to meet ya, cuz."

Clyde shakes my sister's and Whit's hands. I can tell by Whit's silence, the pallor of his skin, and his bug-eyed look that he recognizes them.

"You seen me before, haven't you?" Clyde asks Whit.

"No, sir."

"Seen my picture, though?"

"Yes, sir."

"So you know who I am?"

"Yes, sir."

Clyde tips his hat back on his head, smiles, and says, "Much better looking in person, ain't I?" Whit and Clara laugh.

"Don't pay him no never mind," Bonnie says.

Clyde wraps his arm around Bonnie's shoulder. "This is my wife." I wonder if they found a justice of the peace to marry them, and maybe we are the first to know it, if that is part of the reason they have come to our house, to share the news with the closest relatives.

Clara says, "Hey, Riley, you're taller than both of them, and they're grown up."

"Clara!" I shout.

Bonnie laughs, but Clyde doesn't utter a sound, which makes me wonder if the reason he set out to be a bank robber and murderer was because one too many fools made similar comments. He has a small man's chip on his shoulder.

"That's all right," Bonnie says. "What a pretty little girl." She bends down before Clara.

My mother finally appears and walks slowly toward us, a wary expression on her face. I can tell she knows who's paying us a visit.

"Hello, ma'am," Clyde says. He removes his hat and takes my mother's hand and kisses it. "Mighty pleased to meet you."

My father whistles. "Ain't he a gentleman!"

"Zachary's a cousin of mine," Clyde says. "Haven't seen him since I was a boy."

"Hello," Bonnie chirps, not waiting for an introduction. "It's an honor to make your acquaintance."

"I know who you are," my mother says flatly. She isn't rude, but it's clear that she wants to let these strangers know that she isn't a woman who can be easily charmed or fooled.

Clyde and Bonnie study my mother. The smiles drop from their faces, and then they both nod solemnly, as if they have reached a silent agreement.

"We're just making a little family call," Clyde says, though there's that edgy look in his eyes again, like when he asked my father what happened to his head.

"I suppose you'll be wanting some lunch," she says.

Clyde replaces his hat and then tips it back. "If it ain't too much trouble."

"Will stew satisfy you?" she asks, and again I sense in her question a kind of challenge, if not an insult. It makes me nervous.

"Our favorite, ma'am," Bonnie says brightly.

My mother doesn't smile back, just turns sharply and walks up the ramp into the kitchen.

Clyde says, "I don't think she likes us."

"She's just tired," I say, but of course he's right. My mother doesn't appreciate them and sure as hell doesn't appreciate them being here at our house.

"Riley, you come on and help me with lunch," my mother calls from the window. I don't want to go inside because I figure there will be an interrogation waiting for me, but I have no choice and so leave Whit and Clara with my father, Bonnie, and our famous cousin.

My mother is not old. She had me when she was seventeen, so she's barely thirty, and still pretty, though wrinkles and worry lines have been etched in her forehead and gathered like a spider's web around her eyes and her lips. She does laugh sometimes, especially when she listens to the comedy routines on the radio or when we play dominoes or Wahoo. And she told me once that she had dreams before she met my father of singing on the radio. But now she only sings with the Honey Grove First Methodist choir on Sunday mornings.

"How long they been here?" my mother asks me as soon as I enter the kitchen.

As she stirs the stew she began this morning before she left, and as she puts cornbread in the oven, I narrate what transpired while she was at church, leaving out the photograph. I look out the window every chance I get to see what's going on out there. Clyde does a juggling trick and then limps to his car and retrieves a couple of guns—a rifle and one of the BARs. He shows them to my father, Whit, and Clara. He even lets Whit hold the automatic. And then Bonnie seems to defend Clara's right to hold a gun as well, because she pulls out a small revolver from her purse and puts it in my sister's hand and stands behind her and helps her aim it at the cornfields. Bonnie isn't much bigger than Clara, who is only ten. The gun goes off, and Clara recoils into Bonnie, and they both stumble and nearly topple over. My mother slams the spoon into the big pot, rushes to the porch, and shouts, "Clara, you and Whit get on in here!"

"It's all right, ma'am," Clyde says. "Bonnie knows what she's doing. I taught her myself."

"They're just having fun," my father calls back.

My mother stands there on the porch for a few seconds, wondering, I believe, if she should contradict her husband in front of his relatives. Ever since he's been sick, she's been in charge. Her word is law now, but I know she doesn't want to embarrass my father. She returns to the kitchen, and I can see Whit and Clara coming along after her. They know better than to disobey her. My mother clangs some pots and scowls.

"It's okay," I offer.

"Go wash up and get that table set," she says to Whit and Clara as they slink in the kitchen door.

"They ain't gonna hurt us," I say. "We're family."

She wheels on me, the dripping spoon extended from her hand like a weapon. "No," she growls. "*We* are family."

I bow my head, more afraid at this moment of her than the criminals outside.

A few minutes later, Bonnie stands at the entrance to the kitchen. "Here, ma'am," she says, holding out an envelope. "Clyde and me'd like you to have this. We know you could use it. It's almost three hundred and fifty dollars. I'm sure it will come in handy."

Bonnie steps toward my mother, and the difference in their sizes startles me. I never think of my mother as a large woman, though four children have made her thick through the waist. I am already several inches taller than she is and outweigh her by thirty pounds. But next to Bonnie, she seems suddenly huge—looming above her. My mother keeps her hands by her side and shakes her head.

"Please, ma'am. Clyde'd be awful hurt if you refused."

"I can't take that money."

"I understand what you're thinking," Bonnie says, brushing back a strand of reddish-blonde hair from her forehead. "You're thinking this money's tainted. But you're wrong. Money's just a thing. And the way we figure it, the reason we got this money is so we can give it to folks who really need it."

"I appreciate the gesture," my mother says.

Her mouth is set so that it's clear, to me at least, that she doesn't appreciate it but is trying to be polite. Regardless, this is a lot of money, a fortune for people like us. I wonder if this is the time to be principled.

"I can't take that money," she says again.

Bonnie squints at my mother and then, after a few moments, nods. She returns to the backyard. As my mother stirs her stew, I watch through the window as Bonnie whispers into Clyde's ear. He shakes his head and says something, and then she gives him the envelope. Bonnie kneels by my father's chair and starts to talk to him as Clyde limps onto the porch. He raps lightly on the door, which is polite but not really necessary.

"Mind if I talk to you for a moment, ma'am?"

"Come on in," my mother says, pulling the cornbread from the oven.

Clyde winks at me, as if we're allies. I want to be.

"Ma'am, I gotta ask you a favor."

Without looking at him, my mother says, "I'm not taking it." Clyde silently watches her as she cuts the cornbread with a long knife and puts the pieces in a bowl. When she finishes, she says, "And if you're worried that I'm gonna call the police as soon as you leave, then I can assure you that won't happen. Whatever you've done, you're still Zachary's kin."

I suddenly notice that it's gotten real quiet in the dining room. Whit and Clara must be listening, too.

"I'm much obliged, ma'am. But the favor I'm asking ain't for me. I understand why you got some qualms about how we got this money. But you've got a hard time coming your way. Your kids are a help, but they ain't a man. And by the looks of things, that hard time is coming soon."

"You don't have to talk in riddles," my mother says. "The boy knows his father will die. We all know it. He's lived longer, as it is, than anyone expected. I appreciate your gesture, Mr. Barrow. But if I take that envelope, and I use what's in it, then I'm no better than a thief myself. That money, you and I both know, has blood on it."

Clyde stares down at his dust-covered wingtips and collects his thoughts before proceeding.

"This favor ain't for me. My mother, she loved Zachary like he was her brother. She asked me to come here, asked me to give you this money. He helped us when we was desperate, and he always treated us like we wasn't trash. She never forgot it. Me neither. I ain't a Christian, ma'am. I 'spect you know that. I figure when I'm dead, I'm gone, and the maggots can have me. If there's a heaven and a hell, then I'm sure we both know where I'll be headed. But this gift isn't from me. It's from my mother. She asked that I do this. And I want to grant her that wish. I've brought enough grief on her as it is."

My mother listens to this speech calmly and seems to take it seriously. I stand at the stove, holding my breath, hoping they won't send me out. She wipes her hands on her apron.

After a few moments, she says, her voice warmer now, "I'm sorry, Mr. Barrow. I just can't do that. If it'd ease your mind, you tell your mother that you made good on your promise. I won't naysay you, if it comes to it. But I can't have that money in my house, no matter what good purpose we might put it to. I hope you'll understand and appreciate that and not hold it against me or my husband."

Clyde stares at my mother. He seems like a sheepish boy who's been scolded, though my mother has not raised her voice, and her last words have been as much a plea as a statement of resolve. He nods, as Bonnie did, and puts the envelope in his pocket.

"Would it trouble you too much if we spent the night, ma'am? We would sleep in the barn."

She examines Clyde's face carefully for a few seconds and seems to weigh what she wants to say. "I'm happy to feed you a meal."

This seems to stun Clyde more than her refusal of the money. I wonder how long it has been since someone refused him not only one request but two.

"Yes, ma'am," he says, and puts his hat back on his head. "Sorry to trouble you. We'll be heading out soon."

He touches the brim with his finger in a kind of salute to my mother, and then smiles grimly at me before walking out the door.

I start to say something to her but then stop, not sure what it is I have to tell her. I can't quite believe what I've seen her do, nor the deference that both Clyde and Bonnie have shown her. I admire her, even if I disagree with her. I know we need that money.

"Go bring your father inside."

"But—"

"You heard me," she says and then begins ladling the stew into bowls.

"We gotta be heading out," Clyde is telling my father as I come outside.

"So soon?" my father asks, genuinely surprised. "I thought you was spending the night. We've plenty of room."

"I'm afraid not. Gotta get to Bonnie's mother's house in West Dallas by nightfall."

"Stay for dinner at least."

"I wish we could," Bonnie says. "But we gotta go. My momma would have herself a hissy fit if I was late." I know the lie of this. Policemen are staked out permanently at the Parker and Barrow households. This isn't conjecture on my part. The papers have said as much.

Bonnie leans over and kisses my father's cheek, and then, in a gesture I will never forget, she kisses him on the bad side of his head. It's gentle, and she seems to linger there. It seems to me like a blessing.

And then they are gone.

A few weeks later, the radio buzzes with the news of the deaths of Clyde Barrow and Bonnie Parker. They've been ambushed and slaughtered in Black Lake, Louisiana, their car and bodies riddled with bullets by police.

My father sends me to town to fetch the paper, which proclaims, "Infamous Duo Finally Get Their Due," and tells the gory details of the ambush. Their bodies are being delivered to Dallas, where they will be on public display before the funeral.

"Go see them off, son," my father says when I finish reading him the article. "Your cousin ought to have as much family there as he can."

My father is adamant. My mother, surprisingly, relents without argument and fills a basket with sausage, pickles, cold potato patties, and a thermos of sweet tea for me and Whit. She lets me drive the Ford. Though I drive a lot on the farm and in town, it is the first time I'm allowed to drive in a city. We're to stay with her sister in Fort Worth.

Rumors fly in Dallas. We hear that in Louisiana, where they were shot, people tore off bits of Clyde's and Bonnie's clothing as trophies and that someone even tried to cut off Clyde's ear. We hear that a photographer has taken a picture of their naked, mangled bodies, and it's circulating at the funeral, though I don't see it and know I will tear it up if I do. We hear that someone stole Clyde's diamond stickpin from his jacket, though I doubt that. Clyde didn't have a stickpin on his jacket. I remember everything about him.

Their bodies, still bloody, are put on display in Dallas. Hot dog vendors set up stands on every corner, kids sell iced Nehis and Dr Peppers to the folks waiting in line in the heat to catch a glimpse. A couple standing in front of us in line tells us that a man offered $50,000 for Clyde's body so that he could mummify it and take it on tour. I notice that some of the people—kids you might expect, but also a man and an old woman—are touching them, rubbing their handkerchiefs over my cousin and Bonnie.

"Goddamn it," I mutter to Whit. "I wish I could shoot those sons of bitches."

But when I file past, I touch Clyde's hand as well and then pluck a strand of hair from Bonnie's skull.

"What are you doing?" Whit shouts when I show him. "You want to bring us bad luck?" Whit will steal the hair from me that night and bury it in our aunt's yard.

I will read later that almost twenty thousand people filed past their bodies.

Clyde and Bonnie have separate funerals, which makes me sad since that isn't the way they wanted it, not the way that Bonnie foretold it in her poem. We go to Clyde's funeral, since he is kin, and squeeze with so many others into the old Belo Mansion on Ross Avenue, which has been converted into a funeral home.

At the gravesite, we can't get in close enough to see Clyde's coffin, even when we say we're family.

"Who ain't?" a policeman snarls and then pushes Whit and me back with his nightstick.

Clyde's parents look too old to be my father's generation, but maybe their boys have aged them. They are nearly knocked into the grave when an airplane suddenly drops an enormous wreath on Clyde's coffin. We learn later that the famous racketeer Benny Binion hired the plane. "Binion's Bouquet Bomb," the Dallas paper calls it.

When Whit and I arrive home, my father is already dead himself. My mother says he died on May 26, in the afternoon, at almost three o'clock, the day of Clyde's funeral. I think about where I was at that moment and realize that Whit and I were at the gravesite. I close my eyes and imagine it, the two images superimposed over each other, the bouquet bomb dropping from the low-flying plane as my father exhales his last breath.

Maybe that's just wishful thinking on my part, but there doesn't seem any harm in believing it, though I don't mention this to my mother, who I know might have a different interpretation. I don't want my father dead, and I am sorry I wasn't there for his final hours, but a part of me feels it's appropriate that he died the day they buried Clyde and Bonnie. They had, in a peculiar way, been keeping him alive.

About a week after we bury him, we get a letter. It's postmarked from Louisiana and addressed to my father. My mother opens it up, and inside are a little card and a photograph. The card says:

> Thanks for your hospitality. I sure do hope you're feeling better, Zachary. Enclosed please find an autographed copy of the poem your son recited so brilliantly. I never had a better compliment in my life. Also please find the photograph he took of us. It's a splendid one, I think. Clyde especially likes your hairdo and his toes. See the inscription.

The picture is the one I'd taken, of course, with their Kodak box camera. Bonnie with her skirt hiked up to show her scar, her elbow resting on my father's shoulder. Clyde sitting on the stool with his shoe and sock off and his three-toed foot draped across my father's lap. Just my father smiling. A falling cherry blossom from the tree suspended above my father's head. On the back of the photo, Bonnie had written in a girlish cursive, "The Barrow Gang Display Their Scars."

Bonnie must have sent it from a post office in Louisiana, not long before they died. It feels strange to me—to all of us really—to be getting a letter and a photograph from the dead.

At the sight of the picture, my mother sits down at the table and starts to weep, so hard that she has to rest her head in her hands. She's not a weeper, so this surprises and moves me so much that I start to cry as well. She drops the picture to the floor, and I pick it up.

"Give me that," she orders, and I hand it to her. She wipes her eyes and then tears the picture in two. "That's not the way we're gonna remember him," she says. "With some two-bit . . ."—she stops herself and takes a deep breath—". . . and her murdering boyfriend making fun of him, making fun of us all."

She stands up, drops the two pieces in the trash. "It was all just a lark to them," she says. And then she goes back to her room and lies down on her bed. She doesn't get up for three days.

I retrieve the torn pieces. The rip is precisely through the middle of my father's face, right between his eyes. On one piece of the photo is the bad part of his head, with Bonnie by his side. Clyde's bare, three-toed foot is on that side as well. On the other piece is the normal part of my father's head. Our cousin Clyde sitting beside him, his leg draped across my father's lap. I am intrigued by the precision of my mother's rip. I don't know why, but it seems to me like a signal from the other side, some indication that they might be all right, though I know that such a thought would make them laugh. I keep the two parts of that photograph, hide it in our copy of Milton because I know my mother won't open it. I later tape it together, but you can still see the crease through my father's head, face, and body, as well as the suspended cherry blossom.

Far from ruining the picture, it makes it better.

Sometimes I pull out that picture, still lodged all these decades later between the pages of our old copy of *Paradise Lost*, a fitting place for it, I think. It's the first picture I ever took—and the best one as well. And it's the only one I have of my father. I marvel now at how young he looks, despite the grotesque evidence of his illness and only weeks before his death.

I'm now more than twice the age he was then.

I like to imagine sometimes that I'm in that picture with them, standing behind the three of them, just off to my father's good side. It's a photograph that I could have sold for a lot of money if I'd wanted to. But I never did, not even during the worst years for us, not even after the famous movie came out and it might have fetched a good price.

As I've recounted this event, I've been debating with myself if I should tell the other part, the missing part that I've not told anyone since it happened—not Whit, not Clara, not my mother, nor my children or grandchildren, who have heard this story dozens of times over the years. Certainly not my wife, who passed more than a decade ago. The missing part can't, in the long run, change anything now, though I've hoped it would just disappear with all the other tellings, like an itchy scab that might shrivel and fall away if I stopped picking at it. I'm realizing it will only stop haunting me if I go ahead and tell it, put this part back in the story.

That day, after Bonnie kisses my father, after she blesses him, she and Clyde do not immediately leave. Clyde shakes my father's hand and tells him to take care of himself and stay away from the moonshine, and then he beckons me to help him with the barn doors.

I follow him. Bonnie walks beside me and again hooks her arm in mine. Inside the barn, she kisses me lightly on the cheeks, and I'm disappointed that it's not on the lips, like before.

"You take good care of your mother and daddy," she says.

They get in their car, and Clyde starts the engine. He waves me over to his window and slips the envelope inside the bib pocket of my overalls.

"I can't," I protest, stealing a glance out the barn door across the backyard, where my father still sits in his wheelchair waiting for me to roll him inside, to the kitchen window, where I know my mother is watching, though I cannot see her because of the sun glinting off the glass.

"Your mother's a good woman," Clyde says. "I admire that. But I have a good mother, too. This money belongs to your family. You're the oldest. You don't have to tell her. Just keep it safe and use it how you see fit."

"I can't."

"Please, sugar," Bonnie coos, leaning over in the seat. "It's for the best."

I don't say yes, but I don't protest anymore, and all three of us know that my refusal to say anything is really my answer.

"Watch for us in the newspapers," Clyde says.

"I will."

"You a praying man?" Bonnie asks.

"I guess."

"Well," she says, "don't waste your prayers on us."

Clyde smiles, touches the brim of his hat with his finger in another ironic salute, and then eases the car out of the barn and around the path alongside the house, past our Ford. Then he guns the engine in a gesture that I feel is intended for my mother.

"He sure was a short feller," my father says when I rejoin him. "Don't look like he growed up much since I last saw him."

Though we are on the back side of the house, I see the plume of dust from their stolen sedan billowing over our roof like a tornado.

"Dinner ready yet?" my father asks.

"I believe so," I say and then wheel him up the ramp and into my mother's kitchen.

And what became of that money? I hid it under a loose floorboard beneath my bed. I spent a little on a new Kodak camera for myself, the same model that Clyde and Bonnie owned. I took pictures with it for the next four decades, and I still own it, though it no longer works.

I used seventy dollars to pay for Whit's funeral and another seventy for Clara's. Both of them died when an influenza epidemic swept through Honey Grove in 1938. The rest I gave to the bank that same year for back taxes and mortgage, but it wasn't enough to stop the foreclosure a year later.

I never told my mother about the money, and I don't think she suspected, though I could never be sure what she saw or didn't see through the kitchen window when I stood in the cool darkness of the barn and said my good-byes to Clyde and Bonnie. There were times when she looked at me in a way that made me wonder if she knew about the money, and there were other times when I wondered if she had refused their offer because she knew full well that they'd give it to me. I picked up extra work at the welding shop in town, and she never asked too many questions.

For a while, I believed Bonnie's argument that money didn't have a moral value, was simply paper to be used for exchange. Money could not carry the sins of its acquisition or the ghosts of those who'd died for it. But with my father dying on the day of their funerals, at the very moment that the flowers from the sky nearly crushed the onlookers, with Whit and then Clara dying, and then us losing the farm, I began to wonder if my mother was right after all. But it was too late to do anything about it by then.

I hope she went to her grave without knowing that the money from my famous cousin had tainted our family, after all, despite her efforts to avoid it. During her final moments, I came close to telling her what I'd done, but the more I considered it, the crueler that seemed. To tell her would have been merely to unburden my own guilt on a woman who needed no other burdens.

MELINDA

Judy Doenges

hen I first met James, he was a meth chef. This year he doesn't need to cook, because he has another guy to do it. The chef has runners, guys who take the city bus from drugstore to drugstore to get antihistamine for our special ingredient, one legal box at a time. Now James is our punisher, our savior, our iron-and-brass man. He gives us our worktable and our tools: pens, tape, Change of Address cards, Mountain Dew, cell phones, shards, and pipe.

When he's not cleaning and cleaning, RJ goes Dumpster diving, some-times all the way to Omaha, and rifles through cans and recycling bins for credit card bills and bank statements, sometimes just feathers of paper, and then he dumps the pile on our worktable. Ripped to the winds, no problem, James says today, his hand heavy on Little Fry's neck. She bows her head and starts sifting. There's nothing a tweaker can't do if she sets her mind to it, James says. Right, Fritzie? he asks me.

It's blue-snow December outside, and it stinks of cigarettes inside. Little Fry needs a shower. I need to get busy, James says to me. He tries to put his hand on my neck, but I shrug him off.

When I first met James, I was Melinda Renée von Muehldorfer and I lived at 145 South Poplar. My grandma told me once that "von" means my ancestors were German royalty. James says, You're out of your castle now, babe. After I graduated, ruined my parents' credit rating, sold everything except my ice skates, and moved in with James at the farm, I was Fritzie, no last name, just a girl good at asking for things.

Little Fry tapes strip to strip until she finds a number or a name or both. Today she looks like a cartoon of someone concentrating, the tip of her tongue working around her lips, her hands shaking. She's not very good with numbers and names, so she turns her creations over to me.

Look at this, Fritzie, Little Fry says. Here's one like yours.

She hands me a taped library overdue notice, all the ragged corners perfectly matched, even the split letters lined up and repaired. Richard von Behren it says, 653 Oak. Four streets away from my old house. I picture Richard von Behren with one of those regal profiles, a sharp face like a statue's. He's clearly in a hurry, so impatient with his pile of mail and bills that he doesn't save and shred.

Break time. Little Fry always lights up first because she's the hungriest. She passes to me as we slump on the couch. James walks in to retrieve me, and air comes punching into the room. He carries his own weather, RJ said one time when he was gakked.

In bed is where reputation gets iffy. It's only as good as who's on top of you, a girl named Share, who is no longer with us, used to say. I wonder what that means vis-à-vis James.

Oh, but James goes down, unlike most guys. When you're made of iron and brass, I think, sliding up on the pillow, you're not afraid of anything.

Sex is as selfish as drugs, I think, my nerves undulating inside my arms and legs like earthworms, and I like to be selfish, at least that's what my parents used to say, screaming outside my bedroom door. James doesn't have to work hard or long. He just breathes on me, just shivers me, until I answer back, and then James disappears in a suck of air. I don't open my eyes until he's in and over me. Then I come again while he watches. The sun sets over his shoulder, a red blazing that seems to start the corn stalks on fire while the last of the light slides off the side of the barn. James always leaves me gasping. From the bed, I grab his ankles. He puts on his jeans anyway.

I get dressed and go out to the living room. RJ has turned on the light over the barn door, so we know he's out there with the chef. Little Fry is back at the table, guzzling Mountain Dew. She's just a girl from the eastern sticks of Colorado, solving the puzzle of the paper strips. The house shakes with James's absence, every atom chiding us.

Merilee, she of the cheery name, is James's wife. She lives elsewhere. Sometime in the morning, she comes in her Trailblazer with Riley, the boy she has with James. Merilee lets Riley lay on the horn until James comes out, pulling cash from his back pocket. She does all right—the bitch, James always says after she leaves. Then he laughs. Today Merilee and James talk at the car window, while Riley pulls at the ends of James's long hair.

Fritzie, keep going, RJ says. I'm sweeping in front of his mop: double-team double clean, RJ calls it. He'd lick the floor if he could. Little Fry continues her Good Work at the table, selfless and tireless, like a nun. James sometimes calls her Holy One, she does her one thing so pure.

Oh, Merilee, I think, how have you kept your narrow waist, your big boobs, and your auburn hair to the ripe age of thirty-five? Oh, Merilee, how do you hold onto a husband/boyfriend/father/sugar daddy/fucker like James? Merilee, how? Neither James nor Merilee use anymore. Because of Riley, Merilee says, which James claims too. But I know it's really because James is CEO. You can't run a business and do its work at the same time.

Riley cries in the window of the Trailblazer as it turns around in the yard slush. James comes into the living room, tracking. Get it, get it, RJ yells, pushing me and my broom along.

RJ, James says, you and Fritzie go to town. He gives us a card and the keys to the old Ninety-Eight.

I'm not done here! RJ yells.

James puts his hand on RJ's neck, and he calms down. I'll keep an eye on it, James says. Get going.

RJ holds the steering wheel as if it's made of eggs. If you let me drive, I say, we'll get there lickety-split. Cops, RJ says.

They'll think something is really wrong with you, you go like this, I say.

RJ ignores me and starts on the list of his DUIs, DWIs, driving while fucked up, short stints in the pokey, and I mention that these incidents always center on a wayward girl. Correct, RJ says. Women are the bane of my existence. Were.

RJ and I have this same conversation every time we go to town. Everything is always the same, right down to the number and kind of transgressions. I just go with it. RJ has been with James for a few years, so his stories and his thoughts run in the same tight circle. The cornfields finally give out, and then we're chugging through the outskirts of the city so slowly that I have plenty of time to read "No Soliciting" on at least five doors.

I make RJ go to the Hy-Vee on our side of the city proper so I won't see anyone I know. We do a foilie in the car for courage and strength, RJ says, as if there's going to be heavy lifting. He's right about the possibilities, though.

One day, when he was gakked and ergo superhuman, RJ sawed down a whole tree and cut it into perfect logs even though our fireplace is broken. But here, well. The city is full of people we've never seen and expectations that have passed us by, and we're never sure how we're presenting ourselves. To us, we're just fine.

Inside the store, RJ grabs a cart; I stand on the back and he pushes me. We have a list. We like lists and tasks, but we're never very hungry. Uck, RJ says too loudly, looking around at all the food. I know, I say, but whisper, man. What's first?

When Little Fry eats, it's always bananas and milk because she heard somewhere that it's the perfect combination of food. I point out that there's no protein there, but my opinions on diet don't carry much weight anymore. So RJ and I load up on bananas and the kiwi James likes, then fruit leather for RJ. We tour meat for James's chicken parts, then zoom to dairy for Little Fry's milk and RJ's string cheese, then over to cereal for Cheerios. I've eaten them since I was a baby; my parents have a picture of me sitting in my highchair, those little oaty lifesavers on the tray. Now I like them in a red bowl, one by one, while I work. The last thing for the cart is cigarettes, different brands to please everyone. On the way up to checkout, we swing by the drug section, and even though I didn't plan it, I grab some cold medicine and head back to the bathroom. A surprise for James. I put the foil sheets of pills in my pocket and bury the box under paper towels in the trash. RJ rolls us up to the registers. The checker slides our stuff over the reader, but she also takes some time to look us over. She's seen photos on billboards of guys like RJ, all skinny and snuffly and with that new kind of acne, teeth sprung. I can feel her thinking about calling the manager, but for what? We haven't done a thing but ride the cart. RJ hasn't noticed any of this; he's just holding out the shaking card. I sign in the swiper window—Jacqueline Zingle—and then, thank God, we're out in the parking lot, loading bags. We progress at grandma speed back to James's.

When we get there, the football players' Jeep is in the yard. The team is going to a bowl game, and everyone in the city is in a fever. Part of the proceeds from the sale of RJ's string cheese goes to a fund for the new stadium.

Four huge men stand around the living room, slushing up RJ's clean floor. Hey, he shouts and drops the bag he's carrying.

Let's keep it moving, James says, hustling RJ and me into the kitchen. I go back out, though, just to get a gander at all that healthy flesh. The players are ruddy, thick. Veins pop out on their hands. They fill out their team jackets, and their feet are as big as oars in their matching shoes. One of them looks in my direction, but he stops at my hair and frowns. Little Fry couldn't keep her hands still one night, so I gave her a pair of scissors and closed my eyes. Now my hair is like little blond eruptions all over my head.

There's a new guy this time, the biggest one of the group, wearing a hemp necklace and a small gold cross. You take checks? he asks James.

RJ, James, me, even Little Fry crack up. What? the guy asks, looking around.

Don't be a dipshit, the one black player says. He's the only gentleman of color, as RJ always calls him, who ever comes around, and he tries hard not to look at anything.

The player who looks like an oversized cowboy, down to the Resistol covering his crew cut, pulls out the cash.

They turn to leave, but Player number four, a mammoth redheaded sad sack, looks at me again, this time giving me a morose stare. I gasp. It's Jorge, my conversation partner from junior-year Spanish. I can't remember his real name. *Buenas noches*, Marita, he says, before heading towards the door.

Shit, James says, looking first at me and then at the wide back of Jorge.

Marita, Little Fry says after they go. Marita! Marita! she calls, picking up the pipe. RJ, Little Fry, and I retire to the sofa. James goes into his room and slams his door.

When I first moved in, James said, No way do you go upstairs. Of course I go.

There are four freezing bedrooms and an old bathroom with the sink torn out and a shower that drips. The bedrooms are all the same size, one in each corner, but in each one the windows look out on a permanent piece of anywhere in Nebraska: barnyard, road, clump of trees, pasture. You can go from room to room, as I have, and get a 360-degree view of where you are. It's the opposite of how all of us downstairs live, in our closed fist of work, and that's why James doesn't want us up here.

I figured I'd find old stuff up here like newspapers from World War II or tickets to a county fair or receipts for horses and cows, but the place looks as if RJ's been at it. Not a nail or a shoelace, but I did find a honey-colored curl of hair in a closet once. If I were a different kind of girl, I would have kept it.

I'm up here during the day sometime after the football players' visit, after break time. *Dormitorio*, I say to each bedroom; *ventana* to each window; *árboles*, I say out one window, then *camino* out another one, *pasto* where the cows would be. Translate "barnyard," Marita, *por favor*.

Around dawn, James jumped out of bed, crouching and feeling for cigarettes. Fritzie, he barked, how long have you been here? Quick!

I closed my eyes. Six months, I said. No, eight.

Wrong, babe! James said. Ten months, two weeks. You've got to work on memorization, James said, and he sounded just like my Spanish teacher, Señorita O'Connor. You don't want to end up like RJ, like a CD you can't turn off, James said. Or Little Fry, like all you can do is play with paper.

I didn't say that we were working to his specifications, working for James his very self. I also didn't say that when you don't sleep, like Little Fry, RJ, and I don't, you live in one long hour and that hour takes place during that last minute you're in a class, when you're waiting for the big IBM clock on the wall to make its final click. So why not run on like RJ does? Why not cut and paste like Little Fry?

I'm moving you into a supervisory position, James said, shocking me. I can't afford to hemorrhage any personnel, he says. So you're in charge of Little Fry and RJ, make sure they don't fly away.

Fly away like past chefs and runners, like girls he diddled, like everyone who passes through a business like this.

You're here for the duration, James said at dawn.

When I go downstairs, everything's the same. Little Fry: table, soda, tape. RJ: trying to do some speedy old-school break dancing on the living room floor. My work is done.

You're not going to break anything but your head, I say. I'm going for a walk. Where's James?

Out, RJ says. Who's he doing? I wonder before I can stop myself. RJ's upright now, doing a silly big skip, slide, and sway, like some guy in a boy band.

Little Fry looks up from the table. Take a hat, she says.

Outside the sun is high. It's colder than a tweaker's lungs, as RJ always says, but I've got my old red down jacket with matching mittens and hat. When I get to the end of the driveway, I stick out my thumb and start walking in the direction of the city, even though no one is coming yet on this dinky road. I haven't mailed the Change of Address card yet. It's in my pocket: Richard von Behren, 653 Oak. I haven't planned what I'm going to do or say.

Pretty soon, an old car pulls up. It's an Impala, lumpy with Bondo, and there's a guy I almost know behind the wheel. Cody, he says when I get in, and I know he's a local. There were probably thirty Codys in my high school.

I'm Merilee, I say. Are you going all the way in?

Sure are, he says. What side do you want?

North, I say, Stratford Acres, by the river.

He gives a low whistle. Then there's a long silence. Horses crowd together in the pastures. I see a farmer close by the road, checking a fence post.

Cody clears his throat. I think I seen you before, he says.

Where? I ask quickly. I look to make sure the Impala has door handles that work from the inside.

You're at James's place, yeah? I'm a friend of Tommy's, Cody says.

Tommy's the best chef in three counties, even James says so. People compete for product, not territory, so there're no fights, no shootouts on rural routes. Just admiration and awe. Ah, Tommy, James always says when he hears the name. He kisses the air. Ah, Tommy.

I should have guessed anyway. Cody's got one knuckle rapping the steering wheel, and his nondriving foot is pumping up and down. You can see the sinews in his cheeks.

That would be me, I say with a little laugh. I can't remember the last time I was alone or with a stranger, someone I had to say new things to.

Who're you going to visit? Cody asks. We stop at a four-way, and he sits there too long.

Just a guy, I say. He owes me some money.

Cody snorts. Don't I know it, he says. Then he launches in, telling me all about life at Tommy's place, which he should definitely not do to anyone outside. For miles, he talks about their new satellite dish, his bust last year and how Tommy bailed him, how much product Tommy's putting out, then, inevitably, there's the story of some girl who he has the hots for, this one being Tommy's old lady. Blabbady, blab, blab, blab, goes Cody, as only a meth head can. We get to the city. What will be, will be, Cody the philosopher finally says about life and love at Tommy's.

That's fatalistic, I say, pulling out the word from someplace. You can't do a thing about a life like that, man. Stop here.

Cody pulls into the parking lot at the playground I used to go to when I was a kid. It's too cold for anyone to be on the swings, and the slide would catch even the tiniest piece of skin. I turn and smile at Cody.

Duck down, he says, pulling the pipe out of the glove box. We laugh.

I race the five blocks to Oak on foot, keeping my head down. I practically do the two-step. I rub my fingers together inside my mittens. On Oak, all the houses are bigger than my old one. They're huge blocks of brick—brown, red, cream, with the sun hitting their front windows so the glass glows like porcelain. Richard von Behren at 653 Oak is at the end of the block. The house is two-story, red and brown in alternating groups of bricks, and there are two tall windows in the front, both of them with fake little wrought-iron balconies.

From the skinny window next to the front door, I can see back into one of those kitchens that flow into a dining room. Richard von Behren is getting a plate down from a high shelf. When he answers the door and sees it's me, he scrunches his eyebrows together and purses his lips.

Sorry, he says. But we're not buying anything. I could have put my son through college on what I've paid for candy and magazine subscriptions. A dog snorts and sticks its black muzzle between the man's leg and the doorjamb.

I'm lost, I say, for lack of something else. My car broke down, I add.

What? Richard von Behren asks. Where's your car? He sticks his head out and looks up and down the block.

It's up on the big street, I say, pointing with my mitten. My hand is shaking. I'm sorry to discover that I'm hopping up and down on the front mat.

Jesus, it's cold, Richard von B says. Get in here, and we'll figure this out.

I walk in, and the dog immediately puts its big paws on my shoulders. Batman, down, Richard von B says.

My boots drip water onto the Oriental rug in the hallway. To my right is the flowing dining room and kitchen, everything gleaming; to my left is the living room with deep red walls, bookcases and pictures, and a huge piano. Oriental rugs all the places my parents have carpeting. Richard von Behren is skinny and has the same thick blond hair and pink cheeks as my dad. A blond woman comes down the stairs with an empty laundry basket. Her hand squeaks along the banister.

Dick, Richard von B says to me, holding out his hand. And that's my wife, Sherry. Hi, Sherry says, making the same face her husband did.

This young lady is lost, Mr. von B says. Oh, no, Mrs. von B says.

Share, I say. I'm Sharon. My car broke down a few blocks back. I wave my hand behind my head. I'm stamping my feet, but quietly.

And you came all the way down here? Sherry von Behren asks.

Where are you trying to go? Dick asks, interrupting her.

I thought I went to school with somebody who lives on this street, but I was wrong, I say. I was coming home from band practice, I say, and my car broke down.

It's Saturday, Sherry von B says. She makes that face again.

Sherry, where's the map? Dick asks, heading for the kitchen. Where did you say you were going? he calls back to me.

My car broke down, I say again. But I'm lost too. And I need to tell my brother where to meet me. Somewhere up by my car, maybe.

Here, Sherry says, following Dick into the kitchen. You're no good at finding anything.

So, wait, you're not from around here? Richard calls from the kitchen. I can hear him going through a cupboard and Sherry whispering.

No, I say. I moved here two weeks ago. On a shelf in the living room next to a set of old books are coins in a frame. I take three steps to my left, lift the frame off the shelf, and slide it down inside my jacket. Then I'm back in the hall on the rug, waiting. Batman wags his tail.

What am I thinking? Dick says. He's coming out of the kitchen with a phone in his hand. We need this more than a map. Here, call your brother.

I dial RJ's cell. My car broke down, I say when he answers. What? he asks. Meet me at—, I say. Where should I meet him? I ask Sherry, who is now back in the hall with her arms crossed. What's on the big street? I ask.

Go to Carl's, Dick says. It's a restaurant two blocks west of Oak on Grover. Grover's the big street, he says laughing.

Meet me at Carl's, *Brad*, I say into the phone. It's on Grover. Who is this? RJ asks. What the fuck?

I hang up and say thanks about twenty times. The dog sticks his nose in my crotch. Dick stretches out a leg and pushes the dog back, all the time saying good luck with band, he played trumpet in high school and college, forcing me to say I play glockenspiel, which is the only instrument I can think of at the spur of the moment.

You know, I say, "von" in a name means your family were princes or something in Germany. Way back. I've got it too.

You told her our last name? Sherry asks, her voice high.

Dick just frowns. He's not sure, I think. Royalty, he says. He laughs. Tell it to my accountant.

It's hard to start school in the middle of the term, isn't it, Sherry von B says. She holds herself tight.

Really hard. Unless you get pretty good grades and have extracurricular activities that keep you busy and confident, I say. This last was what the guidance counselor suggested to my parents.

Good for you, Dick von B says.

I had a horse, I say quickly. But the truth is that my parents decided not to buy me one once everything caught up with me, and once my total lack of concern for the welfare of others required a second mortgage. *Have* a horse, I tell the von Bs. His name is Star. He looks like Black Beauty. Dick's face is starting to freeze, but I can't stop myself. I say, When Brad picks me up, we're going out to the stable to see Star. I have some carrots in my trunk. Does your son like sports? I ask.

Well, Richard says.

I was on soccer when I was little, I say. It's suddenly way too noisy under my hat, so I take it off, which is not good, because the von Bs can see my scalp and all its tufts. There's a big bell clanging inside my head. Goalie, the hardest position, I say. We won city for our age group one year. I fought off a lot of balls that season. Then there was gymnastics, five years.

Whose life am I telling? This one belongs to another kid, the kind of kid I never talked to.

Senior play, I was Eliza Doolittle, I say, the bell inside me ringing. They put a notice in the paper. Math was my favorite subject, which is not usual for girls. It's like I'm sure you've said to your kid, find something you're passionate about. All the teachers at school said goals were important. Achieve has an *I* in it, I say.

I stop talking. My brain is clanging like a church. All of this was before, I say. Before I moved here from Illinois two weeks ago. We stand there looking, even the pictures on the walls. That does it for Richard and Sherry von Behren, their son, and my old neighborhood.

Know where you are now? Sherry asks me. She herds me toward the door. Dick manages to get a hand on my shoulder, so I look back. Take care, he says, but he glances away at the end as if I hurt his eyes.

I practically knock myself out saying thanks some more, and then I'm out of the house and the door is closed and I'm trying to catch my breath. I bend down and pretend to tie my boots for a minute, and then I check the mailbox. I take what's there and walk quickly down the street. When I'm a few houses away, I take a sharp left and crunch through a snowy yard until I'm on the next street. Back on Grover, I take the first guy that stops, an old farmer in a pickup. He's silent the whole way to James's, as if I'm just some stock he has to transport.

RJ loves the coins. This one's from 1903 Germany, he says. That's their kaiser on it. He strokes the glass. Man, you know you have a lot of money when it just sits out on display, he says. I'll take that, James says, pulling the frame from RJ's hand. RJ goes back to chasing Riley around the house.

Riley and Merilee are here, picking up money and giving Riley a chance to see his dad not framed in a car window. Little Fry finds a bank statement in the last delivery of mail Richard von Behren will receive for a while, so James gets me on the phone immediately to twenty-four-hour Customer Service.

This is Sherry von Behren of 653 Oak, I say. How are you?

Wonderful! the helpful person says. What can I do for you?

I'd like to get your credit card, but I lost the offer, I say. I give the checking account number.

Password? the helpful person asks.

Batman, I say, and then I'm in.

A while later, Riley wants to go outside. The sun is low again, this time striped with clouds. James makes us all go with Riley, even Little Fry. RJ, Little Fry, and I have a foilie in the pantry before we venture forth. Home, again. The chef stands by the barn with a cigarette, carefully flicking his ash into a tin can.

There's a big cow pond behind the barn that's frozen solid. RJ takes off and slides on his stomach like he's stealing a base. Riley cracks up.

I took Richard von Behren's Change of Address card down to the box myself and put up the flag. The mail truck comes late here, we're so far out. Dick and Sherry are going to visit their own mailbox over and over—nothing there. Every day will be like pressing on a bruise to test the pain. Those two will figure it out quick, but by the time they do, Little Fry, RJ, me, and James will have their finances in a snarl, and then James will sell everything about Richard von Behren to someone else. People get passed around that way. They get lost.

Everyone's standing at the side of the cow pond, watching RJ go crazy on the ice. All that's going to hurt later. Riley is pulling on Merilee's hand. I go inside. My skates are in James's room.

Everyone is slipping and sliding on the pond when I come back out, so no one notices when I sit on a stump and put on my skates. The leather is like soft hands holding my feet. I took lessons until I was fourteen, and when I get on the ice, everything comes back. I do an arabesque and a single Axel.

Wow, Fritzie, Merilee says. That's amazing. Do it again! Riley says. A girl of many talents, James says, but he looks mad.

Everyone gets in a crowd, trying to do my moves, but they can't. This pond is all mine, I want to say. James starts sliding after me. Right away, everyone follows, yelling and laughing. I take off, floating from side to side until my wheezy lungs smooth out. Marita, come back! Little Fry calls.

I skate faster and faster toward the snow bank at the other end of this glassy ground, so fast I can't feel the surface or hear a voice, so strong I could part the clouds over the sun. The wind is wicked.

UNCLE ROCK

Dagoberto Gilb

In the morning, at his favorite restaurant, Erick got to order his favorite American food, sausage and eggs and hash-brown *papitas* fried crunchy on top. He'd be sitting there, eating with his mother, not bothering anybody, and life was good, when a man started changing it all. Most of the time it was just a man staring too much—but then one would come over. Friendly, he'd put his thick hands on the table as if he were touching water, and squat low, so that he was at sitting level, as though he were being so polite, and he'd smile, with coffee-and-tobacco-stained teeth. He might wear a bolo tie and speak in a drawl. Or he might have a tan uniform on, a company logo on the back, an oval name patch on the front. Or he'd be in a nothing-special work shirt, white or striped, with a couple of pens clipped onto the left side pocket, tucked into a pair of jeans or chinos that were morning-clean still, with a pair of scuffed work boots that laced up higher than regular shoes. He'd say something about her earrings, or her bracelet, or her hair, or her eyes, and if she had on her white uniform how nice it looked on her. Or he'd come right out with it and tell her how pretty she was, how he couldn't keep himself from walking up, speaking to her directly, and could they talk again? Then he'd wink at Erick. Such a fine-looking boy! How old is he, eight or nine? Erick wasn't even small for an eleven-year-old. He tightened his jaw then, slanted his eyes up from his plate at his mom and not the man, definitely not this man he did not care for. Erick drove a fork into a goopy American egg yolk and bled it into his American potatoes. She wouldn't offer the man Erick's correct age, either, saying only that he was growing too fast.

She almost always gave the man her number if he was wearing a suit. Not a sports coat but a buttoned suit with a starched white shirt and a pinned tie meant something to her. Once in a while, Erick saw one of these men again at the front door of the apartment in Silverlake. The man winked at Erick as if they were buddies. Grabbed his shoulder or arm, squeezed the muscle against the bone. What did Erick want to be when he grew up? A cop, a jet-airplane mechanic, a travel agent, a court reporter? A dog groomer? Erick stood there, because his mom said that he shouldn't be impolite. His mom's date said he wanted to take Erick along with them sometime. The three of them. What kind of places did Erick think were fun? Erick said nothing. He never said anything when the men were around, and not because of his English, even if that was the excuse his mother gave for his silence. He didn't talk to any of the men and he didn't talk much to his mom, either. Finally they took off, and Erick's night was his alone. He raced to the grocery store and bought half a gallon of chocolate ice cream. When he got back, he turned on the TV, scooted up real close, as close as he could, and ate his dinner with a soup spoon. He was away from all the men. Even though a man had given the TV to them. He was a salesman in an appliance store who'd bragged that a rich customer had given it to him and so why shouldn't he give it to Erick's mom, who couldn't afford such a good TV otherwise?

When his mom was working as a restaurant hostess, and was going to marry the owner, Erick ate hot-fudge sundaes and drank chocolate shakes. When she worked at a trucking company, the owner of all the trucks told her he was getting a divorce. Erick climbed into the rigs, with their rooms full of dials and levers in the sky. Then she started working in an engineer's office. There was no food or fun there, but even he could see the money. He was not supposed to touch anything, but what was there to touch—the tubes full of paper? He and his mom were invited to the engineer's house, where he had two horses and a stable, a swimming pool, and two convertible sports cars. The engineer's family was there: his grown children, his gray-haired parents. They all sat down for dinner in a dining room that seemed bigger than Erick's apartment, with three candelabras on the table, and a tablecloth and cloth napkins. Erick's mom took him aside to tell him to be well mannered at the table and polite to everyone. Erick hadn't said anything. He never spoke anyway, so how could he have said anything wrong? She leaned into his ear and said that she wanted them to know that he spoke English. That whole dinner he was silent, chewing quietly, taking the smallest bites, because he didn't want them to think he liked their food.

When she got upset about days like that, she told Erick that she wished they could just go back home. She was tired of worrying. "Back," for Erick, meant mostly the stories he'd heard from her, which never sounded so good to him: she'd had to share a room with her brothers and sisters. They didn't have toilets. They didn't have electricity. Sometimes they didn't have enough food. He saw this Mexico as if it were the backdrop of a movie on afternoon TV, where children walked around barefoot in the dirt or on broken side-walks and small men wore wide-brimmed straw hats and baggy white shirts and pants. The women went to church all the time and prayed to alcoved saints and, heads down, fearful, counted rosary beads. There were rocks ev-erywhere, and scorpions and tarantulas and rattlesnakes, and vultures and no trees and not much water, and skinny dogs and donkeys, and ugly bad guys with guns and bullet vests who rode laughing into town to drink and shoot off their pistols and rifles, as if it were the Fourth of July, driving their horses all over town like dirt bikes on desert dunes. When they spoke English, they had stupid accents—his mom didn't have an accent like theirs. It didn't make sense to him that Mexico would only be like that, but what if it was close? He lived on paved, lighted city streets, and a bicycle ride away were the Asian drugstore and the Armenian grocery store and the corner where black Cu-bans drank coffee and talked Dodgers baseball.

When he was in bed, where he sometimes prayed, he thanked God for his mom, who he loved, and he apologized to for not talking to her, or to any-one, really, except his friend Albert, and he apologized for her never going to church and for his never taking Holy Communion, as Albert did—though only to God would he admit that he wanted to because Albert did. He prayed for good to come, for his mom and for him, since God was like magic, and happiness might come the way of early morning, in the trees and bushes full of sparrows next to his open window, louder and louder when he listened hard, eyes closed.

The engineer wouldn't have mattered if Erick hadn't told Albert that he was his dad. Albert had just moved into the apartment next door and lived with both his mother and his father, and since Albert's mother already didn't like Erick's mom, Erick told him that his new dad was an engineer. Erick actually believed it, too, and thought that he might even get his own horse. When that didn't happen, and his mom was lying on her bed in the middle of the day, blowing her nose, because she didn't have the job anymore, that was when Roque came around again. Roque was nobody—or he was anybody. He wasn't special, he wasn't not. He tried to speak English to Erick, thinking that was the reason Erick didn't say anything when he was there. And Erick had to tell Albert that Roque was his uncle, because the engineer was supposed to be his new dad any minute. Uncle Rock, Erick said. His mom's brother, he told Albert. Roque worked at night and was around during the day, and one day he offered Erick and Albert a ride. When his mom got in the car, she scooted all the way over to Roque on the bench seat. Who was supposed to be her brother, Erick's Uncle Rock. Albert didn't say anything, but he saw what had happened, and that was it for Erick. Albert had parents, grandparents, and a brother and a sister, and he'd hang out only when one of his cousins wasn't coming by. Erick didn't need a friend like him.

What if she married Roque, his mom asked him one day soon afterward. She told Erick that they would move away from the apartment in Silverlake to a better neighborhood. He did want to move, but he wished that it weren't because of Uncle Rock. It wasn't just because Roque didn't have a swimming pool or horses or a big ranch house. There wasn't much to criticize except that he was always too willing and nice, too considerate, too generous. He wore nothing flashy or expensive, just ordinary clothes that were clean and ironed, and shoes he kept shined. He combed and parted his hair neatly. He didn't have a buzzcut like the men who didn't like kids. He moved slow, he talked slow, as quiet as night. He only ever said yes to Erick's mom. How could she not like him for that? He loved her so much—anybody could see his pride when he was with her. He signed checks and gave her cash. He knocked on their door carrying cans and fruit and meat. He was there when she asked, gone when she asked, back whenever, grateful. He took her out to restaurants on Sunset, to the movies in Hollywood, or on drives to the beach in rich Santa Monica.

Roque knew that Erick loved baseball. Did Roque like baseball? It was doubtful that he cared even a little bit—he didn't listen to games on the radio or TV, and he never looked at a newspaper. He loved boxing, though. He knew the names of all the Mexican fighters as if they lived here, as if they were Dodgers players, like Steve Sax or Steve Yeager, Dusty Baker, Kenny Landreaux or Mike Marshall, Pedro Guerrero. Roque did know about Fernando Valenzuela, as everyone did, even his mom, which is why she agreed to let Roque take them to a game. What Mexican didn't love Fernando?

Dodger Stadium was close to their apartment. He'd been there once with Albert and his family—well, outside it, on a nearby hill, to see the fireworks for Fourth of July. His mom decided that all three of them would go on a Saturday afternoon, since Saturday night, Erick thought, she might want to go somewhere else, even with somebody else.

Roque, of course, didn't know who the Phillies were. He knew nothing about the strikeouts by Steve Carlton or the home runs by Mike Schmidt. He'd never heard of Pete Rose. It wasn't that Erick knew very much, either, but there was nothing that Roque could talk to him about, if they were to talk.

If Erick showed his excitement when they drove up to Dodger Stadium and parked, his mom and Roque didn't really notice it. They sat in the bleachers, and for him the green of the field was a magic light; the stadium decks surrounding them seemed as far away as Rome. His body was somewhere it had never been before. The fifth inning? That's how late they were. Or were they right on time, because they weren't even sure they were sitting in the right seats yet when he heard the crack of the bat, saw the crowd around them rising as it came at them. Erick saw the ball. He had to stand and move and stretch his arms and want that ball until it hit his bare hands and stayed there. Everybody saw him catch it with no bobble. He felt all the eyes and voices around him as if they were every set of eyes and every voice in the stadium. His mom was saying something, and Roque, too, and then, finally, it was just him and that ball and his stinging hands. He wasn't even sure if it had been hit by Pete Guerrero. He thought for sure it had been, but he didn't ask. He didn't watch the game then—he couldn't. He didn't care who won. He stared at his official National League ball, reimagining what had happened. He ate a hot dog and drank a soda and he sucked the salted peanuts and the wooden spoon from his chocolate-malt ice cream. He rubbed the bumpy seams of his home-run ball.

Game over, they were the last to leave. People were hanging around, not going straight to their cars. Roque didn't want to leave. He didn't want to end it so quickly, Erick thought, while he still had her with him. Then one of the Phillies came out of the stadium door and people swarmed—boys mostly, but also men and some women and girls—and they got autographs before the player climbed onto the team's bus. Joe Morgan, they said. Then Garry Maddox appeared. Erick clutched the ball but he didn't have a pen. He just watched, his back to the gray bus the Phillies were getting into.

Then a window slid open. *Hey, big man,* a voice said. Erick really wasn't sure. *Gimme the ball, la pelota,* the face in the bus said. *I'll have it signed, comprendes? Échalo, just toss it to me.* Erick obeyed. He tossed it up to the hand that was reaching out. The window closed. The ball was gone a while, so long that his mom came up to him, worried that he'd lost it. The window slid open again and the voice spoke to her. *We got the ball, Mom. It's not lost, just a few more.* When the window opened once more, this time the ball was there. *Catch.* There were all kinds of signatures on it, though none that he could really recognize except for Joe Morgan and Pete Rose.

Then the voice offered more, and the hand threw something at him. *For your mom, okay? Comprendes?* Erick stared at the asphalt lot where the object lay, as if he'd never seen a folded-up piece of paper before. *Para tu mamá, bueno?* He picked it up, and he started to walk over to his mom and Roque, who were so busy talking they hadn't noticed anything. Then he stopped. He opened the note himself. No one had said he couldn't read it. It said, *I'd like to get to know you. You are muy linda. Very beautiful and sexy. I don't speak Spanish very good, may be you speak better English, pero No Importa. Would you come by tonite and let me buy you a drink?* There was a phone number and a hotel-room number. A name, too. A name that came at him the way that the home run had.

Erick couldn't hear. He could see only his mom ahead of him. She was talking to Roque, Roque was talking to her. Roque was the proudest man, full of joy because he was with her. It wasn't his fault he wasn't an engineer. Now Erick could hear again. Like sparrows hunting seed, boys gathered round the bus, calling out, while the voice in the bus was yelling at him, *Hey, big guy! Give it to her!* Erick had the ball in one hand and the note in the other. By the time he reached his mom and Roque, the note was already somewhere on the asphalt parking lot. *Look*, he said in a full voice. *They all signed the ball.*

DRIVE

Aaron Gwyn

hey were driving back from Wewoka Lake on the narrow stretch of Oklahoma blacktop. They'd been fighting all morning, and she'd been drinking all morning, and now she was drunk. He didn't think she was pretty when she was drunk. Her face turned red and rigid. She was sitting in the passenger seat of the Charger, staring out her window, and he'd turned the radio off so he could think. All his thoughts were mean and desperate. He couldn't get them to stop circling. They hit the straightaway right after the curve by the brick plant, trees on both sides, the black oaks leaning so that the road seemed like a tunnel and the light inside it a strobe of shadow and sun.

His hands were twitching. He was sober. He didn't think he'd been more sober, and looking at things, clear headed as he was, he felt like it was finished. They'd never have kids, get married. They'd never have a lot of things, and when he thought about starting over with another one, something inside him seemed to fall. He didn't know what it was. His sternum felt frozen. There was a cool ache in his throat. He tried to clear it, but he couldn't.

The sun seemed to dim.

A van met them and slipped past. Then a pickup and trailer. He could see the sun reflect off the glass of another about half a mile away, coming their direction, and when the glint of it hit his eyes, he went cold and numb. He couldn't feel his fingers or face. It was like his hands belonged to someone else. They gripped the wheel at ten and two, and he watched them tighten and the knuckles go white, and then he watched, as if on a monitor, them steer the car into the oncoming lane. Jill didn't seem to notice. She probably thought he was trying to pass. But then he started accelerating, up from sixty to seventy to eighty-five, and right before the truck coming toward them began flashing its lights, she glanced up, and then over.

She said, "Jesus Christ, Jimmy! What in the fuck?"

He looked at her. He felt very calm.

When he looked back to the road, the truck coming toward them had begun to brake, and they were about a hundred yards away. He bore down on the pedal and clenched his jaw. He could feel his back teeth grinding. He didn't know what he wanted. He felt like he was floating or coasting. He felt like his mind was stripped bare, low to the ground and gliding fast. Right as Jill began to scream, the approaching pickup swerved into the opposite lane and went past in a blur of paint and chrome and a Dopplering of horn blasts and squealing tires.

She was saying, "My God." She was saying it over and over. She wouldn't look at him, and when he glanced at her, her face was completely drained of blood and she was shaking.

He pulled into the right-hand lane, and when he pulled into the driveway ten minutes later, feeling had returned to his hands and face and he could sense his body. Jill was motionless, mute. She was staring at the console in front of her, the glove compartment. In it was a signature series Dan Wesson .357, five of the chambers loaded with Black Talons. She knew he kept it there. He leaned over and hit the compartment release, took the gun and holster, and then got out and went up the walk to the house. He fumbled with the lock a moment, and then he was inside and through the living room and up the hallway to the bedroom. He walked over to the dresser on his side of the bed, opened the drawer, and buried the pistol under a pile of socks. He sat there and tried to think. His skin was tingling. He decided he'd put the gun back before work in the morning. He decided he needed something to drink.

He went back down the hallway to the kitchen. Jill was standing in the living room. He hadn't heard her come inside. She was short and petite and darkly complexioned: dark eyes and hair and skin. She was twenty-seven years old, and she looked, of a sudden, twenty-one. The years had been burned out of her face. She looked like she'd gotten in from a run. He leaned against the wall a moment and stared at her. She was standing very still in her cutoff shorts and bikini top, her hair pulled into a ponytail, wisps of hair trailing around her ears. She stared at the carpet just in front of her. She had her hands held out to either side as though to steady herself.

She looked up and noticed he'd entered.

Then she started toward him.

One moment she was standing motionless, and the next she was moving, faster than he'd seen her move, and he thought she was going to hit him.

But she didn't hit him.

She came up, and he turned her and pressed her against the wall, and somehow she wrapped herself around him, climbed up, and was at his neck and ears and face. Her body gave off a strange heat. It almost hurt to touch. He held her very tightly, and they were kissing in a way that seemed vicious and fierce. He carried her down the hall toward the bedroom, but they didn't make it to the bedroom. They made it as far as the bathroom, and as he carried her, she came. She squeezed into him and screamed, and her entire body convulsed. It had never happened like that. They were both still clothed. He'd not even touched her there.

Then they were in the bathroom, and she was seated on the counter with her legs around his waist. His belt was off, and he was inside her. She was weeping and grabbing his hips and pulling him into her harder.

She said, "Motherfucker."

She said, "Kill."

She said other things.

She said something that sounded like *grate*.

Afterward, they lay atop the covers of their bed with the air-conditioning prickling their skin and her against him as though she'd wear him for warmth. He didn't understand what had happened, and he thought he loved her very much.

She turned at one point and kissed him gently on the cheek.

She said, "Don't ever do that again."

Of course, he did it again.

Why wouldn't he do it again?

He felt she wanted him to, and it wasn't something she could ask with words. She had to ask other ways. It was something he had to know.

Two weeks and they were coming back from the City after meeting friends for dinner. They'd made the Earlsboro exit and were driving past the county dump. It was just dark, and the stars were swarming up above them, and the trees beyond the bar ditch at either side of the road reflected moon-light in shades of green. Theirs was the only car on the highway. Jill reached over and brushed her nails very lightly against his arm, and he knew at once what she was thinking. She didn't have to say a word. He thought that they'd found something outside sex or speaking. He pressed down the accelerator, and the night began rushing past.

Her breath quickened. The time before, she'd been angry, but this was something else. When they topped the hill and descended the final stretch of blacktop before the 270 intersection, there were headlights in the distance.

They didn't speak. Her nails grazed his arm. She was making a loose fist and then releasing it, making a fist and releasing, letting her nails trail across his skin. The headlights were a mile off, and he gave the Charger more gas and watched the needle on the speedometer track up to 110. The front end trembled. Her nails stopped moving. They stopped moving and settled and then started to dig in. He pressed the pedal to the floor and steered across the centerline.

The headlights were closer. They seemed to hesitate and twitch. You couldn't know what the other driver was thinking, and Jimmy didn't care. He wasn't doing it for the other driver, and he wasn't, he thought, doing it for himself. Something had opened up. He was nearer than he'd ever been. He didn't wonder about losing her. He didn't worry she'd disappear. They'd discovered something on the road by Wewoka Lake, and when you discov-ered something, there wasn't any going back. He didn't even see why you'd want to or how you could. They were going forward, fully forward, faster and faster like the car in which they traveled, on toward the lights which seemed to have stopped moving. They were running at 116 miles an hour with the en-gine whining in fifth gear and her nails clawing his skin and the two of them like one thing, watching, the Charger passing the motionless car, and not even honking this time, no telling what they thought, just wind moving past and the bright blur of the headlamps and the night rushing back to darkness as he eased off the accelerator and allowed the car to coast.

They started calling them *drives*. He'd turn and ask if she wanted to drive, and she'd know what he meant. There were drives that weren't *drives*, but more and more that were. He couldn't come out and say that's what they were doing. If it was a *drive*, he'd have to pretend it wasn't. She needed it to be like that. She'd ask it with her eyes.

She'd ask with her eyes and her cheeks and the way she'd tilt, to him, her face. She'd incline it just so, and he knew she was asking him to ask it.

And he would.

A week later, they pegged out the Charger on the flat stretch of highway headed toward Norman, traveling west. Sundown. Cool and cloudless. Jimmy steered into the passing lane going up a hill, no cars coming, but you couldn't see to know. Anything could suddenly crest out and come barreling into your teeth. When they topped the incline and looked down to see nothing on the road below them, he glanced over to the passenger seat, and she was grazing her nails along her thighs and then she reached with one hand to caress her neck.

She sucked her top lip between her teeth.

Her eyes fluttered.

Then the Tuesday following. This time running slower and at dawn, a fog rising from creek bottoms along 99 and the car pushing through mists and trailing behind it two vortices of turning vapor. You couldn't see anything twenty yards ahead. Jimmy behind the wheel with love and terror churning inside him and thinking, as they parted the morning haze, that the territory into which they traveled was a territory of adoration and fear. Both drew them closer, pressed them, no distance and one mind watching, the old primal mind, reptilian.

And always afterward, after they pulled back into the drive, morning or evening, the two of them having at each other like children, and with the same sense of wonder, and panic, and awe.

Her body was changing. She was changing inside it.

At first it was Jimmy who had changed, or Jimmy who had acted, and the action changed him, and her, changed them together, though somehow at different speeds. She was going faster than him now. She was accelerating, faster and faster. She was astride him, seated atop his hips with her shins braced against his thighs, not bouncing, but actually *riding*, the way a jockey will a horse, faster than bouncing, more controlled, her knees on the bed at either side of him, and now leaning forward, both palms braced against the center of his chest, turning her head as though looking back to someone, someone not in the room, and her eyes clenched and teeth bared, crying out, and him little more than a stump or post, because, in her velocity, she must have forgotten him entirely. He must have disappeared beneath her, because now when she comes and quivers and collapses onto him, her body feels like there is no skeleton inside to sustain it, and he is not Jimmy, he is the thing onto which she's crumpled, boneless, and she just lies like that, heaving slightly and out of breath, and without looking or touching, she rolls off him and onto her side of the bed, and then pulls him to her, uses him to cover herself.

They would lie in the dark in the hours after. He had begun to feel the creep of something. Something very different.

"You awake?" she whispered.

"I'm awake," he said.

They lay there.

The air-conditioning clicked off.

The room was cold.

"Are you hungry?"

He said he wasn't.

"I'm hungry," she said.

"Eat something."

"I'm hungry all the time."

He could feel her toes against his ankle.

"You look like you lost weight."

"I have lost weight."

"You look good," he said.

"I've lost six pounds. It's like I can't get enough to eat. I'll eat, and then, ten minutes later, I'm hungry again."

A minute passed. He thought she'd fallen asleep.

"Do you still love me?" she asked.

He turned his head on the pillow and tried to see her in the dark.

"What?" he said.

"Do you?"

"Of course."

"Say it."

"I love you," he said.

"Say it again."

"I love you."

"Again."

"Jesus," he said. "I love you: I love you, I love you, I love you."

She reached out and touched his shoulder the way someone would to check the burner on a stove.

She said she loved him too.

"Are you going to get something?"

"Get what?" she asked.

"To eat."

"I don't know."

"Are you hungry?"

"Yes."

"Then eat," he said.

She said she wasn't sure.

He almost told her to let him sleep, but he didn't. It used to be something he would've said, not worrying whether it might sting. The drives had changed that, and now he did worry. They engaged twice a week in a ritual that could kill them instantly, and now he worried he might hurt her feelings if he asked to let him sleep.

"You think we'll keep this up?"

"Keep what up?" he asked, knowing exactly.

"You know," she said, and this time her hand on his shoulder was a caress. "The way we've become."

He coughed into a hand and cleared his throat. "I try not to think about that," he said.

She was silent for a time. He couldn't tell if what he said had satisfied her or if his lying had caused her to try a different approach.

"I want us to get married," she said. "I want a family."

He opened his mouth to respond, but he couldn't. He'd wanted that too, at one time, but now he couldn't conceive of that from her, and he realized it was finished.

"Baby?" she said.

"Yeah."

"Did you hear me?"

"Mm-hmm."

"What are you thinking?"

"I just—we talked about that all last spring."

She scooted across the bed and pressed herself against him. "It was different then. I don't think I was ready."

"And you feel like now you are?"

She seemed to be thinking about that. She said that now she felt she needed to be. Without it, she didn't feel safe.

He didn't know what to say. He pulled the covers off his chest and kicked them to the foot of the bed.

"You're hot?" she asked.

"A little."

"I'm cold."

"Here," he said, pulling the sheet back up. "Sorry."

She pressed herself tighter against him, laid her head on his shoulder, and in several minutes, her breathing had relaxed and he could feel her face slacken against his skin.

Jimmy lay there. He was frightened in a way he didn't understand.

He thought he needed to try something to get them out of this.

Then he realized he already had.

The drives ended. He decided to leave. A month and a half ago, he'd almost killed them in a head-on collision because he thought she might move out. And now, just like that, he had to get away.

It was his house they lived in.

It had taken him most of his twenties to pay off, working pipeline jobs in Alaska and out West.

He thought he'd just let her have it and go.

He began to remove items from the den and place them in storage. Fall was coming into the air, and before she woke in the morning, he'd take his grandfather's pair of antique Persian pistols, or his suitcase of baseball cards, or an old photograph album with pictures of his nephews and nieces, take these in the Charger and pull in among the rows of identical aluminum-sided cells—each with a door that scrolled upward like the door on a garage—slip them into one of the cheap trunks he'd purchased, not knowing why it was these items he'd chosen and needed to protect. Standing in the morning cool with the sun not yet fully up, trying to hide his life and reassemble it.

He stood under the shower with his hands trembling.

He watched her as she slept.

Everything about her frightened him. Everything was strange.

He tried to think where he'd be when he told her. He considered moving to another town, going back out to the far West. He considered having a lawyer present, though he didn't know what for.

He thought about discussing it with a friend, but this was not something he could discuss. He couldn't disclose their drives. He couldn't allow another in on that.

And she was getting suspicious. She sat across the car on their way to get dinner, sat squinting and with her arms folded as they circled the drive-through, then sat quietly on their way home, staring out at the road with a look on her he'd never seen.

The sun was down.

The light was failing.

"James," she said, "you're not even here."

He drew a breath and let it slowly out.

"Where am I?" he asked.

"Don't be cute."

"What?"

"Don't get smart."

"I'm not getting anything," he said, braking slightly and slowing the car. "I don't know what you're talking about."

She turned to look out her window. The bag of burgers and fries in her lap and the smell of it made him nauseous. He didn't think he'd be able to eat. They started up the hill toward the airport, the city limits about a mile away.

"Why are you going so slow?" she asked.

"I'm driving the speed limit."

"You never drive the speed limit."

"I do on hills. Patrols set up all through here."

She turned back to face him. "You're worried about a ticket?"

He cleared his throat.

His chest felt thick.

He said he'd just as soon not get stopped.

She looked at him, and her eyes narrowed.

"You're breaking up with me," she said.

"What?"

"Don't lie to me, Jimmy." Her voice was almost a whisper. "Be a man, for God sakes."

"A man," he said. "Two months ago, you were ready to break it off yourself."

Her eyes started to tear. She shook her head. She wiped her face and backhanded the wet from her cheeks and said she thought they were getting married.

He focused on breathing. He watched the road.

She said, "Is there someone else?"

"No."

"Were you going to say something?"

He shrugged and shook his head. "I didn't know what to say."

She leaned back, and Jimmy thought, at that point, the fight was over. He thought he'd been impetuous by moving things out of the den.

She sat slumped in her seat, almost lying.

Then she kicked the dash.

It happened quickly. She kicked with both feet, cracking an air-conditioning vent, and then she kicked the center console and shattered the face of the clock.

He had one arm out trying to push her back. He was saying her name and telling her to calm down.

She began screaming. She released a wail that seemed to come from all the way inside her. She doubled forward, and he was trying to press her back against her seat, and that was when she turned sideways and struck him with her fist.

He hadn't expected that. He raised an arm to fend off a second blow and swerved the car and checked the rearview mirror. He could feel a knot beginning to swell on his temple. She'd hit him very hard.

They passed the city limits. They began to pass construction supply and storage facilities, offices of the various production companies quartered in Perser.

There were a few moments of silence.

She began to shiver.

"Why," she told him, "don't you speed this thing up?"

He glanced at her.

"I'm not going to do that," he said.

"Why don't you give it a little gas?"

"I'm taking you home," he said. "I'm taking you to your mother's."

Her eyes cut sideways and then back to the road, and she pressed her palms together and held them. Then she drew a leg back as if to kick, but she didn't kick. She raised up in the seat and thrust her leg across the column and tried to snake her foot down on top of his and the accelerator.

He managed to push her back. He managed to keep them on the road.

"Speed up," she was saying, fast and barely coherent. "Speed it up."

She tried the thing with her leg again, and again he pushed her back. He was telling her to quit, she'd cause them to have a wreck, and she said she'd show him a wreck and tried it once more.

This time he pushed her harder and with more force than he intended, and as she fell backward, her neck whipped and her head cracked the passenger-side window. The lamination held, but the glass was shattered, spiderwebbing from the point of impact so that the pane behind her was a nimbus of shattered glass.

"Jill," he said, "Jesus," and he reached for her knee, groping air.

She stared at him from beneath her brows, her eyes liquid and trembling. After the first drive, she'd looked younger, but now she looked childlike and wounded. Outraged. Confused.

They drove half a mile. He reached to turn on the lights.

Something peculiar happened. Something strange came into the air. It was almost a scent and almost a breath, and it very nearly had a temperature and taste. It came from God knew where, and it was palpable, sudden. It wasn't there, and then it was. A scent and a breath and a flavor, almost, and also none of these. Jimmy thought immediately of the glove compartment and then thought, by thinking that, he'd bring it to her mind. He tried not to glance over, and then glancing, tried not to move his head.

He thought he should stop the car.

He thought again about the pistol, and this time, he did glance over, just barely turned his head, but it was too much, he knew instantly, and he knew, without any question, they'd been wired to each other or welded, fused in some permanent way, and he made for the glove compartment as quick as he could.

Jill was faster. By the time his hand left the wheel, her fingers had already tripped the compartment release and gripped the pistol, and then she extended it, pressed the barrel to his temple and cocked the hammer with her thumb.

It was fully dark now.

The blacktop clicked against his tires.

"Drive," she said.

LOOKING FOR BOLL WEEVIL

Toni Jensen

t six in the morning, forty miles south of the Twin Cities, I jerked awake in the cold and dark of the bus our school group was sharing with a bunch of touring senior citizens. I was a long way from home, and the air felt different from West Texas air. It was thicker, more humid, and it smelled different, too, like pine trees, maybe, even through the mix of teenager and old-people smells circulating around the bus. My niece slept beside me, her face scrunched into a sleepy frown, thin hands clutching the blanket up under her chin.

Two days ago, my sister Diane had called from St. Paul. It was four in the afternoon, a bright April day, the unseasonable sun blanching the cotton fields, searing the manzanitas in the canyon. My niece Sandra's fifth-grade class was heading out on a bus for the Rosebud Reservation in South Dakota. My sister, a trip sponsor, had been promoted at her job. She was now too important to ride a bus to South Dakota. I was unemployed, and I never had been that important. Still, it was cold in South Dakota sometimes in April. Still, I didn't necessarily want to do Diane any favors.

We are métis, Roubideaux, from near the Blood Reserve in Alberta, and Sandra's father, Pete, is Blackfoot. I didn't see why Sandra had to get on a bus and go all the way to South Dakota to see some Indians.

Look, Diane said, they've been sponsoring Grandma Claw since first grade.

I didn't know we had a grandmother named Claw, I said. Neat.

It's a school trip, Diane said, graduation into middle school, a rite of passage.

I sighed into the phone.

I'll buy your plane ticket here, Diane said.

I sighed again, louder this time, but Diane already was talking over me, explaining the rest fast—how the children gave *Grandma Claw* food and yarn to make blankets or rugs or something, how then they went on a big celebration trip and met *their* elder. I opened my mouth to continue the arguing, but Diane was holding out the phone, and I could hear Sandra crying. Before long, I had my instructions: how I was to bring sleeping bags and pillows, pack sandwiches and fresh fruit but no cigarettes, no booze. Diane said that last part twice, hands clicking double-time against the receiver.

The bus lurched and shrugged down the highway, and a silver-haired woman stumbled in the aisle up front. With her wild hair and hunched shoulders, she looked a little like Bobby Jo, my landlady back in West Texas. In exchange for cheap rent and a house on 500 acres at the top of Blanco Canyon, I watered cottonwood and fruit-bearing trees, peach and apple and pear, mostly pear, row on row of pear, stretching out under the hot West Texas sun.

What are you going to do with all those pears? I had asked Bobby Jo the first time I visited the place.

We, she said. What are *we* going to do with all those pears.

It was unnatural, all those trees out there on the high plains, all the watering. It was almost as bad as Indians riding a bus 400 miles to gawk at other Indians. But I had seen the way Bobby Jo looked at the trees. Every Sunday she drove out from Lubbock and moved her aging body tree to tree, row to row, checking the water hoses and sprinklers, her hands open, her voice rising in what could be construed as prayer.

It was the boll weevils she found unnatural, and, technically, she was right. The cotton-destroying snout beetle was native only to Mexico and Central America and hadn't been introduced into West Texas until 1892, shortly after the Comanche were introduced to smallpox, cholera, and General Mackenzie.

They've done so much damage in such a short time, Bobby Jo said.

Yes, I said. They have.

But it was only April, and the boll weevils were still in diapause, I hoped, were sleeping the spring away, waiting for the lasting heat of July. In the spring, I watered the trees and checked the boll weevil traps for freak, unseasonable activity, which the kind of heat we'd been having could inspire.

I worried over the possibilities, and the Bobby Jo look-alike continued to wander up and down the aisle, one shoe untied. I wondered whether the pear trees had gone dry, whether the boll weevils were waking up and flying, taking over the cotton in my absence. The woman paused by our row, shoe now tied.

My shoe, she slurred, my shoe.

It's tied now, I said. See?

My shoe, she said. Her face contorted, her voice rising. My shoe!

Okay, I said. All right.

I reached down and untied the shoe closest to me. It was standard old-lady issue, tan and thick soled. I leaned in close to retie it and smelled new leather, but the laces were already worn smooth and thin.

There, I said. I leaned back in my seat, the lace double-knotted.

The woman shuffled away, down the aisle toward the back of the bus. My shoe, she said, my shoe.

I wished Diane were here. I'd ask her whether we could give this woman a blanket and all go home. If it would make everyone feel better, we could even call this woman "Grandma." I thought about asking Nancy, the trip leader, but she was quiet, sitting up front by herself behind the driver, and besides, I hadn't figured out why she was here yet, whether she was in it for the children, wanted to see an Indian, wanted to be an Indian, or what. She was dark skinned and dark eyed, but her hair was blond—the opposite of me, with my pale skin and dark hair. Together, I thought, we could make somebody's idea of a complete Indian.

Sandra stirred beside me.

Are we there yet?

She brushed her dark hair away from her face with the back of her hand, eyes squinting in the strange not-quite dark that was bus light.

No, I said. But only a couple hours to go.

Promise? She had her mother's eyes—dark and doubtful and angled up slightly at the corners, even in sleep.

Promise, I said, and she turned back to the window, burrowing down under the blanket.

It was late afternoon by the time we got to Mission and the reservation after letting off the seniors at the Corn Palace in Mitchell. The plan was to eat sandwiches at the casino outside of town, meet our elder, and attend some sort of fifth-grade graduation ceremony the teachers had concocted. I was curious about having snacks with fifth graders at a casino, but when I said as much, four of the five other women in the group scowled, shot me a look that said, *You're not a mother, are you?*

They're giving us a deal, Nancy said. It's the off-season.

As we pulled into the parking lot, though, I was having a hard time imagining this place was ever in season. The concrete lot rose up from the highest point on the rolling plains, majestic, I guessed, but nearly empty. The lot could easily hold a section of cotton, but now held only a handful of cars, huddled together. Rows of baby pine lined the shiny new building, making something like a windrow, except they were only about knee high. They listed out from their shallow, half-filled holes.

The bus shuddered to a stop just as a small tree near the front of the line broke loose and skidded across the concrete, flying end on end, out over the nearest low-lying ridge, and was gone.

Sandra perched on a seat up front, shoulders hunched forward. I could feel her frown before she turned around and gave it to me. I shrugged. This wasn't my idea. The wind rattled the bus windows, a million teeth chattering in unison, and Sandra's frown turned to a scowl. The corners of my face lifted in a feeble attempt at a smile, and we sat there awhile, her scowling, me mock smiling, the rest of the children and parents gathering their things. They were all making happy noises like they hadn't noticed the wind.

I could rent a car, I thought, and be back with the cottonwoods and boll weevils by bedtime if I drove straight through. Tomorrow morning I could be sitting out by the canyon in the sunshine, melting the plastic smile right off my face.

You coming?

It was Nancy, standing over me, my bag in her left hand, another, larger one slung over her right shoulder. You know, she said, you can smoke in the casino part of the casino.

She looked over her shoulder before shaking a pack of Virginia Slims Menthols at me, but we were the only ones left on the bus. Outside, Sandra skipped along with a friend, their hair swirling above their heads in the fierce wind. They broke into a run when they reached the pine trees, and soon were swallowed up by the building. I took a cigarette from Nancy's pack and followed her down the steps, out into the cold.

We stood in the casino entryway, assaulted with its sounds and smells—
the clicks and whirs of the slots, the stale mix of cigarettes and old people's
armpits.

Ugh, I said, lighting up my cigarette, this is awful.

Nancy turned back to me, grinning, hers already lit.

Arrows overhead pointed the ways to the restaurant, hotel, casino, and
swimming pool. Look, I said, the four directions.

Nancy pulled a roll of quarters from her jacket, and we chose north, for
casino. The others must have already gone south, to the restaurant, because
we were the only ones from our group in sight. The place was empty except
for the white-shirted, black-pants-and-tie-wearing waitresses and dealers,
and the old people—they huddled in front of the slots and tables, the women
both Indian and white in polyester, the men in seed-corn or cowboy hats and
thin plaid shirts.

I studied the carpet's geometric design, how the pattern led in all directions but also seemed to circle back to the spot where I stood. I leaned my
back against a slot machine, my head in my hands, dizzy, not quite able to
catch my breath.

You're not going to win like that, Nancy said.

She was still grinning, shaking her half-empty roll of quarters, and there
was another roll in her other hand. A woman with dark permed hair and
a round tray brought Nancy a Coke. She handed me one of her rolls and
pulled a flask from her pocket. I tried to look away, tried to focus somewhere
else, but before long I turned back, swallowed hard, and nodded at her, at
the flask.

Forty minutes passed like that—drinks and cigarettes and the whir of
the machines—and then the door opened and a tall dark-haired man blew
through it, brushing snow from his collar, shaking it off his cowboy hat.

We moved from the machines to the window, rubbed the fog from it.
Snow blew down crazily, covering the baby trees, the huddled cars, the bus.

Crap, Nancy said.

Seriously, I said, it's ninety degrees at home.

Nancy laughed, throwing back her head, her dirty blond hair falling everywhere. You're stuck here, she said, laughing harder, and you're not even
the mom.

I gulped down the last of my drink, and Nancy did the same.

Come on, she said.

The kids and other parents or parent substitutes sat at booths and rectangular tables, finishing off their sandwiches. I scanned the room but didn't see

Sandra. I looked over at Nancy to ask if she saw her, but Nancy's face had gone slack.

Rochelle? she yelled. Has anyone seen Rochelle?

The faces turned, and my face, already flushed from the drinks, grew brighter still. The oldest woman in the group stood and shuffled over to us. Somebody's grandmother, I thought, as she took Nancy and me each by an arm and hustled us into the corner where people had hung their coats. I was trying to remember if I'd brought a coat or just a jacket when the old woman said it—We thought they were with you—when it hit me that Rochelle must be Sandra's friend, that they were both, somehow, gone.

The mothers became a flurry of limbs and bobbed hair, pushing their kids into the opposite end of the restaurant. Like we're contagious, I thought, but then it occurred to me that we *had* been drinking. That we'd lost our kids.

I wished I could will myself home—the lawn chair, the sunshine, even the boll weevils calling me back. I wished Diane were here and then was glad she wasn't. She was going to kill me, I thought, and then felt guilty for thinking only of that and the throbbing that was starting up on both sides of my head.

·The old woman jabbered away to the kids—Did any of you notice—then shuffled back to our corner to report the noninformation. No one had seen anything. Nancy leaned onto her knees, her face two shades paler. I'd lost the sunshine now, was thinking of snow banks, exposed limbs, frozen fingers. I tried to push the thought away, to focus, this time, to try harder.

Look, I said, they have to be somewhere.

It's snowing, Nancy said. It's snowing and—

I circled around the old woman to Nancy's side. I took her hand.

Come on, I said, we'll find them.

The old woman stayed in the south with the children, who sat at her feet on the restaurant floor, and the rest of us fanned out in the other directions. This time, Nancy and I headed west to the swimming pool. This time, I led.

I hurried through the glass door, down the narrow hallway, smelling the chlorine already. My heart beat fast under my shirt, and I was starting to sweat, but I didn't tell Nancy. She was scared, mumbling something about a custody fight and being a terrible mother, about never having taken Rochelle to a powwow.

The blue-green pattern on the carpet zigged and zagged, the geometric shapes leading row on row, straight into the wall. I was dizzy again, but I stood up taller, looked forward. We were almost to the last door, to the sign that said "Welcome to the West." Through the thick walls, I could hear it— the storm growing stronger, the wind picking up speed.

I was hurrying, trying not to picture Sandra flying end on end out of the parking lot when I heard it—a sound cutting through the wind, overriding Nancy, who was starting to cry, who sniffled methodically with each step. I didn't say anything, though; I just squeezed her hand tighter and broke into a run.

We pushed through the last door, and I heard it again, and she was there—Rochelle cannonballing into the center of the pool, throwing up a giant splash—and my heart slowed, some.

The pool was framed by a wall of glass, window on top of window. I saw Sandra's reflection in the glass before I saw her—my niece, hanging on the edge of the pool, kicking her legs, squealing. It took me a second to realize it was her, not some optical illusion, a second more to feel the water on my face, another still to realize I had not let go of Nancy's hand.

Rochelle, Nancy yelled, letting go, jumping into the pool, clothes and all, crying and laughing and hiccupping all at the same time.

Sandra grinned up at me. Hey, she said. Her grin wavered. Are we in trouble?

I tried to answer, but everything felt frozen, and her smile unraveled further. She looked so much like her mother in that moment, with fear creeping into her face, that mine began to thaw.

No, I said, of course you're not in trouble.

I crouched next to her, was reaching down to touch the top of her head when I felt her hand on my back, and I started to fall, end on end, into the pool. My face hit first and then my fists, which loosened on impact. The water was warmer than I would have guessed, and I stayed under, squinting against the chlorine sting, but I kept my eyes cracked anyway. I spread out my limbs. My legs kicked and arms circled, and I headed for the center of the pool, down and down, till I reached the rough, concrete bottom.

I turned over to face the top. Above me, legs kicked fast and water churned. Nancy and the girls were laughing, but it all sounded slowed down, like I was hearing it long after or just before it happened. I started to rise into the sound, but my arms fanned out further, and I kept myself there, waving my arms back and forth, which was a little like flying, a little like its opposite.

By the time I surfaced, Sandra and Nancy were laughing and high-fiving each other, and Nancy came swimming over to me. Her hair was matted to her face and gave off a powerful hairspray stench, and she was smiling.

Welcome, she said.

To the West? I said.

To the sixth grade, she said.

Other than her words and the splashing, it was quiet, peaceful. Outside, the storm was letting up a little now, the wind dying down, the sun coming through the thick barrier of clouds.

Inside, the water was keeping us warm, and I was comfortable there, maybe for the first time, even in my wet clothes. I thought about swimming to the edge, about pulling myself up. I thought about looking for the others, for Grandma Claw and our ceremony, but it seemed enough to splash and squeal and watch the snow come down outside the glass. It fell a little more softly and thickly than before, weighing down the small pines, settling into the half-filled holes, already starting to melt.

TWO YEARS

Tim Johnston

The night Billy came home, a Wednesday night, a storm blew down from the mountains, ripping a limb from one of the oaks in the north pasture and dropping it on the fence line. Friday afternoon, after chainsawing up the limb and splicing the fence back together and stacking the wood, Grant put on a clean shirt and walked out to his truck. The old black Labrador got to her feet and followed but he said, "No, you stay here," and drove off by himself. The dog stood in the sun a moment, then returned to the little place she had under his porch, dark and cool, from which she could watch the other house across the way, the big house, where Billy was.

The old Chevy still had good kick in the mountains but Grant was content not to pass the logging trucks and other rigs laboring up the steep switchbacks. He lit a cigarette and watched the range rear up around him, the patterned thick walls of pine and more pine and now and then a copse of yellowing aspen like a blight on the green.

At the top of the pass was a paved lot, a scenic overlook, a refuge from the harrowing turns—irresistible to a family from the plains, who had never seen such country before.

Why do they call it the Continental Divide, the boy had wanted to know, *if it's not the exact middle of the continent?*

They had their backs to the view while a stranger aimed the camera, found the button.

Because, explained his sister, the thermals tossing her hair, *this is where the water changes direction. On the eastern side, the streams and rivers all flow to the Atlantic. On the western side, everything flows to the Pacific.*

They had looked out, each of them. As if they might see these streams and rivers running obligingly toward their endings.

Grant drove on, over the crown of the pass, and moved his foot from the gas to the brakes. He kept the window down and the high September air was cold, but he was sweating. He looked out over the gorge on his right to the distant vertical forests, checked in with the road before him, then looked left into the racing hillside of trees and rock just a few feet away. He checked again with the road, and again looked out over the gorge . . . all the way down the pass like this, looking, looking, until at last he reached the small resort town that lay in the narrow mountain valley like a tongue in the mouth of a wolf. Here was the restaurant where they ate. Here the little market where mother and daughter ran in for "things." The rental shop where the boy got his bike. The motel where they stayed, the Highland Lodge—he and the boy in one room, Angela and Caitlin in the other. In the morning, after the kids had taken off, Grant had gone through the adjoining door, into the girls' side. Like slipping into her little apartment in college, he remembered thinking: smell of bread from the bakery downstairs. Smell of Angela. Angela lifting the covers, letting him in. A thousand years ago.

He drove to the far end of town, to the Black Bear, and parked, and made his way to the counter. A few faces looked up, looked again, and bent to their sandwiches, their soups. Carlton Reese appeared from the kitchen raising his hand in an automatic wave, but then came forward with his hand held out. He asked Grant how he was and Grant said he couldn't complain, and Grant asked after Carlton's family and Carlton looked away at something and said they were fine, they were all just fine.

He had been one of the good ones, Carlton Reese. Free sandwiches and coffee for the sheriff's people, the rangers, the volunteers. He'd hauled his whole family up into the mountains, Joanne and the two boys, to help look. He'd kept the poster up at the Black Bear long after others in town had taken it down.

A good man who now flipped to a fresh page on his little pad and, staring at it, said, "What can I getcha, Grant?"

A car honked and Grant looked up. The light was green.

He accelerated around the corner and drove down the old street, past the school playground, the town hall, until he reached the sheriff's building, where he took the space between two white, immaculate sheriff's SUVs.

Inside was the woody, dusty, faintly sour smell of a church. The groaning, undulant floorboards. The rack of shotguns aligned ceilingward like organ pipes. He looked over the head of the young deputy to the bulletin board and felt his heart fall out of him—his daughter's face, amid the postings. Her good teeth, her sun-squinted eyes. Black hair whipping away as if she were in full sprint, as if she were flying down the track. It was the picture taken at the top of the divide by a stranger. Grant and Angela and the boy, mountains and sky, all cropped out. He had looked on it a thousand times and it never failed to kill him.

The young deputy sent him on back and at Grant's rap on the jamb the sheriff swiveled and brought his chair level with a sharp mechanical outcry. "Well now," the sheriff said. He got to his feet and Grant came forward to shake his hand, observing that the sheriff's hair was getting paler and thinner, coming into the blown, snowy style of his father, the old man who owned the ranch where Grant was living. But unlike the old man the sheriff was yet a big man, with a high hard gut he wore like part of the uniform.

Grant told the sheriff he'd got a hankering for the Black Bear, and the sheriff, hitching his thumbs in his sheriff's belt, affirmed that it was worth the drive.

In the outer room the young deputy opened a drawer, shut it, and muttered something.

"Do you mind if I close this door one minute, Joe?" Grant asked, and the sheriff said, "No, sir. Shut it and sit down. You want Donny to get you a coffee?"

"No, thanks. I'll only take a minute here."

"Take as long as you like."

On the desk between them a walkie-talkie faintly hissed. Grant knew the exact heft of it and its leathery electronic smell. The sheriff offered him a cigarette and he took it, then leaned to meet the sheriff's Zippo. On the walls were a few plaques and certificates. The framed picture of the sheriff's daughter on her horse at the rodeo, cowboy hat sailing behind her. The big green map of the Front Range.

The sheriff lit himself and said, snapping shut the lighter, "Everything all right down there at Dad's?"

"Well," Grant said, and the sheriff said, "Shit, don't tell me he fell off another ladder—"

"No, nothing like that."

"Man his age, climbing on roofs."

"Nothing like that," Grant repeated. He looked critically at the tip of his cigarette. "I just wondered if you knew Billy's come home again."

The sheriff leaned back and drew on his cigarette. "No, I didn't know that. Last I heard he was in California."

Grant sat forward to tip his ash into the ashtray, a shallow glass bowl with a brass mustang rearing from its center, hindquarters black with soot and tarnish. "Well. He's back. I just thought you might like to know about it, if you didn't already."

"I appreciate that, Grant. But I guess if anything was wrong I'd have heard from Dad."

Grant nodded. "It's not my place, Joe. But your dad and Billy. Well, your dad's getting on."

The sheriff smiled crookedly. "I know he is, Grant. But if you're sitting there telling me he can't handle that dumbshit little brother of mine, well, I'd say you ought to know better by now."

"I'm not trying to tell you anything, Joe. And I probably shouldn't've said anything at all. I just thought you might like to know he's come home again, that's all."

The walkie-talkie crackled, throwing a quick, reflexive flurry into Grant's heart, and the sheriff scooped it up and frowned at it, and set it down again.

After a moment Grant said, "Well," and stabbed out his cigarette and began to rise. But the sheriff motioned with his hand and said, "Now, hold on a minute, Grant. I got something to tell you, too."

"All right."

"It's about Angela."

"What about her?"

"She's been calling again."

"She has?"

"Day, night, it doesn't matter. 'What are you doing, sheriff? What is your plan? What are you people doing up there to find my girl?' She's been working that phone and—I don't know how else to say it, Grant, but she doesn't sound altogether like she's got both feet in the stirrups. I'm sorry for what she's had to go through—what you've both had to go through—you know that. But there's no call for some of the things she's been saying."

Grant studied his hands. The truncated two fingers on his left hand. He'd heard this tone from the sheriff before—that first time, that first morning. Caitlin had wanted to begin her run before the sun came up, as was her habit in the summer, and Shawn had gone with her on his bike. Two hours later a young couple on mountain bikes found the boy and the ruined bike along a high unpaved road. The sheriff called Grant from the hospital, using the boy's phone. Shawn was out from the drugs, and the sheriff wanted to know what a fifteen-year-old boy was doing way up there by himself. Grant and Angela had just gotten out of bed. The mountains were framed perfectly in the window. *By himself?* They stood there in their skins as the world flipped over.

The sheriff flicked at his cigarette, staring fixedly at the brass mustang. He had something more to say but he wasn't going to say it, not today. Behind him was the large green map of the Front Range; in a few square yards of paper and ink it contained all the millions of true, godless places a person might be. How long was long enough when it wasn't your child?

And when it was?

"I'm sorry to hear this, Joe," Grant said. "I'll see what I can do."

The sheriff shook his head and mashed out his butt at the mustang's feet. "I just thought you might like to know, that's all." He came around the desk and opened the door and followed Grant into the outer room. At the front door Grant turned and the two men shook hands.

"I want to thank you for keeping that up," Grant said.

The sheriff didn't turn to look at the billboard. "I haven't forgotten, Grant."

"I know, Joe."

The sheriff looked down at the floor and scuffed the old floorboard with the sole of his boot and he studied the scuffmark a long time.

"All right then," he said looking up again. "You best get back down to the ranch before that old man and Billy decide to kill one another."

They had gone up into the mountains, the boy and the girl, and something had happened up there. The boy had been struck by a car, or a truck—he wasn't sure. And the girl was missing.

The first thing they did after the boy woke up, after they were certain he was going to be all right—his knee crushed but his head all right, he'd been wearing the bike helmet thank God—was get walkie-talkies from the sheriff. Their phones didn't always work up here, and they must always be able to talk, no matter what. They carried the walkie-talkies and they carried their phones and they remembered a show they'd watched about a girl locked in an underground bunker, text-messaging her mother, and they played and re-played the one message, the last one from their daughter, their little girl, her voice breaking on the one word she spoke. The sound of an engine behind her and the sound of wind and then a sound like the phone dropping and then silence, and more silence.

Daddy, she'd said.

In those first days, those early unreal days of this new life in the moun-tains, they did not hold each other and they did not weep in bed at night. They spoke of what had been done that day and what must be done the next and who was going to do it—who would sit with the boy at the hospital and who would take sandwiches to the volunteers and who would get more post-ers printed and who would contact the school back home and who would meet with the sheriff again and who would go to the Laundromat . . . a grotesque fever dream of the domestic, and when they had talked themselves to exhaustion, when sleep was coming at last, she would pull them back to pray. She would pray aloud, and she wanted him to pray aloud too, and he would, in those early days, though it made him nearly sick, the sound of his own voice, the sound of those words in the little room.

Days into weeks. Grant wheeled the boy out of the hospital and the three of them took two rooms on the ground floor of the motel and those rooms were now home and headquarters—papers and supplies and lists and maps on every surface. In town when a poster came down Angela somehow knew, and the poster was restored. Weeks into months. The boy had a birthday; they remembered two days later and went out for dinner. Angela's calls began to be returned less promptly and sometimes not at all, and when she called Sheriff Joe she was no longer put right through but had to speak to a deputy first, and often the sheriff was not in and neither was he up in the mountains searching some unsearched crease of forest.

It may not be just a case of a needle in a haystack, the sheriff told Grant. *It may not even be the right haystack.*

How do you mean?

I mean a smart man don't steal a pony from his neighbor.

You mean he might not be local. This man.

I mean a man might drive quite a ways looking for just the right pony.

Grant returned to the motel and checked with the boy in front of the TV, then stepped into the other room and shut the door and went to her where she sat at the little built-in desk staring at the laptop.

Angie. He needs to go home.

What do you mean?

He needs better care, for his leg. He needs to be back in school. Back with his friends.

She turned to look up at him. *What are you saying?*

I'm saying it's no good for him, keeping him here.

Are you sure you're talking about him?

Grant didn't answer.

We can't go back now, Grant. You see what's happening here. You see what's going on. One of us can go back with him. For a little while.

You mean I can go back. You mean me.

I can keep things going here. I can keep Sheriff Joe going.

And who will keep you going?

He stared at her, and she turned away, and she began to shake.

Angie. He put his hands on her shoulders. He raised her to her feet and pressed her to his chest. He held her as her legs gave out, then he moved her to the bed and eased her down and held her. After a while she stopped shaking and he swept the hair from her eyes and kissed the tears up from her cheeks and he kissed her lips and she kissed him back and then she kissed him truly and something broke in his chest and, kissing her, he put his hand between her legs, and her thighs tightened and she cried into his face *What are you doing, stop it, get off me, God damn you, how could you, how could you?* and she fled into the bathroom and slammed the door and he could hear her in there moaning into a towel.

Dad—?

He got up and opened the adjoining door with a clunk into the footrest of the wheelchair. *I'm sorry, did I hurt you?*

Is Mom all right?

Yes.

What did you do to her?

Nothing, Shawn. We had an argument.

What about?

Grant shut the door and went around the wheelchair and sat on the bed. *Nothing, Shawn. Just an argument.*

She woke up that night clutching at him. *It's all right,* he said, *it's all right.*

No, she said, her eyes white in the dark. *I was driving a dark road. Just me, and . . . she came out of the trees, into my lights. She was naked and covered in dirt. Like she'd been buried alive. But she'd got out! Oh God. She'd got out, and she was trying to come home!*

He held her until she slept again, and then he lay there with his eyes on the pale ceiling thinking about that girl in the bunker, the one who text-messaged her mother. Her abductor had thought she was just playing the games on his cell phone. He had kept several girls down there, one at a time, burying them all nearby. One girl, he said, he kept for two years; they were like husband and wife, he said. He looked like any other man, this man: glasses, blue eyes, halfway bald. In prison now, this man, way back in there, where none of the fathers could touch him.

He came back over the divide and drove down to meet the climbing dusk as the sun dropped behind the peaks. He left the highway while still high above the city and took the county road back into the foothills, to the old mining town that lived on though the copper was long gone.

Inside the Whistlestop, on his way to the back, a man reached out to grab him. "Where's the fire, mister?" It was Dale Struthers, the old veterinarian who owned the ranch down the road from Emmet's. He and his wife Evelyn came by sometimes with a pie still hot at its center and sat a while with Emmet, the way they had when Emmet's Alice was alive and they were a foursome. Now they wanted Grant to join them, but he glanced at his watch and said he couldn't, he only had time for one cold one and then he had to go see what kind of trouble Emmet had got up to.

Dale said, "We were going to stop by on the way here, see if we could feed that old bird. But then we saw Billy's car there, and, well . . ."

"We didn't want to intrude," Evelyn said.

"He been back long?" asked Dale.

"A few days," said Grant, and the old man said, "That right?" and aligned his silverware fussily as if readying for surgery. Evelyn, watching Grant's face, remembered to smile.

He continued back to the bar and sat down. He nodded to Curtis Wieland and he nodded to the man Curtis was serving whom he did not know. He pulled out his cigarettes and got one going and waited. Curtis came and dealt him a pair of cardboard coasters, drew a pint of beer and poured a shooter. Grant tossed back the shooter, chased it, and nodded for a refill.

He sat watching the bar and the restaurant beyond in the mirror behind the counter. He used the mirror to observe the man a few stools down. He looked carefully at the man, but there was nothing to indicate what the man was—what kind of a man he was. His face was ordinary.

Maria Valente came into view in the glass, stopping before a table of high school kids, two boys and a girl, to take their order. The young girl kept glancing around, as if looking for someone, while the boys blowgunned straw sleeves into each other's faces. For a moment, before she went back to the kitchen, Maria seemed to look in Grant's direction, but her face was obscured by a large silver cataract in the old glass.

He thought about ordering another shot and another beer. He rubbed his thumb over the blunt ends of his two shorn fingers, but it was just a habit, such as a man turning and turning his wedding ring. He looked in the mirror again for the man he didn't know, but the man was gone. He ordered another shot and another beer.

"Is this seat taken?"

Maria Valente was there, at his left. A plate of food and a fizzing glass of cola. Her dark eyes and her great dark coils of hair. Her smile. She got onto the stool and set the plate of food between them. "I got the big steak and extra fries," she said. "Here's some silverware."

"No, that's your dinner."

"Are you kidding me? Look at the size of this thing. It should've come with a deed." In her voice, the way she formed her words, were distant scenes of a little girl in Italy. He knew he tended to watch her mouth.

"Are you off?" he asked, and she shook her head, chomping into a fry. "Donna-Lee called in sick. Otherwise known as a hot date. How about you?"

"How about me?"

"Big plans tonight?"

"Oh, of course. Me and Emmet we're throwing a party out to the ranch. Gonna be a hootenanny. You should come by."

"Really. A welcome-home party for Billy?"

Grant looked at her and she said: "He was in here earlier. With that Gatskill girl likes to French-kiss in public." She watched him a moment, his eyes, then she picked up her knife and began sawing into the meat. After a few minutes, Grant joined her.

They had just finished when Maria's daughter appeared at her side, planting her elbows on the bar and levering herself up and forward for a look at the bloody plate. "That is revolting. Did you even cook it?"

"Carmen, *tesoro*—you remember Mr. Courtland?"

"Hi, Mr. Courtland."

"Hello, Carmen."

The girl hung on the bar, humming tunelessly while no one spoke. She had her mother's dark eyes and dark curly hair, but her skin was darker than Maria's. That's all Grant knew about the father.

"Anyway," Carmen said, snapping down a credit card, "here's this."

"Did you have them check the transmission fluid?"

"I checked it myself. It's fine."

"Who taught you how to do that?"

"This hitchhiker dude I picked up."

"Oh, that's funny."

There was a sound, a playful chirrup, and the girl had a cell phone in her hand. She read the message, kissed her mother on the cheek and dismounted from the bar. "Gotta bounce, y'all. Jenna's waiting in the car."

"You two be good," Maria said.

"You too."

"And not one second past midnight, I mean it."

The girl went back through the restaurant, and the three high school kids watched her go, and one of the boys bugged out his eyes, and Grant's heart filled with a perfect violence. He saw himself crossing over and lifting the boy out of the booth by his windpipe.

"So she's driving," he said, looking away.

Maria lifted her eyes to the ceiling, or to heaven, but there was pride in her voice: "I told her if she could save up three thousand, then I'd match it, and we'd find her something when she turned sixteen, something reliable, with airbags. Tell you the truth, I didn't think a girl her age could save that kind of money, but I forgot who I was dealing with."

She smiled, and Grant felt he should say something, but he didn't know what. He sipped his beer.

Maria said, "She drove that car off the lot, just her, sitting behind that wheel, and I thought: This can't be happening, look at her, look how young!" She turned abruptly to Grant and touched his arm. "But you know," she said. "You know exactly what it's like." And Grant nodded, and gave her a smile.

"It's a nightmare," he said. "But you get used to it."

"Do you?" She watched him closely.

"No," he said. "You don't."

At nine o'clock she found him where she'd left him, at the bar, hunched over his drinks. There was a kind of scene outside in the cone of yellow lamplight when he would not surrender his keys. But then with a shrug he dropped

them into his pocket and got into her Subaru. She was not expecting anything. There had been plenty of time for something to happen and it hadn't,
and she was fine with that.

He sat with his knees up high and his hands capping his knees, staring at
the road unspooling in the lights. Maria poked on the radio, listened a moment to some country song and poked it off.

Grant said, "She's a beautiful girl."

"Who is?"

"Your girl. Carmen."

"Thank you."

"And smart. Smart. I bet she's ready to drive that car right off to college."

Maria looked over at him. He pawed at the chest pocket of his jacket, then
stopped and put his hand back on his knee. "You can smoke if you want to,"
she said. "Seriously. I think I've even got one of those lighter things . . ."

"Right here," he said, and he thumbed in the knob. He fished out his cigarettes and got one into his lips and gapped the window. The lighter popped,
and he guided the glowing coil with care. He blew the smoke through the
gap, then held the cigarette as near to the rushing air as he could without
destroying it.

"Well," Maria said. "What about your son—Shawn?"

"What about him?"

"Is he getting ready for college?"

"I don't know."

"You don't know?"

"No, ma'am."

"Doesn't that—" she said. "Don't you want to?"

He nosed the cigarette slowly to the wind, absorbed, until the embers
flared and flew off like tiny hatchlings.

She said, "I'm sorry, I'm overstepping."

"No, you're not."

"I'm taking advantage of the circumstances."

"Which circumstances?"

She glanced at him, and looked back to the road. She slowed for a blind
curve and her lights swept a stand of aspens—white skins flashing for a lurid
instant, then dodging back into darkness.

After a moment he said, "Ask me something I can answer," and she nodded and said, "All right." She said, "All right, I've always been curious: what
happened to those fingers?"

"What fingers?"

She gave him a look, and he splayed his hand before the windshield.

"Was it a work accident?" she asked, "like a saw or something?"

"No. Well, there was a saw, but it wasn't a work accident. It was a drinking accident."

"Oh."

"I used to be a drinker."

"Oh."

"The turnoff's coming up."

"I know. But thanks."

When they reached the property he had her circle around the big spruce and park in front of the old ranch house. He struggled with the seatbelt until she leaned over to get it, the smell of her hair falling across him.

"Maybe I should come in and fix you some coffee," she said. "Do you have coffee in there?"

"Yes I do," he said.

The old Labrador met them on the porch, her tail mildly sweeping. Maria put her knuckles to the dog's nose and tousled the soft ears. Grant held open the door and switched on the light. "Be right back," he said.

"Where are you going?"

"Over to check with Emmet. Come on," he said to the dog. "Come on, girl."

From the window over the sink she watched man and dog cross the clearing in the blue light of the yard lamp, their shadows accompanying them stark and liquid along the ground. He walked upright and steady in a way that made her heart shift. She had once tried to imagine it—what happened to him—happening to her, her daughter, but she couldn't, not even for a second. She shook her head and began looking for the coffee.

Grant stopped short of Emmet's porch and stood before the living-room window. The window was shut but he could hear the argument between two TV crime solvers. Electric auroras of blue and green played over the walls and over the old man's white-socked feet rabbit-eared on the footrest. He held the remote upright in his spotty hand, but his eyes were shut and his stubbled jaw had fallen. Grant thought of his children, his own children—of carrying them to their beds when they were small. The limp human weight of them, the young scent of their skins, the murmurs as he lay them down. He stood outside the old man's window remembering that this had happened, that it was true.

At the end of sleep there was music, low and thumpy and hounding him back into the world. He lay with his knees drawn up on the sofa, her lap replaced by a coarse little cushion she'd somehow slipped under his head. He sat up, boots to the floor, and rubbed at his face. The music was outside, the deep bass pulsing over earth and floorboards. He looked around the darkened room. He'd kissed her, there on the dusty sofa. He had put his hand on her breast, and she had put her hand over his. But when he went for the buttons she stopped him. Rubbed his shortened fingers in hers like coins. She didn't want to be a drinking accident, she said. He put his head on her lap, and she made slow circling patterns on his temple with her fingers. She'd turned off the light when she left.

But no, here she was—the outline of her, at the kitchen window, shaped in the blue light beyond.

"You'd better come look," she said.

Grant got to his feet and went to her and they both looked out.

Six of them over there on Emmet's porch. Three boys, two girls, and Emmet. All but Emmet holding beers. Two of the boys and one of the girls sat on the steps while above them in the rockers like lord and lady sat Billy and the Gatskill girl, the rockers close so she could keep her fingers in Billy's hair. Billy's El Camino was parked before them in the grass, black doors spread like wings and the beat welling up from the crimson deeps of its chest.

"There's your hootenanny," Grant said.

Emmet stood in the light from the screen door, one hand yet on the handle, his white hair wild on his head. He had taken the time to pull coveralls over his pajamas and to put on his old ankle boots though not to lace them. With his free hand he gestured toward the El Camino and spoke to Billy in a series of pale, soundless clouds. Billy said something in reply over his shoulder, and the others ducked their heads in laughter.

Grant raised his watch to his face. "Almost midnight," he said. "Your daughter will be home soon."

Maria stared at him in the dark.

"This is a good time for me to go, you're thinking?"

"No, probably not. But—"

Something was happening over there; Emmet was crossing the porch and making for the steps. He took two steps down between young hips before Billy rose from the rocker and seized him by the upper arm. Emmet looked in amazement at the hand on his arm, then into his son's face. His glasses flashed blue in the yard light.

Maria took Grant's wrist and said his name.

"Hold on," he said. "Hold on."

"He's going to hurt him."

"Hold on."

Billy said something to the old man and the old man said something back, and then Billy was hauling him back up the steps by the arm. Emmet dug at his son's fingers and planted his feet, but with a modest tug Billy yanked him off balance and got him clomping pitifully toward the screen door. Billy opened the door and guided the old man through and shut it again. They stood staring at each other through the screen. Then Emmet turned away, and his shadow on the porch floor grew small, and then it was gone. Billy took his seat again to cheers and raised bottles.

"I'll be right back," Grant said.

"Grant, we should call someone."

"Who?"

"Sheriff Joe."

"He's way up there in the mountains."

"Then Sheriff Dave down here."

Grant opened a drawer and began rooting amid batteries and old tin flashlights.

"What are you looking for?"

"Nothing." He stood and slipped the cartridges into his pocket.

"Grant, you know what he did to that Haley boy in high school."

"I heard about it."

"That boy still doesn't talk right."

"I know."

He went out the door and down the steps, and the old dog came out from under the porch and limped along behind him.

"Evening, neighbor," Billy said, hailing him from the rocker. "Everyone, this here is Grant, the old man's hired gun, as it were. Grant, this here is everyone."

The young people raised their beers and bade him good evening.

"And you brought my dog too, I see. Where's he been hiding you, girl, huh? Come on up here. Come up here, girl. Come on, now." He leaned so that his black western shirt tightened at the shoulders and the white scorpions embroidered above the pockets tensed.

Eyes on the boy, the dog lowered to her belly and flattened her ears.

"Goddamn it," said Billy, slapping his thigh.

"Let her be, Billy."

"Don't tell me what to do, Grant."

"She's just a scared old dog."

"She's my scared old dog. Now get up here girl, goddammit, before I come down there and get you."

Grant turned to look at the dog. She looked up and he made a shooing motion and with a last glance at the boy she rose to all fours and moved away into the dark.

"There goes your dog, Billy," said one of the boys on the step. A lank and pimpled boy with a cigarette caught in his smirk.

Billy stared at the boy until the boy's smirk collapsed and he looked away.

"I think maybe you better call it a night, Billy," Grant said. "I don't think your dad can sleep with all this. And the fact is, neither can I."

"Really," said Billy. "I didn't think you had sleeping in mind, Grant."

"That's that waitress's car," said the pimpled boy. "The one what's got that nigger daughter."

Grant stepped up closer to the boy. "You need to watch your mouth, son."

"Is that right, Dad?"

"That's right."

"Shit, Ray Junior, that is right," said Billy. "You talk like your dad fucked his sister and out you popped whistling Dixie." There was laughter, and Ray Junior bared his bad teeth and said, "Hilarious, Billy."

"I'm going inside for a minute," Grant said. "I'd appreciate it if you all went on home like I asked."

"I am home, Grant," Billy said. "And here's the irony: this wouldn't even be happening if my old house over there weren't otherwise occupied."

Grant glanced back at the ranch house. The kitchen window a dark and featureless square in its face.

"There's nothing to do about that tonight," he said.

"No," said Billy. "I agree with you there."

He went up the steps, past the boy, and on inside. Emmet was in his bedroom, sitting on the edge of the bed. He appeared to be giving great thought to his boots, down there on his feet.

Grant sat beside him.

"I'm sorry if they woke you, Grant."

"Oh, I was up."

"They got no respect. Not one speck of it."

"Em. Maybe we should make a phone call."

The old man looked up, his eyes behind his lenses bleary in their folds. "Who the hell to?"

"Maybe Joe needs to know about this."

"I ain't doing that, Grant. I ain't calling one brother on the other. I told you that before." He shook his head. "These kids will get tired in a bit here and go home."

"It doesn't look that way to me, Em. Looks to me like they're gonna make a show of it, especially now that I've come over."

The old man dragged a hand through his wild hair. "Who is that boy out there? I don't even know who that boy is."

They sat there, the beat from the El Camino like a heartbeat in the bed. Then Grant said, "Where do you keep that shotgun, Em?"

"That what?"

"Just for show."

Emmet looked at the younger man. Then he flung a hand toward the closet.

Grant found the softcase and set it on the bed and unzipped it, releasing a smell of walnut and steel and gun oil. It was an old Remington 20-gauge side-by-side.

"You know how to handle that?" Emmet said.

"I used to have one not too different. It was my dad's. Angela wouldn't have it in the house once the kids got older." He unbreeched the barrels and sighted the bores, then snapped the barrels back. "You took good care of this."

Emmet removed his glasses and worked the papery flesh of his eye sockets. "Hell. Any man can't take care of a gun ought not to have one."

He went down the steps and reached into the El Camino and turned the key, killing the engine and the music. The chromium tailpipe shuddered out a final pale scud in the sudden quiet and was still.

"Fuck me," the third boy said, "the hired gun's got a gun."

"What are you up to, Grant?" asked Billy.

"I asked you to call it a night and now I'm not asking."

"Did that old fart put you up to this?"

"No, he was against it."

"Well, what do you aim to do, Grant? Shoot us?"

"No. I'm going to shoot the tire on one of these cars. After that, if you're still here, I'm going to shoot another one. If I have to buy some new tires tomorrow I will, but tonight the party's over."

"How we gonna leave if you shoot our tires?"

"Shut up, Ray Junior. Grant, I don't believe you've got any ammo in that old gal."

"You're right about that." He thumbed the lever and broke the shotgun, chambered two shells and snapped the gun shut again.

"All right," said Billy. "There's phase one. But I guess we're going to have to see phase two before these negotiations go any further."

"Jesus, Billy," said the girl on the steps. "Let's just go somewheres else before this old man does something crazy."

"Sit down and shut up, Christine."

"These aren't negotiations, Billy," Grant said. "This is what's going to happen next if you go on sitting there." His voice was even, his chest was calm. He thought about that as Billy lifted his cigarette to his lips and crossed a glossy black boot over a knee. The boy tugged on the hair under his lower lip, a shapeless brown tuft that clung there like a deer tick. Then he nodded, and Grant stepped around the El Camino and raised the gun on the front tire of a battered Ford pickup and squeezed the forward trigger. The gun kicked and a flap of rubber flew from the tire in a gaseous cloud and the truck buckled like a stricken horse and swallows burst from the spruce and wheeled amid the stars while the boom echoed away in the hills. The night air bittered at once with the smell of cordite and the rubber tang of old tire air.

"You shot my tire," said the pimpled boy, rising. "You fucking whackjob."

At the sound of the shot Emmet came from his room. He stood back from the screen door watching.

Grant took a step and raised the gun on the toylike tire of a small red Honda.

"Billy!" cried the girl on the steps, and Billy laughed and said, "All right, all right." He put his cigarette in his lips and applauded. He stood from the rocker and offered a hand to the Gatskill girl. "Time to go, those who can."

"What about my goddamn truck, goddamn it?"

"You heard the man, Ray Junior. Said he'd get you a new tire tomorrow, and you've already seen he's a man of his word so quit your crying and get in the car."

As the young people loaded into the El Camino and the Honda, Grant looked up at the stars. The patternless bright birdshot of ancient, monstrous bodies. Forces unthinkable. Passing him, Billy stopped and looked over

Grant's shoulder, peering into the dark foothills. The white scorpions faced each other across the black field of his chest. He squinted and said, "What the hell—?"

Grant knew he wasn't thinking about going for the gun; he understood that shooting the tire was the boy's victory, not his. This was some other game. He didn't turn to look, and Billy dropped his cigarette and ground it into the grass with the toe of his boot.

"Thought I saw somebody," Billy said. He looked up, he looked into Grant's eyes. "But there ain't nobody out there. Is there, Grant?" He smiled. He winked, and swung down into the El Camino.

Taillights receded into the night like the eyes of withdrawing wolves. Grant stood with the Remington on his shoulder, the weight of the barrels, the shapely walnut grip, the warm triggers, the slam of the stock still playing in his bones—all a strange pleasure to him.

Emmet was at the screen door, one hand on the handle as if he were making up his mind whether to step out into the dark or latch the door against it. Grant held the old man's eyes a moment, then turned and began to walk back to the ranch house. The shadows of the spruce gave up the old black dog to follow at his heels, half crippled in her hips, panting softly, halting suddenly when Grant halted: there was movement at the ranch house, someone passing through the dark square of the kitchen window. A woman. She came back and remained there in the frame of the window, doing something with her hands, preparing something, as if she belonged there.

He stood beside the spruce, holding the gun, the dog quietly panting. He looked to the north and made out the invisible mountains by the high and absolute erasure of the stars along the base of the sky. In his mind she was running—always running. Her breath quick, her feet sure on the steep forest floor, dodging left, right, through the trees, never stumbling, never tiring, coming down like water. He looked up there and he began to speak, as he did every night. He began to speak, and the old dog stopped panting and grew alert, cocking her ears to the dark.

SAME AS IT WAS WHEN YOU LEFT

Alyssa Knickerbocker

y sister flies home, but it's too late. When she gets here, she stomps around and fights with the nurses and asks me millions of questions about things I don't know, such as how could this happen?

She yells into his face: Dad!

His face is a cold white-blue, and a machine breathes for him, panting like an approaching wolf.

I know you can hear me! she yells. Wake the fuck up!

A particular type of doctor comes to talk to us today—a neurologist. He is Indian, with smooth caramel skin and the faint lilt of a British accent. He stands to one side, watches Fiona scoop her dark mane of hair from one side to the other and bend over the bed. Her cowboy boots leave rinds of hardened mud and horse shit on the floor, tightly packed crescent moons with fibers of grass sticking out. His eyes drop to the open mouth of her T-shirt, a clean shot to her cattail-thin body, then slide away to the floor.

He tells us his job is to figure out whether our father's brain will be able to wake itself up again. This is confusing to me—I thought that something was wrong with his heart, not his head. But I say nothing. I stay quiet and listen. It is better to listen first than to open your mouth and ask stupid questions. This is what Mr. Devotollo said to me last week when I raised my hand at the beginning of the lesson on genetics, when he was talking about brown eyes beating blue eyes, and asked, What about green eyes?

I asked because green eyes are what I have, and also what my mother has, or so I'm told, because I don't really remember her face, and I urgently needed to know where I stood.

Fiona changes her tack. She speaks reasonably.

Dad, she says. Come on. She pats his hand. She says, Dad, it's time for you to wake up. Okay? Now, please.

She sounds exactly the way he used to when he woke us up for school in the morning. Now, please. Flinging open the door to our room so it clattered against the wall, so that light from the hallway flooded the bedroom and we moaned, writhed dramatically under the covers. I would get up, go down the hall to the little kitchen, where he'd be making breakfast. Every morning it was the same.

There's cereal, he'd say, and put down a box of Raisin Bran. Then he'd plunk down a box of Cheerios right next to it and say, Or cereal.

Cereal, I'd say, and he'd give the back of my neck a little shake, like a dog taking the scruff of a puppy, and say, Good choice.

Fiona stayed in bed until he dragged her out, throwing her over his shoulder and setting her down unceremoniously on the bathmat, where she rubbed at her face as if she were trying to erase something. She always had to shower, blow-dry her hair. He'd stand outside the bathroom door, rattling his car keys, smacking the door with his leather work gloves.

Hey, gorgeous, you're gorgeous enough, he'd yell through the door. Get your gorgeous ass in the truck.

The truck was always cold—chilly, cracked Naugahyde seats, frosted windshield. He had a worn out towel to wipe it with so we could start driving without waiting for the truck to warm up. The cab smelled of American Spirits and turpentine and fresh sawdust. He whistled Mozart while he drove. He could almost hit the high notes in "The Queen of the Night."

In the middle of the night, I go to the bathroom to rinse my mouth out because we've been here so long that even my own tongue tastes bad. When I come back, I see that Fiona is awake too, looking out the window, watching a band of snow-colored light come up over Bellingham Bay. She is gazing toward home, the foggy green island where we grew up together, where I still live with our father. She came straight to the hospital from the airport—she hasn't even been home yet. She hasn't been home in a long time.

I say, Fiona, but she doesn't move.

She's kicking one leg so that her boot beats rhythmically on Dad's hospital bed—clang, clang, clang. Old, hard rinds of dirt rain down while she does this. A janitor comes through, an old man wearing scrubs and heavy glasses, sweeps the whole room, then looks at Fiona: She acts like she doesn't notice, and maybe she really doesn't. He sweeps under her feet, but she keeps her face to the window, keeps on kicking.

What we learn from the other doctor, a woman with a sharp perm, lots of little triangles jagging around, is that our father had a heart attack. This means that there was a tiny piece of clotted blood—like a scab, the doctor says, and I touch the small round bead of scab on my knee—that floated into our father's artery, the big one that leads to his heart, got stuck, and blocked it. Like a stone in a garden hose, she says when I look confused, but how would the stone get in there? It doesn't make any sense.

Anyway—the scab blocked it, and the blood couldn't go forward, and the artery collapsed like a milkshake straw when you suck too hard. This is when my father dropped the board he was carrying, bent over, and then knelt down, put one hand down on the wet ground, the slick damp layers of pine needles sticky with dew. The ground was wet because it was morning. The sun had not come all the way up yet. It was still behind the evergreens, sending spears of light into our shadowy yard.

When I came outside to feed the rabbits, this is where he was. I thought he had found something to show me—a new kind of mushroom. He is always finding mushrooms, bringing them home, cutting them up, and frying them in butter. Some are tough and not good to eat. Others he just shows me and then throws away because they are poisonous. Others are tender and delicious, like the sweet soft flesh of wild salmon—the reddish lobster mushrooms, for example, with their fine droopy caps like the elegant hats of women in old movies.

I ran over to him, excited. I said, What did you find?

But then he twisted and put his back on the ground, and his eyes closed and his mouth opened, his burning cigarette smoking there on the ground, ashy and crackling and dissolving, and I ran around the house twice before I figured out that I should get on the phone. I called Fiona, all the way in Coeur d'Alene. She started shouting at me to call 911, fucking call 911. So I hung up and picked the phone up again to call, but there was no dial tone. I slammed the phone down hard, three times in a row, and then listened again—still no dial tone. Static, a clatter, someone breathing.

Fiona? I said.

She said, Goddamn it, why aren't you calling?

I said, You have to hang up so I can hang up!

Oh God, she said, and then I heard a click, and then the rich low bass of the dial tone, and then I called, and then they came, and they picked him up so easily and got him on a stretcher, like he was no heavier than the long thin board he'd been carrying. I was amazed, because he is large, and dense, and many times heavier than I am. Plus, there is the weight of the clothes he wears—heavy Carhartt overalls that feel as cold as stone when he comes inside, and boots with metal toes, in case he drops something heavy on his foot in the shop. Also there is his old leather jacket, soft and cracked and wrinkled like a tired animal, and his thick flannel shirts, and the tool belt with loops for hammers and wedges and packets of nails—all of these things have weight. Also his skin—he has the roughest, thickest skin. The skin on the palms of his hands, like the pads of his fingers and thumbs, is ice hard, yellowish and smooth. He can pick up a burning log from the bonfire to move it, and he doesn't even feel the heat. He just brushes his hands off on his pants and lights a cigarette. He can take the cap off a beer bottle one-handed, with just his thumb and the edge of a lighter. He moves through the world as if his body is a tool, strong and useful as a hammer or an awl.

He was as still as a hammer—a dropped hammer—as they filed him into the back of the ambulance. They put a plastic mask over his nose and mouth, and I couldn't see his face anymore, and then they shut the two back doors, and I couldn't see him at all.

Tomorrow is my birthday—I will be thirteen. Fiona hasn't mentioned this since she's been here, and it's likely she's forgotten. This seems like a bad time to remind her.

A social worker is here to talk to us—a young guy who has forgotten to shave a small patch of stubble on his neck. He looks as if he's not much older than Fiona, and he sits too close to her at the smooth plastic table in the cafeteria. He wears a tie, but his dress shirt is too big and tents out around his slim body. He flips pages, points with the nib of his pen, forgetting to recap it and leaving thin squiggles on the documents with his shaky hands. Fiona rests her forehead on the heel of her hand. He talks and talks, and she is silent.

I eat a smashed cheeseburger that came wrapped in aluminum foil. I would like to ask Fiona for a milkshake, but she might flip out. When we came down here, I ordered, and the clerk said that would be two dollars and fifty cents, and I looked at Fiona, and Fiona looked at me and said, Oh fuck, who pays now?

It took me a few minutes to realize that what she meant was, who pays now that our father is in a heart-attack-induced coma and not available to offer funds? She had to run back upstairs and get her wallet, and then it turned out she didn't even have two dollars, and she had to dig through her purse for change until she had enough for my hamburger. So I don't see how I can ask for a milkshake.

The social worker is asking whether my father keeps any files, any records of any kind, in the house, where he might have stashed a letter of some kind? Might we be aware of his wishes regarding life support or organ donation?

Fiona looks at him and makes her mouth into a hard heart shape.

He's not even dead, she says, and you want to take his organs?

The guy leans back a little because she's inches from his face, which he probably wanted originally, but now she's making him nervous.

Look, he says. It's something we need to know. In case.

Oh, *in case*, she mimics, with deep scorn.

Fiona looks older to me, but not in any specific way that I can put my finger on. She has no new lines on her face, no real changes in the delicate crescent of her body. It's just that her face seems to have settled, solidified, hardened, like clay in a kiln. She was still malleable when she left; now she is not.

She has had a birthday herself since she's been gone—she's turned twenty—and now she is a whole different person. She and Dale got married at the courthouse in Coeur d'Alene. He calls her Fi. She is now a twenty-year-old married woman named Fi who lives in Idaho.

When I look at her sitting there across the table, saying testily—No, I'm not aware of a living will—I have to make myself remember the ways in which we are close, times when I still felt like she was my sister. Like when she taught me how to stick a spoonful of peanut butter in the sugar jar to make a kind of sticky popsicle, or how we used to pretend to be wild horses and sprint neighing down the beach in a sideways half run that was supposed to be a gallop. She was so good at tossing her dark hair like it was a mane.

So, Fiona says in a dull way, What's new?

We're in our father's room, pretending that he is just sleeping, that we're just hanging out. We haven't actually discussed this, but we're doing it anyway. Fiona acts teenager-ish and put-upon, as though his coma is something he's doing on purpose to irritate her, like the time he picked her up from school with a dead deer tied to the front of his truck. The silver grille was painted with purpling blood, and he had not sawed the antlers off, so they bobbled on the front of the truck like some kind of gruesome hood ornament. I thought it was funny; Fiona did not.

I am less sure about what my role is. I am not yet surly and hormonal, but I know I will be soon, because the school sent us home with a crappy pink booklet with a photo of a smiling girl with wispy, windblown blond hair and sunlight all over her cheekbones. It was called *Congratulations! You're Growing Up! A Guide for Maturing Young Women.* It had drawings of naked people with their cartoonish genitals and exposed reproductive systems labeled. Hannah and I flipped through it and laughed until we couldn't breathe and our faces were streaked with tears. But later, after Hannah went home, I actually read it. I learned that I will soon be on a roller coaster of emotion, elated in one moment and plunged into the depths of misery in the next. I am intrigued by this and want to be ready to play my part. I want to perfect the glassy stare, the moody sighs, the things I remember Fiona being so good at.

So I cross my arms and say, Nothing.

There must be something, she says. She slips a cigarette out of the pack she keeps in the back pocket of her jeans. She doesn't light it, she just taps it against her lips.

No, I say. It's same as always. Same as it was when you left.

Fiona turns her face to the window. When the nurse comes in to suction our father's mouth out, she slips the cigarette into the sleeve of her sweater. She stands by the bed with her arms knitted across her chest, watching intently while the nurse pokes a plastic tube into one corner of our father's mouth, then the other.

When she stops, Fiona says, You didn't get it all.

I did, the nurse says, and she snaps off her latex gloves. There is a puff of white powder.

You did not, Fiona says, pointing. Look.

The nurse looks, says, That's just normal accumulation.

If that's normal, Fiona says, somebody could drown in *normal*.

Look, says the nurse, I can't stand next to each patient and suck up every drop of drool.

Well, Fiona says, I'd like you to suck up this particular drop of drool.

The nurse stares at Fiona for a moment, then makes a big show of poking each finger of her latex gloves right side out again, puts them on with a lot of theatrical struggling, turns the suction machine back on, and pokes the beige plastic straw into the corner of our father's mouth.

Satisfied? the nurse says.

Fiona slips the cigarette out of her sleeve and puts it between her lips. Her lips are blooming, luscious. I overheard Dale saying to her once, when they were making out on the roof outside our bedroom window, Oh my God, I wish I could go inside your mouth and never come out. And Fiona laughed, and then there was rustling, and a different sound—something scraping rhythmically, maybe a boot on the sandpaper rough shingles, and faster breathing that kept time.

Obviously, the nurse says, there's no smoking.

Obviously, Fiona says, I'm going outside.

Good, says the nurse.

Great, says Fiona. Excellent. Superb.

The nurse slams some things onto her little metal cart and wheels it out. The shape of her buttocks is clearly visible through her white pants, squishing up and down as she barrels out the door. I decide that I hate her. Or maybe I am simply absorbing Fiona's hate, which is clear and liquid and spreads through the room like spilled turpentine.

I lied before when I said there was nothing new. A new thing is that Hannah has gotten her period and I have not. She is growing small breasts, and her mother has bought her a training bra. It's white and has flat cups, two shallow clamshells that latch together in the front with a plastic clasp shaped like a rosebud. Hannah let me touch it. It was stiff and thick and felt like a kind of armor.

The other day, Hannah and I decided it was time we kissed a boy. Actually, Hannah decided this, and I said, Sure, okay.

Hannah went next door and got her neighbor Frank, who is one year older than us, to come over. I waited on one of the twin beds in her room, tracing the pattern in the quilted coverlet. It was made from a shiny pink material that was both slippery and sticky under my fingers. When Hannah and Frank appeared, Frank looked curious and excited, and his black-and-white plaid Converse sneakers were untied as if he'd thrown them on in a rush. He was wearing just a T-shirt even though it was cold outside.

Hannah shut the door and just told him, straight up, that we wanted kissing practice and she'd heard he was good at it. I almost laughed out loud when she said that, because we hadn't heard any such thing. But Frank said sure, he could help us out. He kept his hands in his pockets and shrugged his shoulders casually, as if he got asked this all the time.

Great, said Hannah. I'll go first.

And then she told me to go wait in the bathroom. She said, You can't just sit here and watch us. It's weird.

Oh, I said, okay, but then I just sat there, and Hannah said, Now would be a good time.

I said, Are you going to come get me when it's time or something?

Yes, jeez, Hannah said, and rolled her eyes at Frank, and he laughed nervously. She said, We'll come get you. You'll get your turn. Don't be such a Nazi about it.

I locked the bathroom door and stood in front of the mirror, examining myself. I smoothed my hands down the front of my T-shirt and wondered what I would look like if I had breasts like Hannah. I wondered whether Frank would be at the boy-girl sleepover Hannah was planning. I decided I had an okay face. My mouth was a little funny—crooked like my father's, and thin—but maybe if I had a little color on my lips, they would look better. I rooted around in Hannah's medicine cabinet until I found a mug full of makeup products, greasy sticks with missing caps and glitter all over them. Everything in there was Wet N' Wild. There was a rubbed-down pink lipstick, and I smeared it on. I did it badly, and it smooshed almost up to my nose.

Fuck, I said out loud, and I felt bad for swearing, even though I was alone. I didn't sound like myself. I sounded like Fiona. I sounded as though I was faking.

I wiped at the smeared lipstick with some toilet paper, but it just smeared around even more. I rubbed and rubbed and used some water from the tap and a bath towel that smelled like shampoo and mildew, and when I was done, the lipstick was gone, but my upper lip was all red from the rubbing. And then there was a knocking and the door rattling, and Hannah was hissing, Let me in, let me in, why do you have the stupid door locked, so I opened the door, and she came barreling in and slammed the door. Her eyes looked glazed and wet as if she were on some kind of drug, and her face was pink.

Oh my God, she said, breathy and excited. She shoved me out of the way and examined herself in the mirror. What do you think, she said, do I look different? I feel different.

She touched her lips with two fingers. She turned her head to one side, posing, and smiled at her own image. What are you waiting for? she said. It's your turn. Go.

I put my hand on the bathroom doorknob but did not turn it. I felt like I was made of lead.

Will you get over yourself? Hannah said. He's not going to sit there all day.

So I opened the door and walked into the hallway and opened the other door and went into the pink bedroom where Frank was sitting on the farthest pink bed, leaning on his elbows, his legs sprawled open, his head thrown back—a pose meant to look relaxed.

Oh, hey, he said, as though my arrival was an unexpected delight. What's up?

Oh, I said. Nothing much.

I was standing by the door. I didn't want to approach him and seem too eager. I also didn't want to *not* approach him and seem uneager. I took a step forward and stopped. I tipped, almost lost my balance. I felt as though I was walking out onto a tightrope.

Why don't you come on over here, he said.

Why don't *you* come over *here*, I said, and it accidentally came out mean.

He let out a high-pitched little laugh. He said, How about we meet in the middle.

Okay, I said, and then he started walking and I started walking. When he was close enough to me, he put his hands on my waist. His hands felt heavy and hot. He put his mouth on mine. It was as cool and slippery as canned peaches. His belly was against my belly, and it seemed to blaze with heat, as though his whole body was a nightlight and he'd just switched himself to on. I opened my eyes. His eyes were closed, the lashes thick as a girl's, jagging down over his cheeks. Past the peach curve of his cheek, through the window, I could see his house. There was a man on the roof, pushing leaves out of the gutter with the handle of a broom. I could not see the leaves falling to the ground, and I wished that I could. I was curious to know whether they separated and then drifted, gracefully, or fell together in one wet clump.

Frank decided when we were done and let go of me. He wiped his mouth on his sleeve.

You're spittier than Hannah, he said.

I touched my lips. I said, I'm sorry.

You'll get better at it, he said, in a superior way.

When I knocked on the bathroom door, Hannah came out in a cloud of lavender perfume holding up her hands as if I were the police and I'd said, Come out with your hands up! She had painted her nails a glittery silver. She had on the pink lipstick that I had tried to put on, only she had done it well, and the little bow of her mouth glowed. She told Frank that he better go before her mom came up and found him. As soon as the door clicked shut, she started jumping up and down and squealing, her hair bouncing. Hannah's hair always fell in waves, rippled and soft. Once I asked her how she got it that way, and she flicked it over her shoulder and said, It just dries that way.

Oh my God oh my God, she was saying. *Wasn't that amazing?*

She pressed her hands, fingers still spread so that she would not ruin her polish, to her chest and rolled her head around as if in ecstasy. I should have played along and said, Oh yes, it was wonderful, but I just stared at her.

She stopped rolling her head around and fixed me with her bright, water-cooler eyes.

It was okay, I said. I guess.

Okay? she mimicked. You *guess?*

Maybe I just don't like Frank that much, I said.

Maybe it's because you aren't a *woman* yet, Hannah said. She twinkled her fingers and admired the polish. She said, My mom says that when you become a woman, you have stronger feelings about things. But you have to be careful not to get carried away on them.

Carried away, I thought, and I pictured Hannah in a leaky little rowboat, being borne out to sea with the tide, the foaming waves sucking her farther and farther away from shore.

I go over to my father and sit next to him. His skin looks pale under his mustache. It looks like he is already dead. But when I pick up his hand, it is warm and pliable, which is reassuring.

The hospital room is dark, and bleeps with tiny lights and sounds, and smells of lemon floor wash and bad breath. The doctor says nothing's for sure, but it's possible that our father might not make it. Which is a funny expression. As if our dad is running a marathon and maybe he'll decide to drop out before the finish. Or we're having a party, but he's too busy to come. He says he's sorry, but he won't be able to *make it* tonight. Maybe another time, girls, he says, and winks.

Nobody says the word "die"—they just say we have to "be prepared."

When I think about what it might be like—to die, to disappear, to drop into darkness like a stone—I feel the way I did the only time I flew in an airplane, from here to New York City, to see my mother, the one time I ever did go to visit her. When we took off, the stewardess in her too-tight navy blue skirt that showed her panty line came and sat in the empty seat next to me. I think she thought I might be afraid. I was not—the weight of takeoff was heavy and comforting, like putting too many blankets on your bed. She asked me whether I went to school. I said yes. She asked did I like it. I said, Sometimes. She asked did I have a boyfriend, and I panicked and said again, Sometimes. She laughed and squeezed my fingers with her damp hand, and then we were up and the weight was off me, and she unbuckled her seatbelt and clopped off down the aisle.

When the plane landed, there was no one there to meet me. My father had said that my mother would be waiting, that she would be wearing a red dress so that I would find her easily in the crowds at baggage claim. After an hour, I was hungry and bought an egg salad sandwich with the ten-dollar bill he had given me. I also had a check in an envelope in my suitcase, made out to my mother from my father. It was for five thousand dollars. She had called him up suddenly, asked for help. She had also asked to see me. My father had been nervous to put me on the plane alone, but Fiona had said, If there's money involved, she's sure to show.

I ate my sandwich, sat in a hard plastic chair. The baggage claim was noisy and full of people wearing jeans and leather jackets and saris and head scarves and suits and raincoats and everything else you could imagine, but no one wearing a red dress. A recording looped endlessly, the rough, shouting voice of a man: *Please monitor children near the carousel for their safety. Do not sit, stand, or place fingers on the moving carousel.* Bags went around and around, and hands lifted them, bore them away. There always seemed to be a leftover, unclaimed bag, disappearing through the plastic strips into the darkness and then appearing again, stubborn, relentless.

After three hours, I called my father at home. He said, Goddamn it, and then was quiet for a little while, breathing sharply through his nostrils.

Then he told me not to worry, to go over to the United desk and tell them my name, that he was going to call and get me a ticket and get everything taken care of, and before I knew it, I'd be home. And then, almost as an afterthought, he said, Why don't you go ahead and tear that check up, honey, into really little pieces, and throw it in the first ashtray you can find?

Which I did.

On the flight home, I looked out the window and saw the clouds laid out below us like a shining marble floor. The static light of the moon made them look solid, as though I could stand on them the way I stand on the springy layer of pine needles in my backyard. But when I tried to imagine myself stepping onto the layer of clouds, all I could see were the clouds thinning, turning into grey mist, and my own body falling toward earth.

Hannah told me once that if you fall long enough, your heart stops. So, for example, people who throw themselves off the Empire State Building, which I had hoped to see in New York City, often die before they actually hit the ground. Hannah knows things like this because her father is a scientist. People call him when they find dead animals washed up on the beaches—orca whales and harbor seals and Steller sea lions—and he comes and collects them, dissects them to find out about their lives and how they died. This is called a "necropsy," a word that sounds like dirt and rot and peeled fruit.

Hannah got to see a necropsy once. It was a sea otter with a smashed-in face; its paws were folded on its chest just like a person's. She said there wasn't much blood at all.

Later, I saw the skeleton of this very same sea otter in Hannah's house, clean and white and put together in a way that made it look as if it were walking, just strolling along. Hannah's father ran his finger along the spine, telling us the names of each bone. He said the otter had been "articulated," that all the skin and fat and muscle had been removed from the bones, the bones made clean. I thought this was odd, so later, at home, I asked my father what "articulated" meant, to see what he would say, and he said it meant that you pronounced your words clearly. I thought about it and then decided that the two meanings were pretty much the same thing, because sometimes a sentence is like a skeleton strolling along.

The doctor with the triangle hair uses words in a way that erase their meaning. She tells us that we should not be too "optimistic." She says they have had to restart our father's heart eight times now and that the damage has been "considerable." She says the neurologist will have results of the brain scan soon, and at that point we can all sit down together and talk and determine a "course of action."

While the doctor talks, Fiona paces to one wall and then the other. She breathes sharply, like a horse huffing on a cold morning. Perhaps she has been spending so much time with her horses in Coeur d'Alene, where she works at a ranch, that she is becoming like them. She has those same dark shifty eyes that look you up and down and measure you, deciding whether you are pliable, whether you can be kicked or tossed or nipped. She used to take me riding, back when she was still sweet, and she would show me how to take the hard oval brush and press it over the horse's body, making the hair smooth and glossy like polished stone.

Fiona and our father never really fought—not with fists or flat hands or even loud words. There was never any shouting—just a heavy silence in the house, and then a word or a phrase, quiet and snapping and sudden like lightning hitting the sea miles away, too far to hear the crack. Fiona looks like our mother, and our father sometimes points this out.

You look just like Sheila, he'll say, in a way that is not at all kind.

Like, just because she has our mother's upper lip and cheekbones and nearly black hair and high collarbone, she's going to turn out to be a devil and a whore. I have her eyes, but not the collarbone or the lips or the hair.

The day Fiona left, my father went out early to do a job on the other side of the island. I heard his truck clanking out of the driveway when it was still dark out, the sun just a reddish haze out over the water like the inside of a grapefruit. Later he said he forgot she was leaving that day, but there's no way he forgot.

As he drove off, Fiona slept above me in her bunk, open-mouthed, breathing liquor into the room, all her blankets tossed on the floor, burning up with alcohol. She'd been out late the night before. Dale dropped her off in the road so she could creep secretly through the woods. I heard her scrabbling at the back of the house like a raccoon. She came in with pine needles tangled in her hair, smelling like drunken Christmas—the heavy fume of liquor and the fresh tang of evergreens. She climbed into the bunk with all her clothes on. Her other clothes were already packed. I lay there awake until dawn, listening to her breathe, listening to my own heart racing. I had never seen Fiona drunk before.

When she got up in the morning, she threw up a few times in the bathroom. I stood outside the door, worried.

When she came out, she just said, What? and slipped past me thin as a shadow.

She didn't ask me whether Dad was gone, but I saw her check for him in each room and then go outside to see whether his truck was in the drive. She was out there on the porch for a long time. Then Dale showed up in his truck, and she put her stuff in back and she actually hugged me good-bye. It was a hard hug, like a pinch.

Watch the drinking, she said. It's up to you now.

Okay, I said, though I knew that I would not.

Once Fiona took two cases of beer out of our father's private refrigerator in his tool shed and smashed each bottle, one by one, against the side of the house. He was inside, hung over, with a swollen and broken nose from where he had fallen against the porch steps, which is where she'd found him in the morning, a mask of blood on his face, asleep, and thought he was dead, and screamed and screamed until he hauled himself up. He heard her breaking the bottles, but he didn't get up to stop her. He just lay there on the couch with a dish towel full of ice on his face.

Dale didn't get out of the truck, and he didn't turn it off. This was an indication that Fiona was supposed to hurry up and get going. He was blasting the radio, and the truck was seething with white vapor in the cold morning air, a white smoky veil that seeped from the grille and the tailpipe and swirled around it, as if it were some kind of mythic dragon.

I didn't like Dale or dislike him. He was not at all like our father. He was thin and dark skinned and kept his head shaved. He wasn't mean to me—just cool and disinterested. He was always looking around at everything else in the room while you were trying to talk to him, as if he were planning a break-in later and wanted to decide in advance what to take and what to leave.

Shit, Fiona said. I'm probably going to miss you.

Nah, I said. Probably not.

Okay, she said. Here I go.

Yeah, there you go. Look at you going.

You don't have to be mean about it.

I'm not, I said, I'm not trying to be mean about it, but she was already going down the porch stairs and through the churned-up black soil and gravel and pine needles in the driveway in her dirty silver ballet flats and got in the truck, and Dale backed out, and that was that.

When my father came home that night, he didn't ask about Fiona. He acted as though everything was normal and defrosted a chunk of salmon from the freezer and broiled it with maple syrup on top as usual, and we ate while we watched a *Nova* special on volcanoes. Whenever there was a shot of a volcano blowing up, spraying black ash or brilliant neon lava, he said softly, Boom.

It was Fiona's crusade to get our father to stop drinking, not mine. I liked him drunk. He listened when I talked. He laughed. I was funny.

If Fiona wasn't home, I used to open him a beer when I heard his truck in the driveway. He'd act delighted, saying, Why thank you, Madam! And then he'd drink it plus three more while he made us dinner, and by the time Fiona got home from wherever she'd been, he'd want to waltz with her in the living room, which she was never having.

Come on, babe, he'd say. Dance with your old dad.

I'm not your babe, she would reply, and smack his outstretched hand away, and then say something cutting and cruel and intended to hurt him, such as: I wish you'd left instead of her.

It always goes the same way after that: he gets even more jolly and carefree, and we have a bonfire, outside, while Fiona goes into the bedroom and turns out the light. He's talkative and funny and tells stories about our mother that I love to hear, like how she was when they first met, with the knee-high leather boots she wore like a second skin and her boy-short hair that curlicued against her cheekbones, elfish and mischievous. She was so open, so welcoming, people used to come up and speak to her on the street, waiters would start telling her their life stories, and she would nod, and stare at them with her water-green eyes, and sip her coffee. I would always ask, Then *why*? And what I meant was, why weren't they still together? If he'd loved her so much, then why wasn't she here?

She's a sick person, he'd always say. It's not her fault.

When he's fairly sober, he says *It's not her fault* like maybe it's not her fault. When he's pretty drunk, he says *It's not her fault* like he's trying to convince himself that's true, and one time he got so drunk he said she was a selfish and cruel woman who fucked another man in cold blood and then abandoned her children, and then he toppled out of his lawn chair and right into the fire, his outstretched hand landing in the whispering blue-hot center. The burns were so bad we had to go to the island clinic the next day and get antibiotics and OxyContin for the pain and a wet wrap to protect the damaged skin. Fiona drove to the clinic. He had his eyes closed the whole time, and was wearing the same jacket from the night before, even though the lining was bursting out where the sleeve was melted. He kept his good hand over his face. He smelled like sweat and campfire and booze. Fiona was chilly-angry and wanted to know what happened.

He fell, I said. He got up to get another log and he fell.

Fiona said, Because he was wasted.

No, I said. He got drunk after, because the burn hurt so bad.

I even believed it myself when I said it out loud. I could picture it—my father rising to get another log, tripping over one of the stones that encircled the fire pit, his hand going down, into the flames. He would have been stoic, silent—no wailing or screaming or crying for him. He would have clutched his wrist and muttered, *Dammit*, as he does when he nails his thumb with a hammer. Instead of me hauling him up the porch stairs and into the living room and pushing him onto the couch, his boots still on, his tool belt still on, his leather jacket bunched up into his armpits. I got a glass of water and three ibuprofens and brought them to him.

Dad, I said, trying to whisper, trying not to wake Fiona. Dad, wake up.

His eyes drifted open but he was dreaming; he moaned and swatted at me and sent my arm and my hand with the glass into the wall, where it shattered with a dull sound, like a lightbulb popping. He flung his burned hand palm up onto the armrest and passed out. The hand was not bleeding but was yellow and puffed like a cornmeal biscuit and leaking some kind of clear fluid onto the upholstery. When I looked down at my own hand, there was a long red stripe of blood across it, gorgeous as spilled paint. I wiped it off on my jeans, but it welled back up again and again. It bled slowly most of the night, though I wrapped it in an old T-shirt and rolled on top of it, pressing it bloodless with the weight of my body. In the morning, I woke up to the couch springs creaking and his heavy breathing, then his voice: Oh Jesus. Oh Jesus fucking Christ, look at this.

In the truck, on the way to the clinic, I clutched my sweatshirt in my fist to hide the cut, looked at my father to see whether he approved of my little lie, but he didn't open his eyes. His head bobbled as Fiona hit a pothole going too fast.

Yeah, right, is what Fiona said to me. Yeah, fucking right.

A week later, she left with Dale.

The night when my father came home and didn't ask about Fiona, I woke up to a sound like a million raccoons under my window. When I went outside to see what was what, I found him there in the yard, throwing beer bottles at the wall just as Fiona had done that one time, long ago. Each bottle made a dull crunching sound when it hit the house, a soft implosion. The beer foamed madly and rolled down the siding in thick white waves. The bodies of the bottles burst; the necks remained intact and fell to the ground and piled up, caps still firmly attached.

He didn't drink at all after that, not this whole time that Fiona's been gone. I think he's been waiting for her to come back and see, but he doesn't say so. He just sits on the edge of the porch, smoking cigarettes and drinking bottles of soda. He lines them up on the windowsills in our house where they gleam and sparkle, the clear raised lettering—"Coca-Cola"—catching the light like ice.

It seems like we've been at the hospital forever. But then the handsome Indian neurologist gets the test results back, and suddenly, everything is happening too fast. The lady doctor sits us down and tells us that he's not going to wake up. She says there is no brain activity. She says his body is just a shell now and they are pumping more and more drugs into it to keep it going. She says we can keep doing this until his body gives up, or we can choose to let him go. She's leaning toward us with her elbows on her knees, and I notice that she has rose-colored fingernails and that her hands are just beginning to warp—she has gotten to the place in middle age when this starts to happen. Her fingers are interwoven and seem to fit together as neatly as puzzle pieces, knobby and angular. I remember my father cracking his big knuckles, joking, Oh, my aching bones!

I look over to Fiona because she hasn't said a thing this whole time, and I see that she is just sitting there with her legs uncrossed and her arms hanging down at her side. Her head is bent, and her hair is hanging like a curtain, and she is crying, but she isn't making a sound. Her mouth is open, and her eyes are shut, and she shakes as though some invisible hand is trying to shake her awake. Then, finally, Fiona breathes, taking in air with the thick piercing sound of a siren, and the doctor puts her hands over her face and sighs. She stands up, touches Fiona on the shoulder, and goes out of the room.

The nurse tells us to leave while she takes the intubation tube out of our father's throat.

Why! Fiona demands. She says, We want to stay with him.

She is holding his forearm with both of her own hands, the way you might hold the bar in front of you on a roller coaster.

You don't want to see this, the nurse says. It's nasty.

She is already leaning over the bed, taking things out of him. She presses on a wad of cotton taped to the back of his left hand and slides an IV out. She looks at Fiona, stops, and softens her voice for the first time.

You can come right back in, she says. Trust me: you don't want to see this part.

Fiona looks at her for a long moment, then lets go of our father's arm. She leads me out into the hallway, and we start to walk, down one hall, then another. We're moving fast, turning this way and that way, and already I'm lost and don't know how we'll get back to our father, but I look at Fiona and see that she is staring like a searchlight, memorizing the path with her bright eyes, her sky eyes, her blue eyes like our father's. But I got green. Mr. DeVotollo never answered my question about colors. I picture our parents, younger, happier, sitting on the porch of our house, playing rock-paper-scissors to decide whether green beats blue or blue beats green, Fiona just a budding scrap inside our mother, and then later, the same game for me.

Panic rises inside me, a cold nausea—that nurse is killing our father. She is taking away his breath. I will never speak to him again. I will never smell his whiskey-sawdust-sweat smell or watch him move a burning log with his bare hands. The terror of it wells up in my throat, and just as I'm about to start screaming, Fiona starts counting, her hand tightening on mine. The last time Fiona held my hand was long ago, and as she counts our footsteps out loud—seven, eight, nine—I remember that day. It was the first day of school. I was terrified. When the bus came and its doors clattered open, Fiona dragged me forward, my legs in their white-ribbed tights too small for the steps, my knee almost touching my chin, Fiona's black ponytail pointing down her back like an arrow, her pink vinyl backpack as shiny as a shield.

Fiona counts: thirty-eight, thirty-nine, forty. I switch my feet midcount so that my left foot falls at exactly the same time as Fiona's. It occurs to me that it is my birthday. Fifty. It occurs to me that now I will not be able to go to Hannah's boy-girl sleepover. Sixty. It occurs to me that I am a terrible person for thinking such things as my father is dying—a bad girl, an empty girl. It occurs to me that I have nowhere to live, that I will have to leave the island, the only place I know. I will end up living with Fiona and Dale, and Dale will hate and resent me for the space I take up and the food that I eat and the air that I breathe until I get my own surly boyfriend and run away from Fiona the way she ran away from me.

One hundred, says Fiona, and I stop thinking.

When we get back to the room, the nurse has finished. There are no more tubes or needles in our father except a little clamp attached to his finger, measuring his blood pressure in slow, oppressive beeps. I wish I could say that he looks normal, but he does not. He looks like a colder, smaller version of himself, like the stiff little mouse we found once under a leaf, as inert as a bullet. He is pale, but with a gathering darkness underneath, as if he is hardening, turning into stone.

His blood pressure is falling, says the nurse. It won't be long.

The beeping machine says thirty. Then it says twenty-seven. Then it says twenty-two.

The nurse turns on the suction machine and pokes the plastic tube into the sides of our father's mouth. There's no reason for her to do this anymore, but she does it more carefully than she has ever done it before. Fiona sees her do it and turns her face into her shoulder. Her hair falls across her face like a curtain, and I can't see what she's thinking. The machine is going *beep-beep-beep*, but it's getting slower. Each time, there is more silence between each beep. It says fifteen. Then it says seven. The letters are neon red, like an alarm clock. I feel like I do when I wake up before my alarm goes off and I see that it's about to ring and I want to go back to sleep, but I can't, because I know it's coming.

Please, I say to the nurse, turn off the beeping, and she does.

Now we will not know the moment that he dies. At any point he could be gone, or he could still be here. Already he looks like something from the past, like an artifact of love, like a pair of leather boots with no legs inside them.

The nurse squeaks out of the room on her chalk-white shoes, closing the door behind her. The light from the hallway is pinched away, and we are now in perfect darkness and perfect quiet, Fiona and I; there is no more beeping or panting wolf-breath from the ventilator. Fiona is so silent that it's as if she has vanished along with the light. She might still be there, but then again, she might not. The darkness is smooth and deep, and it dawns on me that I probably can't see my hand in front of my face. I hold up a hand to check. I wave it back and forth—nothing. Not even a flicker. Suddenly it is as if my hand does not exist. Then my feet don't seem to exist, or my knees, or my flat girl's chest, or my crooked mouth that is like my father's, and it creeps up and up until only my eyes—green like my mother's—are left. I open and close them and see that there's no difference between open and shut, just a deep and spangled darkness both ways, and then my eyes are gone too.

NEVADA

Kate Krautkramer

ou will think I was shallow. But I was young and passionate and dramatic, and I loved more than anything that I owned a pair of high-heeled shoes that exactly matched the color of my durable automobile, and so I usually dressed in red, and Tom Keegan said he loved this about me. In his most charitable moment of our years together, he pushed me down onto the hood of the car, his lips right there and hot by my ear—and said the way I looked with my car made his knees buckle. It's not the sort of thing a girl forgets.

The car was a toady thing, a reward from my father, who purchased it in return for me not drinking or smoking for all the time I was in high school and college. That's how it happened that I was twenty-two, had never puffed on a cigarette or had a taste of alcohol, and owned the car, a reliable little thing I drove to Nevada and had painted shiny red the day my first paycheck arrived in the mail.

There's no need to tell every little thing that happened, but I loved Tom Keegan very much, and Tom said he liked the way I thought. You cannot imagine the power of these words. In those days (maybe it still is like this, I don't know), boys were constantly doing what Tom never did—groping, feeling, pushing—and here Tom was, asking questions and telling me he loved my mind.

I can't remember now what I had to say that was so captivating. I don't know how I fooled myself into believing he was taken with my brain. But he said he was, and I believed he was and thought myself very clever for wanting him so much.

And while I loved Tom, he would commit nothing to me. So, being rash and thinking to punish him or some fool notion, I finished college in Wisconsin and looked for jobs as far away as I could find.

By mail, I applied and was hired to be the speech pathologist for all of Nevada. I was to cover every town in the state twice per year. Documentation had to be presented in triplicate—notes, reports, and observations on every child in Nevada with a speech defect.

I was exhausted most of the time, but felt myself to be some kind of pioneer—a woman with an expense account. I was based out of Reno and covered a thousand miles a week, hauling my typewriter and a portable audiometer and reams of carbon paper in the backseat of my little red car. I told my employers I had to stay in the best places to be safe, and they paid. Lugging my typewriter into the finest hotels, I spent evenings on thoughtful reports, verifying every cleft palate, every stutter, every case of aphasia for · hundreds of square miles around.

On occasion, when there was far to go, I flew in small planes, pressing my head to the cold windows, trying to understand the vast, untried landscape in aerial view. The first time I flew to Elko, I was met at the airport by a few members of the board of education. The next day, I needed to get an early start in order to evaluate, as a favor to a teacher friend in Reno, her nephew who lived on an outlying ranch. "Maybe you can get him to talk, although it's not really that he can't," my friend had said. Then she added, "And you have such a way." And so I felt important and was anxious to see the boy and anxious for the sort of long dusty drive I was just then beginning to love more than speech pathology.

I had not yet checked into the hotel across the street, but the board members insisted on dinner in the Stockman Casino; photos of Bing Crosby, who owned a nearby ranch, smiled pleasantly at us from the walls. The board members were also adamant about after-dinner drinks, so I stood sipping orange juice at the bar while the men drank Manhattans.

The slot machines *ping-ping-pinged* behind us—you know how they do— and the lights flashed when the president of the board of education turned to me, touched my arm, and said he'd like to take me to bed.

I remember his gin-filled smile, his fitted brown suit, a silk tie. Except for the gin, he resembled my father and must have been something like my

father's age, and so I made a joke about how, technically, he was my em-
ployer and smiled and said thank you, but I couldn't. I knew next to nothing
about sex, of course, but goose pimples rose on my neck. I was thinking all
the while about Tom Keegan.

And what did I know about men? My sisters and I went to school dances
and sometimes afterward to the drive-in for milk shakes and french fries.
Once in a while, we went so far as to neck, usually in the moon shadow of a
cornfield, always in the front seat of a big sedan, where the boy was held in
check by the steering wheel and some very real sense of goodness or piety.
Christian duty reined back our desires—the boys', too, I think, since we were
usually home on time.

And Tom was a Catholic boy, the president of his high school sodality. He
told me everything in such detail, I can picture him in the back pews, leading
prayers, his white-white skin glowing in reverie. I remember the image as if it
were real, as well as I remember coming down the stairs at my parents' house
the first time Tom Keegan came to call.

I was home from college; my sister, Colleen, was a high school senior.
Tom and I were secondary to the arrangement. Colleen had been noticed
and admired by Tom's brother at a regional Catholic Youth Organization
meeting. Colleen was expectant, anticipating the arrival of the boys with the
sort of primping and squealing requisite when charming young gentlemen
were waiting.

It had to have been a formal date, because we wore dresses, and I think
even gloves. I came down before Colleen, who was fussing with her petticoats
or some such.

I was wearing—I don't know what—a dress, as I said, it must have been,
and blue because the shoes are what I do recall, as easily as if I had been
Cinderella, although they were not glass, but satin pumps—light blue and
pointed, which I had purchased that year while I was supposed to be studying
in Milwaukee. I spent a good deal of time looking at those shoes that night,
blushing, I am sure, when I could not look at Tom, because I was smitten
and worked into such a state of self-consciousness, wanting to be perfect for
him from the start, aching for the boy to love me, even then. From the very
beginning it was like that.

We looked a bit like twins; his hair was black, like mine, except it came to
a widow's peak in front. He was maybe more heavyset than you would guess
when I tell you I was in love with a brilliant young lawyer from Chippewa
Falls. But he was tall enough that even when I wore heels, my chin fit under
his head when we danced.

When we had been out together several times and felt we could dance closely, one night I pressed my cheek into the button of his shirt pocket, concentrating on making a clean impression so I could immediately after run to the powder room and look in the mirror to verify the print there, a testament to proximity, my skin flushed.

But you'll see how I lost those years.

While I was in Nevada, Tom went to law school at Harvard, then moved to Chicago, where he was being groomed to someday become head counsel for Brown & Williamson Tobacco, and was a young, competitive trial lawyer but quit because of how he described himself, as a borderline alcoholic with no intention of giving up his vice. And so he went, instead, to Kentucky— Louisville, where he was eventually murdered, it pained me to learn, with a phone cord. But that was after me, after I thought I knew him and knew I loved him, after everything happened and really nothing ever happened. It must not have been love at all, and now I am ahead of my story.

The morning after the president of the board of education propositioned me, I drove south out of Elko. The boy I was to observe was eleven years old and lived on a ranch nearby, "near" being a term all its own in Nevada. The road turned to dirt long before Jiggs, a town I barely saw through the dust kicked up by the yellow Cadillac delivered to me that morning at my hotel and lent by the local superintendent of schools. He had talked with the board president, who believed, he said, I would need some way to get around. The superintendent opened the door for me and watched my legs as I got in. "We sure do appreciate you," he gestured behind him, indicating some absent entourage, then leaned in the open window and winked at me.

A map hand-drawn on the back of a first-grade worksheet suggested a route. The referring teacher had also drawn me a smiley face in red ink. I felt morally obliged to help any child, but especially the nephew of a friend, even if she was someone I knew only because I had moved to Nevada. I watched the Ruby Mountains grow up out of the desert in front of me. Breathing in the bad cologne lingering in the car, I thought about Tom Keegan, how he might look in a cowboy hat.

Some bends in the road led to a log ranch house. A woman, my teacher friend's sister, let me in and squeezed my hand lightly in both of hers. She was older than I was, probably in her midthirties, and petite. Blond hair tufted up on top of her head, and she wore faded blue jeans and a hand-sewn pink gingham top. You think I might be making up details, but I remember her as clearly as any of it. A beautiful, tired face that woman had, and a tiny waist. She thanked me for coming. Never have I seen a person work so hard to smile.

In the living room, an armchair and a sofa sat like forgotten totems. Candle sconces ringed the kitchen and continued down a hallway to the side. The stove used gas; a television was absent. Neither was there a radio, which could have been run on batteries but was unlikely to pick up a station this far out from Elko. There would be no use for the audiometer. I set it on the floor, made of pine—I knew because it looked the same as the floor of my little cabin in Reno, where I suddenly wished more than anywhere to be.

The cabin wasn't in Reno proper, of course, but closer to Tahoe, at the end of a rutted dirt road. I had searched for an apartment and found none that seemed right, and then this, the darlingest little house in a ponderosa forest, with one big floor-to-ceiling window on the Sierra Nevada and the Truckee River, and only a few other little houses, scattered and unseen, a few hundred yards away through the trees.

I had never imagined myself in such a house, but I took it and learned to be a little bold. There were squirrels on the roof, which was not different from home. But black widow spiders that sometimes spun their webs under the chairs, I had to learn to confront myself—which seemed a little risky—the whole situation forming me quickly into the sort of confident young woman who lived alone and would be thrilled when Tom Keegan called to suggest he arrange to visit, in February, for the Olympics. He asked whether he could stay in one of the little cabins near mine when he came.

But now I am ahead again, or behind, because we had been out past Elko, past Jiggs in a ranch house, and got back somehow to Tahoe—which was how it all was then: there was a "somehow" quality to everything that happened. Do you see? Everything so immediate and important at the time and so distant finally, like the tiny little echoes from the audiometer I carried with me everywhere, growing fainter and fainter until there is no discernible signal.

I was so callow before all of this, maybe for the whole of my life before I moved to Nevada, that it had never occurred to me what it might be like, for instance, for a man's hands to travel the particular map of my body. Can you imagine such a thing? A grown woman never really thinking of it? But when I did come to imagine such things, awake in the night, not knowing where he was—in Cambridge or Chicago or Washington—they were Tom's hands I did envision when the time came. His elegant fingers felt the way. His eyes, his mild, sedating eyes, searched my own for signs of surrender, which he would have found, completely, had he ever actually regarded my face as an illustration of emotion.

In those years, I saw Tom sometimes, on vacation or when we were both in Wisconsin at Christmas. We wrote letters and often talked long-distance at night. I sometimes fell asleep with the heavy black receiver a few inches from my ear. We whispered our way through the better part of years.

He paid to fly me places. More than once, we met in Washington, D.C., for lunch, Tom always with his arm around my waist, greeting me with proper little cheek kisses at the airport gate. It was extravagant and thrilling. Absurd, really—to meet for lunch, then fly somewhere else for dinner. Whispering in taxis, convening with lawyers, holding hands, and me covering my face with my fingers, inhaling whatever smell of his was left there, the whole lonely flight home.

You are wondering now why we didn't sleep together. Why we did not have sex, as young people say today. Were we really so controlled, so pious, so wholesome? But maybe you already know, you have guessed what I never guessed until years later, because I didn't even realize there was such a thing as a homosexual, and if Tom knew—he must have known—but still there was duty and upbringing. And here I was, and he loved me, so far as that goes, I swear that he did. And so what was he to do with me when he could not, in the end, want me, even with all our desperate mumbling, the ongoing disappointment for me, what must have been rage for him, and desire for something else altogether?

Still, one night I came to his bed. We had adjoining hotel rooms; we would never have pretended to be married, never would have thought of so much sin. I am sure we had met in a city, probably to visit with company executives and be entertained, as we often were, by men whose faces and names I would not even recognize in dreams.

But this I remember well. I asked Tom to leave his door a little ajar. We were great friends, remember, always laughing and quarreling, his black hair and mine indistinguishable and meshed together while we murmured secrets, our heads bent together like children's. I am sure now he had no idea of my plot.

He was in the bathroom when I came in, took off my clothes, and laid myself in the bed, practically blind with want, my senses crying for his body in a way I surely can't remember and am embarrassed to reveal, although I must have felt it all.

Who knows what he was feeling, if he was feeling anything, when he found me? He may not have noticed I was naked. He was likely drunk. I offer this not as any excuse for him. But it was an almost constant state, a state in which he kept his charms about him, a condition that inspired him to levels of behavior so mannerly and graceful, I admired him, I loved him more for this ability. I believed he would become a senator. And so he may have been drunk when he came to the bed and the light was off and he kissed me politely and fell asleep.

And what could a girl do in this situation? I lay there most of the night, listening to him breathe so offhandedly in his sleep, as if I had offered him nothing. In the shadows, I looked down the length of my body under the sheet for what were some of the longest hours I've known, my toes up and forming a small mountain range there at the end of Tom Keegan's bed.

You want to know how I didn't know, even then. Years of my life I ran to him here and there across the country. Because I thought he needed me. I thought he was testing me. I thought he was waiting until he could afford me, until he had a large enough salary, maybe we'd move to a stone house in St. Paul.

And still Tom phoned me, still we saw each other. Still I was the lovely young girl he presented for inspection at company functions. Still he said he adored my silly little car, and I got another pair of red shoes because the backs of the first pair had worn out against the car floor, driving all those miles, watching brown hills turn to dust, counting tumbleweeds and telephone poles, all the way across Nevada.

The new red heels betrayed me awfully on the ranch out past Elko when the woman motioned me to the kitchen table, pine like the floor and home-fashioned and worn to comfortable condition. Like her sister who had urged me to come here, the woman had a tender way. She waved her hand toward a hall leading away from the living room. "He almost never speaks," she said. "My son, I mean. You understand we love him?"

I am sure I nodded or gave some other smiling response. I didn't have children of my own, and we've seen what I knew about love.

"My husband's a buckaroo, chases cows for a living. He's not home much." She shook her head and poured me a cup of coffee I never drank. Her back was to me as she returned the coffeepot to the stove and said, "I do like your shoes." She turned and looked at me then and leaned against the kitchen counter.

"I used to live in the city," I said. "Milwaukee." I meant these words as an apology for the shoes, the Cadillac, and my electric machine. "Wisconsin," I added. "I grew up in Wisconsin. In a small town. Dairy country. The cows there are all the black-and-white kind."

"I only wear boots," she said, pointing to her bare feet, which were tiny and white. "Except when I'm inside, which is usually. Because of the boy."

My attention strayed out the window to the superintendent's car, which I hoped had enough gas to get me all the way back to Elko.

When I turned back to her, she looked hard at my face. "He's an only child," she said. "Can't stand the feel of the wind. Won't even wear a shirt." She crossed her little arms over her chest and hugged herself hard. She said, "I can only kiss him when he sleeps."

I must have winced, or maybe I managed the expression appropriate to asking a question, but she had said most of what she needed to say. "I know you can't fix everything. Just see if he'll talk, will you? I wish he would say something new. I know he can hear us." She pushed up her pink-checked sleeves.

The boy's bedroom was tidy—a twin bed with a blue spread, a toy box, a bookshelf half full, a glass of water on a little table by the bed. The boy sat in a rocking chair. He had cotton shorts, a naked torso, blond hair, and the same pleading eyes as his mother, although his gaze did not change to meet us. His focus fell somewhere on the far wall, maybe on a knot mark in the pine paneling.

His mother opened her arms at the room in general. "This is Ambrose." She squared an already perfect stack of comics on his dresser top. She walked to the boy and stood in front of the chair, careful not to interrupt his rocking. "Ambrose, someone is here to see you. Do you like her pretty shoes?" The boy's focus did not shift, but his hands flapped around each other once in his lap. "All right then, I'll leave you." She turned and took two steps to the door, then looked back at me. "He's quite smart," she warned before closing the door. "It's not how it looks." Her voice stayed even, but I saw the tendons rise on either side of her neck like twin asps ready to administer the merciful bites.

I stood still with my back against the boy's bureau, watching him rock and watch the wall more attentively than if it had been a Hopalong Cassidy movie. His bare feet hit the floor like a metronome clocking time. "One, two, three, four," I began counting with his footfalls. "One, two, three, four." For a minute or more I went on, waiting for the boy to acknowledge me or pick up on the pattern, which he did not.

I went and sat cross-legged on the floor in front of him, pulling my skirt over my lap. "Can you speak, Ambrose?" I asked.

The boy's eyes did not shift from the wall. "How do you do. My name is Ambrose," he said. His voice landed as steadily as his gaze—even, clear, and without inflection. His hands gave a few flaps in his lap.

Really, I need not bother you with all of the details of this visit, except to say I had no idea what to do. Ambrose would not speak to me, except to answer all of my questions with a question of his own. "Are you here to see me," he said, always punctuating the sentence with the flutter of his graceless hands, for he did not deliver it with the rise in voice needed to make a proper question.

I tried for an hour, watching and listening, looking for any behavior, any clue to help me understand. I understood very little, of course, but the boy was lovely, with high pink cheeks and eyes clear enough to reflect all of Nevada or an even bigger space, like his mother's heart.

When I believed enough time had passed that his mother would feel I had made some kind of adequate effort to connect with the child, I stood to go. "One, two, three, four." I made a final attempt. "Can you count, Ambrose?" Really, I was convinced the boy would say nothing. All the while I sat at his feet, I felt he was holding me in some kind of aura, some kind of calculated, controlling spell that cared for nothing but predictability and rhythm. It cared not for Ambrose, not for his mother, and certainly not for me. His silence hung about, deliberate and invasive, and like a wicked child, I suddenly wished to tease him. So I said, "Can you count, Ambrose, with the lovely bare feet?"

"How do you do," Ambrose said. "My name is Ambrose. I am not a bear."

He rocked, watching the wall for comfort. Or watching the wall for changes. Or watching the wall to steady himself against the wind, which, even inside the sturdy ranch house, I heard kicking its heels outside the walls.

I walked to the door and looked back at him. "Good-bye, Ambrose," I whispered.

"How do you do. My name is Ambrose," he said to the pine wall.

Out in the kitchen, his mother leaned against the counter, as she had done before. Her face appeared calm and disappointed, as if she had been listening at the door, although I guessed from the sincerity in her posture she had not.

I stopped by my audiometer and stood still. "He is a beautiful boy," I said. "He looks like you."

His mother glanced away from me and out the window, to where a dust devil cut across the driveway. She shook her head but did not cry. "Thank you for coming," she said without moving.

I lifted my clunky machine and walked to the door. I pushed the screen to let myself out. Still she did not move. The dust devil petered out, and for a half a moment, the wind stayed calm.

"It's nothing you did," I told her. I barely saw her nod before I let the screen flap closed behind me.

All that was before Tom and I split. It was in the fall before the winter when he came to visit me in Nevada. I never saw Ambrose again. I don't know what happened to him or his doe-eyed mother. I compiled the report in the hotel that night, sat staring at the typewriter, etching out what had happened. And when I finished, I tore the carbons up, left them there in the wastepaper basket, and said a prayer. I got on my knees on the hotel carpet and prayed that things could be different.

Of course, one day I knew it was finished between Tom Keegan and me. I walked in the pine forests around my house. I drove my car to the edge of Lake Tahoe and stared, trying to discern how far from shore I could still see the bottom.

And one day I bought my own ticket to Chicago. I arrived at Tom's office unannounced and told him he had to marry me or I would leave forever. On Lake Shore Drive, the office showed off windows to the floor and dark leather furniture. Tom sat behind the desk, taking me in or trying me on or something like that. After a few moments, he said, "Well, let's go have a drink then!" Which we did—highballs, not champagne—and it was the last time I ever saw Tom Keegan.

You think, still, it was impossible I didn't know. Or you think Tom Keegan never loved me or that he can't have been so adroit as to string a clever, beautiful girl, such as I then was, along for years, to make her believe and believe. Or you think he was cruel and cool and lovely, doing what he had to do to succeed or not be found out.

But you haven't imagined how sincerely tall he was. Imagine floating across some waxy country-club dance floor in tall Tom Keegan's arms when John Kennedy had just been elected and we were full of hope.

Or, imagine this, a little earlier. I was still living near Reno, and Tom came for the Olympics, as I said. In preparation for his arrival, I knit matching sweaters—his and hers, with complicated Fair Isle yokes in six different colors. This because I guessed he was bringing a ring. We had not seen each other for Christmas, and he had made me agree to not send him a present. He made me agree to wait. We would be together for the Olympics in Squaw Valley, not far from my cabin in the woods. He said he had a gift to give me then.

I stayed up late every night, imagining God knows what sort of scene. I knit and knit, working the yarn, letting it slide over my fingers, around and through, over and under—my body still craving what it did not understand.

I folded his sweater, smoothed it down, and laid it in a box, covering it with tissue paper and wrapping the whole thing with a spectacular velvet bow.

By this time in the story, you are not surprised that Tom came with a large package. When he went back to the car for a bottle, I quickly tore open the sweater and rumpled it, throwing it casually over the arm of my couch, where it would not seem to be a monument to undying love.

Tom's gift was an abridged version of the *Oxford English Dictionary*. He thought I would love it. And I tried, stroking its cover, opening the volume and letting my hands run over the words, lifting it to my chest like a schoolgirl, pressing it into my breasts.

And Tom wore his sweater. We both did—the matching sweaters in Squaw Valley, where a miraculous twelve feet of snow fell right before the games began. And Tom posed with me, one hand holding a martini, the other arm around my waist, a cigar clamped in his mouth. I remember thinking the cigar was cavalier and rebellious, at home among his even, immaculate teeth.

It was the first time the Olympics were televised nationally; Walt Disney himself choreographed the opening ceremonies, and we wanted to look exactly right. I wore thick-rimmed, plastic, dark glasses and plenty of red, red lipstick. The snow kept falling. Cameras flashed everywhere, and we smiled as if going to heaven depended on it.

LUNCH ACROSS THE BRIDGE

Peter LaSalle

hey wouldn't know about it until the next day.

Later they would read about it in the paper, eventually hear it on TV. The couple would learn that what happened that day at the restaurant called Arandas was all part of what Nuevo Laredo across the border was at the moment. But, as said, they didn't know that then, when it happened there at Arandas.

It was a fine restaurant just two blocks off the city's main street, a modernistic villa-style setup—pale lavender stucco and tinted glass, walled in for its own little enclave with a courtyard offering gardens of fleshy hibiscus and the stars of oleander, a hissing fountain—and they had simply walked over the international bridge from their hotel in Laredo to have a late lunch.

They didn't say much as the meal was ordered. Closing the big menus, they smiled and thanked the waiter. They smiled at him again when the food was served. They both surely realized that they were beyond talking any more about the sadness in their lives right then, losing a child like that. They had driven from Austin, going south for four hours or so on the interstate—over the dusty flats peppered with mesquite and prickly pear, always a dreamlike landscape, admittedly—only because they had often done that when younger and during college years at the university, gone to the border for a weekend to relax. Maybe they now thought that just getting out of Austin for a weekend, being somewhere else, would help.

The restaurant was half full, if that, in mid-afternoon, the waiters moving around the tables in their black trousers and very white shirts; there was the low buzz of talk and the soft clinking of china and silverware.

If he was thinking anything in the long stretches of silence at the table, it was how beautiful she always looked, even now after what she had been through. He was maybe thinking how that very day, in the lobby of the stately old hotel in Laredo on the Texas side, he had noticed people glancing at her—tall and willowy, her auburn hair loose, her gray eyes large; even the lines lately fanning out from those eyes possibly made her more lovely still, being a bit older and having carried beauty gracefully into a next stage in life, rare. She wore simple white Capri slacks and a simple white blouse, and the blue canvas rope-soled espadrilles were quite comfortable for their walk this warm and sunny spring afternoon. And if she was thinking anything, it was maybe how it had broken her heart even more, what she thought about often, the way that he, her husband, had maintained his hope for so long. It wasn't a hope that he had expressed anywhere else in life before that, she knew, and for at least the last few years he had admitted that granting he was supposedly as successful as he was in the old and respected Texas law firm in Austin, the youngest full partner, the work had come to attract him less and less; he often said, good-naturedly, that he probably should have forgotten about law school altogether when young, dared early on to try something more interesting. But this past year, as the doctors kept cheerily lying to the two of them—all those doctors inevitably with diplomas neatly framed and from the very best universities on their office walls, doctors inevitably wearing horn-rimmed glasses and blue button-down shirts, or it sometimes seemed to her, they were all interchangeable—true, as the doctors all talked only of more options, the new experimental treatments for William and rates of possible success, she knew deep down the situation to be otherwise, she knew that the blood tests and the marrow samples told another story altogether; doctors had to convince themselves of their cures, that was their daily business, it justified who they were. She had to admit that in the course of that, his keeping up hope as he did—believing the smug doctors and refusing to do otherwise, repeatedly becoming excited at what he saw as the slightest hint of a good turn for William—could have been the saddest thing of all.

But maybe they weren't thinking things like that. They were just a couple, still young enough, both attractive, educated people—they had strolled across the bridge spanning the weedy river bed, and they had simply come to the restaurant for lunch and weren't thinking of much whatsoever, or saying much besides the small talk concerning how good the meal was, how good even the wine was at this restaurant, Arandas.

The waiters were attentive yet maintained full dignity, like European waiters, and the food, touted as "interior" Mexican cuisine, was actually exceptional; the place surely deserved its reputation.

"It's very good," he said.

"Yes," she said, "and I'm glad we came for the weekend."

After a few minutes, she said it was also good that they had decided to take the walk over to Nuevo Laredo for lunch instead of coming in the evening, as they had originally planned.

"Yes," he said.

The news reports would later say that it had to do with a public appearance, to make a point. That meant asserting power and announcing, so there would be no mistake, that Paco Villarreal was out of the Mexican federal prison in Zacatecas at last. The escape, in all likelihood, had been not so much a matter of any adventurous derring-do as large payoffs to guards. And free again, Paco Villarreal was in Nuevo Laredo again to let the opposing cartel know where he physically was, tell them boldly that he had no fear and they couldn't ignore the Helios cartel, headed by his brother Esteban, in the ongoing Mexican drug wars currently playing themselves out in Nuevo Laredo; the local police would leave him alone, of course—they were easily paid off. The city itself was strategically important because the Pan-American Highway passed right through Nuevo Laredo and then Laredo. The highway, which became Interstate 35 clear up to Minnesota, was a main conduit for drug transport into U.S. markets.

But it wasn't like anything in the movies, the way they took over the restaurant that afternoon. And how it happened was that nobody seemed to have noticed the two young men, neatly groomed and dressed in casual clothes, who came in to look around, politely enough, and then leave for a few moments. They came back with three other young men accompanying a rather short man of fifty or so in a loose-tailed light-blue *guayabera* shirt, with a pockmarked face and aviator sunglasses, who the couple dining would later learn was indeed the man named Paco Villarreal. And nobody eating seemed to have noticed that the twin large carved wooden doors leading to the outside courtyard, the entrance to the restaurant, had been latched, and that there was another young man posted to stand watch there. A middle-aged woman had been called over to the table where the man, having removed the sunglasses, was now seated with the several younger men. She must have been the manager or perhaps the owner, and as she sat down at the table with the men, that, too, probably didn't seem to be anything out of the ordinary, if anybody in the restaurant did notice her doing so; it could have been but a greeting to a regular customer, let's say. Only when she stood up from the table, remaining very calm—a petite, dignified woman in a linen suit, she had substantial makeup and carefully coiffed hennaed hair—did people look that way, and she had already motioned for two of the waiters to come to the table. She spoke to them in low tones, and then one waiter made the announcement to the room in Spanish and the other in English, obviously for the benefit of Americans, of which the couple might have been the only ones there. The people eating were told that Señor Villarreal would like all of them to be his friends for the moment in celebration of his return to Nuevo Laredo after a long absence; a round of drinks for everybody—wine or a cocktail—would all be paid for by Señor Villarreal.

The couple looked around, and everybody was raising glasses in a toast, there was even some applause; people didn't recognize the name—or didn't do so at first, anyway, there in the restaurant, it was later noted—and they were now certainly appreciative of the magnanimous gesture of this man, whoever he was.

The couple smiled to one another. She reached over and put her long slim fingers on his on the table.

They continued with their meal. The waiter came with a bottle and re-filled their wine glasses without their asking him, and they both nodded, smiled. If a table of people who finished their own meal had gotten up to leave and had been deterred from doing so, discreetly spoken to at the door by the muscular young man in the pink polo shirt and gray slacks and soft leather slip-ons, advised maybe to have an after-dinner drink or a dessert, even enjoy some dessert champagne, compliments of Señor Villarreal, as the reports later would say—and such details were included in the extensive coverage the next day in the big Laredo Sunday paper—the couple didn't notice that. And if some of the other people eating gradually understood, or suspected, that what was going on was that nobody, in fact, was being allowed to leave the restaurant before the group of men at the table had finished what probably were just drinks and appetizers—the men were in the restaurant for no more than a casual twenty minutes—the couple didn't notice that either. All of which is to say, there was never any commotion whatsoever. And the reports would also explain that a few observers pass-ing on the street had seen several armored black Toyota Land Cruisers, a convoy of sorts, parked outside the iron latticework gates to Arandas on its side street, and while nobody in the restaurant who was later interviewed had seen any arms being carried, there certainly must have been armed men, a contingent of them, in those gleaming black Land Cruisers parked outside. Still, for the locals, customized armored vehicles were rather routine in Nuevo Laredo.

After the men had left the restaurant the check came, and the couple tried to pay the waiter for the extra glasses of expensive wine, but the waiter said it was entirely out of the question: all drinks had already been paid for by Señor Villarreal.

In the balmy late afternoon, the couple walked around Nuevo Laredo for a while before they crossed the bridge, to return to Laredo. They strolled through the two squares of Nuevo Laredo, first the older one with its fine baroque church and big leafy green trees with trunks whitewashed lower down and handsome statues, bronze gone to black, of honored heroes of the Republic. And then they strolled through the larger square, which served as a terminal where sooty local buses pulled up around its periphery, a tall, ornate clock tower exactly in its center; with precise Bavarian workings from the nineteenth century, the clock, they knew, had always been a landmark for the city.

They lingered over coffee at a sidewalk place. Music played from a vendor's cart selling tapes and CDs across the street, *norteño* and pleasantly scuffling *cumbia*. The smell of exhaust from those rattling buses hung rich and nearly tangible in the air, yet it was somehow appreciated, too, because it became almost a fragrance that had always seemed to define Mexico.

By the time they did head back toward the bridge—the older silver-painted bridge, a long trestle, with a pedestrian walkway and without the traffic of the sleek new multi-laned international span for the highway—the lights were already coming on in the places along Nuevo Laredo's main street leading up to it, a soft, buttery illumination in the string of tacky gift and souvenir shops with their clutter of rugs, pottery, T-shirts, and countless swivel racks of faded postcards. And, of course, there were also the many open-fronted *farmacias*, entirely clinically white within; in the *farmacias* stood the pharmacists themselves, men and women, dressed in white lab coats and always silently waiting for business behind the long, very white counters, like just so many mannequins staring out, perpetually, at those strolling by.

The couple entered the empty U.S. customs and immigration terminal, and the uniformed agents politely waved them through. They returned to the hotel, an especially well-appointed older one, in fact, Spanish architecture and located beside the river and not far from the customs concourse on that side of the bridge in the currently deserted downtown of Laredo; they would start on the drive of several hours back to Austin the next morning.

Yes, as odd as it may sound, it would only be when they were in the lobby the next morning, waiting to check out, their bags packed and sitting around in the big yellow easy chairs and paging through the Laredo Sunday paper taken from one of the polished mahogany coffee tables in that spacious lobby, that they learned what had transpired; they indeed learned and realized how—as the paper emphasized in a prominent front-page editorial right beside the detailed news article and with no shortage of dramatic rhetoric—it was a wonder that the situation in the restaurant hadn't turned into "yet another bloodbath in the current, never-ending tragedy of senseless violence plaguing our sister city." Paco Villarreal certainly had announced to his enemies that he was out of prison and back in Nuevo Laredo. If nothing else, he had provided the full confirmation of his presence needed, and such presence had already become newsworthy; word would travel fast—and then some.

They even heard two other couples—very loud and very garish and, well, very Texan—talking about it in the lobby, and the violence in general in Nuevo Laredo, too. One of the overweight men told the other some story about how he had been in Nuevo Laredo just the year before and shopping for silver jewelry with his wife on the very day when the new police chief had been gunned down outside the central police station only three hours after he had been sworn in. The other man, not to be outdone, told his own story about how one time, returning from a beach vacation in Mazatlán, he and his wife had been driving straight through in an attempt to get back to Houston by the next day, and they had actually witnessed a fiery, full-fledged shoot-out—in the middle of the night at the newer international bridge for the Nuevo Laredo–Laredo crossing—involving one group of *narcotrafficantes* in a large semi truck defending it from assault by another group, with the U.S. agents stationed there soon caught up in the heavy automatic gunfire themselves.

But, to repeat yet again, the couple, he and she, wouldn't know exactly what had happened in the restaurant until they read about it in the paper in the hotel lobby the next morning, well after they had been over to Nuevo Laredo for the late lunch. In fact, they had simply gone up to their room once they got back to the hotel that evening and remained there, not needing any dinner.

And they had made love that night after the walk across the bridge, there in their room in the hotel—lovemaking with its own kind of sadness to it, really, because they hadn't made love for so long—and afterward they lay in bed side by side. All blue shadows, the room was large, and they had turned off the air conditioner and opened up the row of big French doors to the balcony overlooking the river and the sparkling blanket of lights beyond, which was Nuevo Laredo, and then the silhouetted low hills of Mexico proper; there was a slice of an ivory moon. It was then, as they lay in bed in the darkness, that she told him something that she said she had been thinking about; she spoke slowly and softly, almost more to herself than to him, it seemed. It concerned something that had happened after their son William had gone through the long summer of intense radiation and chemotherapy and then transferred to the private school in the fall, St. George's Episcopal Academy in Austin, doing so because, unlike the public junior high, St. George's would let him make up what he had missed the year before without having to lose a grade standing. She told him how William came home one afternoon and William was smiling, gently so, telling her about how a kid from his eighth-grade class had come up to him after school let out for the day, introducing himself to William, and the kid had told him that his, William's, hair was wonderful—the kid said that he personally envied somebody with a head of hair like his, which was, in fact, William's wig.

"We were in the kitchen at home," she said, "he was having an after-school snack at the table and even laughing quietly a bit about it, how the boy said he was sure that he himself was destined for early baldness—his father was bald, all his uncles. The boy said to William that he, the boy, would be lucky if he ever had a girlfriend, that he had always wished he had a full, thick head of hair like William's. William said he couldn't believe that the kid couldn't see that it was a wig."

Lying there on the bed, he didn't say anything and he just listened to her speaking—somewhat vacantly, very softly—in the darkness. In truth, after she told the story, neither of them said anything for a while.

He finally got up from the bed, and in the blue shadows, he walked across the room's cool terra-cotta tile floor and to the bathroom, to take a glass tumbler from the vanity and let the water run, let it get very cold, before filling the glass. Back in the bedroom, sitting on the edge of the bed, naked, he asked her if she would like a drink, and, naked, she nodded. She hoisted herself to her elbows, her auburn hair still tangled from the lovemaking, her gray eyes large, and he held the glass as she sipped and swallowed some, then she nodded to indicate she had had enough.

He then gently removed the tumbler from her lips, sipped some of the water himself and placed the tumbler on the night table, next to the telephone there, its dial faintly glowing green in the dark.

It was warm with the windows open like that, but comfortable.

He looked at her. He reached out to lift a ribbon of her hair that had fallen across her damp forehead and slowly put it back in place, saying nothing.

"We walked an awful lot today," she finally said, smiling tentatively, "though, didn't we?"

"Yes," he assured her.

ALONE

Yiyun Li

hen the waitress came to take the order, she asked how Suchen was doing with the smoke. Suchen replied vaguely that all was well with her, though she had no idea what smoke the waitress was talking about. The man sitting at the next table, an elbow away—the patio was barely large enough for the six tables it held, three of them unoccupied—must have been observing the exchange; he leaned over after the waitress had left and explained that up north the wildfire was just a few miles from the state highway.

The October sky was blue, empty but for some still wisps of cloud. The restaurant, Mony's, was the last on the block, and the road running past the patio narrowed into an unpaved footpath that vanished into an open field. Apart from the bushes and the grass, green and unaffected by the season, there was not much between the town and the mountains. Ski lifts idled above aspens, their leaves just beginning to show a tinge of yellow. Suchen could sense no trace of smoke in the air.

An old couple, sitting at a third table on the patio, were also discussing the fire, their voices loud enough to be an invitation, and the man next to Suchen wasted no time chiming in. The couple wore matching polo shirts the pale yellow of newborn chicks, and their hair had faded to a similar sandy shade. They lived two valleys north, the wife explained, where fall was already descending with all its colors, and what a beautiful season it would be if it weren't for this fire. The man eating alone expressed sympathy, and then began musing about fire control: wildfires had existed long before America—or, for that matter, the earth—was claimed by human beings, he said, and there was no point in trying to beat something that was part of nature. The old couple listened, neither agreeing with the man nor withdrawing their smiles, careful not to embarrass a stranger. Suchen looked at the slice of lemon floating among the ice cubes in her glass and blushed, as though the man were her companion. She imagined what the couple would say to each other on their drive home. A husband and wife who behaved so courteously toward the world must have ways of dealing with awkwardness like this—a subtle reference to someone similar they'd encountered, or perhaps just a benign dismissal of the man's opinions. Suchen wondered what it would be like to be understood without having to speak, the comfort of silence without the threat of misunderstanding or estrangement.

Pure greed, Lei had said, shaking his head mockingly when she had told him that this was what she had dreamed of for their marriage. Of course, he was right, Suchen had readily agreed. If a woman did not desire clothes or jewels or children, she'd said, taking up his tone, although she was the target of its mockery, she would harbor some other form of unreasonable greed, no? He did not reply but poured more wine for her, and then for himself. It was the night before his flight back to China. When they spoke again, it was about his trip, the few things he needed to pack in the morning in his carry-on, and what she should do with the clothes and other belongings he was leaving behind. What they had not talked about at their last dinner was that they would be taking the most natural and least hurtful course to becoming strangers: their marriage would no longer be on his conscience when he went with his business associates to the nightclubs and karaoke bars of Beijing, where young women blossomed under the dimmed lights, eager to be chosen. In time, he would choose a woman, not one he'd met in a nightclub but someone more companionable and trustworthy, who would not oppose the idea of having children with him, and whose greed—if she had any—would be easier for him to understand and to satisfy.

The divorce papers had arrived six months later, mailed to the cottage that Suchen had rented, not far from their old house. She had signed them at once and mailed them back. She had wondered what to do with the wedding ring—a thin, unadorned band; when they had married, sixteen years earlier, they had not been able to afford a more lavish one—and in the end she had put it in the plastic folder where she kept her passport and her green card. She had brought the folder with her, in the car trunk.

After the couple left, the man told Suchen that his name was Walter. When the waitress came with Suchen's salad, he asked for a refill of coffee. He appeared to be in his late sixties or early seventies; his hair and beard, both patchily grayed, were bushy. He had on a light-blue shirt, buttoned to the top and wrinkled by sweat—it was a warm day, and there was not much of a breeze on the patio. He was in town from Seattle for an event organized by the alumni association of his alma mater, he said; he and his wife had been invited as the top donors from their region.

Suchen stabbed at a slice of pear and wondered whether there was a death or a divorce she would learn about. But what difference did it make? A change of circumstance had led the man to eat alone at a ski resort before the first snowfall. Outside the town, there were trails to hike and rivers to fish, but those activities were for people with companions or for those with solitary souls. It was loneliness that had led him to seek a conversation on a restaurant patio long past the lunch hour, as it was loneliness that had made her empty the refrigerator in the cottage and pack her belongings into five megasized black plastic garbage bags and drop them outside a Goodwill early one morning. Suchen had left a check in the cottage to cover an extra month's rent and a note apologizing for breaking the lease. The landlady, who lived next door, was a widow in her seventies. On holidays, her children and grandchildren would visit her, their cars crowding the driveway and spilling onto the street, the lights in the house burning late into the night. Suchen wondered what the landlady would tell her children about the runaway tenant at the next Thanksgiving dinner—or perhaps the incident would have been forgotten by then, and an ad would already have brought a replacement for Suchen.

Walter asked Suchen where she was from. Los Angeles, she said, although she knew he'd meant where she was from originally. China was not an answer Suchen gave people these days; there was no point in making unnecessary connections to strangers, in discovering whose neighbors, friends, or acquaintances had travelled to her country. The last time she had been there was for her mother's funeral, eight years ago, and before that, two years earlier, for her father's. She had not kept in touch with her siblings—a brother and a sister, both younger than she—whose attitude toward her had gone from intimidation in their youth to indignation as adults.

They must have been given some explanation after the accident, as their parents had insisted on calling it, when Suchen's picture was printed in the county and province newspapers alongside the pictures of five other girls, hers the only one not framed in black. The pictures had been taken the previous year, when the girls had entered middle school, the standard one-inch black-and-white photos for school registration. Suchen's mother had immediately thrown out any newspapers that had come into their house, though Suchen later read about the incident at the town center, where newspapers were displayed in glass cases. A senseless tragedy, it was called, and she was described as a reticent and prematurely aged survivor. Her report card, which demonstrated neither excellence nor deficiency, was reprinted, a proof, along with her neighbors' comments confirming that her family was a respectable one and she a normal child, that the tragedy had been beyond any adult's ability to foresee. Information about the five other girls was given, too, but in a less detailed manner, as if the dead deserved respect rather than understanding.

Had it happened now, Suchen thought, she would have been sent to a psychologist, but the talk twenty-nine years ago had been whether she should be allowed to return to school or whether other options—a reform school, for instance, or an asylum for the disturbed—were more suitable. In the eyes of her neighbors and her schoolmates, Suchen had seen fear and awe, as if she carried a rare infectious disease, and in the end it was her family's move to another province that had ended the episode. Suchen had always wondered whether her siblings remembered their childhoods as severed because of her; their parents, after the move, had forbidden them to talk about their old home.

When Suchen asked the waitress for her check, Walter finally picked up his. The waitress gave Suchen a sympathetic look, but did not make any comment.

He had been in town for two days, Walter said as he followed Suchen into the street. The waitress's name was Antoinette, he continued, and she was from Boise, one of those kids who would never leave their home state. The manager was the niece of the owner, who lived in Colorado. Come to think of it, Walter added, it was funny that a man would choose to live in a skiing state and open a restaurant at a ski resort in another state.

At the corner, Suchen paused, waiting for Walter to step into the crosswalk first so that she could choose another direction. Walter stopped, too, and pointed at the broad, unmarked street. "See how the streets of the wild Wild West are different from the streets of your Los Angeles. Imagine a hundred, a hundred and fifty years ago: folks drove their horse carriages down this same street, and they were probably too busy to think about us."

Suchen had driven along the Pacific Coast for five days before turning inland. She had originally planned to cross the border into Vancouver, where years ago, on her first trip to North America, she'd spent an eight-hour layover on the way to Austin, Texas. She had looked up the schedules of ferries, and was certain that at this time of year night would have fallen by the time the last ferry left Horseshoe Bay. She was planning to leave her car in the parking lot, along with her suitcase and her legal papers. It would appear to be an accident at first, a woman slipping into the dark sea and never surfacing again. After a while, the police would gather the other pieces of the puzzle, the easy parts, but by then she would be beyond reach and would not be expected to explain her decision, as had been the case years earlier when, as the one who had lived, she had been made to account not only for her own survival but also for the deaths of the other five girls.

Suchen hung the "Do Not Disturb" tag on her hotel-room door and let herself out onto the balcony, where two chairs and a small table, made to look like solid wood but with less weight, fitted snugly. She imagined a vacationing couple sitting where she was now, a bottle of wine left untouched for as long as the silence lasted. She and Lei could have ended their marriage on a balcony like this—on a mild day during the snow season, their last shared memories the white mountains close by, the ski lifts moving tirelessly and smoothly uphill and downhill, and small colorful dots sliding down the slopes: actions viewed from afar. When they had first come to America, Lei had insisted that they be active in their local Chinese community. Later, when he had secured a position at an investment bank, he had pushed for a more mainstream American life. For years, Suchen had felt as though she were standing at the edge of a beach, holding a line that flew Lei into life like a kite over the sea—or was it the other way around? But even the most trustworthy hand could eventually find it difficult to keep its grip on a taut line. Suchen had continued watching from afar while couples their age began to have children, and when Lei had joined the other overseas Chinese returning to the mother country to make their fortunes, she had not accompanied him on his trips. Soon he had begun to spend more time in Beijing, flying back to Los Angeles every other month, out of some sense of duty.

An autumn breeze drove a few leaves across the street. Suchen tried to imagine this sleepy town engulfed by a raging fire, but she couldn't picture it. There were places that would never be destroyed by a fire or a tornado or an earthquake, just as there were those lucky people who escaped disasters unscathed. Once upon a time, she had been considered one of those people, by her husband and the few friends to whom she had revealed her version of the story. A boating accident, she had told Lei when he was courting her in college. A boating accident that had killed five girls age twelve and thirteen and left another feeling forever on the verge of drowning—she could see, from the look of concern and pity in his eyes, that he had interpreted her melancholy air that way. Any man who'd had a happy childhood and an uncomplicated adolescence could mistake the initial shock of encountering the senselessness of life as a sign of falling in love, the desire to protest and protect confused with a desire to love. He had been worn out by her, Lei had said toward the end of the marriage, not without bitterness. Sixteen years was a long time for anyone to endure a wife who had neither faith nor interest in the worldliness of marital life, he said, and she wondered whether, by letting her go, he had finally outgrown his youth. His next wife would certainly not stand as a trophy in the tug-of-war between Lei and fate, death, and any mystery beyond his understanding.

A man stopped on the other side of the street and waved up at Suchen. She recognized the bushy hair and the blue shirt, yet for a moment she willed her face to stay expressionless, hoping that Walter would think that he had waved at the wrong woman. But without a trace of doubt, he crossed the empty street. Would she care for a cup of coffee? he called up. From where she stood, her elbows resting on the railing three floors above, he looked, despite his gray hair and beard, like a small child waiting for permission that he was almost certain would not be granted. She would have refused him politely had they been standing together on the ground, but looking down at his upturned face, she felt that any excuse would be trivial. She signaled for him to wait, and when she entered the bedroom, the air-conditioned atmosphere made her shiver as though she had just stepped into a pool of cold water. Suchen thought of Walter wandering the strange town, searching for a friendly face on a restaurant patio or a hotel balcony, and tried to convince herself that she had agreed to the coffee because of the helplessness that an old man could not erase from his face.

Walter took her to a café at the back of a gift shop. Apart from an idle man halfheartedly flipping through a book of local attractions, there was no one in the front of the shop, where miniature carved boats and model fish aged unwanted on the shelves. At the back of the shop, dim but for a single lamp hanging from the ceiling, there were a few unvarnished wooden tables. An old man at the counter nodded in greeting when he saw Walter. It was three o'clock in the afternoon, the best time for those in the mountains to revel in the joys of hiking and fishing before the sunshine thinned into dusk, but in the shop, time seemed to be stranded, day taking forever to turn into night. The browser picked up a snow globe and shook it; when his cell phone beeped, he perked up and left abruptly. Out of reflex, Suchen fumbled in her purse and found her phone.

"Are you waiting for a call?" Walter asked.

Suchen nodded and then shook her head. For a year, when she had not yet given up trying to be the wife Lei had hoped her to be, she had let herself be absorbed into a group of women who met one Saturday a month at a local café for brunch and gossip. After a while, she began to set an alarm on her cell phone; when it rang, she would apologize for having to take an important phone call and leave. She could see the suspicion in the other women's eyes: she, a childless woman whose husband was enjoying a round of golf with their husbands—what urgency could she have but a secret love affair? If any of the women had ever mentioned this to their husbands, or if any of the husbands had mentioned it to Lei, Suchen would never know. Soon afterward, she had stopped replying to the group e-mails, and eventually the invitations had stopped coming.

The waiter came over to take their order: iced tea for Suchen, a strangely named energy drink for Walter. The waiter's face, tanned to a dark brown and deeply wrinkled, reminded Suchen of a walnut shell, yet his eyes, even in the dim light, glimmered with alertness, like the eyes of a mountain lion. He was wearing a T-shirt that was too big for his skinny body, and his hair, grayish white, was pulled up into a bun on top of his head. When he talked, his tone was unhurried. He did not chat with Walter as a waiter would with a returning customer, yet there was something in his manner that showed friendliness.

"He spent forty-plus years in India and only came back two years ago," Walter said when the man had gone back behind the counter. "Grew up in Connecticut and was a hippie for a while, but look at him now—all you see is an old sage, something this country could never produce."

Suchen wondered why the man, after spending almost a lifetime in India, had chosen to return. Once you knew a slice of someone's story, you wanted to understand more, she thought. Yet when Walter walked around town gathering other people's stories, his curiosity led him not to understand the world better but only to marvel at it.

"Are you in town just for tonight?" Walter asked.

"Yes."

"I'm leaving tomorrow, too," Walter said. "The event is this evening, but I came early to have a bit of time to myself. It's a nice place when it's not busy."

There was not much to say to this, so Suchen agreed that indeed the town was quiet and lovely.

Walter waited a moment, and then said that the hosts were a couple who produced a popular HBO show. Suchen apologized and said she did not watch TV, and Walter seemed disappointed. Not that he watched much TV either, he said, but he thought that she, being from Los Angeles, would be familiar with these things. When Suchen did not speak, he asked her where she was going.

It was the most natural question to ask a traveler. A waitress with her hair dyed purple, in a town called Fortuna, had called Suchen "honey" and asked her where she was headed; a mechanic in a coastal town, whose name Suchen had forgotten, had changed a flat tire for her and then asked, too. Vancouver, she had replied both times, and both times her questioners had seemed impressed by the distance she had travelled. She was not in a particular hurry, she had said when the waitress asked how many hours she had to put in each day. More of a road trip than seeing the city, she had replied unconvincingly when the mechanic, with a mild stutter, commented that he wouldn't care for that long of a drive, even though Vancouver was said to be a fine city. She did not tell anyone that she spent much of her time looking out at the Pacific from empty beaches, some of them narrow with coarse sand, though farther north, many of the beaches were rocky, desolate in the falling dusk, when seagulls circled hungrily and waves deposited dead seaweed. Those beaches made Suchen think of a ragged shoreline in Ireland or the clashing waves of the North Sea at the mouth of a Norwegian fjord. She did not know why she thought of these places, only that she would never have a chance to visit them, along with many other places on many other continents, to confirm or correct her imaginings. The morning before, she had decided to leave the coast, convincing herself that she wanted to drive across the Rockies and see the big sky in the western states. She would always be able to find a patch of water, she told herself, but even when she was studying the rivers and lakes in the road atlas, she knew she was procrastinating.

"Say, do you want to come with me to the event this evening?"

Suchen looked up quickly, but there did not seem to be a trace of guile in Walter's face. She didn't have the right outfit for a social gathering, Suchen said—not the best excuse, but the first to occur to her.

Walter glanced at Suchen, and she knew he wanted to say that she would look just fine in her blouse and skirt; she knew too that he could tell she was inventing an excuse. "Is there anything that's bothering you?" he asked in a gentle voice, leaning over his dark-green drink.

Travelling alone must have made her sink too easily into her own thoughts, she said.

"My wife died earlier this year," Walter said. "Leukemia. We were married for thirty-five years."

"It must be hard for you," Suchen said, looking into her iced tea. She wondered whether he had informed the townspeople he had met of his loss: the waitress at the restaurant, who was too far removed from death to be sympathetic; the old man here at the café, who, despite his kindness, would not feel sufficiently attached to this ephemeral world to acknowledge the loss as irreplaceable.

"She asked for a divorce when she knew she wouldn't live long."

"Why?" Suchen said, though as she spoke, she realized that she might already know the answer. She imagined the wife watching Walter and herself aging, waiting to endure his death, aware that the solitude afterward would be enough of a compensation. Her illness must have come as a disappointment; life had not been lenient enough to let her keep her secret. Her desire to be alone while still alive must have ultimately trumped the guilt that came from making an incomprehensible request of a husband who would soon lose his wife.

"If only I knew the answer," Walter said, his voice hoarse; but when Suchen looked up, he was studying his palms, dry eyed. On his ring finger was a wedding band, aged though not dulled. "My children told me that sometimes illness makes people act strangely."

"Did you agree to divorce her?"

"No," he said, his tone defensive. "How could I?"

"I thought that was what she wanted."

She had asked twice in one week, Walter said, but when he had said no both times, she had not mentioned it again.

Why dwell on a minor episode when death was the more lasting tragedy, Suchen wanted to ask, although she knew that long after he accepted his wife's death, he would remain tormented by her request for a divorce. When the dead departed, they took away any falsehoods that they might have allowed us to believe while alive; we who are left behind have to embark on a different life, since the dead are no longer here to help us deceive ourselves. Suchen had often wondered how she and the five girls would have turned out if the others had not drowned. They would have drifted apart, she suspected, becoming wives and mothers, and if they had ever reunited, they would have been too occupied with their earthly duties to let the memory of their scheme surface. Yet through their absence, the girls had made themselves more present than anyone else in Suchen's world, and she had lived not only for herself but also for their unconsumed lives: when she sat in a movie theatre on a weekday afternoon, the tears she shed were not for the romance on the screen but for a love story that might have broken the heart of one of the girls; when she reluctantly mingled with strangers at a party, she was convincing the girls that they had not missed much in this life; at the farmers' market, she picked up fruits with exotic names and fragrances because the girls had not heard of or tasted them in their small hometown; when she was having sex with Lei, she watched them watch him with pity in their eyes, because only they knew that he would never be able to touch her the way their deaths had touched her. "You should feel lucky you are the one alive," Suchen said. "There are many things in life that are stranger than death."

Walter looked up, stung, Suchen thought, by the cruelty of her words. She unfolded her white paper napkin and began to dab her straw on it, leaving faint tea-colored dots. "When I was thirteen, five friends and I decided to commit suicide together," she said, and without meeting Walter's eyes, she shook her head. "You want to ask why. Everyone did. The truth is I could not answer that question at the time and I still can't answer it. All I can tell you is that it was not an impulsive action. We talked and we planned and we carried it out almost to the end."

Almost: Suchen watched Walter flinch at the word and then let hope flicker in his eyes. A scheme like theirs could have failed easily. They could have stopped it at any moment: when they had looked in the almanac to choose the date (there was no day described as good for killing oneself, so they had settled for a day on which it was good to take a journey). Or when they had pooled their allowances to buy an expensive bottle of liquor and hidden it in the tall weeds on the far shore of the reservoir the day before the chosen date. The field had been awash with May sunshine when they set out after lunch, their schoolmates returning to classes while they, buoyant in their truancy, gathered nameless blue and white flowers that they later scattered carelessly near the dock. An adult bicycling on his way out of town could have yelled at them from the road, asking why they were not in school. Uncle Liang, the town's hermit, who lived in a shack by the reservoir, could have woken from his midday nap early and caught the young thieves clumsily rowing his boat into the open water.

They had taken turns rowing in pairs until they were out of immediate sight of the town and the road, and when they stopped, the boat rocked slightly under their shifting weight, the water almost even with the rim. For a while they sat, and Suchen remembered the splash of a fish breaking the surface of the water, and two egrets taking off with unhurried elegance, one after the other. The girls could have decided to row back and face the questions from their parents and teachers, spending an extra Saturday afternoon in school for their misdemeanor; such a possibility, however, had not occurred to Suchen, and if any of the other girls had thought of it, they hadn't brought it up. They had giggled as they divided the liquor among six identical enamel cups, their school registration numbers printed in red on the bottoms, and when they had encouraged one another to drink, they'd done so with laughter and coughing and, later, tears. Why, her parents had asked her when it was all over; so had the parents of the five girls, wishing her dead, no doubt, so that their own daughters could be revived; the schoolteachers and the reporters had asked, and now, too, sitting across from her, a man whom she barely knew. "Why?" Walter said, his voice faraway, as if coming to her in a dream. "What happened?"

"The other five girls drowned," Suchen said. She did not say that none of them had known how to swim; nor did she say that after they had swallowed the liquor, they had cried, not out of fear or regret but because there was nothing left, by then, for them to do. When they had stepped into the water, the boat had overturned, and the chaos afterward seemed to last only a few seconds—not much of a chaos, because Suchen did not remember any of her friends making a noise or struggling. For years, she had tried in vain to make sense of that moment of farewell, but all she could recall was two heads bobbing before vanishing under the boat, the linked arms of two other friends, and a wave from Meimei, the youngest of the six, as she sank beneath the surface. Suchen never understood what had driven her to grasp the oar at the last moment. The water had been cold, her teeth had chattered, but her hands had not let go of the oar—perhaps she had been a true coward, or perhaps she had been overcome by animal instinct, hanging on to life blindly. We had to, she had replied when her questioners would not leave her alone, although no one had understood her. At the border of life and death, said a folktale, there was a river called the River of Forgetting, and on the bridge an old woman called Mrs. Dream offered tea to travelers; once you drank her tea and crossed the bridge, you would forget everything on this side of the world. Many times, in the five weeks during which their talk had gone from a hazy idea to a concrete plan, they had promised one another that they would not drink Mrs. Dream's tea. They would travel together in the next world as they had in this world, their love and understanding of one another free from families and other earthly burdens.

"But why? Why did six young girls want to do a crazy thing like that?" Walter said, the gentle concern in his eyes replaced by an angry and disapproving look.

"If only I knew the answer," Suchen said. Afterward, while the girls' parents and teachers groped for any possible explanation—divorced parents for one of the girls; an older sister's failed affair that had ended with the birth of an illegitimate baby; difficult schoolwork; the unhealthy influence of cheap romance novels; hormones and adolescent mood swings—Suchen had remained contemptuously silent, the last warrior standing between the world and her felled comrades.

Walter fidgeted in his seat, unable to find the right words for his curiosity— or perhaps he was simply eager to end the conversation. People would have shaken their heads in pity had one young girl decided to kill herself, but when six girls took a journey like that together, people felt threatened and rejected by a bond they could not understand. Suchen imagined what Lei would have said had she told him the truth; over the years, she had thought of making the confession, thinking that a man who shared his life with her deserved more than a lie, more than silence. But how could she have explained to him that she had never guessed the meaning of Meimei's wave, that she would never know if Meimei had been beckoning her to come along on a joyous journey or begging her, the last one afloat, to save her? Lei had insisted that a new life in a new country—marriage, friendship, children—would save her from her despair, but why would she want to be saved when her friends and their memories would become the casualties of her battle to live on?

Suchen looked up at the afternoon sunshine, framed by the rectangular door, waiting to claim Walter and herself. Perhaps Walter would invite her once more to join him for the evening; perhaps she would say yes, another procrastination, like the detour from the coast. When they parted, both would feel vaguely comforted, he by the momentary warmth he had offered another human being whose senseless tragedy had eclipsed his bewilderment, she by the knowledge that it had been good of her to let Lei go, that he would not become an old man seeking companionship among the strangers in the world.

HORN HUNTER

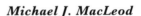

Michael J. MacLeod

ardin Graves shot his first deer just before his seventh birthday. His old man held the rifle across one knee and said pick a doe and put it right behind her shoulder.

"What does a doe look like?" the boy asked.

"They have big ears."

"I see one with *huge* ears."

"Then shoot it."

Hardin hit the doe behind the shoulder, but to be both precise and accurate it was a fawn shot in the buttocks. The boy was so embarrassed that he practiced on gophers all the next summer with his new .243 bolt action. That fall Dad missed a nice four-by-four whitetail buck at 350 yards twice. Hardin shot it dead.

Over the next five years the boy killed a dozen deer using his father's tags.

Friends said you're creating a monster Gravey Graves.

At twelve the boy was legal to hunt elk, and though men of the valley struggled to "get their elk" year after year like some beauty contestants come with guns, he took a calf just days after his birthday on a morning of minus five and hasn't missed a year since.

Hardin took up bow hunting at fourteen. Since he made good marks, Mom allowed some truancy. He and Justin showed up with some alleged notes from Mom, but when the desk lady called, Mom always said yes she had. In those days, nobody cared that they had bows and rifles and ammunition in the white Blazer parked in the school lot, not in Belgrade, Montana. He killed his first moose that year.

Then in the spring, he and his dad drove to the Elkhorn Mountains to find elk antlers shed the previous winter. Elk sheds. It was a new sport. Antlers just lying on the ground. To Hardin it was the goldfields. His dad bought new tires for the Blazer with $800 won gambling. Hardin and Justin began hunting elk sheds in earnest, not missing a single spring weekend. At nineteen, Hardin earned $1,482 from the horns he'd collected, sold to some middleman who sold them to the Chinese for better luck in the sack. There was lots of beer in those days, and motorcycles, "hicked up" buddies with pistols, and a bachelor camper for extended stays at trailheads. The old men acquired Gore-Tex and competed with Hardin and his buddies for the biggest and the most horns, youth and vigor versus old age and treachery. More and more, horn hunting took the boys into the heart of grizzly country, and Justin carried more beer and ever-larger canons into the woods until the weight and the alcohol and the bears killed his interest altogether.

"All you want to do is find them horns. You don't even want to kill any more," Justin told Hardin.

It was true, Hardin had begun recording his horn-hunting efforts on ROTC calendars from high school, how far he hiked, how many horns, how deep the snow, how high up, what cover, what position, what nearby. He took pictures of every horn he found as it lay and filled scrapbooks like tiles of Bible text. He took pictures of all the new country he'd seen and studied the pictures for potential horn hunting. Why elk do what they do gave way to why horns lay where they lay.

He bought a black Lab and taught her to wind horns.

"Them chipmunks want to eat the horns," he told the dog. "We've got to save 'em all, big and small."

Scarlett could wind a horn at two hundred yards. She preferred to find deer horns because she could carry them in her jaws. Raghorns she could drag, but larger horns she just sat next to and waited for Hardin with the frame pack.

When he drove through Yellowstone to the antler auction in Jackson Hole, park rangers knew and watched his truck, and just to addle them sometimes Hardin would horn hunt in the park and leave only with photos and that was worse for the rangers in many ways.

Private land was sometimes fair game, especially the big ranches where elk sheds were poorly picked and left to rot and feed rodents. Anger at such waste Hardin could barely hold down, and the guards on those ranches knew his truck, too.

When Hardin got to college, he plotted important dates, tests, and papers on his ROTC calendars, but he forgot to tally the number of days he'd missed. It so happened that he'd missed three weeks one spring, and the school kicked him out. A cowboy school even. That gave him more time to horn hunt. He started to smoke.

There is a place on the Rocky Mountain Front where nature has forsaken the mezzanine altogether, and in that jarring articulation from prairie to peak it is not uncommon to find both prickly pear and grizzly bears at once. To this country Hardin and his buddies went bow hunting for elk one autumn. Hardin had already shot his elk, he was along just to see shit die, so he said.

"I ain't going out with you. You'll just go someplace to find horns," was the common complaint.

Fuzz had been there before. He was hungry for his first bow kill. Rigby liked to hunt by himself, even long-legged Colby didn't like trying to keep up all day. Colby used to go with him, then just Colby's dog. Hardin was a large young man, and though he held fresh memory of Dad's hunting buddy Tommy calling a fat youngster the Poppin' Fresh Doughboy, there wasn't nobody could keep up with him nowadays, even with the smoking. Twenty miles was nothing for him day after day.

"Fine. I'll go by myself."

He usually did anyway.

"Hardin, you walk too far and you'll find yourself in the corn rows of North Dakota," Colby said.

Fuzz said whoa at the thought of that. "Hardin's never even been on a plane let alone left Montana. Mama's milk, ain't that right Hardin?"

"That ain't true."

"Disneyland don't count, you jagoff."

"Don't you have any goals other than finding horns and living with your parents 'til thirty?" Rig asked. Rigby worked for his uncle on a construction crew that sometimes went out of state, what felt to the others like some kind of deployment to be awed.

Hardin said to himself where's the crime in liking your parents. Living with the folks to twenty-five was in fact a goal, so he could stay in the valley, buy a place someday, be near them. Where's the crime?

"You've never had a lick of bad luck or hardship what your parents don't fix," Colby said. "Everybody knows old Gravey Graves takes care of his kids."

"Borrowing money from your mom."

"All your rifles are your dad's."

Hardin didn't say it, but what people called the pink elephant in camp was the fathers who hadn't been called to table, the one who died when Fuzz was fifteen, the one who broke Justin's jaw, the two who left Bud and his mom and sister before the third one stayed. Fools will fool themselves. This talk irritated Hardin only when his girlfriend said a little hard luck would do him good.

Early morning, he set off from a camp they'd made at the base of a mountainside with steep cliffs, headlands to a prairie that ended somewhere in Iowa. Day was just breaking, and Hardin saw it as like being under a great stone and some giant come along and lifted just the edge like he were looking for snakes or humans, and one bright crack of light shot through you could barely look at with your slit-eyes. He thought about these things. He could think like a snake.

The prairie was flat as glass. He was searching for mule deer antlers, and he wished he had Scarlett along. After some time, he stopped for a smoke. His long bent fingers working the flint, covering his eyes, tapping the ash, scratching. This is dumb, he thought. Ain't no cover for mulies. Nowhere. He headed north parallel to the mountains, not because he saw a break or a hill, but this way when he turned west he'd hit the mountains close to a winter range that was sure to hold ores of elk sheds.

He spied an odd shadow on the land, long and thin, inumbrate only of itself for there were no trees, not even one. As he approached, four mule deer bounded from a hole in the ground, does and fawns. The hole was like a coulee with no outlet, some alchemed crater of prairieland, a limestone drain hole, he didn't know. He was curious.

He kept walking. After a while, he had his theories. Meteors, hit so hard they closed in behind themselves and left these pocks, like when skin heals with a divot from some invasive trauma as with bad acne. His uncle had some. He saw another dark line on the prairie. From this hole he counted ten fleeing mule deer, one of which was a nice four-point buck. The next hole held seventeen, and he suspected the next would hold some thirty.

There were thirty-two. Gushing like the Yellowstone mud pots blowing clay deer. As does and fawns and buck deer scrambled up the powdered sides, over his head a golden eagle sailed in on great broad wings and sank its talons into the least, a small fawn, bleating, twisting, and finally falling to the deck. The eagle made some hasty aerobatic stall and was back after the fawn now fleeing pell-mell into the pit. Pull up or crash, Hardin thought. The eagle pulled up, shied from the man, and flapped away toward the mountains like that's what it'd been intending all along.

Hardin caught movement in the rocks below him. A raggedy bobcat was putting the sneak on the same luckless fawn. It was a haggard old cat, and Hardin wasn't about to let him take the fawn after all that. He picked up a chunk of earth and tossed it at the cat's head, but the cat shifted and continued its stalk. He winged a rock, and another. Hardin was beside himself. He was a better shot than that. All that basketball at the college. Some ten rocks and no hits. Meanwhile the many deer had themselves come to the fawn's rescue, herded around it and swept it up and over the rim.

Hardin smiled all the way to the mountain. There was much to consider, the craters, the deer—where did they water? The protective herding beyond the social aspect, and the unlucky eagle that flew off to these mountains. Where was he? More probably a she it was so big. He thought about these things as he climbed into open ponderosa park, and then he found his first antlers, a matched set of massive seven-point elk browns—last year's horns.

"Bingo!" He lifted one out of a sage bush. "Holy moley," he laughed. Each a ten-pounder. He strapped them to his frame pack and continued up the mountain. There would be a triumphal entry into camp tonight. You just wait. *No goals.* Rig could cram it. Holy moley.

An elk bugle stopped Hardin dead. Immediately in his head was the bull that carried these horns last year, and he almost dropped in a hot flash. The elk screamed again, grunted and screamed. Hardin stumbled up the hill to the fringe of an old fir forest.

He listened, breathing too hard to smoke. There were two bulls. He crept into the undergrowth, careful not to step on the rattle-dry leaves of arrowroot and cornflower. Antlers were cracking. What commotion now. He closed, he saw horn tips, he heard their heavy panted breath. The ground beneath them. Saplings like ragdolls. He peeked through.

They were giants, battled and gored, ripping the earth, stinking with urine and musk, but before Hardin could count their tines, a ruffling caught his eye off left. Bright green pine boughs swishing, and then the big ovoid face of a grizzly bear. It was the breath, a hot and fetid meat scavenger's flatus that sent Hardin scaling the nearest tree. Hardin didn't remember climbing, he was just in the tree, and the bear was below him, a terrifying effluvium of rushing brute, breathing, pacing and lunging with snapping teeth, and each time the bear hove to, his tree swayed a little more, and the bear didn't stop.

He was up higher. The bear bit the abandoned pack frame and flung it well beyond the clearing where the elk had been, now gone. The bear rushed the tree. It shook like a blending carrot, top aflurry. He moved lower, afraid of some doomsday leverage. To his good fortune, the roots had given up what play they had and now had a talon's grip on the slope.

Hardin couldn't figure this bear out. There were no cubs to defend. He thought he'd seen the stub of a pecker. He wasn't angry at the bear. Hardin rarely got angry at anyone. Fuzz was always trying to get his goat with some unprovoked raillery, but Hardin understood that was the point and couldn't even force himself to be riled. He wished that bear would go away.

After a while a cool wind blew through the treetops. The shadows held only bad news. The bear had moved off in some over-swaggered ruseful gait, but of a sudden, he was behind the tree again with those Pleistocene eyes, panting like some obese retriever on the first day of duck season. Again he moved off, and Hardin watched keen-eyed from the fastness of his perch. In a clump of brushy saplings, the bear had grabbed hold of some object. Muscles rippled along its bulbous shoulders, a tugging.

"I'll be a—"

The sword of a great bony crown swung over the bear's head and nodded with the bear's feeding. It was the antlers of the monarch whose year-olds were strapped to Hardin's frame pack. Unmistakable. No wonder the bear had treed him.

"Son-of-a—" he whispered.

Hardin wanted those horns like he'd never wanted anything. Yet the specter of bear and darkness was so close he could feel them in his teeth. There was nothing to throw, and even if he could, it would only enrage the bear.

The bone saw was in his pack. While the grizzly's face was buried in car-rion, he could sneak down, run for it, and climb another tree. No, this tree was a good tree with good roots. Perhaps the bear would soon be full and need a nap. Better yet, perhaps the carcass was nearly consumed. Hardin decided to wait and see, and when, a moment later, he realized there really was no choice, he felt like he'd just won some prize he had not signed up for.

With the crepuscular twilight the bear faded into the forest. Hardin was not surprised. He knew bears like he knew anything you could shoot. He didn't expect tricks this time. That bear had to be full of elk meat. Yet with reluctance he let go of the last branch and dropped to the ground. He wait-ed. He knew how long animals waited, and he waited longer. Convinced the bear was gone, he retrieved his buckled frame pack with the antlers.

From a pouch he took his bone saw and headlamp. He looked at the empty bear-spray holster. He'd loaned it to Fuzz on account of his heading into the prairie.

"Real bright, Graves," he muttered.

He scanned his surrounds one last time and then marched purposefully to the carcass, sawed off the grisly skulltop and seven-by-seven rack, strapped it to his bent pack frame, and made haste into the dark forest. A grouse blew up at his feet and sent him toppling backward downslope directly on the bear's outbound tracks. He knew this without actually seeing the tracks. He squirmed and clawed at the air, and in his mind he saw himself as some mutant flightless beetle sprawled on its back flailing toward the nameless oblivion of upended insects and turtles, and that settled him down. He kicked his feet hard over his head, and the whole mass of man and antlers tumbled over and popped up just like a beetle.

Hardin kept to the most open forest for visibility and berth for the broad rack strapped upside down on his back. More than once he was jolted by unforgiving trunks of trees and spidery alder limbs. Twice he stopped to study his backtrail, holding cigarette smoke in his lungs until it burned. He smoked to the filter five times in less than a mile, and even when he was certain that camp was just ahead, he couldn't shake the feeling of being followed.

At last he felt a void before him, and in the starry dark, he held fast to a sticky subalpine fir and peered over the lip. Cliffed out. He had traversed too high. Some three hundred feet below, Hardin saw a pulsing campfire and blue halo glow of an electric lantern. He was too worn to backtrack. He groaned and bent to, picking a path through crenellated rocks. Shale slid, he grabbed a root and watched the rocks and the dust and listened for the inevitable clinking far below.

The antler tines dug at the slope and nearly sent him sprawling headlong into the blackness. He gasped and turned white-faced to the mountain, continued down. He stopped for a much-needed smoke and to consider the situation. It wasn't too late to climb back up and around.

"Grave Grave Graves," he prattled.

Hardin found what looked to be a sheep trail and traversed to a barren rock chute, a natural chimney that he was able to descend with ease, and he felt quick and smart, and for the first time since climbing the tree, he started running through this remarkable day with Fuzz and Rigby and Colby in a pre-telling of his story, a trial run. What he did and what all hunters do on a walkout regardless of what happened. To decide what happened, how the telling of it would go. And it dawned on him the utter stupidity of taking these horns from the bear's dead elk. That his buddies would see it less an act of bravery than depravity, a sickness for horns taken too far. Because he was so far ahead of them. They did not understand him. Mama's boys don't do this crazy shit. He was a horn genius.

Soon the chimney petered out into a broad fan of igneous scree that tore at his hands and boots, and some cascaded down the cliff beneath him like cinders from a firebucket.

Another precipice, another smoke. A rock clattered to the side, and immediately he thought he might be killed from above by his own latent avalanche. Another rock smacked just below him, and then lights flashed in his face.

"A bear!" somebody yelled. More rocks pelted his position. He panicked.

"I'm not a bear!" he yelled. "It's me, Hardin!"

The rocks kept coming.

"It's me! Don't shoot!"

"It's a bear!"

"No it ain't!"

"Yes it is!"

"It's a bear with a flashlight and a cigarette! Shoot him!"

"Don't shoot!"

Hardin flushed. The boys were laughing hysterically.

"Get down here you knucklehead. Supper's almost gone." It was Fuzz.

"I'm stuck."

He heard muffled talk, and then Colby hollered, "We're sending food up to you."

An apple exploded to his left.

"You guys are assholes."

They were talking again. Two lights returned to the fire.

"What the hell are you doing up there, you dumb Mexican?" Only Fuzz called people Mexicans because only Fuzz worked as hard as one.

Hardin was already shimmying down the flotsam of some wrecked patch of forest slid long ago. He thought if he could just ease out onto this old pine without snapping it, he might be able to drop the last twenty feet to the ground without breaking anything.

"Help me get this pack down."

He didn't tell about the horns. He'd let the mammoth antlers introduce themselves at the table, and he would bask in their shock and awe.

Hardin had a theory about horns and horn hunting, and it goes something like this. Pound for pound, it takes as long to find forty whitetail basket racks as it does to find one magnificent elk matched set. Big horns take a long time to grow and a long time to find. Time is money. Money is wealth. Big horns are big wealth, but so are many small ones. Never leave a horn behind. He wished he could tell somebody that.

There's more to life than horns, of course. There's memories, for instance. In an unfinished basement hung and stacked on bare studs are some six hundred pounds of elk and deer antlers from the past few years that will be sold only when there's no more room. Scarlett can't take being down there, sot in a wine barrel. Hardin's daughter only gums them, and his young wife puts up with it all, though when asked about his frequent absences she'll tell you it's like vacation to have him out of the house.

To Hardin it's something different. Big and small, he can say where he found nearly every antler, the browns, the ivories, the bone-bleached and cracking partials, the heavy-tined truncheons, the raghorns, and single spikes—even the rodent-gnawed—and if that ain't enough, he can show you where. Somewhere near home in southwest Montana. He ain't really saying where. And don't even bother stealing through his notebooks because all the locations are written in a code even his daddy don't understand even though it was his fault originally.

They told old Gravey Graves he was making some kind of monster. They said who knows what will come of this boy—said with some collective vision of a great meat locker stocked with the carcasses of most of the valley's wild game hung by their hocks in the Graves' basement on Alder Street, but his wife says he could have done worse. She signed the notes, she said, so really they made their son together.

WHAT YOU DO OUT HERE,
WHEN YOU'RE ALONE

Philipp Meyer

ax had a name for what had happened to his son: the Accident, he called it. He wondered if his wife had her own name for it, though it wouldn't be the same, because she didn't think of it as an accident.

For the first few days, they had cried almost constantly. They had made love constantly as well, more than they had in the entire year previous, which seemed surprising to Max but also correct, and he had begun to wonder, guiltily, if Lilli might come back to him.

At this moment, he was lying on the floor next to the couch. Ligne Roset, picked by his wife, just like the other furniture. He was on the floor because he did not feel like taking off his shoes, though of course Lilli would not have known. She had disappeared somewhere—it was Sunday and they were both off work; Sunday and their entire future was in question; Sunday and Lilli had left without leaving a note. The previous Christmas, Max's brothers had sat him down and told him what they thought of her. An intervention, they'd said. He'd defended her, he was used to doing so, but meanwhile, at this moment, Lilli was nowhere to be found.

Before they moved to the Oaks, Lilli was the sort of person who didn't appear to care what anyone thought of her, was always joking at her own expense—about growing up in a trailer, about how you'd better not turn your back or she'd steal your TV. In Huntsville they'd made quite the couple, he the owner of the Porsche shop on the Speed Channel, she the loud, funny, slightly outrageous wife.

After they moved to the Oaks, she'd changed her hair, got a Martha Stewart wardrobe, and stopped cursing overnight. Max, meanwhile, remained himself. With the result that they were not exactly snubbed, but they were not invited to parties, either. Max did not care about this.

He knew he had to get up. It had been three weeks since the Accident, and there was a lot to be done: bills, the mortgage; it had been raining steadily and the lawn was returning to nature. The sun was coming through the big windows. He felt slightly drowsy and his back hurt, but that was just from lying on the floor. He was a small man, and fit; his body had not changed much since his youth, his hair was thick and his arms stronger than they looked, and it seemed to him that, in the past few years, other people had finally begun to see him the way he had always seen himself. The women who came to the shop would leave him presents—bottles of wine, invitations to come hunting on their husbands' ranches.

As for the shop, it was always busy. They serviced Porsches, mostly; they did frame-off restorations, setups for the track. Max was the best Porsche mechanic in Texas, the entire Southwest, if he was honest—he could sense what was wrong with a car before the factory computer did. He'd worked for a series of dealerships before opening his own shop, ten years ago, at the age of thirty-one. At thirty-three, he was making appearances on TNN and the Speed Channel. At thirty-seven, he'd been talked into buying this house.

Which was too big, for one. He had never thought he would say that about a house, but it was true—it made you feel exposed. He had got it for half the asking price, as it was widely considered the least desirable home in the community (no pool, the lot an awkward wedge shape), and, while Lilli had planned on lots of entertaining with their new neighbors, hardly anyone ever visited except their old friends from Huntsville, who drove the hour to see them. So far as people in the Oaks were concerned, all Huntsville had going for it was the state prison and its death chamber.

He had been on the floor all morning—Brazilian cherry—and he knew that if he did not get up now he would end up spending the day like this. Which was fine. Something had changed since the Accident. Something was trying to communicate with him. He felt it in every molecule of air, in every sip of water, even in the sore muscles in his back: you are alive. The longing for his wife, the shock at the near loss of his son, had all been submerged under that simple, insistent fact; he might have been a man lost at sea who has woken to discover that a wind has blown him ashore, an Arctic wanderer stunned by the onset of spring.

But there was plenty to do. The lawn, for instance, which had not been mowed in three weeks; any minute now a neighbor would report them. It was not a small offense in the Oaks, and to say he hated it here . . . No, it was just that he had never wanted to buy this house. In the first place, it was too expensive; in the second, it was in a community of lawyers and oilmen. You could be sued for painting your mailbox the wrong color, for putting up the wrong fence, for installation of unapproved roofing materials. And for a three-week-old lawn—he didn't know. There was probably a firing squad, all-volunteer.

They'd heard about the Oaks from Lilli's boss at Goliad Associates, the hedge fund. Lilli ran their office. The Oaks was a new development, designed by an architect, and Max thought the houses bore a resemblance to storage buildings—flat metal roofs, cement walls. Of course, there were also floor-to-ceiling windows and various decks and balconies. Frank Lloyd Wright is what people said, and Max guessed there was some beauty in it, maybe in the way the houses contrasted with the tall pines the developer had left standing. Or maybe it was just a case of the emperor's new clothes. Meanwhile, Lilli and all the other neighbors collected *Dwell* and *Architectural Digest*, and sometimes driving along the streets at night you saw things through those tall windows that you were not supposed to see: Buck Hooper touching himself in front of the pay-per-view; Jeanne Winston throwing a Bottega goblet at her much younger husband; Clyde McCay, who owned an island off Mexico, having a long visit with the commode.

But those things were all distractions. At some point, they would bring his son home, and there were big decisions to be made, though he would have to make them on his own; he could not depend on Lilli. He stood up quickly and did a lap of the first floor—living room, den, kitchen, garden room. It was very modern; it was all the same big room, really, big and white and open, no nooks or crannies, filled with the expensive furniture they'd bought to go with the house, artsy leather couches, chairs, side tables. Everything had an intentional look. He stopped by the windows overlooking the back-yard and saw a neighbor sunbathing on her deck. He wanted to linger and watch, but after a minute he made himself go back into the living room.

He considered turning on the radio; his son always left music playing, even when he wasn't home, its presence in the house like the buzzing of insects. There are parts of his mind that are dark—that was how the doctor had put it. It will take time before he recovers, he'd said. Meaning months, possibly years. Harley was in an induced coma, the bones of his skull still knitting, his brain just beginning to repair itself. In the scope of Harley's life, the doctor had told them, this will seem like a very slight interruption, and Lilli, of course, had been furious. She had wanted to sue the doctor for saying that; she wanted things to go back to the way they had been. Pure impossibility. It was only Max, in his heightened state, who understood how right the doctor was.

Back in Huntsville, Harley had not exactly been popular but he'd had enough friends, he had been ensconced at the top of his class; at thirteen he was already planning to go to Rice when he graduated. Moving to Houston, to the Oaks, had thrown him off-kilter. Just as it had Max. Harley had ended up with the goths, teenagers who wore their clothing stuck with safety pins and white makeup on their faces. Most likely, that was when he'd got into drugs. Max was just speculating. Until quite recently, until the Accident, Lilli had done a good job of hiding their son's problems, taking him to a therapist that Max had known nothing about.

It didn't matter. There was work to be done. He would mow the lawn—he was the only one on the block who did his own yard work. From his deck, he could see out over the other homes in the development, the pines swaying above them. He could see the Welches' kids playing behind their fence at the near end of the yard, and at the far end he could hear Joy Halloran—the sunbather—laughing about something into her phone. She was thirty-eight and separated. She was one of the few people Max liked in the Oaks—she was comfortable with herself. She smiled a lot, but you got the feeling that she might be smiling even if you weren't there. Lilli despised her. The former trophy wife—that was what Lilli called her.

Joy noticed Max crossing the yard and waved to him.

"Morning, sunshine," she called down.

"Morning," he called back.

She put her phone away and leaned over the steel railing to talk. From her position on the deck she was ten feet higher than he was, her black hair wet from the shower, wearing her bathrobe loosely over a swimsuit; he could see the tan lines around her collarbones, the freckles on her nose. He wondered if she had heard about Harley, but of course she would have—the news had gone all over the neighborhood.

"How are you guys holding up?" she said.

"Fine, I guess."

"If you want a drink, I was thinking I'd make a batch of mojitos. Kill the day in proper style."

He wondered if he ought to make up some excuse about Lilli, but then Joy said, "I ran into Lilli this morning. She was with Tom Stockton—they said they were going to the river."

"I wondered where she'd gone," he said.

"Judy was with them, of course."

"Of course."

She pulled her bathrobe around her. "You're a good man, Maxwell. I'm sorry as hell about what happened."

"He'll be fine," Max told her. "It's just going to take a little while."

"He's a brave kid," she said.

Max had gone into Joy's house once, when Lilli wasn't home. They'd had a few drinks, and he'd admitted to her that Lilli was only the second person he'd ever slept with. He'd expected something to happen, and he guessed Joy had, too, but he hadn't been able to initiate it. She had seemed a little hurt, but then she had forgiven him, maybe even respected him for it.

"I've been thinking a lot," he told her. "I've been getting this feeling I ought to move away and just start my life over."

"Why not," she said. This was how they talked.

"That's the conclusion I've come to."

"I think you should."

He grinned and they looked at each other.

"Anyway," she said, after a minute, "come over anytime. You don't have to knock."

"I will," he said.

"I'll keep reminding you."

His throat got tight, and everything inside him began to feel warmer. "I better get mowing."

Joy smiled and cracked an imaginary whip at him before walking off the deck into her bedroom.

All around Max, the grass was lush and nearly shin-high, the sound of the Welches' kids drifting over the fence. He ought to be jumping the pickets to Joy's house right now. Instead, he made himself cross the lawn to his woodshop, where he kept the mower and gardening tools. He had not been in there since the Accident, and the order of it all, the way there was a space for everything—saws, clippers, trimmers, all outlined in marker on pegboard—almost made him cry. He was embarrassed—Joy knew, everyone knew, how badly Lilli treated him. Knew how long he had put up with it. It seemed like a miracle, or maybe a curse, that since the age of twenty he had only slept with one person. There had never seemed to be any hurry. He was not enough of a risk taker. That was what his brothers had always told him.

He pushed the mower out to inspect his lawn. It was a sunny day with a few big white clouds, the skyline of Houston visible ten miles away. With the grass so tall, the mowing would not be easy, but it was a fine time to be out. He was about to start the machine when something caught his eye. There were bees everywhere and flowers, thousands of them. Some sort of purple-and-white wildflower. He knelt down to examine them and was again filled with emotion—this was just what he'd been thinking, there was life everywhere. The universe in a handful of dirt. These flowers had lived here forever, but he'd never known it. He'd been cutting them down since the day he moved in.

He was certain that Lilli had not noticed the flowers either, just the over-grown lawn. Things had been bad for a year, he figured. But that was not even true. Things had gone bad the minute they moved there. She had be-come embarrassed by him. If you do wear a T-shirt in public, she said, you definitely shouldn't tuck it in. And you shouldn't wear those jeans. Or your running shoes. He had allowed her to buy him new clothes, but it did not seem to matter how many times he gave in. There had never been real equal-ity; he had never been the decision-maker. He looked at the lawn and all the color—their yard was a sea of flowers. Forget-me-nots? Spiderwort? The fact that he didn't know, that he could not identify this tiny flower, felt like a crime against himself. Against everything that was good. He would never cut them down.

Of course, there were practicalities. Any day now, they'd be reported to the community association. Lilli would be furious, yet she should have been here to see these flowers, which had come from nowhere. He pushed the mower back into the woodshop, then unscrewed the sparkplug, and hid it in a jar of screws. Max Callahan: protector of flowers.

Meanwhile, his wife was out with Tom and Judy Stockton—his least fa-vorite people in the development, a serious accomplishment given the com-petition. Tom Stockton had a pair of 1960s Corvettes that he told everyone he'd restored himself, but one look around his garage and you knew—there was not a single toolbox. That was the problem with most of the men who lived here—despite their pride at being Texans, they'd grown up in cities, worked in office buildings, and, truth be told, they had more in common with people from New York than they did with their own parents.

Max remembered again where he was, standing in his yard. Joy Halloran was back on her deck, talking into her phone, the sun directly behind her. She had taken off her robe, and for a moment it looked like she was wearing nothing at all; she looked like something nature itself was offering him. He lost awareness of everything but her—if she would just make a gesture he would go to her, but she was distracted by her phone call, and she stepped back suddenly from the railing and disappeared from sight.

He knew that he was in a fragile state, but, at the loss of her, he had the brief feeling that he had left his body, a sense of such overwhelming despair that he wanted to obliterate himself from the earth. If he could only summon the energy, he would walk out of the yard, past the gates and into the traffic on the highway. Instead, he sat down in the flowers, which came nearly to his chest now. He was aware of his own heart, wearing itself down to extinction. The End—he had always known what it would look like. Things would simply get dark, a ring of blackness closing around you; he had seen it happen to his father. He eased himself down onto his back. From the ground, he could see only the pine trees bordering the yard, the very blue sky with the fat clouds of a nearly pure whiteness. He wondered if he was dying, if his heart was about to stop, but after some period of time he began to feel settled again, returned to his body. Of course he was not dying. It was the opposite: he was alive. Lying in a bed of flowers. And, Christ, the sky and those clouds: he ought to be up there among them, an actual pilot. He ought to have been a pilot in Alaska, flying a small plane just big enough for one, a vast wilderness beneath him.

His mind was moving quickly now. Their old neighbors in Huntsville were selling their house—five acres in the Piney Woods, close to Max's brothers, a small house but well kept. If he and Lilli sold their place here, even in this market, they could buy the Huntsville one for cash; they'd have no payments except taxes. He could sell the shop—business was steady, but he'd been bored with it for years, bored with being in charge. He had not laid hands on a car in months, there was so much to do in the office. He could sell the shop and this house and have breathing room to figure out exactly how they would adjust to their new situation. When Harley was better—anywhere from six months to several years from now, according to the doctor—Max would turn the house over to him and begin his journey.

Lilli stayed out with the Stocktons all day, and Max turned in early. He was barely aware of her coming to bed. Later that night a noise woke him, and he thought, It's just Harley coming in, and then he heard another noise and woke up all the way.

Lilli was lying on her side with her back to him, and he reached and touched her hip lightly. She was small and delicate; she looked like a pixie, like something from the movies. Even now, at forty-two, she seemed to glow in the dim light. She didn't pull away from him, and he stayed there with his hand like that, looking at the curve from her shoulder to her small waist and up to her hip, aware of the feeling of her not pulling away. Put all your weight on me. That was what she used to say to him, but she hadn't said it in more than a year, not even during those few days of intense lovemaking after the Accident. They had both been sore, but they had not been able to help themselves; it had felt like having a new partner.

"No," she said now.

"I didn't know you were awake."

"Well, I am."

"Did you hear that noise? I think a window might be open."

It was quiet. Lilli said, "You know there isn't even a word for what we are, leaving him in there like that."

"You shouldn't think that way."

"We should have had more children," she said.

"You should have told me he was doing cocaine."

He wondered if he'd gone too far, but then he didn't care. He got out of bed and went into the bathroom. He heard Lilli begin to cry, softly at first, and then she was sobbing. He wanted to go back to her, but he stood with his hands on the sink, looking at himself in the mirror. In the soft moonlight that came through the window, he really didn't look much different from the way he'd looked at twenty, and at forty-one he was not even old—he had plenty of time and life left. He had recently told Lilli this, and she had laughed at him. But he was certain he was right. They were not the same person. When he first met Lilli, his love for her had been so intense that he had wondered if he would survive it. He had dropped out of college for her, changed his path on earth. Whereas Lilli was the opposite. She would survive anything. He had always thought of this as an admirable quality, but now he was not sure.

Of course, he himself was not perfect. It had occurred to him that maybe this love he felt, this intensity of feeling, maybe that had not really been about Lilli after all. Maybe it was simply the way he preferred to feel. He had begun to feel the same thing for Joy Halloran that afternoon at her house, which was why he had not slept with her, because compared with that feeling the sex would have been nothing.

He could hear his wife crying in the other room. He could feel his feet trying to move on their own, but he forced himself to stay put. It was a large bathroom, all polished cement, two sinks, two showers—they shared nothing. Lilli's guilts were not the same as his, either. At some point after they moved here, she had become more of a friend to Harley than a parent; Harley had been miserable at his new school, and Lilli had stopped setting boundaries. A sort of club had formed, a family within the family that did not include Max.

And yet this question—the question of who was responsible—would not change anything. Max passed back through the bedroom, where Lilli was now silent. Naked, he went down the stairs and out onto the deck, to look out at the skyline of Houston, all the buildings lit, even on a Sunday night. He touched his toes and felt the muscles of his back stretch, then reached forward and kicked up into a handstand, holding himself with his feet straight up in the air, naked on his own deck. Then the feeling left him. He eased back onto his feet. The light in Joy Halloran's bedroom was on, but Max was thinking about his son. He was thinking, You are the one who did that to him.

Which was true but not the entire truth. The truth being that he, Max, needed to get away from this place. Needed to walk out, turn his back on all of it, leave Texas and never return. He had good hands; he could support himself indefinitely. Porsche, tractor, chain saw—he could fix it. Remake himself as his ancestors had done: they had left Kentucky with just the clothes on their backs. Meanwhile, he'd lived his entire life within sixty miles of his hometown.

Yes, he would leave. It was that simple. It felt good to have a plan, even a vague one. It felt good to stand out there, a slight breeze in his hair, only the sound of the crickets. Lilli could have the house, his car, his business, everything; she could sell it all. He would start again from nothing. She would not have trouble finding a husband, and wherever Max's legs gave out, that's where he would settle. He would not make any of the same mistakes. He would not surround himself with people who wanted to be anything but what they were.

He wondered if Lilli would do that to him, if she were able. Part of him was sure of it. He wondered if that was why he had made the decision to leave Harley in jail that second night; he wondered if he had done that to punish his wife. But he did not think so. It was simply the sort of choice you made, a hard decision for which there would be consequences, the sort of decision that showed you your life was different from what you'd always thought it was.

Harley had been pulled over for speeding, and the police had found a vial of cocaine in the car. Texas was not a good place to get caught with drugs, even if you were white, even if you lived in the Oaks, but Harley was not the sort of kid to think about those things. He had just turned eighteen, he was just like his mother, and in that sense maybe it had been his destiny for this to happen.

Neither Max nor Lilli had come from anyplace important. Max had grown up sharing a room with two brothers, but he'd been taught to be proud. When he was sixteen, a tornado had touched down in Huntsville, torn the roof off his house, and knocked down plenty of others. Most of the neighbors had spent months living with blue tarps, but Max's father had pulled all three boys out of school and in a week they'd had the roof reframed, sheathed, and shingled, all the fallen trees limbed and bucked, as if no storm had ever occurred. Max's father was a machinist, a man who came from cedar choppers, from laborers; a man who had plenty of excuses to be hard on his children. Except that he was the opposite. When their church's steeple was infested with pigeons, when even the minister had resigned himself to shooting them, Max and his father had climbed up there in the dark, while the pigeons were night-blind and reluctant to fly, and caught them by hand, a hundred pigeons. They'd stuffed them into burlap sacks, then released them thirty miles away.

Whereas Lilli came from a different sort of family, had grown up in a double-wide trailer, the kind that looks like the owner is a collector of things. She had left home, moved in with a boyfriend at age fourteen, but maybe you never escaped your family. She'd met Max at nineteen, finished her associate's while Max supported her, and then she got pregnant just after their wedding. Max dropped out of A&M the same year. He hadn't wanted to keep the baby—they were barely into their twenties and broke—but Lilli was suddenly desperate to be a mother; it was as if Max's love was no longer enough.

The light went out in Joy Halloran's bedroom, and Max went back inside, down the steps to Harley's room. There were clothes all over the floor, posters, and he didn't know what, cocaine probably, hidden somewhere. The only drug Max had ever tried was alcohol, and this saddened him now—he should have had those experiences. He looked around as if someone might be watching. It was strange being naked in your son's bedroom. He picked up a T-shirt from the floor and smelled it: it smelled like his son, and also like his son's sweat, and also like cigarette smoke. He draped the shirt around his neck. The Cure, it said. He picked up another shirt from the floor. This one smelled like his son and something else, something sweet. A girl's perfume.

He wondered who the girl was and realized he had no idea so he put that shirt down, the one that smelled like the girl, and sat on his son's bed.

He didn't remember falling asleep, but when he woke up he felt more rested than he'd been for weeks; he'd had the kind of sleep you get from good dreams. It was the best he'd slept since Harley had left the house that night.

At two in the morning, they'd got the call. Max would have expected Harley to sound different, humbled maybe, but he was the same.

"I'm in jail," he told Max. "I'm going to be here at least till morning, when the judge comes through."

"What happened?" Max said.

"I dunno. They're saying I had drugs in the car."

"Did you?"

There was a long silence, and then Max realized that Harley must be standing in a room surrounded by police officers and was probably more scared than he'd ever been in his life. "Don't answer that question," he said. "I'll call a lawyer."

There was another pause and Harley said, "Tell Mom to come and bail me out tomorrow."

It was an order. Max felt all the sympathy go out of him.

"Dad, did you hear me?"

Max still didn't answer—he was thinking about the time he'd been arrested in College Station for driving drunk. He was twenty, two years older than Harley, but he'd been too scared to even consider calling his father, not scared of punishment but scared of disappointing him. And so he had stayed in jail until his brothers collected the money to bail him out.

"Dad?"

"I heard you," Max told his son.

"They said I can call again when the judge sets the bail."

One extra day. It had not seemed like a long time, and Lilli, to Max's surprise, had agreed. She was ashamed; it was as if she herself had been arrested. It was clear to both of them that a bit of scared straight would be healthy for their son, that an immediate rescue would do more harm than good.

When Harley called the next morning, Max told him it would take another day to get the bail money. Harley asked to speak with his mother. I'm sorry, honey, she told him. Well, Harley told her, I guess that's the way it is. Max had felt simultaneously proud and awful. They retained a lawyer in the Skyline District, but Max spent all day worrying that they had made a mistake.

WHAT YOU DO OUT HERE, WHEN YOU'RE ALONE

The guards found Harley the next morning. They claimed he'd fallen down the stairs. Of course it was a lie. Harley had mouthed off to the wrong person, guard or inmate, or maybe he had not done anything wrong at all. Maybe he had just been in a place he was not meant to be.

The day after Max slept in Harley's bed, he stayed late at the shop to finish some paperwork, and when he got home there was no sign of Lilli. He walked around looking for her, room to room, but there was no note. Her car was still there, and there were any number of things she might be doing. Recently she'd been spending a lot of time with the Stocktons. People told stories about them, threesomes and foursomes. Max did not entirely believe those things, but the fact remained that whenever Lilli went over there she came back acting like she'd smoked pot. Tom Stockton was hairy and barrel-chested, and Max imagined him penetrating Lilli from behind, his enormous body pressed against her small frame. It made Max sick to think about. He went to the kitchen and fixed a rum and Coke, then found himself standing by Harley's room again.

The door was open, and there was Lilli, asleep in Harley's bed. She had not gone to the Stocktons' after all. He stood for a long time and watched her breathe; she was in a deep sleep. It was a thing they had in common now, and he thought about getting in bed with her but decided against it.

The next morning he ran into her in the kitchen. He looked past her, out at the yard. The flowers were continuing to spread; you could see their color now from a distance, and he tried to recall what they had smelled like.

"I talked to the doctor yesterday," Lilli said. "I forgot to tell you."

"We didn't see each other," he replied, which was not entirely true.

"They're going to wake up Harley tomorrow. They said we'll be able to bring him home soon."

"What time?" he said.

"What time what?"

"What time are they going to wake him up? What time should we get there?"

"I didn't ask."

"I guess we'll have to call them back."

"I'm sorry," she said.

"Did they say anything else?"

"I don't think so."

"Are we going to need a nurse or someone like that to watch him?"

"I don't know."

"I'll call them back."

"Fine," she said.

"This is good news," he told her. "I don't understand what's wrong."

"I guess I'm worried they should keep him there longer, maybe. I'm worried something could happen if he comes home too soon, like maybe it's just the insurance company trying to push him out before he's ready."

"We have good insurance," he said, but he could tell she wasn't listening. She was looking at her reflection in the glass door.

"We got married so young, Max. Don't you ever feel that way?"

Max felt such disdain then that he could barely stand to look at her. His wife might have been a strange woman he'd seen on a street corner. He had the feeling that if he never saw her again he would not mind. It was quiet for a while before he said, "I'll take care of Harley."

"What are you talking about?"

"He can live with me. I'm not staying here anymore."

"Max," she said.

"You can come with me, or you can do whatever you want, but I'll take care of him."

He was surprised he'd said it, and so was Lilli. He could tell it knocked her right off her tracks, and he could see her mind working to catch up.

"Do you want me to come?"

He could see himself with Joy Halloran, in her bedroom and elsewhere—she was the sort of person Lilli would never be, and he could see himself making a life with her, only it was a more distinct, more real version of himself. They would be living in the hills beyond Austin—Joy's family had a ranch there, her father had a collection of airplanes; she had told him that afternoon. Max had always imagined himself in a place like that, dry air and forty-mile views. Harley would be off at college. Then things closed in again, and he could see Lilli alone, living with her family in Huntsville. Things would not be as easy as she thought. It would not be easy for him, but it would be even harder for her; she would not understand until it was too late.

"Yes," he told her. "I want you to come with me."

That night after work, he picked up Chinese food from a place Lilli liked. He had spent the entire day with a feeling of lightness, although there had been nothing but problem customers, the type who could not really afford their expensive cars. The type for whom owning a car like this meant they had accomplished something with their lives, the type who spent their weekends rubbing fenders with carnauba wax, taking their kids for long drives, not telling their wives that they were one big repair bill away from having to sell. Anyone else would have told them all to go to hell, but Max felt sorry for them. Gave away parts and labor. And today that hadn't bothered him.

The lights were out throughout the Oaks when he got home; some sort of power outage; the city was always having brownouts. He took a flashlight from the garage and carried the bag of food into the kitchen and saw Lilli sitting by herself in the enormous white dining room, eating by candlelight. She wasn't wearing any makeup. He couldn't remember the last time he'd seen her without makeup. She was a beautiful woman, better than Max had ever deserved. He'd known that since they first met—it was the end of summer, and he was about to return to A&M, but he'd realized that he was making a mistake. So he had made his way back to her. It had been twenty-one years, but at this instant it seemed to him that this feeling had not faded; it had only grown richer, more complex.

But, when he looked at her again, something was wrong. She was eating cold leftovers. Eating without him.

"I brought the Chinese," he said. He set the bag on the long table that seated twelve people. Nothing in this room was his—the furniture, the pictures on the wall. It might have been his money, but it all belonged to his wife. "I said I'd get dinner."

"I don't know, Max. The power went out and I guess I just got hungry and I wasn't sure."

"I said I would bring Chinese."

"I know you did. I just wasn't sure."

He sat down across from her.

"I think I want to eat by myself."

He carried the bag of food into the kitchen, but it wasn't right—Harley's room was just there, on the other side of the wall. He got up and went outside, through the big glass door.

It was pitch black, a cool, clear night, and even the Houston skyscrapers were dark. He went to the far end of the yard and sat in the grass. A familiar feeling—he had thought he was doing the right thing, only to learn he wasn't.

He sat there in the darkness, listening to the crickets and night birds, a whip-poor-will; the lights of the city were out, and there was not a single human sound. It might have been the end of the world. The last instant. His father asking them to open the blinds and Max looking at his brothers; they all knew, and then his father was gone, just like that, his light winked out the same as any murderer's. Pure biology. A habit of breathing. Harley would be no different, and at the thought of that Max lay on his back. He could sense the dew settling on his face, above him were all the stars, uncountable—the black universe would swallow them up, he himself, everyone he had ever known.

Only . . . he did not really believe that. He could not explain why; he knew it was true, but he did not agree with it. There was Lilli sleeping on the couch at his shop while he pulled all-nighters. There was Harley swimming at Lake Livingston. The last time they had gone, Max had got out because a storm was coming, a big norther, but Harley had paddled out to the middle so that he could float on his back and watch the storm blow in over top of him. To raise a son like that, who was not afraid—he was not sure how he'd done it. Men like that built empires, they crossed oceans, they became the stuff of history.

As for his own life, he was barely to the middle of it, and his son's was just beginning. He realized that he had been looking up at the sky, the stars visible as in his youth, and his dark house seemed strange to him now, a place from some half-forgotten dream, a place he had gone to pass his days. The next morning, or the morning after, he would go and pick up his son. He could see them both clearly, two figures on a remote highway, at the saddle of some unnamed pass. They were carrying their burdens easily. They were already fading from sight.

IFF

Antonya Nelson

Failure to yield," my neighbor says knowingly, nodding at the crooked stop sign. The accident had not quite knocked it over, and the city has not quite made repairs. On the tilted sign today is a poster. It appeared the way all the posters of the lost beloveds do, taped fluttering in the wind, wrinkled with weather, cheaply produced and faithfully hung, flagging—nagging—every tree and pole.

"Weird," says his companion, squinting at the print. A gay couple, Dave and Raymond, past their scandalous prime, now just two elderly men trying not to trip on the broken sidewalks.

But the photo is not of a dog or cat, but of a teenage girl, and the description is far lengthier—typed font rather than Magic Markered scrawl—than the ones describing pets. Pets are so simple by comparison. For starters, they want to be found.

"Does somebody have to die before they fix that sign?" Raymond himself is dying, his partner, Dave, now his nurse, holding an elbow, navigating the oxygen tank. In the old days, their roles were reversed: Dave was the needy one, an alcoholic loose cannon, likely to be rip-roaring down the street mid-morning drunk as a skunk, accompanied by his dog, Plato the black Lab, also drunk. And Raymond, who sold cars, whose voice on the radio for years promised Albuquerque listeners they'd be "Toyotally satisfied!" would be summoned home by one nosey parker or another to retrieve his errant boyfriend.

"This wasn't here yesterday," Raymond says angrily. "We'd have noticed." We study it the way we do the others, hoping to be the hero, to perform the neighborly deed, to sight the lost, notify the owner, reunite the duo. Never mind the reward; virtue is its own.

"A mystery," Dave savors, he who's never had a child, he who's lately been charged with finding fun wherever he can. He and Raymond routinely tour the blocks surrounding the park at dusk. The bicyclist who pulls over and uses his muscled leg as a kickstand is also a regular, as is the woman being dragged by her three riotous dogs—*working* dogs, she will proudly inform you—as are the recently arrived retirees from Minnesota, and the grumpy hermit watercolorist. An impromptu neighborhood meeting convenes beneath the sign; we begin discussing the missing girl. Her name is Ashley Elizabeth MacLean, but she also answers to Madonna Rage.

"Madonna *Rage*?" says the young mother with the elaborate stroller. She and her husband divided local opinion several years ago when they demolished an ancient adobe home and built in its place a modern mansion. Our neighborhood has fallen on hard times; that a young couple wished to live here impressed us. That they also wished to rip out a historical structure sullied the matter. Addicts and pigeons had been holing up in the old house. Feral cats. The place didn't so much fall down as disintegrate when the wrecking ball swung, a drift of ashy pink sand. The couple's new baby has softened some hearts. Not all hearts. Dave and Raymond are not fond of the little family, although they'd been very kind to my family when we were young and our son was a baby. Their dog, Plato, was a puppy then; in some square piece of wet concrete across the park, both Plato and Jules left their youthful footprints.

The new mother furrows her brow as she reads the rest of the poster's description. Her expression says that the swaddled infant in her care will never run away. Never dye her hair blue or pierce her tongue. Never be identified for any passing stranger as someone with scars on her arms from having cut them. Her stroller's complicated wheels rotate smoothly into reverse, bumping over the curb without rousing its occupant. Her smugness sends up in me an urge for disaster—where's the driver who fails to yield when you need him?

"I wonder if she's one of those gangsters at the gazebo?"

"When I call the cops, they say to call the school. When I call the school, they say blame the parents. The parents throw up their hands." Mrs. Minnesota throws up hers. "Typical pass the buck."

"The noise!" says the watercolorist. He is grizzled and unpleasant, yet his paintings are sentimental landscapes, the Sandias, Santa Fe, Mexican field-workers in gold and periwinkle meadows. "Noise is pollution, too," he adds, as if expecting argument. There's always something to complain about, and these days it's the teenagers in the park. Like flocks of birds to certain trees, they've recently been mysteriously drawn here. We turn as a group to appraise the centerpiece gazebo, empty now, innocuous. Site of weddings, barbeques, *quinceañera* parties. Only an hour or so earlier, high school students were smoking and shrieking and stomping on the benches, music beating like jungle drums from their car stereos. From a distance—from my kitchen window, for instance—you can't tell whether they're playing or fighting, celebrating or rebelling. They probably don't know either. At Christmas, they methodically broke every single tiny bulb in the strings woven through the trellising, a labor far more elaborate than the city's in hanging the lights.

"Seventeen," Mr. Minnesota says wistfully, concerning Madonna Rage. He and his wife are newest to the neighborhood, zealous busybodies, scrambling to catch up on decades of gossip. They exchange a look that maybe means they had a teenage girl themselves, once upon a time in the Midwest, that this trouble isn't unfamiliar, and also that they are glad it is no longer theirs. Their troublemaker would maybe be a mother now, her offspring—their grandchildren—not yet old enough to raise this particular kind of hell. "Take care," they call as they resume their evening's power walk, hands cinching rubber weights, legs in military conjunction.

The working dogs are restless; off duty, they have been known to urinate on people's feet; "OK, OK, OK," their owner scolds ineffectually, letting them drag her away. In her yard, she and her husband and father practice roping; more than once, I've been startled by the steer-sized sawhorse, that crazy creature fitted with longhorns. The woman was a rodeo queen, back when, Miss Bernalillo County; her father occupies the attic, like a rumbling thought in the mind.

"Kids take their health for granted," the weathered cyclist says, refastening his helmet, straightening his blaze-orange safety vest. The poster's author had noted Ashley Elizabeth MacLean/Madonna Rage's pills, the appointments she must keep. She isn't stable.

"What does it mean 'permanent retainer'?" asks Dave, stalling. I think it must be he who insists on these evening constitutionals, he who needs air, to escape the house and its smothering atmosphere of illness. When he was hauled away, caterwauling in the street, all those years ago, he berated Raymond, slapping at his arms, blithe and slippery, "I'm a kept man! I'm humiliating my meal ticket!" But he grew up, and then old. Plato the dog died long ago.

"I'm guessing for her teeth," I say, of the retainer. "My cousin had one. She used to pop it out to scare people." Like a mechanical drawer ejected from her face, two bright bits of porcelain on a tray.

"Excellent," he says, nodding. Raymond clutches his arm—those tusk-like fingernails, the particular guilt-producing grip that signals the stalling is over, time to go home. Dave gives me a rueful smile over Raymond's head. "Gay *and* gay": I always approved of Dave; my ex-husband dismissed both men. He eventually dismissed the whole shabby neighborhood, its hundred-year-old houses, its cranks and misfits, packed himself up and moved to a gated golf-course community carved out just below the mountains. *Seemly*, I suppose you'd call his new place.

The men make for their house down the block—their forsaken garden, where once there were roses; their smudgy convertible, once waxed every weekend—oxygen machine trailing like an old pet.

The watercolorist's cell phone begins singing, although it's hard to imagine who would call him; he'd severed ties with his sister after a shouting match with both her and the fire department when she'd reported the amount of potential accelerant he kept in his garage studio. "For your own good!" she had pleaded, weeping on the sidewalk. "Interfering *cunt!*" he had shrieked in response, and then the uniforms had restrained him.

The jogger restores his earbuds. "Bye," we say to one another. We all head toward our houses around the park, to the cloistered business that goes on inside them. Only occasionally is there evidence of a flaw, a public announcement of failure, rescue summoned in the wee hours, the open spectacle of something gone horrendously wrong. The drunk man singing in the street with his drunk dog. Maniac painter and frantic sister. Today, this poster.

The last part of the message is in italics, as if whispering directly into the child's ear: there is still time for her to graduate from high school, this voice promises, all will be forgiven, her father loves her. The bald appeal, the father's pain, the girl's desperation seem to require shelter. Seeing their intimacy exposed makes my heart hurt, my face hot, as if there were something I ought to be doing for these strangers, some action I should have taken ages ago.

I was a difficult girl, myself, growing up, causing my parents heart-hurting hardship. Also, my son is a teenager, so I feel for this parent, especially the evident fact of his being the only parent. I imagine him tragically widowed, although I am that more pedestrian sort of single parent, divorced.

But maybe what interests me, what stopped me at this stop sign today, involves another teenage girl, my son's girlfriend.

I wish *that* girl would disappear.

Do you go to school with the missing girl? I text Jules. School ended hours ago, but he won't be home. He is with The Girlfriend. When he is with me, he texts her; with her, he texts me. But he is always more with her than me.

He responds immediately. *Used to. Now she's at the Bad Girl school.*

Pregnant?

Druggy. Also knives. Armed and dangerous. Before I can reply, he's sent another, speedy on the keypad. *You said pregnant girls weren't bad.* He's good at reminding me that my ideal self is better than my daily one. In the middle of my composition of a suitable response, another of his arrives. *Her dad's a tranny.*

Really? I have neither the manual dexterity nor sufficient patience to ask for clarification via text.

Wouldst I lie to you?

He wouldn't. I peer into the girl's eyes with new guesses about her trouble. Her father now seems more vividly defenseless. Albuquerque would not necessarily be friendly to a man like him. Its citizens might understand and sympathize with the child who wished to abandon such a parent. The girl's half smile possibly reflects her ambivalence toward everything and everybody. It might hold her own prospect of change, of the scissors and dye and razors and rings—*knives!*—she would use to transform herself, of the escape she would make of her home. Of the parent she left behind, who is now out hanging signs on signs, begging for mercy.

I glance around for witnesses, then snatch the poster.

"Looky here," I say to my mother-in-law. Gloria is startled, as always, by someone entering the house; pensive, and elderly, she rarely steps outside, spending the day studying catalogues and the newspaper, adrift in her relationship with the world, first alarmed and then grateful when her grandson or I come home to interrupt her solitude.

"What's this?" she peers through cat-eye bifocals at the girl.

"Jules says she's at the Bad Girl school. He says her dad's a tranny." Though it is evening, Gloria still wears pajamas and a bed jacket; her life is convalescence. She presents a kind of nostalgic, 1940s glamour-girl-in-the-boudoir fashion statement, face glossy with makeup, white hair teased in an updo. Vain, she keeps the lights low and seems ever ready to drop supine and sultry onto a chaise.

"What does that mean, 'tranny'?"

"Either he dresses like a woman, or he is a former woman. One of those, I think."

We settle into cocktails and speculation. For many years, Gloria ran a beauty school and hair salon in Ohio. She feels a lot of affection for young girls, and also a lot of impatience. Like me, she doesn't trust Jules's girlfriend. She stares at the "Missing Girl" poster and hazards guesses both suspicious and bighearted: Spoiled child grabbing at attention! Poor confounded thing in need of a mother!

Gloria says she once knew a boy who dressed as a girl, back in Columbus. Also, she's wondered whether our alternate mail lady might not once have been a man. She finds it sad that people cannot be happy with who they are. This overarching insight leads her, as most of our conversations do, to her stepson, Nathan, my ex-husband. His real mother died while Nathan was in high school, and his father married Gloria a few years later. Because she has no children of her own, Gloria was eager to declare Nathan as her son. But Nathan didn't feel he needed another mother; he vaguely resented his father's needing another wife. Since his father's death, he seems to have forgiven Gloria her blameless presence, her unrequited affection for him. But he can't muster a responding love. He tried to explain it to me, shrugging helplessly, claiming that he shared no blood relation with the woman.

"Me, either," I said.

"So you shouldn't feel an obligation to her," he said, mistaking what I'd meant.

"No," I told him, "you and *I* don't share blood." And he went opaque, that therapist talent he has. It is as if he can fall into a detached trance right before your eyes. Willfully decline to face facts.

"I hate Friday night," I pronounce. "It's by far the most anxious night of the week." The sirens have started up. There's a high school football rivalry to settle. A girl has gone missing. My son isn't home, and it's already dark, not even a moon this evening.

"Maybe that's why I miss cigarettes the most on Fridays," Gloria sighs; she'd still smoke if it weren't for Jules. "Shall I shampoo you?"

"That sounds wonderful." I smile at her effort to rally me; usually, it's the other way around. "Have you decided about tomorrow?"

"I haven't." Gloria is debating whether to attend Nathan's wedding. Her loyalty has shifted from him to me in the year and a half since she moved into our home. After his departure, Gloria stayed.

"I can't even bring myself to dislike that woman," I admit. "Don't not go on my account."

"Oh, I don't dislike her either," says Gloria. "Just sorry for her. For that matter, I feel sorry for Nathan. He has no idea what he's getting himself into. But she's just pathetic." The fiancée is a far needier person than I, an innocent. You can see it in the way she greets you, grabbing with two palms to shake your hand, to detain you in her clutch, the watchful face that wants to please, her childlike smallness, the frizzy hair that suggests frightened thoughts.

"When I used to see her playing piano, back before I knew about her and Nathan, I kept thinking of her as that busy little tyrannosaurus. The BLT." I make Gloria laugh by illustrating the fiancée's attack on the keyboard, her fierce concentration and her too-small, nail-bitten hands. Gloria has a great laugh. It's good to live with a laugh like that.

"Do they really want me there, Nathan and the BLT?" she asks.

"Go with Jules. I know they want Jules there." If Jules weren't around, we would all fly apart. What would be the point without him? "You're hard," Nathan explained, when he left me. He couldn't meet my eyes, but what he said is true: I peer at the world through an ever-narrowing skeptical lens. I make no new friends, and I trust strangers less. Nathan and I are the same age, but I've had to deduce that women grow hard over time while men grow soft. He lived with what I called "realism," and he named "cynicism," long enough; our marriage had accrued it, each year another layer of shell. Finally, he decided to climb out. I could sense what he'd shed, witness his heart's expansion—like something formerly root bound, prepared to embrace the waiting pathos that is his next wife. "He needs a project," I told my mother-in-law, but understood, privately, that he merely needed to be able to smile.

Nathan will never acknowledge the true beginning of our demise as a couple. It was Gloria's coming to live with us. She moved in after a failed suicide attempt. Nathan and I disagreed about it, me believing (believing yet) that the woman was entitled to determine her own fate, my husband the therapist doggedly taking another view.

"It wasn't a very good attempt," Gloria has admitted. "Maybe Nathan is right, I was crying for help." She downed a bottle of Xanax. The dose was too low to kill her. For a few weeks afterward, she was incarcerated in a mental institution, finally phoning Nathan, in New Mexico, to come spring her. She moved into our guest room; sixteen-year-old Jules was good for her. I like to think that I was also good for her, the two of us trading stories at the kitchen table at the end of every day. "What was there left for me?" she will ask rhetorically. Her husband died and her business went bankrupt. She was bored, tired, done. This was in Ohio; part of the trouble may have been the weather, that annual midwestern mourning, damp and gray. Here in Albuquerque she marvels daily at the forecast: mostly sun. Here, "mourning" and "gray" describe the ubiquitous, querying doves.

Nathan's new marriage might grieve my mother-in-law, yet it might also distract her, give her one more thing to live for, its uncertain but surely jagged plotline. Nathan has not stopped compelling her concern.

As Jules has not yet stopped compelling mine. He too is a conversation touchstone. Gloria retrieves the wine bottle from the refrigerator and refills our glasses. She drinks all day—mimosas in the morning, chardonnay after noon—yet never seems drunk. It pleases her to have company in it, and in the snacking that will become our evening meal, the two of us dining on little bites of cheese or meat on crackers, shrimp, baby carrots and tomatoes, chips and dips. We pass the hours this way, as if at a cocktail party for two.

"Is The Girlfriend going to the wedding?" Gloria asks.

"I don't know. It's an occasion to put on fancy clothes and be admired." If I insist, Jules will come home, will leave his loitering post at the coffee shop where The Girlfriend works on Friday nights to join me and his grandmother. He would be present yet texting her, politely ours, but not passionately. "I was thinking that I wished it was The Girlfriend who'd run away," I confess, "instead of poor Madonna Rage."

Gloria nods in understanding; as a suicidal person, she has an expansive empathy. "But then Jules would be crushed," she says. We both know that The Girlfriend's moods are like natural phenomena, rolling over the house and determining its atmosphere. "He loves her too much," Gloria says. "She has him wrapped around her little finger. It's not good."

"I know." I had that power over Nathan once, and for a long while. Gloria had had it, too, with Nathan's father.

"He's too nice to her. She's toying with him. She's waiting to trade up."

I sigh unhappily. It is all true, a fact of femaleness that Jules could not know but that his grandmother and I understand with chilly certainty. Every few months, The Girlfriend breaks up with Jules, sending him into a terrible despair. Its depths are frightening; I would rather suffer it myself than witness it in him. Already thin, he has to be forced to eat. At night, I have to sit beside him on his bed, stroke his forehead, hold him shuddering in tears against me, waiting for sleep. "You have to learn to step away," I counsel. "Turn off your phone," I beg him. It seems terrible to have to advise indifference. But even if he'd take the advice, he can't turn off his feelings. He sleeps with one of The Girlfriend's sweaters, a bundle of orange angora like a wadded blankie. For Christmas, he gave her a diamond ring. Both Gloria and I were horrified when he showed us, his face wounded when we didn't congratulate his thoughtfulness, his generosity, his large, vulnerable heart. That diamond like an evil twinkle in a villain's eye.

He would want to kill himself if The Girlfriend left him for good. Neither of us mentions this, but the thought is with us in the room. It has been punctuated by the lost-girl poster, by her father's similar fear clearly lingering between the lines.

"Shampoo?" Gloria reminds me hopefully.

At the kitchen sink, she massages my wet scalp with her seasoned, professional hands. I luxuriate into the intimacy, my mother-in-law's scrubbing nails vaguely erotic near my ears, the fragrant suds popping, warm water flowing over my head, a cool trickle leaking along my neck and down my shirt. At first, Gloria was suspicious of my request for a cut, sensitive to being condescended to. But over time, she's let herself enjoy her old talent. She cultivated a new hairstyle for me, something backward-looking, an asymmetrical bob from the '60s, dyed a purple brown named "aubergine." She likes to say the word. Though shaky and tentative at other chores, her fingers move confidently when in possession of a pair of scissors and a comb. She does Jules's hair, too, finishing him with a burring electric trimmer around the neckline and sideburns that always ends with a highly satisfying frisson crossing his face. "Too hot?" Gloria asks loudly.

"Just right," I reply. I could stay under the water, under these skillful fingers, for hours. At the beauty school in Ohio, when Nathan and I traveled there for his father's funeral, all the girls, employees and students and alumnae alike, clucked protectively around Gloria, supernaturally teary for her loss. The group was exuberant and chatty, physically affectionate, brash and pretty. When they didn't have customers, they practiced on one another, all day grooming and debating. They'd treated Nathan's father, Woody, like a mascot. Apparently, he had taken to hanging out at the salon with them, sitting under a dryer hood, reading the newspaper, making conversation, flirting. "Dotty old sot," Gloria said of him, fondly enough.

Gloria, Nathan said, was nothing like his mother, the only fact that made him curious about her, or maybe more curious about his father. The man who would spend his days in a beauty parlor wasn't the Woody that Nathan had grown up with. He'd been a bastard dad, Nathan always claimed; but then Woody had grown old and sentimental, disarmed and harmless, a character in his second act. Nathan had finally chosen to see his father as reformed, penitent; his stepmother had some other thoughts on the matter. "Senile," she said, finger twirling at her ear. "Brain all turned to mush. He would have been horrified to see himself. I'd've left him if he wasn't so wretched. And if I wasn't already so old and lackadaisical," she acknowledged. "You know, you ought to have to renew your license to live. Some people are no longer qualified. Some people wouldn't pass the test."

Jules chimed in then, as he occasionally did when we didn't realize he was listening, when we sort of forgot he was in the room. "A liver's license," he said.

Gloria shuts off the faucet and squeezes water from my hair before performing a tidy upsweep with a towel, tucking the end into the bundle. "I'll get the dryer, you open a new bottle."

We discuss transvestites. We discuss transsexuals. Doesn't a sex change usually go the other way, from man to woman? Isn't it the boy who more often feels he's been wrongly assigned his gender? And would Madonna Rage's mother-father have had surgery? Aside from the obvious subtractions and additions, what small touches might be attended to? Adam's apple, for instance? The weathered flyer on the table serves as a coaster for Gloria's wineglass; the girl's color image is blurring.

We both look up at the sound of a car door slamming outside. A second slam follows. We straighten our spines, take girding sips of wine, and then Jules and The Girlfriend are in the kitchen, she with her haughty tossed head and aggressive ballet stances, the faint floating odor of coffee and coconut. "She got fired," Jules says. "Her boss is a sexist asshole," he adds, which explains The Girlfriend's quivering, righteously indignant expression. "Hi, Grandma," he says to Gloria, bending to put a kiss on her cheek. He has lavender circles under his eyes, my old-souled son.

"Oh, honey," she says. The Girlfriend chooses to think this is directed toward her, while I know it's Jules for whom Gloria feels sorry. He will suffer The Girlfriend's bad news. Her business is the house's business, her tempers paramount.

A year ago, I would have challenged them, saying, "Define 'sexist asshole,'" because a year ago, it was The Girlfriend trying to earn my approval. Now that's changed. Back then, I was delighted by her, a smart and arrestingly striking child, one who had not only skipped ahead a grade, but whose poise and confident costumes were a pleasure to behold, a girl who was seemingly obedient to her parents, a teenager with a job, straight As, and who had the good taste to find Jules worthy, to become his first girlfriend. But as my marriage eroded, so did the enthusiasm and respect I'd been accorded by The Girlfriend, as if she found me guilty, even though it was Nathan who left. Her contempt feels specifically female, her judgment on my skills at old-fashioned womanhood: I failed to keep my man. Perhaps it seems I've traded him in for an old woman who drinks too much and never changes out of her pajamas. The Girlfriend rakes her gaze around the room, establishing a distance between herself and me as if fearful of contagion. So I say, "I'm sorry."

She blinks a slow, one-eyed bit of restraint. "That chick's a skank," she says, spotting the poster of Madonna Rage. "We were in sixth grade together. Before I got accelerated."

"Maybe she was kidnapped," Jules says.

And all three of us, in unison, tell him quite confidently, "She wasn't kidnapped."

"Unless she kidnapped herself," says The Girlfriend, voicing my precise same thought. Do I not like her because she reminds me of me? Maybe.

Then Gloria asks, "We've been wondering: did her father used to be her mother, or does he just like to put on women's clothes?"

"Limited options," Jules notes.

The Girlfriend lifts her lip in disgust. "*Grotesqueness*! All I know is, that girl wore the same pants every single day of sixth grade." Can I realistically wish that The Girlfriend were the missing girl without also dooming Jules to heartache? No, I cannot. I do what I always do: invite her to Sunday dinner. Compliment her outfit. Ask whether she and Jules have decided about the wedding, whether they would like something to eat, something to take with them as she leads and he follows to his bedroom.

It's a room that shows two influences: the innocent accessories and pastel adornments of childhood, for which I am responsible, and the newer, brasher colors and business of adolescence, which accoutrements The Girlfriend supplied. Retro cowboy-and-bronc wallpaper now covered by sneering musicians. Finger-paint table suddenly groaning beneath a perilous stack of pachinko machine and television. Post-it notes of The Girlfriend's Red She Said lipsticked kisses on every toy and shelf and remaining childish object. And, finally, snapshots of her face, like that lost girl's face on the street, everywhere. During the times when she breaks up with him, he lies immobilized and surrounded, four walls' worth of mocking, taunting images.

When his door slams behind them, Gloria leans across the table and confides, "What do you want to bet that boss is not so much a sexist asshole as that girl is a royal pain in his behind?" Like me, Gloria is relieved when Jules's relationship is going well, and distressed when it is going badly. His unhappiness brings up her own, reminds her that joy cannot be trusted. It is understood that Gloria will decide one day to die. She will commit suicide in such a way that Jules will be spared. He doesn't know about the overdose. He will be told that she died of old age; to a seventeen-year-old, the whole household could believably perish of this affliction. Nathan would know the truth; he would accuse me of being an accomplice. What did he expect me to do? Abandon Gloria, as he had? "She should be in therapy," he said, stubbornly defending his profession, also, maybe, defending his lack of interest. He does not want to think about the ways that living no longer appeals. To him, she is another woman grown cold.

"Sometimes it seems like I'm inside a room with a too-tiny door," Gloria once told me, her pale blue eyes dilating as she tried to capture the feeling, to put it into words, "and the room is shrinking. As is the door . . ."

"That sounds *awful*," I said, shivering.

Out of nowhere, Jules chimed in. "That's why cats have whiskers, so they won't get into a space they're too big to escape. That's why it's cruel to trim their whiskers." He was fiddling with his movie camera on the floor. Gloria and I had yet again forgotten he was with us.

"I did something naughty," I confess to Gloria now.

"What'd you do?"

My bit of sabotage was to forward The Girlfriend's mail. On a whim, I filled out the form while at the post office forwarding Nathan's, forging his signature, then pulling another card from the stack, checking the box for individual (as opposed to family) forwarding, so that only The Girlfriend's mail would be sent to Montana. This is the season of college applications; she scored nearly perfect on her SATs. Now, all her acceptance letters will be winging their way to Anaconda.

"I *love* it!" Gloria declares, smiling hugely. "That child needs to be taken down a peg or two."

"Maybe getting fired will improve her."

"Ha!"

Gloria falls asleep on the couch. "Passed out," Nathan would say, superior to such an impulse himself. She prefers sleeping here, on the couch in the living room in the middle of a cinematic drama, to the small dark guest room and daybed. She prefers for sleep to take her unaware. She lay down holding the television remote in one hand, her wineglass cupped by the bell in the other. I remove each from the grip of her elegant, manicured fingertips. Her hands fold automatically into one another at her throat. It's the position of the dead. It's the position of the fetal.

"It's the only saving grace of not being a mother," she said to me once. "I have permission to kill myself. You don't."

When the house phone rings, its shrill jangle passes over her face like a burst of air on a still pond.

Nathan. He sighs when I answer, his usual disappointed salutation. "Checking in," he says. "Hoping to speak with Jules. He's not picking up his cell." Usually, I let the machine answer the landline. I like to treat Nathan to Jules's ten-year-old, chiming voice requesting that the caller leave a message for the members of our former nuclear family. The injury of that gone-forever time.

"Not here," I lie. "Off with The Girlfriend." At the kitchen table, I pick at the wine-stuck corner of the rippled poster. Madonna Rage is streaked blue, her father's pleas draining away. It's quite possible Nathan knows them; the man's eloquent way with words and his complicated situation suggest that he is not a stranger to therapy, to seeking help. But I would learn nothing by asking. For years, I've carried on a taunting, imaginary conversation with Nathan's professional self and his rigid code, me playing the brat against his steadfast droning advice, in my head alternately resorting to tears or telling him to go fuck himself.

"You want me to encourage or discourage Gloria about your wedding?" I ask. Time teaches this, that you are astonished at what winds up coming out of your mouth.

"It's a little bit of a hike," he says. The aspen trees. The wilderness forest just above his manicured new home. He will never say that he wants nothing of his former life except his son, that singular, culled, impeccable emblem of the future. For this reason alone, I will insist on sending both Gloria and Jules tomorrow; The Girlfriend can make her own decisions. In the midst of his lengthy explanation of the rutted parking lot, the exorbitant BLM fees, the unknown quantity of the weather, I reach for my mobile and text Jules.

It is almost midnight. Jules always makes fun of my inability to operate the keypad's apostrophe.

She's upset.

Take her home.

I don't want to.

She will get in trouble. Before I can add *She will get you in trouble,* Jules's message comes flying back.

To me it seems like everybody's in trouble all the time anyway.

"Goodbye, Nathan," I say to his final breathing ponderousness. He prefers having the last word.

"Don't let her drink," he chooses to say.

Jules's bedroom door remains resolutely closed. I debate knocking, nagging. I worry that The Girlfriend's parents are going to blame Jules for keeping her out beyond curfew. For getting her fired. For having a mother who plays juvenile pranks like forwarding mail. For the other juvenile prank of having put Jules's old baby monitor beneath his bed, the receiving end in my own bedroom. I can tune in, listen to what they say or do. Once, I heard them talking about calculus, The Girlfriend teasing while Jules struggled to finish his homework; she didn't mind being coy and ditzy, wasting time, idling and flirting and distracting, making him prove over and over his extravagant affection. "I remember 'If and only if!'" she squealed. "I always thought that sounded like wedding vows!" Jules gave a grudging laugh. Another time, he told me the names he and The Girlfriend had picked for a boy baby, for a girl baby, including me in an improbable fantasy future that made my chest ache.

I listen to the monitor only occasionally, only in quick bursts, his privacy something I invade like a wasp sent whizzing through a small gap into the room, then swiftly out, frightened of what might happen.

I move through the house, switching off lights, extinguishing the television. With every muted room comes another sensation of opening vastness, as if I were carrying a candle, bearer of the last small illumination. On the bed I shared for nineteen years with my husband and now occupy alone, I find the cat. "Hello, cat," I say as she, sleek and impassive, pours herself to the floor and slides away toward the cat door, toward the night. If she is ever lost, if ever I find myself tempted to make a poster, I will be reminded of this evening. "Do not get run over," I order her vanishing tail in vain.

For that wasp's flight's worth of time, I switch on the monitor. On it, The Girlfriend cries. My son consoles, more like a song than words proper, a murmuring litany of steady care. My ex-husband would offer the curt opinion that I'd dislike any girl Jules chose, and perhaps that's true. But I can't hate her, crying. She sounds too much like the child she was, too much like somebody so well loved that losing her could not be survived. In the summer, Jules will go to Europe—the grand tour, Gloria's exorbitant graduation gift—without The Girlfriend. Maybe the time zones, and the technology, or its absence, will divide him and her. Maybe he'll meet someone else. I might even have the heart to feel bad for The Girlfriend if that's what happens.

Because, of course, he will be leaving me too. He has already left me.

Around the bed, the room expands exponentially, not like Gloria's shrinking coffin but like space. It will be during this summer, I think, while Jules is gone, that Gloria will end her life. Or she might postpone until fall, when he's away at college. Then what? I ask myself, beginning to slip away into sleep. *What then?*

Hours later, I am brought upright and alarmed by a car outside. It screeches hideously at the tilted stop sign, slides screaming over the pavement for an unthinkable length of time. I brace to absorb the impending, certain crash; surely all my neighbors do the same—lonely Dave as he cruises the Internet, Miss Bernalillo County's father-in-law the insomniac, Madonna Rage's vigilant parent—our breath collectively held. But it does not come and does not come. We blink in the black, waiting.

CREATURES OF THE KINGDOM

Stephanie Reents

I drove for gas. It was mixed up, using some when we needed more, but we lived a gallon's worth from town. My wife, Trish, said, *There is nothing for the table.* The boy said, *The animals need to be fed.* Then I drove for supplies, and on these errands, I liked the variety, the windows of the truck open, the air whipping back and forth. Making something from nothing, wind when there was none, not on summer days. But I wondered whether it was right. Because God said the earth would make grass, the herb making seed, the tree making fruit, everything after its kind. But on a still day, when the fields were still and the grasshoppers were still, and even the ligers and the tigons and their offspring were still, though only in the heat of the afternoon, here was the wind, so swift that when I stuck my arm out the window, the wind tried to snap it off, and would have but for the fact that I was strong.

My boy, Tyce, was stronger. He could haul three bags of concrete for my two. Boise State had recruited him for football, and he said, *Look at the horizon!* I was proud, but I did not know how I would manage without him: he built the fences, poured the concrete, carried the meat in the gate instead of heaving it over the fence.

Ten days ago, he came in the house and said, *One of them has died, and they are eating him.*

Boise was not far, but I was still afraid because of what had happened when I went away, a boy just like him. Africa was farther.

I drove because we lived outside Lava, and it was a place you had to want to visit to get there, two gallons of gas to the highway, another three to Pocatello. A different truck might have been less thirsty, but if we had had the money for a different truck, the gas would not have mattered. We thought the people who came for a dip at Lava Hot Springs would swing by Ligertown, but we did not have a sign or bleachers or refreshments or a microphone for running the show, and there were other obstacles: insurance, the sky-high premiums, the shenanigans the state jumps you through. People rushed to the hot springs, returning to the water that brought them forth, to the springs the Indians had deemed holy and a businessman had built a pool upon. I heard the high dive closed because nowadays people are bigger and could sink like stones to the tiled bottom of the pool. For every three feet up, the state required five feet down. The same was true with the dead. You needed a permit to bury your kin, though not your animals. And then you had to shut them up in a box or burn them to dust. To lay our boy to eternal rest, we had to promise to dig the grave ten feet deep and pay a fee in cash or check at the county courthouse. After that, the sheriff wanted to know how he died, and the Fish and Game men found a hole in the fence. They have killed three cats already, and they are coming for more.

Trish and I sit in the front room, waiting for the men. She has not left the davenport in more than a week. It is covered with white sheets to keep it cool and clean, and the drapes are pulled to keep the newspapermen from peeping in the windows. The calendar says summer, and outside agrees, dust lifting along the road to the highway, coating everything with powder, even the inside of the glove compartment, but the house is a different season, an in-between one, unlike anything we have ever seen before. Trish's sleep is un-settled. She has strange dreams at all hours of the day. People knock, but we do not open the front door. We let them traipse through the dried-up garden and prowl around by themselves. We pretend we are not here, though we are very much here. In the garden, the tomato plants are bleached stems, and the cucumbers are stunted, no larger than a pinky, and rough with stubble. These days when I venture out, it is dark, and I cannot see the dust, though I know it is there because I feel it between my teeth. I know there is a ragtag parade of animals circling because I can hear the steadiness of their steps, the crack of the sagebrush when they pass too close. I feel the movement of the air when they swish their tails, and I smell their hunger.

I want to talk about the rifles, the cost of a steer if the cats take one down, what will happen to my animals. Tyce is dead. I want to talk about how he is gone, more gone than if he left for Boise later in the summer to start football practice, but Trish will not talk about this. I wanted him to go to Boise, and I feared it. Three weeks ago, he turned eighteen. *Otherwise, you'd be charged with child endangerment,* said the sheriff. *But I suppose it was technically of his own free will that he went into the enclosure. If I were you, I couldn't live with myself. There will be an investigation.* Trish does not want to talk about anything except her disturbed sleep, the dreams about the woman who tries to drown herself.

"She kept throwing herself over the railing into the ocean," Trish says. "They had to fish her out."

"Who?"

"The men on the boat."

"In this heat."

"It wasn't hot there. The woman wore a long dress, like *Little House on the Prairie.*"

"Why?"

"Why anything?"

She raises herself from the sofa. In the summer, she wears a see-through white nightgown, but only at night. She is tall and thin with fancy hands, even though she works hard in the house and garden, and long feet with second toes that dwarf the others. The women in her family are all the same. Trish says it is because they have been on their feet for generations.

"I hear the cats now," she says.

"It's too hot. They'll be sleeping."

"Poor woman, she wanted the water so badly," she continues.

"You're frightened. Everything that's happened."

"No. No, I'm not. The only part that was scary was when they took her out. It was like reeling in a fish."

"Do you miss him?"

"I don't want to talk about that. The point is the underwater part wasn't scary for the woman, but being reeled back in was."

"Tyce loved the ligers."

"She wanted to stay in the water, but they wouldn't let her."

"The man said there's a place in California that will take the wolves, but they don't know about the cats."

"I want to go swimming."

"You don't know how."

"I don't care." Trish goes to the kitchen to get a glass of water from the faucet. Walking, she makes a breeze that shows her body, and I remember how beautiful she is. The phone rings. "Yes," she says. "I see."

Neither of us learned to swim. Every year, kids drowned in the Snake or broke their necks diving when the river was already running slow. My mother said it was unnatural to swim: *We have two legs. Fish don't.* I never asked Trish why she did not learn. Trish insists that Tyce could swim, but I think she just wants a secret to overcome the sadness. She does not know that secrets are also burdens.

"I'll tell him," she says to the person on the phone, but when she returns to her spot on the couch, where the outline of her body is always present, she does not say anything.

Out back are sheds, a maze of posts planted in concrete and strung with barbed wire, and large corrals made of tall cyclone fencing. Sagebrush grows, and this grants a little shade. I nailed together the shelters from scrap wood I hauled from the construction jobs I worked until two years ago, when we were almost ready to cut the ribbon for Ligertown and shatter a bottle of sparkling cider beneath our feet. I fashioned the troughs and mended them when they began to leak. I built the windowless sheds, roofed them with tin, and divided them into stalls. This is where I kept the cats when they had just arrived. This is where they awoke from their drugged journeys from the penny breeders and roadside zoos; this is where I unloaded the back of the truck when I came home from exotic animal auctions, jittery from driving all night and the knowledge of all the creatures I could buy. This is where they first roared, first met their mates, first came together and gave rise to animals not frequently seen before.

Ligertown was my creation. I made it, I populated it, encouraging natural acts between unlike ones. There were not laws for this. No one cared if you wed a male lion and a female tiger. Penned together long enough, they stopped being shy, mingled, and made a liger. The ligers were bigger than the sum of their parentage, with striped hinds and spotted abdomens and sweet tempers. If you reversed the pairing and put together a father tiger and a mother lion, they would produce a tigon, a stunted cat with a barbered mane. Further down the tree—or up, I hadn't decided which—everything got more mixed up: li-ligers and li-ligons, ti-ligers and ti-ligons. Their coats looked like the cloth on the floor that catches spilled paint. The males were sterile, and they all died young, though that was after cycles of food and starvation. I was not sure why they died, whether from disease or weakness. Beyond Ligertown, we had a bit more land before the neighbor's fence. It took many hours to dig a hole in the desert, and my boy also learned to do this faster. Fake flowers bloomed from unfertile land, and among them stood the plastic army men that the boy offered when he was still young. *Bang, bang*, he pretended. *You're dead.* The edges of our property were a cemetery.

I did not know everything. In the beginning, I made mistakes. I lost the three wolves that came from a traveling circus in Alaska that I had bought with a money order. At the end of their crated journey, they stood wobble-footed and squinty in the bright sun. I tossed them in with the ligers, because there was only one permanent corral back then, and I thought it was big enough to be like nature. Pressed against the metal fence, the boy watched the first one go down. Afterward, he hid in the front coat closet for a day and a half. Then, he was just a little boy, didn't haul nothing, had pale skin that burned if we did not keep him covered, and a tendency toward earaches. He cried his voice dry, kicked the wall, and Trish said it was abominable what had happened in our backyard, too scary for a boy, too scary for her. Her voice was stern.

I wanted to tell her that I was scared, too. I wanted to say that I was scared "shitless," but we did not use that kind of language in our house. I had just seen the second one taken, the way the big cats fanned across the corral, like kids in a marching band, but quiet, low to the ground and pressing closer until the wolf, penned to the fence, tried to scamper up, his claws splintering in the diamond-shaped metal openings.

The next day, I intended to save the last one and not see all my wolves go for dinner, but the cats were whipped up such as I'd only seen on *Wild Kingdom*, but never in the Ligertown, and I was afraid to set foot in the corral, even to water their troughs and bring them more meat. I could not afford the luxury of being nervous or the whole operation would fail. I asked for bravery, for strength and wisdom. I promised myself I would return to the pens the next day.

They took the third wolf in the night. I heard the howling.

I got another pair of wolves—a girl and a boy—from a private zoo in Florida that was going under. Before they came, I built a separate compound for them, as far away from the ligers as the property allowed. I planted a wall of bushes and trees, most of them dug up from nearby parks. I could have gone to jail for stealing them, but not for possessing wild animals. It was a hot summer, and it was hard to keep the plantings moist enough. The trees turned brittle and did not root. When the first wind came, they toppled over like a house of cards you build on a rainy day. The shrubs flourished, and it smelled like Christmas, except when the animals ignored the meat I threw them and I did not have time to clean.

This system worked, except sometimes the wind blew, and the ligers thought the wolves were coming, or the wolves thought the tigers were on the prowl, or the ligers and the tigers thought they were a pack that had been separated, and bellowed and hollered until the wind changed direction or died completely, and then we were back in Lava, where it was usually so quiet you could hear the splash of someone jumping from the high dive at the hot springs, only it was off-limits on account of the accident. Because of this, you knew that quiet had a sound, or inside your head did.

We lived far from the nearest neighbor, off the road and down a lane of dirt. The closest were the Maddocks, and they had fifty head of cattle that grazed their land and spent summers in the foothills. They brought their kids to see our animals but did not understand the scale of my dreams. Tyce played capture the flag with the Maddock boys while their stock looked on. When he got to high school, there was always a football tucked under his arm. He was a normal boy. At home, he did not talk much about school, except to tell me when I could see him on the field, and at school, I assumed he did not talk of home. That was how I had been. I bought him a motorbike for going back and forth, and Trish took him to Pocatello for Wranglers and Birkenstocks. At his games, I was so nervous for him to keep the quarterback untouched, I could barely watch.

There were other things I tried not to consider. In Africa, I had seen three lions bring down a giraffe like a tree timbered by loggers. As it fell, the small birds perched on the giraffe's head chirped and flew away. It brought tears to my eyes. I tried not to think too much about Africa. Instead, I thought about elephants for sale in South Carolina and cushioned bleachers. Elephant rides, snake charmers, girls in sequined dance uniforms who could tightrope-walk an elephant's trunk. Barnum and Bailey's in Lava, Idaho. I plotted and plotted, and in the plotting, I tried to forget the past.

My boy had a shadow boy, both of me and not my kind. A shadow boy with longer arms and legs, or so I imagined, but then Tyce grew up, and they wanted him to play football in Boise: *Can you believe it, Dad, they only lost one game this year*—and it was possible Tyce filled the space made by my other boy, the image of me and not me. That one the shadow, this one the body. I thought often about my shadow boy, even though these thoughts never bore the fruit of words. I did not tell Trish or anyone. Pastor Christiansen said: *We're all creatures of God.* He said: *Spread the word.* Rumor was they sent the dumb ones to Africa because the smart ones would not stay. *We're all creatures of God,* Pastor Christiansen said. *Let us make man in our image, after our likeness,* the Bible said.

In Uganda, the son of God was brown, sometimes black. I saw into their churches, though I did not enter. I wondered: who was he who spoke the Word? I was eighteen years old, graduated from Pocatello High, dressed in a dark suit from Alexander's—blue or black, it changed color with the light. The suit and everything was from my grandparents, their barley crops brought the money for tithing and getting grace and buying plane tickets. Who had heard of such a place as Uganda?

I saw my shadow boy for only one month and six days, and then I left. His mother was Josephine, the girl who sold chapatis from the little wooden shack near the house where Coles and I boarded. We were supposed to stick together, closer than a husband and wife, the way men can be with men in fellowship, never alone to question God's deed and our missionary work or give in to temptation, but Coles said our homes were so far away the rules did not hold, and after dinner he went out. At night, the streets of Kampala were beautiful and frightening, the smell of burning charcoal everywhere like on the Fourth of July, the small light of candles and lanterns giving the appearance of a spooky movie.

Josephine knew about Road Runner and Coyote. She had seen the cartoons in South Africa, where she had gone once with a girls' dance troupe. She'd been there only a week, but she was well acquainted with the characters' ways. *That Coyote, he is a very determined dog,* she said. *I know he will get the bird next time.* I thought maybe she was correct, because no one knows which cartoon will be last. The palms of Josephine's hands were soft. I could not wait for them to touch me after I had walked from house to house, corn on the cob roasting over the coal fires in the front yards. It was like a year-round picnic, except when the rains arrived, and then I thought of Noah and his ark, and of God telling him to bring aboard all the creatures: *Of fowls after their kind, and of cattle after their kind, of every creeping thing of the earth after his kind.*

It rained and rained, and the dark-colored umbrellas we brought were useless because the water came down so hard it ricocheted off the ground, raining from above and below, and the crazy men with no feet or hands lay down in the dirty puddles and drank from them. I thought God was destroying this land, and as Coles and I sloshed through the streets, wearing plastic bags over our suits, the skin of our feet growing thick and rough in our wet shoes and making blisters, my mind wandered to the procession of creatures, man and fowl, cattle and creeping thing, and I wondered who would be my other half. It could not be Coles, because we were too much of the same thing, but perhaps Josephine and I would take our place together in the long line of chosen creatures for the ark.

At the end of the day, when Brother Coles went away to wherever he went, Josephine and I lay together on the foam mattress in the narrow cement room where she lived with her aunt, and we lay together, and Pocatello became the place where Coyote finally caught Road Runner, not the town itself, but the empty acres of sagebrush and cheatgrass around the town. *Coyote knows about a secret gully,* I told Josephine, *but for his plan to work, he must wait for it to fill with water. He is patient for many months, and then he becomes fanatical, wondering when it will finally rain, and at last, just when he is about to give up hope, the skies open up and it pours. Now, he can lure Road Runner into his trap, chasing her toward the gully that is too wide to jump, chasing a bird that can neither fly nor swim.*

Does she drown? Josephine asked.

It was a logical question, but the whole point was that there should be a happy ending. I told her they made peace.

I thought that Josephine and I would go together aboard the ark. We would be holding hands. When I was small, I had seen a picture of a pair of elephants boarding Noah's mighty ship, their trunks tied up like a splendid bow. I thought it would be like this, serene and wonderful. But then Josephine had her baby, and we were three, and I had to repent for the boy who could never be my own.

Your work is done here, Pastor Christiansen said, even though the date of my departure was still three months away.

You know the Road Runner cartoon? I asked him. *Do you think it's possible that Coyote catches Road Runner?*

He shook his head, as though I were speaking nonsense or an obscure dialect that even he had not mastered, and he gave me my passport, which he had kept safely for me. *The whole point of the cartoon, Brayden, is that the coyote never gets what he wants. It's impossible for it to be any other way.*

In the next batch were two female lions and a male tiger, and they did nature's work, flourishing and multiplying. Each year brought a crop of cubs that delighted Trish and the boy and swelled me with pride, as though I were the father of all of them. With a straw hat tied to her head in the summer and rabbit-fur muffs in the winter, Trish saw to the niceties, brushing the ligers and other cats as well as she would have cared for the tender skin of a new baby. She talked to the mothers in a low voice when they drew close to their due dates, sharing knowledge only women possess, and she brought them balls of peanut butter and corn syrup as treats. She made a bridle for one of the friendlier wolves, and just like that, our son got a pony. We only had Tyce. Children are lost so easily.

I watched my brood grow, my boy getting big and strong, bigger and stronger than me, and my pack of wolves and ligers and tigers getting bigger and bigger until we had twenty-seven ligers and tigons and ti-ligers and li-tigons and li-ligers and ti-tigons. I dreamed of cars lining up to see Ligertown. I studied the front of the house, trying to decide where I could pour concrete for the parking lot or whether it was better for the people to park on the road and walk. If they were thirsty by the time they reached the entrance, we could sell them pop by the name of jungle juice. Maybe we would sell ice cream too, and little plastic bags of meat that could be tossed to the animals. The details were what I liked. I imagined myself in beige, like a park ranger, and Trisha in a ruffled blouse and skirt, her hair in two long braids down her back, small green sparkly studs in her ears, and Tyce in a blue tuxedo, like the one he wore to his first high school prom.

"Sweetheart," Trish had asked every week or so for the past two years, "when are we going to open up?"

But Ligertown was never perfect. We needed to clean the pens or repair part of the fence. I needed to build bleachers or buy red collars for the wolves, research our tax status or write a radio jingle. A liger was too young to be seen or too close to death for visitors. And then about a year ago, there was a rash of deaths, eight or nine sick and suffering in half a year, which made me wonder whether disease had struck the whole lot of them and they would all die together. I waited to see what would happen. I waited too long, and after a while, it was beyond my means to buy enough meat. That was when I stopped driving so much and lived with the stillness, and Tyce was going to go to Boise and *play for a real good team*, and the animals did what all animals do when they grow desperate.

"Dad," Tyce said, "one of them is dead, and they are eating him."

My son was strong and fearless. He played offensive line. The coach said he was tough, the way he held his own. When the bigger boys hurled their bodies at him, he never flinched, and I felt pride in him, and I was proud myself, thinking he might have gained his fearlessness from walking among the creatures in Ligertown.

We went out back. The sun was directly overhead, so nothing made shadows. Objects were just what they were, and in the clearing of the pen, a litiger lay quiet and unmoving. Half its skin was pulled back, the ribs exposed like dirty teeth. Flies covered the flesh like thick paste, buzzing persistently. I handed Tyce my leather gloves. "It might get messy." He pulled up the hood of his sweatshirt. When we got near, the flies flew up in a cloud and, once up, became small flecks, tiny things that assumed their rightful place in the world.

"Jesus," Tyce said, pressing his gloved hand across his face. Another time, I might have reprimanded him for taking the Lord's name in vain, but the scene unnerved me. There were dozens of paw prints in the soft dirt, a stain of viscous blood like a shadow. The li-tiger's tongue lolled out of one side of her mouth, and her eyes were milky. I looked around for the other cats but, except for a female liger named Miss C., saw none. The rest must have been sleeping in the wooden shacks or in the middle of clumps of sagebrush, waiting for the cool part of the day. I wondered which one was responsible, whether the li-tigers were loyal to their kind, whether distant relations were more likely to fight. Tyce grabbed the dead cat by the tail and was pulling her toward the gate. Miss C. swiveled her head in our direction and yawned. Her coat was rubbed bare in patches along her haunches. For three weeks there had been no money for food. We ate the vegetables canned by Trish, while I told myself the lack of food was like a small famine, not an unnatural occurrence for the cats. Someone might see my ad in the magazines and buy one of the animals that I'd put up for sale. The mailman might bring a check. I walked to the box at the end of our drive every morning, and Tyce reminded me he was leaving for college at the end of the summer, and I was so proud of him when he assumed his place in the offensive line, crouching down, swinging his left shoulder forward, standing his ground. I also hoped he would stay and help us survive in the kingdom I had created.

I went to open the gate for Tyce. At the same time, Miss C. rolled off her side and onto her feet and swaggered toward us.

"Are you coming for a visit, Missy?" Tyce said. "Gonna pay your respects to this one?"

All at once, Miss C. sprang, and when she had ceased being a blur through the air, she was knocking Tyce over, sending him to the ground. He screamed, and I grabbed a shovel and swung it at the liger's head. Her mouth closed around Tyce's neck, and she shook him. I hit her with all my force, the shovel ringing against her skull. She shook him again, ripping off the hood of his sweatshirt, and I could see Tyce's bloody face. He curled, like a hand balling up into a fist, and I hit the liger again, this time along her spine. She turned and swatted me, dragging her claws across my thigh.

"I'm going to get help," I screamed at Tyce, and I ran toward the house, leaving my son with the animal.

My loaded rifle was in the top of the coat closet. I did not waste a second looking for bullets. I aimed. I fired. I killed Miss C. All this was done as quickly as possible.

After Tyce died, Trish claimed that he could swim, that he even went off the high dive. It was just a rumor that it had closed. "I saved money from my housekeeping so that he could learn," she said. "No reason not to swim if you live in Lava. It's the one thing we're famous for."

"Weren't you afraid?"

"I met a nice woman from California at the springs," she says. "Half-Indian, but not like the Blackfoots. She had a tiny diamond in her nose. She told me about her beliefs, how nothing goes away, at least not permanently. Things change into other things. After that, I saw no reason to be afraid."

"We don't swim," I told her. "We don't swim." The force of how I said it surprised me.

"Tyce swam," she repeated. "You should have seen the way he went. So high up on that board, I could barely tell he was mine. And he didn't just jump: he dove. A clean streak through the air."

Our boy, a bird or fish: I wanted to believe the truth of what she said. But all I could see was the body of our boy, not Tyce, since his spirit had already risen, or so I hoped, but just the mangled body of my son left in the corral and my liger feeding from his blood.

Trish has not moved from the davenport in the front room. The day is still hot, but the sky has turned to the same tan color as the land. I sit next to Trish. She takes my hand, and her fingers find the callous on my palm. They always find this spot, the roughest part, the skin so thick I do not feel her touch, just the pressure.

I want to tell her about my shadow boy, about Josephine and the lie I told her about Coyote and the Road Runner because everyone knows that Coyote never wins. You do not have to see the final cartoon to know this. All this is my fault, thinking I could lie with Josephine and raise animals that God, in his infinite wisdom, did not see fit to bring to life when he was making the world, animals that will never propagate after their kind because they are sterile.

My son is dead.

He could have gone to Boise and played football, but he is dead. I wanted him to go to Boise. I wanted him to go, and I did not want to lose him.

They found three cats hunting in the neighbors' pastures and shot them. Two more may be loose, though I do not know for certain. The other cats are prowling small, worried circles in the pens, wearing out the land. The paths they walk are old and dirty, like the nightgown that Trish hasn't changed in over a week, not since our boy was taken from us.

"The men are coming any minute," Trish says.

These are men with badges pinned to their breast pockets or tucked in their wallets. My boy had just started shaving, and these men wear mustaches and carry long slender guns. I could unlatch the gate, set fire to the sagebrush and the wooden shelters, and send the animals into the neighbors' pastures and beyond our town, into the semiopen range. I've seen dogs cross freeways. I could say that I lost control, and this would not be far from the truth.

"You better put on some clothes," I tell Trish.

I am afraid I will not be able to watch them kill what I have spent my life creating, and I am afraid that I will be able to watch them. Even with the windows closed, I can hear the car approaching. Trish returns in a pair of jeans and sandals, a yellow T-shirt. She looks normal.

Out front, three men ease their way out of a sedan. They are of a kind, large and broad with heads that sit directly on their shoulders and slits for eyes. They stand in the doorway. They nod at Trish. They are polite with their rifles, angling them down like canes. The biggest one with heavy steps says, "My condolences about your son."

Out of Trish's mouth comes a new, terrible sound.

The air outside is so thick, it is difficult to breathe. There is dust, and there is the smell of rotten meat. One man whistles under his breath. One man breathes heavily through his mouth. The man from the state, dressed in normal clothes instead of a uniform, takes out a red handkerchief and puts it across his face. Three cats huddle around a corpse, one of them lapping up the blood that has spilled out of the li-tigon's side. I do not know whether these three are the strongest or the biggest, or whether there is something else, something I cannot know, that makes them hunt their kind.

"My God," the sheriff says.

"There's a good chance those three are diseased," the Fish and Game man says. "The humane thing is to kill them."

"What were you thinking?" asks the man from the state in a muffled voice.

I see how it looks to them: the holes in the fence that I have repaired with chicken wire, the filth that has built up in the enclosure since I have been too afraid to enter, the scattered piles of wood that I intended to use, the crooked row of bushes that runs like a scar across the land, the shovels and rakes, the rusty axes and handsaws strewn across the yard, the wheelbarrow overflowing with glass bottles that might have lined flowerbeds, the bags of concrete that have hardened after years of being left in the rain.

I see what they see.

The cats, stretched out in the shade of the small shrubs and sagebrush, do not move. They are stretched out on their sides in a way that would seem peaceful, except they look tired and thin. None of them moves except the three who understand that their survival depends upon eating one of their own.

The man from Fish and Game raises his gun and pulls the trigger four times: pop, pop, pop, pop. It is so quick, the three cats in the clearing don't move until after the shots have been fired.

"No," I shout. It is too late.

The cats race away from the li-tigon as though they had just woken from a dream and realized what they were doing. They run, but there is nowhere for them to go, no escape from Ligertown, no dignified place where they can quietly slip away. They run circles, blood spurting from their wounds and raining down on the dry land. They run. It seems like they run for hours, but it is over in minutes. The smallest one slows first. His mane is streaked with red, his tail limp. They slow down but keep moving forward, trying to get away from the terrible thing that has happened, the pain that has entered them. They wobble forward, and before they choose to stop, they fall, and nothing happens, nothing rises, except for dust.

FIVE SHORTS

Sam Shepard

CRACKER BARREL MEN'S ROOM
(HIGHWAY 90 WEST)

I understand there was a man who got trapped inside a Cracker Barrel men's room, once. (I've heard the story three or four times now in various convenience stores and gas stations just outside of Butte, so there must be some germ of truth to it.) He was trying to take a dump in peace in one of those oversize stalls for the handicapped (even though he wasn't). He liked the extra space around him, the aluminum hand-rail, the hooks to hang his hat and coat. It must have been after closing hours, I guess, because the night manager had mistakenly locked him up in there and had also left the sound system on and, evidently, Shania Twain songs played all night long in an endless loop. Over and over, that's all he heard was Shania Twain. She sang songs of vengeance and good riddance, infidelity of all stripes, callous treatment at the hands of drunken cowboys, maudlin ballads of deprived youth, the general inability of men to see into her hidden charms; songs where she refused to be a slave anymore to the whims of men, like for instance making toast, doing the dishes, washing clothes, frying an egg, shopping for groceries. She wasn't buying into any of that stuff. Then she had songs full of praise for her mother; prayers to her baby sister, her great-aunt, her sister-in-law, her sister's sister-in-law. She praised God for making her a woman. She praised Jesus for her spectacular body and her luscious red mane falling down to her luscious ass. The man became desperate to escape the Cracker Barrel men's room. He tried to dismantle the door hinges with his trusty Swiss Army Knife. He tried pounding the walls. He tried screaming his head off but there was nobody there. No dishwasher, no waiter, no cashier, no janitor, no night manager, no one but Shania Twain, over and over and over and over again. There was no escape from the onslaught. The man collapsed to the tile floor in a heap of resignation and tried to fall asleep but sleep wouldn't come. Shania's voice taunted and tortured him. She clawed at his ears with her long silver talons. He hauled himself up off the floor and turned all the water faucets on full blast. He punched all the hand-dry blowers. He flushed every toilet but nothing would drown out the piercing voice. He could still hear it pealing through the background somewhere; whining away in mawkish misery. He tried climbing up on top of the toilet stall and unscrewing the speaker but he stripped all the screwheads with his trusty Swiss Army Knife and fell backwards to the floor, impaling himself with the open blade. He writhed in pain and managed to extract the knife from his left thigh but blood gushed freely into the overflowing water of the sinks and steam was rising like out of some primordial stew. He dragged himself through the darkening red mess of it, back toward the door, moaning like some butchered stockyard animal. He kicked with his one good leg and flailed his hands and screamed one last time but nobody answered; nobody but Shania Twain in her endless refrain. Then he surrendered completely and did something he'd never done in his entire life. He prayed. He prayed to Jesus to stop the bleeding. He prayed to God for a little peace and quiet. He prayed someone might find him before he drowned in his own fluids. Then a miraculous thing happened (and this has been verified by at least two eyewitness accounts—window washers at the very scene); the men's room door swung slowly open and there she was—Shania herself, towering before him in her spectacular body, her spectacular red hair, her spectacular lips, her spectacular tits. She was singing her head off. She was singing like there was no tomorrow. She didn't seem to notice the man on the floor, bleeding to death. In fact she stood right on his chest in her green satin stiletto high heels and kept right on singing. She seemed to be focused on something in the far, far distance but it was hard to tell through the steam.

DEVIL'S MUSIC
(MONTANA, HIGHWAY 2)

From Culbertson to Cut Bank, all along the High Line, he ripped his voice out completely. At first he was just managing to sing along politely with the Howlin' Wolf Chess collection; dodging in and out of feeble harmony attempts on "Back Door Man" and "Moanin' at Midnight," but gradually he became carried away in a frenzy of exultation. By the time he hit Kalispell his throat was actually bleeding but he couldn't stop himself. Something had taken over. He kept desperately trying to find the shift from the high nasal megaphone pitch down into Wolf's deep growling groans of lost love and tortured treachery but he just couldn't find it. He was stuck somewhere smack in the middle. Torn apart. Truckers blew by him with American flags flapping from every possible fixture; staring down in bewilderment at his bloated purple face, screaming to the wind: "I asked her for water but she brought me gasoline!" He passed ranchers on three-wheelers gathering calves as he belched out "Smokestack Lightnin'," torturing himself with the failure to make the transition into the shaky howls and terrible haunting swings of Wolf's paranoia: "Don't you hear me crying?" "Where'd you sleep last night?" The sky dipped into great bars of plum-colored clouds as the sun set behind the Bitterroots and he pressed on hypnotically toward Bonners Ferry. He checked into the Motel 8 there but his voice wouldn't work at all. Nothing came out but a faint wheeze. He kept smiling apologetically to the little gray woman behind the desk and pushing his credit card toward her so at least she'd know he was good for the rent. He took the Wolf CD with him into room #6, on the ground floor, but there was nothing to play it on so he sat on the edge of the bed and read the liner notes: How Wolf ended up weeping for his mother on his deathbed but she never came to visit. She had forsaken him a long time ago for singing the Devil's music.

WYOMING

(HIGHWAY 80 EAST)

The long haul from Rock Springs to Grand Island, Nebraska, starts out bleak. After two runny eggs and processed ham I hit the road by 7:00. It's hovering at around nineteen degrees; light freezing snow and piss-poor visibility. Eighteen-wheelers jackknifed all along the high ridges between Rawlins and Laramie. Tow trucks blinking down into the black ravines. Through wisping fog, things loom up at you with chains and hooks and cranes; everyone inching along, afraid to drop off into the wide abyss. Just barely tap the brakes and the whole rear end slides out from underneath you. I'm trying to keep two tires on the shoulder in the chatter strip at about five mph hoping the ice will get dislodged between the treads. Only radio station is a preacher ranting from Paul—something about the body as a tent; "this tent in which we groan." Same preacher segues into a declaration that, for him, 1961 was the absolute turning point where the whole wide world went sour. I don't know why he landed on that particular year—1961—the very year I first hit the road, but he insists this is the date of our modern dissolution. He has a long list of social indicators beginning with soaring population then family disintegration, moral relaxation, sexual promiscuity, dangerous drugs, the usual litany. But then he counters it with the imperious question: "What must the righteous do?" As though there were an obvious antidote which we all seem to be deliberately ignoring. If we could only turn our backs on this degeneration and strike out for high ground, we could somehow turn the whole thing around. It seems more political than religious. "What must the righteous do?" An "Onward, Christian Soldiers" kind of appeal. I've lost track of the centerline. Snow boring down into the windshield so fast the wipers can't keep up. Your heart starts to pump a little faster under these conditions; not knowing what might suddenly emerge. Not knowing if the whole world could just drop out from underneath you and there you are at the bottom of crushed steel and spinning wheels. What *must* the righteous do?

WOUNDED KNEE, PINE RIDGE RESERVATION

The large metal sign on the dusty shoulder of Highway 27, explaining, front and back, the horrific events that took place here in December 1890, has been altered. The word *battle* has been covered over with a patchwork metal plate riveted to the sunbleached narrative reading *massacre* in bold black letters. "Massacre" replaces "battle," as if that's all the correction we need to alter our thinking about it. As if now we are able to digest the actuality of carnage, one hundred and twenty years in our past.

Pathetic little lean-tos roofed with pine boughs shelter wrinkled-up Lakota women selling beaded crafts and crude jewelry. It's 103 degrees and the wind is swirling across the broken highway sending up dust devils. White plastic coffee cups and potato chip bags go whipping by. A dark hawk high above a field of burnt grass tumbles and swoops through the hot-air currents, hoping for some sign of varmints below. I decide to park beside a line of glittering Harleys directly across the highway from the monument; thinking that driving up the hill to the site might be disrespectful. There's also some nagging notion that walking up the hill in this sledgehammer heat might be some slight form of penance. (I don't know where these notions of guilt originate.) I'm staring down at my boots in the powdery clay as I climb toward the two brick columns, arched by a steel span with a small cross in the middle. "Walking through time," I whisper. I reach the top and pull out my disposable Kodak that I've been using to record catch-and-release Rainbows. I've only got a couple shots left. As I'm trying to focus on the raggedy monument, a boy's face jumps into the frame then darts back out. A skinny teenage Lakota boy with wide eyes and a crooked smile. He peeks out at me from behind one of the brick columns. I take my eye away from the lens and see two more boys hiding behind the structures. I call out to them and ask if I can take their picture in front of the monument. They shyly reveal themselves, barefoot in grimy T-shirts, clutching aluminum cans of Pepsi. I ask if they can bunch together under the steel arch. They giggle and line up facing me then, suddenly, as I raise the Kodak to my eye, they all throw their fists to the sky mimicking the Black Panther salute of the sixties. I have no idea what era I'm living in.

MILES CITY, MONTANA
(HIGHWAY 94 WEST)

Seven young firefighters from the BLM Forest Service are looking for rooms in the War Bonnet Inn. I'm standing, waiting in line right behind them in the lobby. Their exhausted faces; red eyes, hooded in ash, the steel toes of their boots burned black. Montana's on fire. Miles of open rangeland in flames right up to the shoulder of the interstate. That's all anyone talks about around here. How to contain it. Where exactly the giant Caterpillars have cut the breaks. How often the planes are bombing the wild ridges with water canisters. How many new conflagrations have spontaneously erupted from Bozeman to Missoula and beyond; up into the High Line, threatening the ski resorts from Kalispell to Hungry Horse? Blame it on Big Bad Nature, touching down. Lightning from the Thunder Gods. They're laughing at us from far away; watching us scramble in earthly horror. As soon as one blaze gets extinguished another flares up. We're chasing our tails down here.

By the time I step up to the desk all the rooms have been taken. More long pickups loaded with young firefighters are pouring into the parking lot as I come out of the lobby into the glowing red dusk. The air smells strong of burning pine and sagebrush. Your eyes sting of ash. Maybe Billings has a room. Down the burning highway. Maybe Billings.

OPPOSITION IN ALL THINGS

Shawn Vestal

I

hen I awoke. Sea the color of stone curled away in every direction, tucking itself beneath a bright mist that blotted out the sky. A tinge of lilac bleeding into the frosty air. A rocking, a lulling. Was this the celestial kingdom? I had believed I was dying into God's glory. Now I was seeing through someone else's eyes and could but hope this was a passage, a way there. The ashen sea rocked on. I stared into the haze, longing to see it open upon a wide shore, a sacred light, the heavenly host.

But the mist did not part, and no shore appeared, and I remained behind the eyes of a stranger, a sailor on an armored warship, standing ready beside a big gun on the foredeck, a bigger gun than I had ever seen. I watched with him from the deck, and from his seat at the mess, and as he read his letters in his cramped bunk, sour water swishing on the floor below. It was no heaven and no hell, and soon I realized, from the letters, that he was no stranger. He was Rulon Warren, the son of a niece whom I had known only as a girl. And what was I? Angel or spirit? And what was my purpose?

When we returned from the war in Europe and all we had seen there, Rulon Warren wanted nothing but the silence no one would allow. He was assaulted by talk. Everyone called for an accounting. I wanted so much to help him then, to ease his way or strike down his enemies, but I held no such earthly powers.

His parents wanted to speak to him at all hours—his mother, my niece, about church services and socials, young women in town, his plans for the future; his father about the barley, canal weeds, young women in town. His mother could talk for hours, it seemed, while his father spoke only three and four words at a time, but they both wanted the same from him, a future parceled out in syllables.

At church on Sundays, the older men came up one by one, shy, like courters at a dance. *Didn't it make you seasick, all that time on the boat? How many of those Huns did you send into outer darkness?* Rulon sometimes could not think of a single word. He would blush and shrug and look at the ward-house floor, and the men would do something similar, rebuked. They'd pat him on the shoulder and retreat. Other times, the answers came as if from another place. He was never once seasick. "Best sea legs on the ship came from right here in Idaho," he'd brag. And in his job on the ship, navigating the fixed gun on the foredeck, he'd probably helped kill thirty-five or forty of the kaiser's boys. "My share," he would say, and try to smile. "Maybe a few more."

I could feel his temptation to tell them, the men with their fingernails cleaned and hair slick for Sunday, that he'd stood next to a gunner whose head had vanished in a pink mist, and that hours later, below deck and pulsing with adrenaline, he had found bits of skull clinging to the shoulder of his uniform. Or that he had watched as his fellow sailors fired on the survivors of the *Gotthilf,* the destroyer they'd sunk in the metal-gray North Sea, the Germans bobbing in the water, waving their arms in surrender, and then jerking and sliding below the churning water while the sailors laughed. I could feel Rulon's desire to unsettle the brethren, to terrify them—it was the selfsame desire I had brought to church during my own life, Sunday after Sunday, and in those early days of our coexistence, it made me feel we were aligned.

And yet we were not. Rulon's guilt boiled at him. He pitied those Huns, which had struck me as weak when he'd first felt it, out on the ship. Like the response of a child. I had only recently joined him then and was lost inside my new existence. I had died, bleeding onto the earth in the Tetons, killed by a posse, and then thirty-two years passed in a black instant and I awoke inside Rulon's vision. We were sailing into a sea that spread in every direction into a cloak of fog. The bliss of death was already fading, and the first sensations of my new life were the salt air, the roll of the horizon, the anxiety burning within Rulon, and the fear that I had awakened to something never-ending.

Weeks later, after I had discovered, from his letters, the passage of time since my death, Rulon couldn't let the deaths of those Huns go. He would pray at night for forgiveness, and he dwelled upon the souls of the Germans, pondering how their eternities would be affected by their foreshortened lives. What if they had died before they'd had the chance to achieve their full righteousness? He worried about his own sin as well, and I was there with him in all of it. I saw what he saw, and I sensed his thoughts and shared in the images that spun relentlessly through his mind. He thought back to the time, before he had shipped, when he'd asked the bishop whether it was a sin to kill an enemy in warfare. Bishop Lawton, a short thin man who curved forward at the shoulders, had seemed surprised.

"You're serving your country, son," he said. "That's no sin."

Then the bishop cited the warfare in the Bible, the battles in the Book of Mormon between Nephites and Lamanites. The sixth commandment was a prohibition on murder, he said, not war. As Rulon brooded, I thought of my own life—my desire to be exalted for slaying the Lord's enemies and my fear that I would be damned instead. I now doubted that either was true. Was this damnation? Exaltation? I could see no punishment in it, nor any reward. When Rulon prayed in his bunk at night, doubt hounded my thoughts. What was this life? Where was God's hand?

When I was alive, I prayed daily, over meals and with my parents and sister, and by myself before bed. I prayed before every decision. I prayed before asking Sally Bartram to marry, and then we prayed together once she said yes. I prayed before I bought my own cattle—the fifteen head my father told me I was a fool to purchase. The cattle sold at a profit, and I knew that I would discard the wisdom of my elders and listen only for the answers to my prayers. I prayed when I left the church and my parents and faithless Sally Bartram, and I received an answer, the knowledge that I was walking in the Lord's light. I knew it then the way I knew how to strike with a maul or knot a length of rope, but I did not know it any longer. Every new day showed me that I must have been wrong. Rulon would get no help from beyond but for me, and I pitied us both.

In his bunk on the ship, Rulon had often wondered why no one else was concerned about the killing. The whole town of Franklin, it seemed, had come to wish him farewell when he left for the navy. They had all appeared happy he was going, so proud. He fretted over these memories, unable to overcome his fear that everyone—the ward, the town, the whole country— was wrong about this: *Thou shalt not kill,* he thought. They had papered over sin with happy lies.

Now that he was back, the bishop was after him to give a talk to the ward. Rulon could share how the Lord had helped him through his times at sea. "Maybe not yet," Rulon said, but what he did not say was that he had experienced no help from the Lord at sea. He had ridden on that ship beyond the sight of land and beyond the hand of the Lord, which he had not thought possible.

He returned certain he was fallen.

All that talk. How I wished to draw a curtain of silence around him. To describe for him the eternity of silence awaiting him, how comforting it might be before it turned to torment. To say: *Peace be with you.* To say: *May peace cast its shadow on your heart.* But my words weighed nothing, and even then—when I still wanted him to live—I had no honest desire for peace.

Rulon had been honorably discharged in May 1918 and had spent a week in San Francisco with some of the other men from the USS *Gooding*. At night, he had stayed in his hotel room, paid for by the navy, and had tried to adjust to the idea that he was back in this world. San Francisco was as foreign as the sea. Sailors roamed the streets drunkenly, arms flung over shoulders, calling obscenely to passing women. The wharves reeked of fish and salt, and nights were smudged with lamp soot and weak yellow light. Every time he met another sailor, he'd be told once again where the best brothels were. "Nickel a throw," they'd say, unashamed. "Get yourself a dollar's worth." Rulon prayed and prayed, and remembered the exhortations of the brethren—their appeals to chastity and purity, their warning of the Lord's watchfulness over everything.

Lust tore at him. He couldn't stop thinking about what it would be like. Finally, he went to the address in Chinatown. The woman had light brown hair that smelled of chemicals and flowers, and her lips tasted waxy. Afterward, Rulon was not quite sure what had happened between them—could not picture the way their bodies had come together. He knew only the surge of intensity that wrapped his hips and shot up his spine. "Already?" the woman said in a teasing voice, and Rulon opened his eyes and noticed she was much younger than she had at first appeared, the skin around her eyes smooth and unwrinkled, the pores on her nose tiny.

Her scent haunted him, back to his hotel and through the night, and as he thought of her, I thought of faithless Sally Bartram, my fiancée, whom I had never kissed, who had smiled with half-closed eyes as we'd danced at the ward house on Friday nights, her hand light on my shoulder. I remembered how I was choked with the desire to press into her, *through* her, and I wanted Rulon to go back now, to return again and again.

For two days, he prayed inside his room. He told himself he must have passed through the war and into hell. The city was never quiet, and the lights burned all night. The third day, he went back and spent a dime. He told himself it didn't matter whether he committed this sin, because he'd done worse, but he felt watched and ashamed as he walked the narrow streets and went up the stairs to the door marked by a sign in Chinese characters. In the front room, men sat on couches, murmuring with the girls. Sheer red cloth draped the lamps, shading the room in crimson. Rulon asked for the woman by name: *Irene*. Walking home, he could smell her perfume, now familiar, and taste her smoky breath, and he knew he had stained his soul. He left for home the following day, and he could not stop thinking of Irene, of her cheap stockings draped over a bedpost, the thrill of her carnal smile, the fleshy rub of her belly against his.

He rode the train first to Boise and then to Pocatello, where his folks waited for him at the train platform. His father's beard seemed longer, spreading like an apron below his collarbone. He wore simple wool clothing, threadbare gray pants hemmed high above the ankles of his boots. His mother— my niece, a girl I had barely known, now grown into a woman who carried weariness in her frame—wore a gingham dress made from a pattern of pale blue with tiny flowers. They took a room in a hotel—Rulon on the floor and his parents in the small bed—and then caught the one daily train to Franklin the next morning. Rulon watched the landscape as the train lurched and smoked, the tan floor of the desert spotted with dusty sage. Franklin was the state's first settlement, formed sixty years before by the Warrens and thirteen other families who had followed the Mormon Trail out from Illinois to the Salt Lake Valley, and then north, after years of pestilence and drought.

"They thought they were in Utah!" Rulon's father would say with a roar, any time he had the chance to tell the story. It was true. My own father was among those who had crossed the territorial border unaware into Idaho. He built our home at the foot of the Tetons, the heavenward mountains, and used to say that God meant for this land to be in Utah—in Zion—but that men are often deaf to His intentions.

Rulon settled at the farm and worked with his father. Spreading across the wide valley floor to the east of the town, the Warren place was one of the biggest in the county, a range of wheat and barley and cattle pasture that Rulon's father had expanded year after year. In the center sat the magisterial two-story house, painted white, with a steeply pitched roof and a row of box elders on the west side. A grid of ditches and culverts, hand dug, lined the fields, and Rulon's father was often consulted by the other men in town about irrigation and farm practices. Rulon's older sister had married while he was still in school; she lived four miles away on a smaller farm, on the other side of town, with her husband and children. When Rulon returned, the planting was done and everything was greening, the land fresh and bristly under the warm sun. Rulon loved getting out into the fields and emptying his mind, carrying a shovel along the ditch bank or hauling hay to the cattle.

He didn't know what he would do and didn't wonder. He wanted only cool mornings in an empty room as the first line of sunlight traced the horizon, hot afternoons on a dusty ditch berm, cool evenings with the moon white in the window. Empty rooms and dreaming. Empty rooms and the remembered feel of sheer stockings, the taste of lipstick, the motion of Irene's head on the pillow, her mocking little laugh. He could no longer picture her face, but could envision the skin under her eyes and along her nose, could remember the moment he realized how young she was—seventeen? sixteen? younger? He eyed the girls in church now and felt intense impurity. He could make a whole life out of doing that, pants folded over a chair, an hour's rest and back at it. Sin was sin, and how much could it compound? He had already broken a commandment many times over: Thou shalt not kill. All those Germans. That, plus three times with Irene and, more appalling, his delight in it, his continued delight. How could his eternal reward be worse now if he abandoned himself to a life of murder and fornication? And yet he could not. He yearned for sin, and then forgiveness, and then for sin, and he could not decide, moment to moment, where the wickedness was greater: in himself, in the church, or in the world.

I wanted to tell him they were only Huns. Pile them up. I would have fired those guns myself and laughed as the Germans sank. I wanted to tell him he was but a man upon the earth. But I could not influence him, could not make my presence real in any way. Sometimes I concentrated thoughts and tried to send them to him, tried to wish him into acting. *Close it now,* I would think as he read from the Book of Mormon during church. *Close it.* I tried to focus my command into a beam of light. *Close it, Rulon. It is folly.* I was desperate for him to hear me. What was my existence otherwise? I tried and tried to make a ripple in the world. To be there.

Rulon's parents invited Ann Lawton to dinner without telling him. She arrived one Sunday after church, in a new-looking dress of pale blue that hung so low it covered her feet and rose snugly to her neck and traveled down to her wrists. She was seventeen, the bishop's daughter, quietly bold. She wore her long brown hair in a single braid and was delicate but for her chapped red ears. Her father was the bishop who had blessed Rulon when he shipped out, the one who had reassured him, and he felt false before both father and daughter.

After church that Sunday, before Ann arrived, Rulon had gone to his room, up the narrow stairs and at the end of a dim hall. He had taken off his tie and dress shoes and lain on his bed, watching the play of light on the wall as the curtain lifted and fell before the open window. An eddy in time arrived, and he entered it. He drifted near sleep. His legs and hips lightened as though they were lifting with the curtain, and his head became warm and damp, and the sound of his breath lulled him, until his mother called.

Going downstairs in his stocking feet, he heard his mother say, "Rulon, come say hello to Ann." He stopped. He was aware that from the living room below, where his family and their guest sat waiting for him, his feet and the legs of his trousers were visible. The room was bright with sunlight, and he could hear his nieces and nephews clattering about on the porch. Resentment filled his mind. He had gone to sea and done what he had done, and now was being denied peace, the only thing he sought. His fury covered all the people he knew, all the people who continued to live, to eat Sunday dinner and hang clothing on the line and take baths in fresh water and have picnics and parades and ask smiling questions about the war. Sometimes at church, he imagined the heads of the Saints exploding silently—the bishop's head as he stood at the pulpit, the heads of the men who sidled up to him, the heads of the people in the pew in front of him, one by one in time with the hymns, a wave of magical death bursting amid the empty talk of sin. Now he imagined it happening with his family, a popping sound repeated throughout the house—his mother in the living room, sister in the kitchen, her husband on the porch with his father, leaving his nieces and nephews out of it—the bodies strewn about while he slept the silent day away. I experienced it, too—the throb of adrenaline, the rushing thrill of anger, flooding me just as it had in the days before my death—and I could not begrudge him.

At dinner, though, Rulon was fine. He talked to Ann about the crops and teased her about boys in the ward. His parents and sister mostly listened to them talk, joining in when there was a pause, pressing them along. They passed the large crockery bowls filled with potatoes and beans again and again. Rulon looked at Ann and saw Irene, and beneath the table he swelled. He felt guilty for besmirching Ann with his thoughts, and yet he didn't try to stop. He imagined her bare shoulder blades, placing a freckle on the right one. He imagined the dip in her collarbone, pink nipples, pale belly, a wild thicket of hair. He imagined her embarrassed whispers. Rulon could not tell, but I could see in the speckled flush that bloomed on Ann's neck and face when they talked, and in the way her eyes darted away from his, that she had already decided she loved him.

After dinner, Rulon walked her down the dirt lane to her house, his irritation having vanished in the easy pleasure of her company. A ditch ran alongside the lane, and insects spun above the thick green grass, catching the coppery afternoon light. I thought: *Take her hand.* She told him of the scandals from the ward dances: which girls disappeared and returned with which boys. She told him the gossip about Brother Lundeblad drinking whiskey, how his sons had to keep the farm going. His hands swung loose at his sides. *Take her hand, Rulon. Turn her toward you.* When they reached her house, she reached for his hand while he said good-bye, and it froze his words. Back in his room, he tugged at himself furiously, thinking first of Irene and then of Ann, and fell to his bed in shame.

I was with him then, as in all moments. There was nothing in Rulon's mind that made me sorry for his soul. *Do not be ashamed.* I imagined my voice, rich with the cadenced tones of a prophet. *You are but a man upon the earth. You are forgiven.* I watched, and I wondered again about my own existence. *You will need no forgiveness.* I had been with him for eighteen months now, but no part of me could reach him. He brooded over every little sin. I dreaded the idea that this was all of life left to me and that it might plod on and on. I wanted to press against Rulon, to force him into action. Any action. *There is no forgiveness you will ever need.*

For weeks, Rulon did little but work on the farm, irrigating the fields, clearing weeds from the ditches. The wheat turned golden, the heads of barley grew heavy, and the warm afternoon breezes made waves of the fields. His parents suggested daily that he walk up the lane to the Lawtons, that he pay Ann a visit, that he sit beside her at church. But he could not. When he was with Ann, he would turn her into Irene. It became impossible to sit comfortably with her. He was convinced his lust was apparent to all. He spoke less and less. Sometimes when his mother asked him a question, he walked away without answering or merely kept his eyes on his plate. He could not marry Ann Lawton, or any other righteous woman, for he no longer desired their righteousness. And yet he could not stop thinking of Ann. At church, she looked for him when he came in, and despite himself, he would smile or nod. He felt his every glance was a lie, and that he should no longer live around people.

When he learned that the government was going to open a post office in Franklin, he applied for the position. He got the job—mostly, he was told by the visiting postmaster from Pocatello, because he was a war hero—and decided to move into a room in the back of the new pine-smelling post office they had built on the town's main street.

The news shocked Rulon's parents. Though he would be in town, just three miles away, it was a larger departure than they had ever expected. He was their only son. His mother wept, and his father told him the farm would be there for him when got tired of the post office.

"I always figured you'd take this place over," his father said. They were sitting in the living room before supper. Fall was coming, twilight sifting down earlier each day. Soon harvest would begin.

"I'll help you get the wheat and barley put up, and then go," Rulon said. "I'm not sure it was ever really for me."

His parents were confused, I could tell, because it was a lie. Rulon took naturally to farm work, walking the fields and testing the moisture of the soil, checking for stripe rust on the wheat, calming cows to put medicine drops into their great glassy eyes. But Rulon wanted silence at meals. Freedom in the afternoons. He wanted never to discuss the war again with any smiling face, never to sit across a family table laden with bread and jam and roasted meat and pretend to chastity with any woman.

Go, I thought. *Go*. I wanted something new. I had followed his dreary routine, day upon day, and sensed his desperate faith, his clutching need to be righteous, and I sometimes thought this was a hell after all, one that revealed itself slowly. A hell of Rulon's making, which could end only when he did.

Rulon rode into town together with his father. He was calm as the wagon clattered along, and was grateful his father didn't speak. I sensed the moment was right for me then. *Rulon*. If my existence was all there was to eternity, why should he be deviled by sin, by guilt, by propriety? Why should he not live a life of happy moments? *Follow your will*. I could not fathom my existence. Were there others like me? Out there among the living, behind their eyes? The days were pale, emptied of meaning. *Follow your will*. I wanted Rulon to burn down the tedium of my days. But he was like a branch floating downriver, and I was a leaf fallen beside him, drifting without weight on the water.

II

Rulon loved the post office and his simple little room in back: his bed, a small table and one chair, his navy trunk, and a couple of shelves. His belongings had fit neatly into four boxes. On the shelves were his Book of Mormon and a few novels his mother had used as a schoolteacher, before she married: *Great Expectations*, *The Scarlet Letter*, *Les Misérables*. And the notebooks in which he had begun keeping a journal, pages filled with the turmoil of his mind.

In this room, he wrote, *with this one candle flame, the wind in the darkness, I can believe that I am alone upon the earth, perfectly, peacefully alone. Here is where I can worship. Here is where I can feel the Lord's spirit. Here, not in the lukewarm clamor and stink of the ward house, where everywhere you look is compromise and cowardice.*

The mail arrived every afternoon, a gray canvas bag that shuffled with secrets. Rulon welcomed it with a kind of reverence, and he handed over the outgoing sack with the same solemnity—the same reserve that animated his actions when he took the sacrament on Sundays, the gentle way he held the trays, the tiny cups of water, the bits of torn bread. The body and the blood. The sacrament had become real for him. He had held bits of flesh and bone between his fingers, just as he held the bread now, and when he tasted the bread, he believed he was tasting the living flesh of Christ, and some days he believed it saved him, and some days he believed there was not enough holy flesh in all the world to erase his wickedness.

Winter came hard. It snowed in mid-October and stayed cold for weeks, hardening the coarse snow. Rulon wore all his clothes and burned wood in his stove, but the wind slipped through the walls of the post office and chased away the heat.

Each day, Rulon sorted the letters into PO boxes and waited on customers and filled the gray sacks to go back to Pocatello and beyond. He enjoyed the order and predictability of the work and missed the open space and days of the farm less than he had imagined he would. His parents stopped by more than they needed to, and he always greeted them formally, like a servant, until his mother, baffled and hurt, stopped coming altogether.

His father kept at it, quietly. "Okay, son," he would say, taking his mail and preparing to leave. "I know your mother would like to see you sometime. You could come for supper on Sunday."

"Sunday would not be possible," Rulon said, flipping through a handful of envelopes.

"Some other day, then."

Rulon didn't answer, though it made him sad to keep silent. His father left, a wintry gust banging into the room. Rulon could not explain what had happened inside him, but he did not want to be with others.

He riffled the envelopes in his hand again. Rulon loved handling the mail, the thick brown envelopes and the smudged white ones, the letters and the packages, stamped red and blue, the announcement of all the world outside Franklin. He paid attention to who got what. Families got a lot of letters from Salt Lake. The Johansens got a letter a week from North Dakota; the Popes two a week from Nauvoo, Illinois. Frank Staley got special orders for fabric and dry goods from wholesalers in San Francisco or Minneapolis. One day, Rulon saw a letter for Ann Lawton, posted in Chicago, from "Elder Britton." Two weeks later, he saw another. Jake Britton, a kid Rulon used to torment at ward picnics and youth nights. On a mission in Chicago and writing letters home to Ann. Like most returning veterans, Rulon hadn't served a mission, but most other young men did, two years spent trying to bring far-flung people into the fold.

Rulon had told himself he was finished with Ann, but when he saw the third letter from Elder Britton, he slid it into the front pocket of his apron. Later he burned it at his table, wrote three angry pages in his journal about the spiritual weakness of the young, consumed as they were by lust and worldly emotions, and was then embarrassed before himself for his hypocrisy.

I came to hate the post office for just what Rulon loved—its tedious repetition, the sanctuary of routine. It was not so different from the plodding days on the farm. His days were my days, and I yearned for them to pulse with blood, with lust. *Go see Ann.* I'd send the futile messages. *Go to her.* Sometimes I thought Rulon was weakening and we were floating toward one another. As he sat in sacrament meeting, seething at the bishop's milky tones, I'd think: *Challenge him, Rulon. Denounce him.* He wanted peace, and I daydreamed of his violent end. It had been so thrilling to die. *Scatter their letters, Rulon. Make a fire in the night.*

In the early evenings, after work and before he settled into his reading and writing, Rulon walked outside town, along the fields—places that reminded me of my life. Once he stood on a ditch bank east of town, watching the gold and purple light on the Tetons and the gentle apron of hills easing into the valley. It called me to a specific moment from my own life—an exact replay of the light on the mountainside, the melancholy beauty of the dusk, the comforting silence that follows a day of noise and effort. I was walking home from Brother Miller's farm after an afternoon of putting up hay, flush with exhaustion. The memory brought back a keen surge of love for my physical self. How I missed my body! I missed swinging my arms and scratching my neck. I missed the sensation of meat and milk in my mouth, the crust of drool on my cheek upon waking.

I thought of my father, reading from the Book of Mormon at the family table, interpreting it for the rest of us. "There shall be opposition in all things," I could hear him say, in his whispery baritone. "Without darkness there can be no light. Without weakness, no strength. Without evil, no good."

I was waiting along with Rulon for an opposing force, for something to press against. Something in this world, some person or idea, was the opposite of me, and I needed to crash into it to become whoever or whatever I was.

Every morning, Rulon arose before dawn and read in his Book of Mormon or in Revelation. He was hounded by guilt over the war, over the iron-handed lust that seized him at night, and he repented daily. But he also became more concerned with the sins of others, and he sometimes felt righteous by comparison. He saw the end days all around him and believed he was surrounded by corruption and hypocrisy. He came to think that, through the war, the community was built on a foundation of killing, contracted and paid for, to be done quietly and beyond the curtain of the everyday.

In his journal: *Today, a parade in Richmond for three returning seamen. A murderer's parade. The brethren there wanted me to greet the men, welcome them back, form friendships, etc. They came to me to ask it, and I told them I could not.*

Rulon started missing church. The only reason he'd been going at all was guilt over his mother—she seemed drawn and shocked all the time now, as though she had never imagined anything as bad as this estrangement.

Again, in his journal: *The Church has become the whore of Babylon, calling forth the last days. It has strayed from the hard path of righteousness. It loves comfort and compliance, and respects no suffering but submission.*

I, too, had broken with the church, had cried out for a more vigorous gospel. Now I didn't care about any of that. *Hear me, Rulon. Heed me.* I didn't care what Rulon believed or what the bishop believed or what the people in the ward believed, because I knew they were wrong. *Make a fire in the night.* None of their hells described my hell. I did not understand what was happening to me, but I knew—with a faith surpassing any I'd ever had—that it had all been false, everything I had believed, it had all been a fantasy or a joke, and this imitation of life was all I would ever have. Sometimes I hated Rulon, hated his weakness with Ann, hated the dull and pointless struggle in his soul. *Listen.* I prayed to him at all hours, not without hope that he might one day answer. *Listen, brother. Listen.* I craved his death, to find whether I would perish with him or live on.

One night as Rulon slept, he dreamed he was in a field in spring, holding the smooth wooden handles of the plow and standing behind the sagging rump of the family mule. A fog of dust surrounded him. Shapes floated into clarity before his face. He saw his shipmate from the *Gooding*, a plug of tobacco in his cheek, saying with a wink and a leer, "You look at her right, sailor, and her drawers fall to the floor." His father floated forward and said, "Nephi said barley out back and potatoes here." His sister, saying, "Ann Lawton, Ann Lawton." Then a face he didn't recognize, the pinched, unhappy countenance of a woman, hair pulled into a bun behind her head. "John Wilder," she said, "your father paid a dime to have that sharpened."

The words rushed to me across time, as clearly as sound over water. The woman was my mother, exact in every way, and the moment returned to me: I was eight years old and, because of some misdeed, was hiding from my father in the firewood lean-to behind the house. After a while, when it became clear my father wasn't coming after me, I took up his ax and walked around the dirt yard, chipping it gently against the cross posts in the fence and on the rocky ground.

I hadn't tried to send Rulon the dream. He had drawn it from me somehow. Or I had melted into him. I tried even harder then to send him my thoughts, often the simplest things—*Take one more bite of beans. Now another. Now the bread.* Sometimes he would do as I said. *Open the letter.* Was it coincidence? Every life needs its faith. I longed for a voice. A prophet's voice. A patriarch's. If Rulon ever heard me, he might think it was the voice of the Lord.

Soon after the dream, Rulon attended sacrament meeting for the last time. He listened to Bishop Lawton's placating tones, his soft calls to righteousness. He watched the back of Ann Lawton's head, the stray strands of hair that caught the light and burned as golden filaments, and he could not chase away the lust. *Go to her. Find a way.*

That night he slipped into sleep and awoke inside a dream, a vision of Franklin and the surrounding valley from a rocky promontory in the Tetons. It looked like a view from heaven, from some impossibly high place. A voice spoke in words of an unknown language, and when Rulon turned, he looked upon a face that I knew well.

The man was Hiram Jensen. As Rulon floated toward him, Hiram spoke, calling him by my name. "They are coming, Brother Wilder. Our moment is nigh."

Rulon was dreaming my life, dreaming my last days on earth.

We had fled into the mountains—Hiram, myself, and five others. The Idaho territory had passed the Test Oath Act, banning Mormons from voting or holding office. This, after some counties had thrown good Mormon men in jail for celestial marriage and fired Mormon teachers. When the bishop called on the Saints to obey that law, to refrain from voting, I knew my break with the church had come.

"Render to Caesar the things that are Caesar's," the bishop said, in his ignorance and weakness.

Hiram organized the resistance—we would render nothing to Caesar. We would formally renounce the church and go to the polls, where we could honestly present ourselves as non-Mormons. Afterward, we would rebaptize each other into a new church with a new mission. A true church, which would not bow and truckle. When we arrived at the polls in Pocatello, a mob stood already in the street. They held signs with vile slogans and shouted as we tried to make our way inside. I blazed with hatred for those faces, the black pits of their eyes, their rotten mouths. We had settled this land—Mormons had, our families had. We should have been the ones guarding the polls and turning away the wicked.

Our plan failed. We were well known as the faithful. Despite our claims, the deputies tried to arrest us for voter fraud, and we fled into the mountains. After our first night, Hiram led us down to the valley, where we killed and half skinned a calf on the ranch of one of the town marshals, carving off as much as we could haul back. They might have left us alone if not for that, but peace was not what we wanted.

In Rulon's dream, he watched—and I watched, watched and remembered—as the posse came slowly up a field of shale toward our position behind a ledge. It was just as it was then, everything just as it was. I rested the sights of my rifle on the brown hat of the posse's leader. The rifle shot cracked and echoed through the mountains. The man fell. A ruby shadow grew from his head on the shale.

Hiram floated into Rulon's view. "Now you know," he said. "Now you know." And Rulon awoke, certain he had been sent a vision from the Lord. He spent the night praying for guidance. I thought: *Do not pray, brother. Act.* I wanted to be the answer to his prayers. I wanted him to know the joy of my final days, the joy that came from the force of our opposition. I wanted to live it again. *Act, Rulon.* After I shot that man, we spent two weeks in the mountains, the nights so cold we clung to each other for warmth. The first posse had been coming to arrest us; we knew the next one would not be so docile. During the days, Hiram preached to us a new gospel of righteous resistance—calling for the homeland for the faithful that we had come west to establish—and we burned with it. We baptized each other one day in an icy stream.

This was a holy war, Hiram said. I never sorrowed for killing that man, and yet I feared the only atonement would come through blood—my blood spilled upon the earth. But Hiram said there was no need for the blood sacrifice.

"Scripture tells us, Brother Wilder, that it is the murderer whose blood must spill. The warrior will live forever in God's light."

I was unconvinced. One night, I slipped away and knelt beneath a pine tree. I prayed to the Lord to forgive me, and I pricked my finger and squeezed three drops of blood onto the ground. They formed tiny black beads in the moonlight, and I knew how paltry I was before the Lord because I was not remorseful in my heart.

The sheriff's men returned, with a bigger posse. They swarmed us from all sides and made no attempt at capture. Before I felt the blade in my ribs, I saw a man open Hiram's throat with the slash of a knife. A horrific red gape appeared and rained down his chest. Lying on the ground, I watched my own blood pool on the soft earth, creeping among the pine needles and stones, a true atonement at last, and I slept in the certainty of my salvation, rushing, rushing toward the celestial kingdom, my eternal reward.

Rulon opened the next letter from Elder Britton, who wrote of his disappointment at not having had a letter from Ann for two weeks.

Rulon studied the close, tiny handwriting. Much of the letter was simply news of Britton's life—he was serving in Chicago, working in the urban neighborhoods, "baptizing few." Rulon wondered how far it had gone between Britton and Ann. It had been months since he had last walked the lane with Ann. He slid Britton's letter between the pages of his Book of Mormon.

Ann came to the post office three days after the letter had arrived. It was March; a smell of chill air and water lay under everything and rushed into the room with her. Rulon sorted letters behind the counter, and when she entered, his face flushed, tightening around the eyes. He feared his voice would tremble and show everything about him.

"Hello, Rule," she said.

"Hello, Miss Lawton," he said with mock formality, but the words were awkward in his mouth. "I'm glad to see you."

"I'm surprised to hear you say it."

She smiled thinly, holding something back. Rulon's heart boomed in his ears, and I heard it too, thinking, *Take her, take her*, his lust my own, instantaneous, everywhere.

Ann said, "I might have thought you hadn't taken any notice one way or the other. Shut up in here all day." As usual, her dress was buttoned to the neck and covered her to her ankles and wrists, but for Rulon, the room was suffused with the warm breath of her flesh, damp and eager.

"You know better," he said, and, after a pause, added quickly, "There's no mail for you."

"There's a dance Saturday at the ward house."

"I heard that."

Ann went crimson to her hairline, turned, and left.

Fluttering light filled Rulon. It was only 4:20 p.m., but he pulled the shade on the door and hung the closed sign and went back to his room. He retrieved the letter from Britton to Ann and read it again. He took out his notebook and pen, smoothed Britton's letter beside it, and began to write a new letter in close, tiny handwriting like Britton's own.

He copied the first paragraph exactly. And some of the next ones too. Then he wrote: *I heard of the fire at the ward dance from Jenny Monson. Jenny writes me fairly regular. She is a funny girl that I love to hear from and one who can tell a good story. Her letters don't hold a candle to yours, Ann, but they are entertaining.*

He tucked the letter into an envelope, copied the address, stamped the envelope, and put it in the box labeled "Lawton."

Rulon went to the dance Saturday. He stood along the wall near the door and watched as the dancers moved in and out of the lantern light. He hated every laughing face. He dreamed of their glorious deaths. Then he saw Ann, serving drinks and popcorn balls at the folding tables, and his anger ebbed. She looked at him, tipped her head toward the dance floor, and smiled. Rulon blushed. He walked to her and offered his arm, and they joined the next dance. He was a terrible dancer, but he stomped through the steps with vigor. Ann smiled at him and laughed often. A couple of times, as she turned past him, he smelled talc and cream, and he knew that it rose from under her clothes, and lust inflamed him. Coming off the dance floor, he ran into his mother and father, standing awkwardly to the side as though they were not waiting for him. Seeing them, he felt caught, and he could barely bring himself to speak. His father asked formal questions about the post office, and his mother asked him what he was eating, desperately trying to sound casual, and she laughed once, a shrill, false note. They parted after a long pause, like strangers forced together at a funeral.

Later, in his bed, he imagined Ann coming to him, emboldened, roughened, remade as Irene, red lips opening on teeth of pearl gray, breathing a stream of forbidden cigarette smoke through her pursed lips into the night air, lowering herself onto him, hair hanging in his face, talking to him all the while, talking in Irene's throaty voice, talking.

Ann wrote back to Britton. Hurt and reserve lay under every word, though she didn't mention Jenny Monson. Rulon took out a sheet of paper and wrote his own letter to Britton, carefully, in Ann's handwriting, saying she'd met someone new: *I have become closer to this man than I intended, and now I feel it would be dishonest of me to say otherwise. I feel I owe you that, you've been such a dear friend to me.*

They were the words Sally Bartram had written to me in 1865, mere weeks after she had moved with her family to Salt Lake City. Faithless Sally Bartram. When I saw those words come from Rulon's hand—"such a dear friend"—I remembered the moment I had first read them, on our porch, an autumn day in the heat of the afternoon, and I remembered my mother coming out while I read.

Rulon sealed the letter and mailed it to Elder Britton.

He began opening other letters. Sometimes he wrote replies. He wrote to one family that their sister in Nebraska had died of smallpox the day after everyone thought the fever had broken.

It was the precise manner of my mother's death.

He wrote a letter denying an extension on a loan payment to Roy Kalper, the largest landowner in the county. The words he used were the very words I had written—over and over again—as a clerk in my uncle's bank in Minneapolis, when my parents sent me to stay with him the summer of 1858.

Rulon believed he was inventing the stories, that he was being inspired to sow chaos in these placid lives. They would learn the truth eventually, he thought, and their sorrow would not last. But a nervous sliver would be left in their hearts, and he knew that they would trace the letters back to him eventually, and he wanted that. I wanted it, too, whatever it meant for Rulon.

Several weeks after he forged the letter to Elder Britton from Ann, she stopped at the post office on a Sunday afternoon. Rulon was lying on his cot, reading a Natty Bumppo novel. He read for hours every day now, Scripture and novels borrowed from the little "library" shelf set up at the store, and he began to consider the idea of writing something more himself, something more than journal entries or the tales he was spinning in the letters. An accounting. A testament.

Ann knocked and said his name quietly, and he sat up on his cot, silent for nearly a minute before deciding to open the door. The sun was behind her, throwing her face into shadow, ringed by a corona of light. She held a basket with a cloth folded over the top.

"Hello, Rule," she said, smiling.

I pitied her then, to be chasing him so. She was losing her pride. But Rulon's desire flared, and it raised in me again how I missed my human form.

"What are you smuggling in that basket?" Rulon asked, and he was thrilled at his easy tone, his clerk's glibness. "Come in so I can get a look."

She had brought him cinnamon rolls, and they shared one at his little table. He sat on the bed and she used the chair. No one else had been inside the room. As they ate, Rulon realized with a start how shoddy it looked, as though he were waking up to something he had ceased to see. His thread-worn clothing sat in a pile on his trunk. Sheets of paper, covered with scrawls, were scattered about. Pieces of mail lay on the floor, on the bed, on the little shelf. A package to the dry goods store sat in the corner, unopened. It occurred to him, too late, that he ought to have hidden the mail before he invited Ann in. She noticed it, and uncertainty entered her attitude.

He told her he had been reading in the Book of Mormon and praying about it; he didn't want his absence at church to give her the idea that he was losing his righteousness. I wanted him to put that aside. I was remembering Irene and thinking that Rulon could simply take Ann. Overpower her. *Embrace her.* He struggled to explain himself to Ann. He could not tell her how he had become convinced the Lord was warning him away from the church, because her father was the bishop and because it was the foundation of her entire life. It would sound only like wickedness to her.

Finally, she said she had to leave. *Kiss her. Take her skirt in your fists.* Rulon stood beside her as she wrapped the rolls and put the empty basket on her arm, and he looked down at the fine hairs on the back of her neck, the final flesh before her blue dress rose and covered her. He reached out his hand but did not know how to begin. *Seize her.* He placed his right arm around her shoulder abruptly and buried his face in her neck, sensed the warmth of her skin. *Kiss her on the mouth.* He pressed his lips to her neck, feeling she might turn to him, but she stiffened and remained rigid. Her silence told him the depth of his mistake. She simply waited, playing dead, then left when he released her, not once raising her head. Rulon sat on his bed for hours, as it grew darker and darker.

I whispered to him all through that night. *Scatter the letters. Make a fire in the night.* I could feel his shame, his conviction that he did not belong among people. Was there room for me inside him now? *Be a force against. A force opposed.* And the rushing flume of his anger, growing out of all of it, washed us closer and closer together.

III

Rulon didn't open the post office the next day. He stayed in the back as people came and knocked, shouted for him, and then left him to silence. He emerged only when he heard the mail wagon, in the afternoon. After collecting the canvas bag silently from Broom Janson, he turned back toward his room.

Rulon dumped the contents of the bag on his bed. Something about it nauseated him. *Burn it.* A network of human connections, built on lies and comfort. He picked up the first letter and tore it open. News of the Nebraska prairie to Glenda McDevit from a niece. He opened another. A report from a missionary to his parents. Another. A bill for milk delivery. *Burn it.* He opened every envelope and package, and when he was finished he stuffed it all back into the canvas sack and lifted it over his shoulder. *Burn them all.* He went out and walked to the middle of the street, the short graded dirt road that ran between the five buildings of downtown Franklin—the dry goods store, the post office, the ward house, the livery, and the tiny jailhouse. Rulon emptied the sack in the street and kicked the torn pieces of mail as though they were autumn leaves. It was a weekday afternoon, and the street was not busy, but the few people there stopped what they were doing and stared at him.

We were moving, the two of us, and gaining speed.

Sister Bingham came out of the dry goods store, and behind her, Brother Barry, the store's owner. They squinted against the lowering sun at Rulon as though he presented an enduring mystery.

"Greetings, Sister Bingham! Brother Barry!" Rulon waved in an exaggerated manner. He was filled with the Lord's pulsing light, and would not have been surprised to find himself rising above the earth. He laughed. "See you in church on Sunday!"

He marched back to the post office. For the first time, he found the room uncomfortable. The space leaned against him. He imagined they were out there, everyone, the whole town. He pulled the curtains on his little window.

No one came to his door. He heard them outside in the hour after he had dumped the mail, heard voices and confused laughter, heard the patient tones the brethren applied to him, knew the patronizing manner in which they were speaking of him. He prayed at his bedside, on his knees, hands clasped together so firmly his knuckles ached, and he asked the Lord how he should begin.

He didn't open the office the next day either, and no one knocked. He sensed the town's knowledge surrounding him, but could not imagine what they might do. He heard the mail wagon pull up in the afternoon, and he rushed out once again to greet it.

"Good afternoon, Doctor Warren," Broom said jovially. This was one of his standard jokes—to call people "Doctor." "Here's some more of your medicine."

Rulon despised Broom, despised his nonsense and his happiness. He lifted the canvas sack from the back of the wagon and looked up at Broom, sitting on the buckboard seat. *Knock him from that seat.*

"Shut your ridiculous mouth," he told Broom quietly, and turned back toward his room. As he reached the door to his room, he heard Broom mutter, "All right," and then the brief slap of the reins before the wagon rattled into motion.

A few minutes later, when he could no longer hear Broom's wagon wheels outside, he reemerged with the bag over one shoulder and his kerosene lamp in the other hand. I stayed silent. I knew. Rulon heard his blood in his ears. He dumped the sack on the same spot he had the day before. The street was silent. A young woman and a child watched him from down the street, and a curtain peeled back in the upstairs window of the store before falling back into place. He held the burning wick to the corner of one letter, and then another. Soon the pile curled and blackened, wavering in the flames of gold and orange, and it was beautiful.

Deputations came and went from Rulon's door for three days, and he stayed silent in his room, lying on the cot, eating hard biscuits and dried meat, while they knocked and demanded and left. Bishop Lawton came twice, and Verl Gentling, the part-time sheriff, three times.

The mail stopped arriving. Soon, someone would break down the door.

Rulon tried to imagine what he would do. He thought about leaving everything behind. He believed the Lord was calling him to a radical act, and I wanted him to answer—to something, to whatever. *You are outside them. You are their enemy.* I was sick of his prayers, of his constant yearning for God, but he wanted to die a righteous death, and in this we were one. I wanted that thrill once more. And then I wanted him gone, to see what shape my existence would take.

In his room, he felt adrift on a raft, floating ever farther from the ship. He thought the ship might no longer be visible. Sometimes he stayed on his cot for hours, imagining he was surrounded by water and safe only there. Sometimes he imagined he was underground, burrowed into the earth, and no one could reach him.

On the third night after he had burned the mail, Rulon left his room after midnight. He stood in the street and peered at the town; the April night was cool, freshening him like water. He started walking toward his family's house.

Make a fire in the night.

The night sky was blue and the land black, and a bright curve of moon reclined above the mountains to the east. Rulon followed the dirt road toward the mountains, whose night shade hid the homes that spread outward from town. As he walked, he remembered the gunner's mate from the ship, Sawicki, a Pole from Chicago who talked like no one Rulon had ever met, who told vile stories about women and swore more than any other sailor on board, and who still prayed each night, holding a necklace with a cross in his hands as his lips made their silent ministrations. On the day of the battle with the *Gotthilf,* in the North Sea, Rulon had been navigating, working the wheel that spun the big gun. Sawicki was the gunner, and his head had vanished almost in silence, everything around them so loud. The nose of the gun slumped forward, and Sawicki collapsed onto the deck. Another gunner took over, and it was three hours later when Rulon realized that he had been covered in a spray of sticky pink and slivers of bone. He picked a bit of something from his shoulder and what he saw there, pinched between his fingers, took in the whole human world: a fragment of bone, three black hairs, a red-black clump.

He came to the crossroads now and turned south, toward his family's home. The more he walked, the brighter the night seemed, though there was scarce light from the crescent moon. Rulon's spirit vibrated at a perfect pitch between calm and discord. It seemed natural to me, as though I were sliding alongside him in a groove.

The war seemed long ago to Rulon, and he was surprised at the heat and energy that accompanied his memories. Whatever he might do now, he thought, he was justified. He remembered the Germans in the ocean. He imagined what it must have been like for them in the icy water, desperate to live and waving their arms in surrender, begging to be spared, only to feel the metal burn of the bullets. Now he knew what he should have done: He should have defended the Germans. He should have stopped his fellow sailors, attacked them. He should have acted as a lone righteous soul.

I thought he was foolish to care so much—still, after all this time. But I loved what was happening inside him, as if his mind were reaching for mine.

Act, Rulon. Act.

When he reached his parents' house, he went to the shed and selected an ax, a heavy one with a sharp, gleaming blade, and he walked to the house and went quietly in the front door. He stood in the entryway and listened, and hearing only his own galloping blood, he stepped to the closet under the stairs and lifted his father's rifle and a box of shells from the top shelf.

Be a force against.

He went outside to the barn, where he harnessed his father's mule and led him out to the road, and then back toward town. As he walked, I sent him thoughts in an unending stream. I imagined them as commands.

Be a force against. An opponent. Make a fire in the night. Act, Rulon. By your actions will you prove your righteousness. Act. Act. That word, like a mantra.

He stopped abruptly in the middle of the road and whispered angrily: "I *am* acting. I *am*."

His words came into me like a hot blade. Like a beautiful wound that tells you you're alive.

You are my brother, Rulon. You will follow me into eternity.

But there was only silence after that. Silence and the sound of his steps in the pale night.

At the post office, Rulon took his trunk and packed it with his bedroll, his notebooks, his Book of Mormon, a sack of beans and a piece of pork fat, extra pants and shirt. He strapped it onto the back of the mule and returned to the rear of the post office, where he had leaned the rifle and the ax. He picked up the ax and held it with both hands. It felt like an instrument of balance. *Make a fire.* He carried the ax to the front office, lit a kerosene lamp, and stood before the PO boxes, the rows and columns of square holes, the names of the townspeople listed below: Jansen, Bingham, Lawton, Strengel, Pope, Miller, Warren. The boxes made a grid, and Rulon's first swing buried the ax with a splintering crack in its exact middle. His second swing sent a foot-long piece of wood careening past his head, and his third brought four boxes off the wall completely. He swung again and again until the boxes lay in splinters at his feet, and then he turned the ax on the desk and the partition where people came for their mail and on the tables where he sorted it and then on the floors themselves, the planking, and then the walls, the door, the windows with a glassy shatter. *Bring it down.* By the time he rested, he had turned it all back to simple wood, piles of fuel. The night shone through gaps in the walls where he had driven the ax through. *Make a fire.* I thought then that Rulon wanted to do it, to burn it all, but he saw the chaos he had made and he changed his mind. He wanted to leave it as a monument. In this, he was right. I wanted it then, too. He took the ax and rifle and mounted his father's mule. The street was silent, and no lights appeared in the windows of the nearest houses, well down the lane. He began riding slowly into the desert.

As the mule swayed under him, Rulon sank into warm weariness. He wondered how long it would take the brethren to come for him. Then, for the first time, it occurred to him that they might not follow.

They might forgive him.

This was not what he wanted. He wanted them to come for him, and I wanted them to come for him, to come relentlessly, so many he could not kill them all.

He was riding past a small herd of cattle asleep on their feet, head to tail in a group. *The cattle, Rulon. The rifle.* He checked the mule and slid off. He set the rifle against his shoulder and fired four times into the herd. Two cows thudded to the ground.

No one would forgive him now. He climbed back onto the mule and rode toward the horizon, which was beginning to brighten with the new day's light.

Rulon went on into the desert, to the cave where he had played as a boy. It sat under an outcropping of lava rock; the desert floor sloped downward and into a dark mouth surrounded by dusky gray blocks of basalt. Inside was a roomy cavern that trailed backward to an opening too narrow for anyone to pass through. When he was a boy, Rulon and his friends would crawl back as far as they could, moving on their bellies, and call into the gap to hear the echo.

Rulon unpacked his belongings and set them inside the cave. He unspooled his bedroll, laid it beside his trunk, and retrieved water from the tiny stream that cut a little notch in the basalt to the east. Morning light filled the sky, but it was dark in the cave, and Rulon lit his lamp, casting harsh shadows on the walls. He took apart the rifle, cleaned it, and reloaded it, leaning it against the rock at the cave entrance.

I knew Rulon's mind completely. I thought of my own last days, in the mountains looming now above us. I thought of how fully I had left behind my life, my parents and my sister and my church—I could not have gone back. I had prepared to die, and had I survived, it would have been a failure. My whole life had been filling itself with the possibility of striking the ultimate mark. Even now, though I had lost my faith in God, I had not lost my faith in that. My faith in death. I could feel Rulon's mind gathering strength—he could live alone in the cave, he thought, a hermit's life, but it was not what he wanted. He wanted to go to an ultimate place, and there to end.

The sun crawled upward in the sky. The mule grazed. Spring showed on the land, green and tan and cool, and Rulon had an overwhelming eagerness to leave this wicked world and enter God's embrace. I hoped he would not be too disappointed. I wondered what would happen to him, and what would happen to me. The world rolls on and on. We cannot imagine it without us, even as we dream of death.

The crunching of cart wheels sounded across the desert. A wagon drew closer, and soon we saw a little cart and a mule, and then Brother Pope, sitting in the seat, forearms on his knees and hands holding the reins loosely, face sunk in the shadow of his hat brim. Rulon came out of the cave and stood with his rifle propped over his shoulder, squinting toward the sun. The cart passed twenty yards away, and Rulon waved briefly at Pope, who kept his eyes rigidly ahead. When he was out of sight, Rulon heard him clack at the mule, and the sound of the wheels sped up, and he knew that Pope would not be coming back alone.

Twilight settled onto the desert. Rulon made a fire outside the mouth of the cave and built a tripod with lengths of sage wood. He hung a pot over the fire and filled it with beans and water and a chunk of salt pork. Then he retreated to his bedroll in the cave and dropped into a thick, dreamless sleep.

In the morning, he awoke with a clarified mind. For the first time I could remember, he did not pray. He walked out to the pot to stir the beans and add wood to the fire. The smoke rose like a signal above the desert. Rulon considered what would remain of him, how the stories would be told. I stayed silent behind his eyes. He did not need me now.

He took a ledger and a red pencil from his pack and returned to the cave. He sat cross-legged on his bedroll and began to write, and I found myself entering a dream of my last hours on earth, and he bent to his task, writing faster and faster, and I stood in the clearing with Hiram and the others as we watched for the posse. Rulon wrote, and I smelled the pine air, the mountain cold, and Rulon imagined he was leaving a testament, a scripture, a vessel to carry forth his righteousness. I heard the crunch of boots and looked into the trees, and Rulon filled the ledger with his furious red scrawl, and the posse slipped out from behind the trees as though they were spirits of the mountains, and Rulon sharpened his pencil with a pocket knife, and I felt a blade in my side, between my ribs, and then came the sound of horses in the desert outside the cave. Rulon put down his pencil and took up his father's rifle, and I felt the blade again, a second wound, a fire in my side, and someone called, "Warren! You come out of there!" and Rulon stepped from the mouth of the cave into the desert, and the knife slipped from me, and Rulon saw seven men on horseback, the sheriff and the bishop and five brethren, but not his father, and I tasted my blood, warm and thick in my throat, and Rulon raised his rifle and rested the sights on the bishop's gray felt hat, and I dropped to my knees, as if to pray, and Rulon tightened his finger on the trigger, and I fell to my side and tasted dust. The bishop toppled from his horse, and Rulon was filled with nausea and bliss and felt a sharp tug in his shoulder, a blossom of bright pain, and I saw my blood puddle and thicken on the earth, and Rulon's left arm hung useless, and I watched my blood and knew I was ascending, and Rulon braced the rifle against his hip with his right hand and fired, then the answering bullets tore into his chest and thigh, and he sank to his knees as if to pray, and I dreamed of my ascension even as I knew it was a dream, and Rulon rode a wave of bliss and heard a voice, *the righteous need have no fear of death*, the words as clear as a rifle shot, coming to him in his own voice, *for it is a joy to enter the celestial kingdom, to spend eternity at the side of the Lord*, and his blood joined all the blood of the earth, and he sank toward it, we sank toward it, a cloak fell across our eyes, and we soared.

THE LAST THING WE NEED

Claire Vaye Watkins

July 28
Duane Moser
1077 Pincay Drive
Henderson, Nevada 89015

Dear Mr. Moser:

On the afternoon of June 25 while on my last outing to Rhyolite, I was driving down Cane Springs Road some ten miles outside Beatty and happened upon what looked to be the debris left over from an auto accident. I got out of my truck and took a look around. The valley was bone dry. A hot west wind took the puffs of dust from where I stepped and curled them away like ashes. Near the wash I found broken glass, deep gouges in the dirt running off the side of the road, and an array of freshly bought groceries tumbled among the creosote: Coke cans (some full, some open and empty, some still sealed but dented and half-full and leaking). Bud Light cans in the same shape as the Coke. Fritos. Meat. Et cetera. Of particular interest to me were the two almost-full prescriptions that had been filled at the pharmacy in Tonopah only three days before, and a sealed Ziploc bag full of letters, signed M. I also took notice of a bundle of photos of an old car, part primer, part rust, that I presume was or is going to be restored. The car was a Chevy

Chevelle, a '66, I believe. I once knew a man who drove a Chevelle. Both medications had bright yellow stickers on their sides warning against drinking alcohol while taking them. Enter the Bud Light, and the gouges in the dirt, possibly. I copied your address off those prescriptions. What happened out there? Where is your car? Why were the medication, food, and other supplies left behind? Who are you, Duane Moser? What were you looking for out at Rhyolite?

I hope this letter finds you, and finds you well. Please write back.

Truly,
Thomas Grey
PO Box 129
Verdi, Nevada 89439

P.S. I left most of the debris in the desert, save for the medications, pictures, and letters from M. I also took the plastic grocery bags, which I untangled from the bushes and recycled on my way through Reno. It didn't feel right to just leave them out there.

August 16
Duane Moser
1077 Pincay Drive
Henderson, Nevada 89015

Dear Mr. Moser:
This morning, as I fed the horses, clouds were just beginning to slide down the slope of the Sierras, and I was reminded once again of Rhyolite. When I came inside, I borrowed my father's old copy of the *Physicians' Desk Reference* from his room. From that book I have gathered that before driving out to Rhyolite, you may have been feeling out of control, alone, or hopeless. You were possibly in a state of extreme depression; perhaps you were even considering hurting yourself. Judging by the date the prescriptions were filled and the amount of pills left in the bottles—which I have counted, sitting out in the fields atop a tractor which I let sputter and die, eating the sandwich which my wife fixed me for lunch—you had not been taking the medications long enough for them to counteract your possible feelings of despair. "Despair," "depression," "hopeless," "alone." These are the words of the *PDR*, 41st Edition, which I returned to my father promptly, as per his request. My father

can be difficult. He spends his days shut up in his room, reading old crime novels populated by dames and Negroes, or watching the TV we bought him with the volume up too high. Some days he refuses to eat. Duane Moser, my father never thought he would live this long.

I think there will be lightning tonight; the air has that feel. Please, write back.

Truly,
Thomas Grey
PO Box 129
Verdi, Nevada 89439

September 1
Duane Moser
1077 Pincay Drive
Henderson, Nevada 89015

Dear Mr. Moser:

I slept terribly last night, dreamt dreams not easily identified as such. Had I told my wife about them, she might have given me a small quartz crystal or amethyst and insisted I carry it around in my pocket all day, to cleanse my mind and spirit. She comes from California. Here is a story she likes to tell: On one of our first dates, we walked arm in arm around downtown Reno, where she was a clerk at a grocery store and I was a student of agriculture and business. There she tried to pull me down a little flight of steps to the red-lit underground residence of a palm reader and psychic. I declined. Damn near an hour she pulled on me, saying what was I afraid of, asking what was the big deal. I am not a religious man, but as I told her then, there are some things I'd rather not fuck with. Now she likes to say it's a good thing I wouldn't go in, because if that psychic had told her that she'd be stuck with me for going on fourteen years now, she would have turned and headed for the hills. Ha! And I say, honey, not as fast as I would've, ha ha! This is our old joke. Like most of our memories, we like to take it out once in a while and lay it flat on the kitchen table, the way my wife does with her sewing patterns, where we line up the shape of our life against that which we thought it would be by now.

I'll tell you what I don't tell her. There is something shameful in this, the buoying of our sinking spirits with old stories.

I imagine you a man alone, Duane Moser, with no one asking after your dreams in the morning, no one slipping healing rocks into your pockets. A bachelor. It was the Fritos, finally, which reminded me of the gas station in Beatty where I worked when I was in high school and where I knew a man who owned a Chevelle like yours, a '66. But it occurs to me perhaps this assumption is foolish; surely there are wives out there who have not banned trans fats and processed sugars, as mine has. I haven't had a Frito in eleven years. Regardless, I write to inquire about your family, should you reply.

Our children came to us later in life than most. My oldest, Danielle, has just started school. Her little sister, Layla, is having a hard time with it. She wants so badly to go to school with Danielle that she screams and cries as the school bus pulls away in the morning. Sometimes she throws herself down to the ground, embedding little pieces of rock in the flesh of her fists. Then she is sullen and forlorn for the rest of the day. My wife worries for her, but truth be told, I am encouraged. The sooner Layla understands that we are nothing but the sum of that which we endure, the better. But my father has taken to walking Layla to the end of our gravel road in the afternoon to wait for Danielle at the bus stop. Layla likes to go as early as she is allowed, as if her being there will bring the bus sooner. She would stand at the end of the road all day if we let her. She pesters my father so he sometimes stands there in the heat with her for an hour or more, though his heart is in no condition to be doing so. In many ways, he is better to my girls than I am, Duane Moser. He is far better to them than he was to me. I am not a religious man, but I do thank God for that.

I am beginning to think I dreamt you up. Please, write soon.

Truly,
Thomas Grey
PO Box 129
Verdi, Nevada 89439

October 16
Duane Moser
1077 Pincay Drive
Henderson, Nevada 89015

Dear Mr. Moser:

I have read the letters from M., the ones you kept folded in the Ziploc bag. Forgive me, but for all I know, you may be dead, and I could not resist. I read them in my barn, where the stink and thickness of the air were almost unbearable, and then again in my truck in the parking lot of the Verdi post office. I was struck, as I was when I first found them out near Rhyolite on Cane Springs Road, by how new the letters looked. Though most were written nearly twenty years ago, the paper is clean, the creases sharp. Duane Moser, what I do not understand is this: why a Ziploc bag? Did you worry they might get wet on your journey through the desert in the middle of summer? Then again, I am reminded of the Coke and Bud Light. Or am I to take the Ziploc bag as an indication of your fierce, protective love for M.? Is it a sign, as M. suggests, that little by little you sealed your whole self off until there was nothing left for her? Furthermore, I have to ask whether you committed this sealing purposefully. She says she thinks she was always asking too much of you. She is generous that way, isn't she? She says you didn't mean to become "so very alien" to her. I am not so sure. I love my wife. But I've never told her how I once knew a man in Beatty with a '66 Chevelle. I know what men like us are capable of.

Duane Moser, what I come back to is this: how could you have left M.'s letters by the side of Cane Springs Road near the ghost town Rhyolite, where hardly anyone goes anymore? (In fact, I have never seen another man out on Cane Springs Road. I drive out there to be alone. Maybe you do, too. Or you did, anyway.) Did you not realize that someone just like you might find them? Duane Moser, how could you have left her again?

I have called the phone number listed on the prescription bottles, finally, though all I heard was the steady rising tones of the disconnected signal. Still, I found myself listening for you there. Please, write soon.

Truly,
Thomas Grey
PO Box 129
Verdi, Nevada 89439

P.S. On second thought, perhaps sometimes these things are best left by the side of the road, as it were. Sometimes a person wants a part of you that's no good. Sometimes love is a wound that opens and closes, opens and closes, all our lives.

November 2
Duane Moser
1077 Pincay Drive
Henderson, Nevada 89015

Dear Duane Moser:

My wife found your pictures, the ones of the Chevelle. The one you maybe got from a junkyard or from a friend, or maybe it's been in your family for years, rotting in a garage somewhere because after what happened, nobody wanted to look at it. I kept the pictures tucked behind the visor in my truck, bound with a rubber band. I don't know why I kept them. I don't know why I've kept your letters from M. or your medications. I don't know what I would do if I found what I am looking for.

When I was in high school, I worked the graveyard shift at a gas station in Beatty. It's still there, on the corner of I-95 and Highway 374, near the hot springs. Maybe you've been there. It's a Shell station now, but back then it was called Hadley's Fuel. I worked there forty, fifty hours a week. Bill Hadley was a friend of my father's. He was a crazy sonofabitch, as my father would say, who kept a shotgun under the counter and always accused me of stealing from the till or sleeping on the job, when I did neither. I liked the graveyard shift, liked being up at night, away from Pop, listening to the tremors of the big walk-in coolers, the hum of the fluorescent lights outside.

Late that spring, a swarm of grasshoppers moved through Beatty on their way out to the alfalfa fields down south. They were thick and fierce, roaring like a thunderstorm in your head. The hoppers ate anything green. In two days, they stripped the leaves from all the cottonwoods and willows in town, then they moved on to the juniper and pine, the cheatgrass and bitter salt cedar. A swarm of them ate the wool right off of Abel Prince's live sheep. Things got so bad that the trains out to the mines shut down for a week because the guts of the bugs made the rails too slippery.

The grasshoppers were drawn to the fluorescent lights at Hadley's. For weeks, the parking lot pulsed with them. I would have felt them crunch under my feet when I walked out to the pumps that night, dead and dying under my shoes, only I never made it out to the pumps. I was doing schoolwork at the counter, calculus, for God's sake. I looked up, and the guy was already coming through the door at me. I looked outside and saw the '66 Chevelle, gleaming under the lights, grasshoppers falling all around it like rain.

I tried to stop him, but he muscled back behind the counter. He had a gun, held it like it was his own hand. He said, You see this?

There was a bandanna over his face. But Beatty is a small town and was even smaller then. I knew who he was. I knew his mother worked as a waitress at the Stagecoach, and that his sister had graduated the year before me. The money, he was saying. His name was Frankie. The fucking money, Frankie said.

I'd barely touched a gun before that night. I don't know how I did it. I only felt my breath go out of me and reached under the counter to where the shotgun was and tried. I shot him in the head.

Afterward, I called the cops. I did the right thing, they told me, the cops and Bill Hadley in his pajamas, even my father. They said it over and over again. I sat on the curb outside the store listening to them inside, their boots squeaking on the tile. The deputy sheriff, Dale Sullivan, who was also the assistant coach of the basketball team, came and sat beside me on the curb. I had my hands over my head to keep the grasshoppers away. Kid, it was bound to happen, Dale said. The boy was a troublemaker. A waste of skin.

He told me I could go on home. I didn't ask what would happen to the car.

I drove out on Cane Springs Road to Rhyolite. I drove through that old ghost town with the windows rolled down, listening to the gravel pop under my tires. The sun was coming up. There, in the milky light of dawn, I hated Beatty more than I ever had. The Stagecoach, the hot springs, all the trees looking so naked against the sky. I'd never wanted to see any of it ever again.

I was already on my way to college, and everyone knew it. I didn't belong in Beatty. The boy's family, his mother and sister and stepfather, moved away soon after it happened. I'd never see them around town or at Hadley's. For those last few weeks of school, no one talked about it, at least not to me. Soon it was as though it had never happened. But—and I think I realized this then, up in Rhyolite, that dead town picked clean—Beatty would never be a place I could come home to.

When my wife asked about your pictures, she said she didn't realize I knew so much about cars. I said, Yeah, sure. Well, some. See the vents there? On the hood? See the blackout grille? That's how you know it's a '66. I told her I'd been thinking about buying an old car, fixing it up, maybe this one.

Right then she just started laughing her head off. Sure, she managed through all her laughter, fix up a car. She kept on laughing. She tossed the bundle of photos on the seat of the truck and said, You're shitting me, Tommy.

It's not her fault. That man, the one who knows a '66 when he sees one, that's not the man she married. That's how it has to be. You understand, don't you?

I smiled at her. No, ma'am, I said. I wouldn't shit you. You're my favorite turd.

She laughed—she's generous that way—and said, A car. That's the last thing we need around here.

When I was a boy, my father took me hunting. Quail mostly, and one time, elk. But I was no good at it, and he gave up. I didn't have it in me, my father said, sad and plain as if it were a birth defect, the way I was. Even now, deer come down from the mountains and root in our garden, stripping our tomatoes from the vine, eating the hearts of our baby cabbages. My father says, "Kill one. String it up. They'll learn." I tell him I can't do that. I spend my Sundays patching the holes in the fence, or putting up a taller one. The Church of the Compassionate Heart, my wife calls it. It makes her happy, this life of ours, the man I am. Layla helps me mend the fence. She stands behind me and hands me my pliers or my wire cutters when I let her.

But here's the truth, Duane Moser. Sometimes I see his eyes above that bandanna, see the grasshoppers leaping in the lights, hear them vibrating. I feel the kick of the rifle butt in my sternum. I would do it again.

Truly,
Thomas Grey
PO Box 129
Verdi, Nevada 89439

December 20
Duane Moser
1077 Pincay Drive
Henderson, Nevada 89015

Dear Duane Moser:
This will be the last I write to you. I went back to Rhyolite. I told my wife I was headed south to camp and hike for a few days. She said, Why don't you take Layla with you? It would be good for her.

Layla slept nearly the whole drive. Six hours. When I slowed the car and pulled onto Cane Springs Road, she sat up and said, Dad, where are we?

I said, We're here.

I helped her with her coat and mittens, and we took a walk through the ruins. I told her what they once were. Here, I said, was the schoolhouse. They finished it in 1909. By then, there were not enough children in town to fill it. It burnt the next year. She wanted to go closer.

I said, Stay where I can see you.

Why? She said.

I didn't know how to say it. Crumbling buildings, rotted-out floors, sink-holes, open mine shafts. Coyotes, rattlesnakes, mountain lions.

Because, I said. It's not safe for little girls.

We went on. There behind the fence is the post office, completed in 1908. This slab, these beams, that wall of brick, that was the train station. It used to have marble floors, mahogany woodworking, the first telephone in the state. But all that's been sold or stolen over the years.

Why? She said.

Because that's what happens when a town dies.

Why?

Because, sweetheart. Because.

At dusk, I tried to show Layla how to set a tent and build a fire, but she wasn't interested. Instead, she concentrated on filling her pink vinyl back-pack with stones and using them to build little pyramids along the path that led out to the town. She squatted over them, gingerly turning the stones to find a flat side, a stable base. What are those for? I asked.

For if we get lost, she said. Pop Pop showed me.

When it got dark, we sat together listening to the hiss of the hot dogs at the ends of our sticks, the violent sizzle of sap escaping the firewood. Layla fell asleep in my lap. I carried her to the tent and zipped her inside a sleep-ing bag. I stayed and watched her there, her chest rising and falling, hers the small uncertain breath of a bird.

When I bent to step out through the opening of the tent, something fell from the pocket of my overalls. I held it up in the firelight. It was a cloudy stump of amethyst, as big as a horse's tooth.

I've tried, Duane Moser, but I can't picture you at 1077 Pincay Drive. I can't see you in Henderson period, out in the suburbs, on a cul-de-sac, in one of those prefab houses with the stucco and the garage gaping off the front like a mouth. I can't see you standing like a bug under those streetlights the color of antibacterial soap. At home, at night, I sit on my porch and watch the lights of Reno over the hills, the city marching out at us like an army. It's no accident that the first step in what they call developing a plot of land is to put a fence around it.

I can't see you behind a fence. When I see you, I see you here, at Rhyolite, harvesting sticks of charcoal from the half-burnt schoolhouse and writing your name on the exposed concrete foundation. Closing one eye to look through the walls of Jim Kelly's bottle house. No, that's my daughter. That's me as a boy getting charcoal stains on my blue jeans. That's you in your Chevelle, the '66, coming up Cane Springs Road, tearing past what was once the Porter Brothers' Store. I see you with M., flinging Fritos and meat and half-full cans of Coke and Bud Light from the car like a goddamn celebration, a shedding of your old selves.

It's almost Christmas. I've looked at the prescriptions, the letters, the photos. You're not Frankie, I know this. It's just a coincidence, a packet of pictures flung from a car out in the middle of nowhere. The car is just a car. The world is full of Chevelles, a whole year's worth of the '66. You know nothing of Hadley's Fuel in Beatty, of a boy who was killed there one night in late spring when the grasshoppers were so loud they sounded like a thunderstorm in your head. I don't owe you anything.

When I woke this morning, there was snow on the ground. Layla was gone. She'd left no tracks. I pulled my boots on and walked around the camp. A thin layer of white covered the hills and the valley and the skeletons of the old buildings, lighting the valley fluorescent. It was blinding. I called my daughter's name. I listened, pressing the sole of my shoe against the blackened rocks lining the fire pit. I watched the snow go watery within my boot print. There was no answer.

I checked the truck. It was empty. In the tent, I found her coat and mittens. Her shoes had been taken. I scrambled up a small hill and looked for her from there. I scanned for the shape of her among the old buildings, on the hills, along Cane Springs Road. Fence posts, black with moisture, strung across the valley like tombstones. Sickness thickened in my gut and my throat. She was gone.

I called for her again and again. I heard nothing, though surely my own voice echoed back to me. Surely the snow creaked under my feet when I walked through our camp and out to the ruins. Surely the frozen tendrils of creosote whipped against my legs when I began to run through the ghost town, up and down the gravel path. But all sound had left me except for a low, steady roaring, the sound of my own blood in my ears, of a car rumbling up the old road.

Suddenly, my chest was burning. I couldn't breathe. Layla. Layla. I crouched and pressed my bare palms against the frozen earth. The knees of my long johns soaked through, and my fingers began to sting.

Then I saw a shape near the burnt remains of the schoolhouse. A panic as hot and fierce as anything—fiercer—rose in me. The slick pink vinyl of her backpack. I ran to it.

When I bent to pick it up, I heard something on the wind. Something like the high, breathy language my daughters speak to each other when they play. I followed the sound around behind the schoolhouse and found Layla squatting there in her pajamas, softly stacking one of her stone markers in the snow.

Hi, Dad, she said. The snow had reddened her hands and cheeks as though she'd been burned. She handed me a stone. Here you go, she said. She softened into me.

I took my daughter by the shoulders and stood her up. I raised her sweet chin so her eyes met mine, and then I slapped her across the face. She began to cry. I held her. The Chevelle drove up and down Cane Springs Road, the gravel under its tires going pop-pop-pop. I said, Shh. That's enough. A child means nothing out here.

Truly,
Thomas Grey

OTHER NOTABLE WESTERN STORIES OF THE YEAR

Christopher Feliciano Arnold, "Laidlaw"
Ecotone, Volume 8 (2009)

Paula Belnap, "The Road to Chimayo"
Alligator Juniper, Volume 14 (2009)

Heather Brittain Bergstrom, "Farm-In-A-Day"
Narrative, Winter 2009

Rod Dixon, "Growing as It Goes"
Red Rock Review, Volume 25 (Spring 2010)

Zach Falcon, "Bridge to Nowhere"
Sycamore Review, Volume 22.1 (Winter/Spring 2010)

Amber Folland, "The End of a Long Season"
Ruminate, Volume 14 (Winter 2010)

Abby Geni, "Terror Birds"
Indiana Review, Volume 31.2 (Winter 2009)

William Giraldi, "Sasquatch Love Song"
Idaho Review, Volume 10 (2009)

Charley Henley, "Satellite Mother"
Copper Nickel, Volume 13 (2010)

Drew Johnson, "Leave"
New England Review, Volume 30.4 (2009–2010)

Laurel Leigh, "Shoeless"
The Sun, Volume 414 (June 2010)

Peter Levine, "La Jolla"
Southern Review, Volume 46.2 (Spring 2010)

Jerry Mathes, "Birth of the Hippo"
Narrative, Story of the Week, 2009–2010

James Miranda, "All In"
Storyglossia, Volume 38 (February 2010)

Candice Morrow, "Touch"
Colorado Review, Volume 37.2 (Summer 2010)

David Mullins, "This Life or the Next"
Yale Review, Volume 97.4 (Fall 2009)

Bonnie Nadzam, "Devil's Circle"
StoryQuarterly, Volume 44 (Fall 2010)

Kent Nelson, "Going Dark"
Sewanee Review, Volume 118.1 (Winter 2010)

Jeff O'Keefe, "Anniversary"
Greensboro Review, Volume 86 (Fall 2009)

Shann Ray, "The Miracles of Vincent Van Gogh"
Ruminate, Volume 15 (Spring 2010)

Ethan Rutherford, "John, for Christmas"
Ploughshares, Volume 36.2 & 3 (Fall 2010)

Rob Magnuson Smith, "The Harvester"
Greensboro Review, Volume 86 (Fall 2009)

Maggie Shipstead, "The Mariposa"
Missouri Review, Volume 32.4 (Winter 2009)

Mark Slouka, "Crossing"
Paris Review, Volume 190 (Fall 2009)

Renée Thompson, "Farallon"
Narrative, Story of the Week, 2009–2010

Josh Wallaert, "Geography"
Bellingham Review, Volume 33 (Spring 2010)

Joe Wilkins, "Crow Road"
Berkeley Fiction Review, Volume 30 (2010)

Evan Morgan Williams, "Ivory"
Kenyon Review, Volume 32.2 (Spring 2010)

Christian A. Winn, "False History"
Bat City Review, Volume 6 (2010)

The following online and print journals, magazines,
and newspapers were consulted for this volume:

PUBLICATIONS REVIEWED

12th Street · Afro-Hispanic Review · Agni · Alaska Quarterly Review · Alimentum · Alligator Juniper · American Letters & Commentary · American Literary Review · American Scholar · American Short Fiction · Antigonish Review · Antioch Review · Antipodes · Apalachee Review · Appalachian Heritage · A Public Space · Arkansas Review · Arroyo Literary Review · Asia Literary Review · Atlantic · Austin Chronicle · Bat City Review · Bellevue Literary Review · Bellingham Review · Berkeley Fiction Review · Bitter Oleander · Blackbird · Black Warrior Review · Blue Mesa Review · BOMB · Boston Review · Boulevard · Briar Cliff Review · Brick · Bridges · Callaloo · Calyx · Canteen · Cavalier Literary Couture · Cerise Press · Chariton Review · Chicago Reader · Chicago Review · Cicada Magazine · Cimarron Review · Cincinnati Review · Collagist · Colorado Review · Commentary · Confrontation · Conjunctions · Copper Nickel · Crab Creek Review · Crab Orchard Review · Crazyhorse · Cream City Review · CT Review · CutBank · CUT-THROAT · Daedalus · Dalhousie Review · Dappled Things · descant (Fort Worth) *· Descant* (Toronto) *· Dialogue: A Journal of Mormon Thought · DIAGRAM · Dirty Goat · Downstate Story · Drash · Ecotone · Electric Literature · Eleven Eleven · Epoch · Esquire · Exile · Exquisite Corpse · Failbetter.com · Fairy Tale Review · Farallon Review · Fence · Fiction · Fiction International · Fifth Wednesday Journal · First Line · Five Points · Florida English · Flyway · Front Porch · Fugue · Gargoyle · Georgia Review · Gettysburg Review · Glimmer Train · Grain · Granta · Great River Review · Green Mountains Review · Greensboro Review · Gulf Coast · Hanging Loose · Harper's*

Magazine · Harpur Palate · Harvard Review · Hawaii Review · Hayden's Ferry Review · Heat · High Desert Journal · Hobart · Hopkins Review · Hotel Amerika · H.O.W. Journal · Hudson Review · Idaho Review · Image · Indian Literature · Indiana Review · Interim · Iowa Review · Iron Horse Literary Review · Isle · Isotope · Journal · Kenyon Review · KGB BAR LIT · Knee-Jerk · Lake Effect · La Petite Zine · Lapham's Quarterly · Laurel Review · Literary Review · L Magazine · Long Story · Louisiana Literature · Louisville Review · Main Street Rag · Make · Malahat Review · Manoa · Marginalia · Massachusetts Review · McSweeney's · Memoir (and) · Meridian · Michigan Quarterly Review · Mid-American Review · Minnesota Review · Mississippi Review · Missouri Review · Mizna · n + 1 · Narrative · Natural Bridge · New England Review · New Letters · New Madrid · New Ohio Review · New Orleans Review · News from the Republic of Letters · New South · New Yorker · Nimrod International Journal · Ninth Letter · Normal School · North American Review · North Dakota Quarterly · Northwest Review · Notre Dame Review · One Story · Open City · Opium · Overland · Overtime · Oxford American · Oyez Review · Paris Review · Passager · Paterson Literary Review · Paul Revere's Horse · Pearl · PEN International · Persimmon Tree · Persona · Phoebe · Pilgrimage · Pilot · Pinch · Pindeldyboz · Ping Pong · Platte Valley Review · Pleiades · Ploughshares · PMS poemmemoirstory · Potomac Review · Prairie Fire · Prairie Schooner · Prick of the Spindle · Prism International · Provincetown Arts · Puerto del Sol · Quarterly West · Queens Quarterly · Quercus Review · Red Cedar Review · Redivider · Red Rock Review · Reed · Regarding Arts and Letters · Rio Grande Review · River Styx · Ruminate · Sakura Review · Salmagundi · Salt Hill · Santa Fe Writers Project Journal · Santa Monica Review · Saranac Review · Saturday Evening Post · Seattle Review · Seneca Review · Sewanee Review · SFWP.org · Shenandoah · Sierra Nevada Review · Sinister Wisdom · Slake · Slice · Sonora Review · South Carolina Review · South Dakota Review · Southeast Review · Southern Humanities Review · Southern Quarterly · Southern Review · Southwestern American Literature · Southwest Review · Stand · Storyglossia · StoryQuarterly · Subtropics · Sun · Sycamore Review · Talking River Review · Terrain.org · Texas Review · Thema · Third Coast · Threepenny Review · Tin House · Tonopah Review · TriQuarterly · Virginia Quarterly Review · Walking Rain Review · War, Literature, and the Arts · Washington Square · Water-Stone Review · Weber: The Contemporary West · West Branch · West Coast Line · Westerly · Western Humanities Review · Whitefish Review · White Fungus · Willow Springs · Witness · Women's Studies Quarterly · Workers Write! · Writer · World Literature Today · Yale Review · Yellow Medicine Review · Zahir · Zoetrope · Zone 3 · ZYZZYVA

NOTES ON CONTRIBUTORS

RICK BASS is the author of twenty-five books of fiction and nonfiction, in-cluding, most recently, a novel, *Nashville Chrome*. He divides his time between Missoula and the Yaak Valley, in Montana, and is a board member of the Yaak Valley Forest Council (www.yaakvalley.org).

T. C. BOYLE is the author of *A Friend of the Earth*, *Riven Rock*, *The Tortilla Curtain*, *The Road to Wellville*, *East Is East*, *World's End* (winner of the PEN/ Faulkner Award), *Budding Prospects*, *Water Music*, *Drop City* (nominated for the 2003 National Book Award), *The Inner Circle*, *Talk Talk*, *The Women*, and nine collections of stories, including *Wild Child*, published in January 2010 by Vi-king Penguin. In 1999, he was the recipient of the PEN/Malamud Award for Excellence in Short Fiction. His stories appear regularly in major American magazines including the *New Yorker*, *Harper's*, *Esquire*, and *Playboy*. He lives near Santa Barbara, California.

RON CARLSON is the author of ten books of fiction, most recently the novel *The Signal*. His short fiction has appeared in *Esquire*, *Harper's*, the *New Yorker*, *Gentlemen's Quarterly*, *Epoch*, the *Oxford American*, and other journals, as well as in *The Best American Short Stories*, *Prize Stories: The O. Henry Awards*, *The Pushcart*

Prize Anthology, *The Norton Anthology of Short Fiction*, and other anthologies. Among his awards are a National Endowment for the Arts Fellowship in fiction, the Cohen Prize at *Ploughshares*, the McGinnis Award at the *Iowa Review*, and the Aspen Foundation Literary Award. He directs the Graduate Program in Fiction at the University of California–Irvine.

ANA CASTILLO is the author of two collections of stories, *Loverboys: Stories* and *Bocaditos: Flash Fictions*, and six novels, including *The Guardians*, *The Mixquiahuala Letters*, *So Far from God*, and *Watercolor Women/Opaque Men: A Novel in Verse*, which won an Independent Publisher Book Award for outstanding book of the year. She has also published numerous collections of poetry, including *My Father Was a Toltec, and Selected Poems, 1973–1988* and *I Ask the Impossible*, as well as a collection of essays, *Massacre of the Dreamers: Essays on Xicanisma*. She has won two National Endowment for the Arts Fellowships in creative writing, a Mountains and Plains Booksellers Award, and the Carl Sandburg Literary Award in fiction, and she was also recognized as a distinguished contributor to the arts by the National Association of Chicano Studies. She currently lives in New Mexico.

K. L. COOK is the author of *Last Call*, a collection of linked stories that won the inaugural Prairie Schooner Book Prize in Fiction, and *The Girl from Charnelle*, a novel that won the 2007 Willa Award for Contemporary Fiction and appeared on several lists of best books of 2006. His stories and essays have been published widely in magazines and literary journals, including *Glimmer Train*, *Threepenny Review*, *Shenandoah*, *Harvard Review*, *American Short Fiction*, *Brevity*, *Writer's Chronicle*, and *Poets & Writers*. "Bonnie and Clyde in the Backyard" appears in his new collection of stories, *Love Songs for the Quarantined*, which won the 2010 Spokane Prize for Short Fiction. He teaches at Prescott College in Arizona and is also a member of the faculty for Spalding University's brief-residency MFA in Writing Program.

JUDY DOENGES was born in Elmhurst, Illinois. She is the author of a novel, *The Most Beautiful Girl in the World*, and a short-fiction collection, *What She Left Me* (a *New York Times Book Review* Notable Book). Her stories and essays have appeared in many journals, among them the *Georgia Review*, *Kenyon Review*, and *Western Humanities Review*. She has received fellowships and awards from many sources, including the National Endowment for the Arts, the Ohio Arts Council, and the Artist Trust. She teaches at Colorado State University.

DAGOBERTO GILB's latest book is *Before the End, After the Beginning* (Grove Press). He is the author of seven previous books, including *The Flowers*, *Woodcuts of Women*, and *The Magic of Blood*. His fiction and nonfiction appears in a range of magazines, most recently the *New Yorker*, *Harper's*, and *Callaloo*. He is writer in residence at the University of Houston–Victoria, where he is also executive director of Centro Victoria, its center for Mexican American Literature and Culture.

AARON GWYN is the author of the story collection *Dog on the Cross* (Algonquin Books), and a novel, *The World Beneath* (W. W. Norton). *Dog on the Cross* was a finalist for the 2005 New York Public Library Young Lions Fiction Award. His stories have appeared in *New Stories from the South*, *Esquire*, *Glimmer Train*, *McSweeney's*, the *Gettysburg Review*, and other magazines. He teaches fiction writing at the University of North Carolina–Charlotte.

TONI JENSEN is métis and is from the Midwest but has spent most of her adult life in the American West—in Arizona, South Dakota, and West Texas. Her story collection, *From the Hilltop*, was published through the Native Storiers Series at the University of Nebraska Press in 2010. Her stories have been published in *Fiction International*, *Passages North*, *Nimrod*, and other journals, and have also been anthologized in *New Stories from the South* and *New Stories from the Southwest*. She teaches creative writing at Penn State University.

TIM JOHNSTON is the author of the story collection *Irish Girl* and the novel *Never So Green*. Published in 2009, the stories of *Irish Girl* won an O. Henry Prize, the *New Letters* Award for Writers, and the Gival Press Short Story Award, while the collection itself won the 2009 Katherine Anne Porter Prize in Short Fiction. His stories have appeared also in the *New England Review*, the *Iowa Review*, the *Missouri Review*, *Double Take*, *Best Life Magazine*, and *Narrative*, among others. He holds writing degrees from the University of Iowa and the University of Massachusetts–Amherst, and is the recipient of a MacDowell Fellowship and a grant from the MacArthur Foundation. He currently lives in Los Angeles, California, where he is at work on his second novel, from which "Two Years" is excerpted.

ALYSSA KNICKERBOCKER is the Axton Fellow in fiction at the University of Louisville. In 2010, she received her MFA from the University of Wisconsin–Madison; previously, she lived in the San Juan Islands of Washington State, where she worked in environmental education. Her work has appeared in literary journals including the *Bat City Review, Meridian, Sou'wester*, and *Avery: An Anthology of New Fiction*. A novella, "Your Rightful Home," was published in 2010 as a stand-alone book by *Flatmancrooked*. She lives in Louisville, Kentucky, with her husband.

KATE KRAUTKRAMER's work has appeared or is forthcoming in publications such as the *Colorado Review, Creative Nonfiction, Fiction*, the *Mississippi Review, National Geographic*, the *New York Times*, the *North American Review, So To Speak*, the *Southern Humanities Review*, the *Seattle Review*, the *South Dakota Review, Washington Square, Weber: The Contemporary West, Quarter after Eight*, and *Zone 3*, as well as in the anthologies *The Beacon Best* and *The Best American Nonrequired Reading*. She has also been featured on National Public Radio's *Morning Edition* and *Day to Day*. Kate lives with her husband and children in rural northwest Colorado, where she teaches writing at South Routt Elementary School.

PETER LASALLE is the author of the novels *Strange Sunlight* and *Mariposa's Song* (forthcoming 2012) and three short-story collections: *The Graves of Famous Writers, Hockey Sur Glace*, and *Tell Borges If You See Him: Tales of Contemporary Somnambulism*. His work has been selected for many anthologies, including *Best American Short Stories, Best American Mystery Stories, Best American Fantasy, Sports Best Short Stories*, and *Prize Stories: The O. Henry Awards*. He lives in Austin, Texas.

YIYUN LI is the author of *A Thousand Years of Good Prayers, The Vagrants*, and *Gold Boy, Emerald Girl*. A native of Beijing and a graduate of the Iowa Writers' Workshop, she is the recipient of a 2010 MacArthur Foundation fellowship as well as the Frank O'Connor International Short Story Award, the Hemingway Foundation/PEN Award, the Whiting Writers' Award, and the Guardian First Book Award. In 2007, *Granta* named her one of the best American novelists under thirty-five. In 2010, she was named by the *New Yorker* as one of the twenty writers under forty to watch. Her work has appeared in the *New Yorker, A Public Space, The Best American Short Stories*, and *Prize Stories: The O. Henry Awards*, among others. She teaches writing at the University of California–Davis, and lives in Oakland, California, with her husband and their two sons.

MICHAEL J. MACLEOD, a combat correspondent with the U.S. Army's 82nd Airborne Division, covered the army's first "advise and assist" brigade deployed to Iraq's restive Al Anbar province, in 2009–2010. He has taught college courses in field zoology and ecology, published the nationally distributed outdoor magazine *River*, and written *The River What*, a coming-of-age memoir of his graduate years spent studying wolves, cougars, and elk in Montana's Glacier National Park. Originally from Bozeman, Montana, MacLeod and his family currently live outside Fort Bragg, North Carolina, where they will be until his service ends in 2013. He has two teenage children and has been married to Barbara MacLeod for twenty years. "Horn Hunter" comes from *Valley Boys*, a collection of hunting-based short stories drawn from the lives of young men, all natives of Montana's Yellowstone region, with whom MacLeod framed houses for many years.

PHILIPP MEYER was recently named one of the twenty best American writers under forty by the *New Yorker*. His first novel, *American Rust*, was an *Economist* Book of the Year, a *Washington Post* Top Ten Book of 2009, a *New York Times* Notable Book, one of *Newsweek*'s "Best. Books. Ever," and appeared on numerous other best-of-2009 lists. *American Rust* also won a Los Angeles Times Book Prize and is being published in eleven languages. Meyer's other writing has been published in the *New Yorker*, the *Guardian*, the *Independent*, *Esquire UK*, the *New York Times Book Review*, *McSweeney's*, the *Iowa Review*, *New Stories from the South*, and Salon.com. Meyer is the recipient of a 2010 Guggenheim Fellowship and a 2010 Dobie Paisano Fellowship. He lives with his wife in Austin.

ANTONYA NELSON is the author of four novels, including *Bound* (Bloomsbury, 2010), and six short-story collections, including :*Nothing Right* (Bloomsbury, 2009). Her work has appeared in the *New Yorker*, *Esquire*, *Harper's*, *Redbook*, and many other magazines, as well as in anthologies such as *Prize Stories: The O. Henry Awards* and *Best American Short Stories*. She is the recipient of a USA Artists Award in 2009, the 2003 Rea Award for Short Fiction, as well as NEA and Guggenheim fellowships, and teaches in the MFA program at Warren Wilson College, in Asheville, North Carolina, as well as in the University of Houston's Creative Writing Program. She lives in Telluride, Colorado; Las Cruces, New Mexico; and Houston, Texas.

Born and raised in Boise, Idaho, STEPHANIE REENTS has published fiction in *Epoch*, *StoryQuarterly*, *Gulf Coast*, *Pleiades*, the *Denver Quarterly*, and *Prize Stories: The O. Henry Awards*, among other places. Her first collection of stories, *The Kissing List*, will be published by Crown in January 2012. She is an assistant professor of English at the College of the Holy Cross.

SAM SHEPARD is the Pulitzer Prize–winning author of more than forty-five plays. He was a finalist for the W. H. Smith Literary Award for his story collection *Great Dream of Heaven*, and he has also written the story collection *Cruising Paradise*; two collections of prose pieces, *Motel Chronicles* and *Hawk Moon*; and *Rolling Thunder Logbook*, a diary of Bob Dylan's 1975 Rolling Thunder Review tour. As an actor, he has appeared in more than thirty films, including *Days of Heaven*, *Crimes of the Heart*, *Steel Magnolias*, *The Pelican Brief*, *Snow Falling on Cedars*, *All the Pretty Horses*, *Black Hawk Down*, and *The Notebook*. He received an Oscar nomination in 1984 for his performance in *The Right Stuff*. His screenplay for *Paris, Texas* won the Grand Jury Prize at the 1984 Cannes Film Festival, and he wrote and directed the film *Far North* in 1988 and co-wrote and starred in Wim Wenders's *Don't Come Knocking* in 2005. His plays, eleven of which have won Obie Awards, include *The God of Hell*, *Buried Child*, *The Late Henry Moss*, *Simpatico*, *Curse of the Starving Class*, *True West*, *Fool for Love*, and *A Lie of the Mind*, which won a New York Drama Desk Award. A member of the American Academy of Arts and Letters, he received the Gold Medal for Drama from the Academy in 1992, and in 1994 he was inducted into the Theatre Hall of Fame. He lives in New York and Kentucky.

SHAWN VESTAL's short stories have appeared in *Tin House*, *McSweeney's*, the *Southern Review*, *Ecotone*, *American Short Fiction*, and other journals. His story "The First Several Hundred Years Following My Death" was selected for the anthology *Real Unreal: Best American Fantasy*, published in 2010. A graduate of Eastern Washington University's MFA program, he is a columnist at the *Spokesman-Review* in Spokane, Washington, where he lives with his wife and son.

CLAIRE VAYE WATKINS is a Nevadan and a Presidential Fellow at Ohio State University, where she received her MFA. A graduate of the University of Nevada–Reno, her short stories and essays have appeared in *Granta*, *Ploughshares*, *One Story*, the *Paris Review*, and elsewhere. "The Last Thing We Need" is from her short-story collection, *Battleborn*.

CREDITS

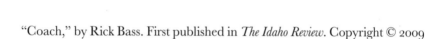